WITHDRAWN

THE SECRET MISTRESS

THE SECRET MISTRESS

MARY BALOGH

THORNDIKE
WINDSOR
PARAGON

This Large Print edition is published by Thorndike Press, Waterville, Maine USA and by AudioGo Ltd, Bath, England.
Copyright © 2011 by Mary Balogh.
The moral right of the author has been asserted.
Thorndike Press, a part of Gale, Cengage Learning.

Thorndike Press® Large Print Basic.
The text of this Large Print edition is unabridged.
Other aspects of the book may vary from the original edition.
Set in 16 pt. Plantin.

LIBRARY OF CONGRESS CATALOGING-IN-PUBLICATION DATA

Balogh, Mary.
  The secret mistress / by Mary Balogh.
    p. cm. — (Thorndike Press large print basic)
  ISBN-13: 978-1-4104-3891-1 (hardcover)
  ISBN-10: 1-4104-3891-0 (hardcover)
  1. Nobility—Fiction. 2. Large type books. I. Title.
  PR6052.A465S428 2011b
  823'.914—dc22   2011025526

BRITISH LIBRARY CATALOGUING-IN-PUBLICATION DATA AVAILABLE
Published in the U.S. in 2011 by arrangement with Delacorte Press, a division of Random House, Inc.
Published in the U.K. in 2012 by arrangement with Little, Brown Book Group.
U.K. Hardcover: 978 1 445 85878 4 (Windsor Large Print)
U.K. Softcover: 978 1 445 85879 1 (Paragon Large Print)

Printed in Mexico
3 4 5 6 7 15 14 13 12 11

THE SECRET MISTRESS

CHAPTER 1

Lady Angeline Dudley was standing at the window of the taproom in the Rose and Crown Inn east of Reading. Quite scandalously, she was alone there, but what was she to do? The window of her own room looked out only upon a rural landscape. It was picturesque enough, but it was not the view she wanted. Only the taproom window offered that, looking out as it did upon the inn yard into which any new arrival was bound to ride.

Angeline was waiting, with barely curbed impatience, for the arrival of her brother and guardian, Jocelyn Dudley, Duke of Tresham. He was to have been here before her, but she had arrived an hour and a half ago and there had been no sign of him. It was very provoking. A string of governesses over the years, culminating in Miss Pratt, had instilled in her the idea that a lady never showed an excess of emotion, but how was one not to do so when one was on one's way to London for the Season — one's *first* — and one was eager to be there so that one's adult life could begin in earnest *at last,* yet one's brother had apparently forgotten all about one's very existence and was about to leave one languishing forever at a public inn a day's journey away from the rest of one's life?

Of course, she had arrived here ridiculously early. Tresham had arranged for her to travel this far under the care of the Reverend Isaiah Coombes and his wife and two children before they went off in a different direction to celebrate some special anniversary with Mrs. Coombes's relatives, and Angeline was transferred to the care of her brother, who was to come from London. The Coombeses arose each morning at the crack of dawn or even earlier, despite yawning protests from the junior Coombeses, with the result that their day's journey was completed almost before those of more normal persons even began.

The Reverend and Mrs. Coombes had been quite prepared to settle in and wait like long-suffering martyrs at the inn until their precious charge could be handed over to the care of His Grace, but Angeline had persuaded them to be on their way. What could possibly happen to her at the Rose and Crown Inn, after all? It was a perfectly respectable establishment — Tresham had chosen it himself, had he not? And it was not as if she was quite alone. There was Betty, her maid; two burly grooms from the stables at Acton Park, Tresham's estate in Hampshire; and two stout footmen from the house. And Tresham himself was sure to arrive any minute.

The Reverend Coombes had been swayed, against his better judgment, by the soundness of her reasoning — and by the anxiety of his wife lest their journey not be completed before nightfall, and by the whining complaints of Miss Chastity Coombes and Master Esau Coombes, aged eleven and nine respectively, that they would *never* get to play with their cousins if they had to wait here forever.

Angeline's patience had been severely tried by those two while she had been forced to share a carriage with them.

She had retired to her room to change out of her travel clothes and to have Betty brush and restyle her hair. She had then instructed her drooping maid to rest awhile, which the girl had done to immediate effect on the truckle bed at the foot of Angeline's own. Meanwhile Angeline had noticed that her window would give no advance notice whatsoever of the arrival of her brother, so she had left the room to find a more satisfactory window — only to discover the four hefty male servants from Acton arrayed in all their menacing largeness outside her door as though to protect her from foreign invasion. She had banished them to the servants' quarters for rest and refreshments, explaining by way of persuasion that she had not noticed any highwaymen or footpads or brigands or other assorted villains hovering about the inn. Had they?

And then, alone at last, she had discovered the window she was searching for — in the public taproom. It was not quite proper for her to be there unescorted, but the room was deserted, so where was the harm? Who was to know of her slight indiscretion? If any persons came before Tresham rode into the inn yard, she would simply withdraw to her room until they left. When Tresham arrived, she would *dash* up to her room so that when he entered the inn, she could be descending the stairs, all modest respectability, Betty behind her, as though she were just coming down to ask about him.

Oh, it was very hard not to bounce around with impatience and excitement. She was nineteen years old, and this was almost the first time she had been more than ten miles from Acton Park. She had lived a *very* sheltered existence, thanks to a stern, overprotective father and an absentee overprotective brother after him, and thanks to a mother who had never taken her to London or Bath or Brighton or any of the other places she herself had frequented.

Angeline had entertained hopes of making her come-out at the age of seventeen, but before she could muster all her arguments and begin persuading and wheedling the persons who held her fate in their hands, her mother had died unexpectedly in London and there had been a whole year of mourning to be lived through at Acton. And then *last* year, when all had been set for her come-out at the indisputably correct age of eighteen, she had broken her leg, and Tresham, provoking man, had flatly refused to allow her to clump into the queen's presence on crutches in order to make her curtsy and her debut into the adult world of the *ton* and the marriage mart.

By now she was ancient, a veritable fossil, but nevertheless a hopeful, excited, impatient one.

Horses!

Angeline leaned her forearms along the windowsill and rested her bosom on them

11

as she cocked her ear closer to the window.

And carriage wheels!

Oh, she could not possibly be mistaken.

She was not. A team of horses, followed by a carriage, turned in at the gate and clopped and rumbled over the cobbles to the far side of the yard.

It was immediately apparent to Angeline, however, that this was not Tresham. The carriage was far too battered and ancient. And the gentleman who jumped down from inside it even before the coachman could set down the steps bore no resemblance to her brother. Before she could see him clearly enough to decide if he was worth looking at anyway, though, her attention was distracted by the deafening sound of a horn blast, and almost simultaneously *another* team and another coach hove into sight and drew to a halt close to the taproom door.

Again, it was not Tresham's carriage. That had been apparent from the first moment. It was a stagecoach.

Angeline did not feel as great a disappointment as might have been expected, though. This bustle of human activity was all new and exciting to her. She watched as the coachman opened the door and set down the steps and passengers spilled out onto the cobbles from inside and clambered

12

down a rickety ladder from the roof. Too late she realized that, of course, all these people were about to swarm inside for refreshments and that she ought not to be here when they did. The inn door was opening even as she thought it, and the buzz of at least a dozen voices all talking at once preceded their owners inside, but only by a second or two.

If she withdrew now, Angeline thought, she would be far more conspicuous than if she stayed where she was. Besides, she was enjoying the scene. And besides again, if she went upstairs and waited for the coach to be on its way, she might miss the arrival of her brother, and it seemed somehow important to her to see him the moment he appeared. She had not seen him in the two years since their mother's funeral at Acton Park.

She stayed and assuaged her conscience by continuing to look out the window, her back to the room, while people called with varying degrees of politeness and patience for ale and pasties and one or two instructed someone to look sharp about it, and the someone addressed replied tartly that she had only one pair of hands and was it *her* fault the coach was running an hour late and the passengers had been given only a ten-minute stop instead of half an hour?

Indeed, ten minutes after the coach's arrival, the passengers were called to board again if they did not want to get left behind, and they hurried or straggled out, some complaining vociferously that they had to abandon at least half their ale.

The taproom was soon as empty and silent as it had been before. No one had had time to notice Angeline, a fact for which she was profoundly grateful. Miss Pratt even now, a full year after moving on to other employment, would have had a fit of the vapors if she could have seen the full taproom with her former pupil standing alone at the window. Tresham would have had a fit of something far more volcanic.

No matter. No one would ever know.

Would he *never* come?

Angeline heaved a deep sigh as the coachman blew his yard of tin again to warn any persons or dogs or chickens out on the street that they were in imminent danger of being mown down if they did not immediately scurry for safety. The coach rattled out through the gates, turning as it went, and disappeared from sight.

The gentleman's carriage was still at the far side of the yard, but now it had fresh horses attached. He was still here, then. He must be taking refreshments in a private parlor.

Angeline adjusted her bosom on her arms, wiggled herself into a more comfortable position, and proceeded to dream about all the splendors of the Season awaiting her in London.

Oh, she could not *wait.*

It did seem, however, that she had no choice but to do just that.

Had Tresham even left *London* yet?

The gentleman whose carriage awaited him at the far side of the inn yard was not taking refreshments in a private parlor. He was doing so in the public taproom, his elbow resting on the high counter. The reason Angeline did not realize he was there was that he did not slurp his ale and did not talk aloud to himself.

Edward Ailsbury, Earl of Heyward, was feeling more than slightly uncomfortable. And he was feeling annoyed that he had been made to feel so. Was it *his* fault that a young woman who was clearly a lady was in the taproom with him, quite alone? Where were her parents or her husband or whoever it was that was supposed to be chaperoning her? There was no one in sight except the two of them.

At first he had assumed she was a stage-coach passenger. But when she had made no move to scurry outside when the call to board again came, he noticed that of course she was not dressed for the outdoors. She must be a guest at the inn, then. But she really ought not to have been allowed to wander where she had no business being, embarrassing perfectly innocent and re-spectable travelers who were trying to enjoy a glass of ale in peace and respectability before continuing the journey to London.

To make matters worse — *considerably* worse — she was leaning forward and slightly down in order to rest her bosom on her forearms along the windowsill, with the result that her back was arched inward like an inverted bow, and her derriere was thrust outward at a provocative angle. Indeed, Edward found himself drinking his ale less to slake the thirst of the journey than to cool an elevated body temperature.

It was a very shapely derriere.

And to make matters even worse, if that were possible, the dress she wore was of fine muslin and clung to her person in places where it would be kinder to innocent males for it *not* to cling. It did not help that the dress was of a bright, luminous pink the likes of which shade Edward had never before encountered in a fabric or anywhere else for that matter. The woman could have been seen with the naked eye from a distance of five miles. He was considerably closer to her than that.

He was further annoyed over the undeniable fact that he was ogling her — or one part of her anatomy, anyway. And, while he was ogling her with his eyes, his head was fairly humming with lascivious thoughts. He resented both facts — and her. He prided himself upon always treating ladies with the utmost respect. And not just ladies. He treated *women* with respect. Eunice Goddard had once pointed out to him during one of their many lengthy conversations — not that he could not have worked it out for himself — that women of all walks of life were *persons,* despite what the church and the law might have to say to the contrary, and not mere objects to cater to man's baser instincts.

He respected Eunice's opinions. She had a fine mind, which she had cultivated with extensive reading and thoughtful observations of life. He hoped to marry her, though he realized that his family might find his choice disappointing now that he was Earl of Heyward instead of plain Mr. Edward Ailsbury.

His carriage — his ancient embarrassment of a carriage, which his mother had begged him to bring to London because she could never seem to get comfortable in any newer one she had ever ridden in — was ready to leave, Edward could see through the window over the pink lady's head. He had intended to eat something as well as drink before resuming his journey, but she had ruined that plan. It was not right for him to be here with her — though it was not *his* fault that he was placing her in such a potentially compromising position. And it was not *his* fault that the ale was not cooling his blood one iota.

Though Eunice might argue with that, about its not being his fault, that is. The woman had done nothing to provoke his re-action, after all, beyond being here with her bright-pink-clad derriere elevated in his direction. And he could have gone to the dining room to eat, though he would then have felt obliged to order a full-blown meal.

He set his not-quite-empty glass down on the counter as silently as he could and straightened up. He would leave and take his grudge against her with him. He had not even seen her face. She might be as ugly as sin.

An unworthy, spiteful thought.

He shook his head in exasperation.

But then, before he could take a step toward the outer door and freedom from temptation and other ills, the door opened from the outside and a man stepped inside.

Edward recognized him, though *he* clearly did not recognize Edward. That was hardly surprising, since Edward was quite unremarkable in his own person, and his title had been lending him consequence only for the past year, since the death of his far more imposing and charismatic older brother, Maurice. And the year of mourning had been spent at Wimsbury Abbey in Shropshire, where Edward had stayed to familiarize himself with his new duties and gird his loins for the inevitable removal to London this spring to take his seat in the House of Lords — and to take a bride, a step his female relatives deemed essential despite the fact that he was only twenty-four years old. Maurice and Lorraine had produced only one daughter before Maurice's demise, and the succession must be secured. Edward was the spare of his particular generation; he had two sisters but no other brothers.

The new arrival was Lord Windrow, a member of Maurice's old circle of friends and acquaintances, and as wild and rakish as the best of them. Tall and handsome, neither of which attributes Edward shared to any noticeable degree, Windrow moved with an indolent swagger and regarded the world from cynical eyes over which his eyelids habitually drooped as if he were about to nod off to sleep at any moment. He was dressed in the height of fashion.

Edward would have liked nothing better than to nod genially at the man and be on his way. But he hesitated. The pink lady was still present and was still posed as before. And if *he* had ogled her, what would Windrow do?

It was absolutely none of his business what Windrow might do, Edward told himself. And the pink lady was certainly none of his concern. Let her look to the consequences of her own indiscretions. Let her family look to them. Besides, this was the public tap-room of a respectable inn. No real harm would come to her.

He urged himself to be on his way.

But he found himself instead resting his elbow on the counter and picking up his glass again.

Confound his misplaced sense of social responsibility. The fact that Eunice might applaud him for staying was no consolation.

The landlord appeared behind the counter and served Windrow with a tankard of ale before disappearing again.

Windrow turned to survey the room, and his eyes alit almost immediately upon the pink lady. But how could they not unless he was totally blind? He leaned back against the counter, resting his forearms back along it while clutching his tankard in one hand. His lips pursed in a silent whistle.

Edward was all the more annoyed at the blatantly sensual look on the man's face because his own must have looked very much like it just a few minutes ago.

"Sweetheart," Windrow said softly, obviously having dismissed Edward as a man of no account whatsoever — or perhaps he had not even noticed him, "may I persuade you to share my ale? Better yet, may I persuade you to share it and a meat pasty? There is only one comfortable-looking chair over by the fireplace, I see, but you may sit on my lap and share that too."

Edward frowned at him. Could he not see that the woman was a *lady?* The evidence was glaring enough in the fine muslin of her dress, despite the bright shade, and in the intricacy of her coiffure of dark hair. He glanced at her, expecting to see her stiffen with horror and fright. She continued to stare out the window. She either assumed that the invitation was directed at someone

21

else, or — was it possible? — she simply did not hear the words at all.

He should *leave*, Edward decided. *Right now.*

He spoke instead.

"I doubt you know the lady," he said. "Calling her *sweetheart,* then, would be inappropriately impertinent."

Maurice had often called him, affectionately enough most of the time, a staid old sobersides. Edward half expected to see dust emerge from his mouth along with the words. But they were spoken now, and he would not recall them if he could. *Someone* had to speak up for defenseless female innocence. If she *was* innocent, that was.

Windrow's head swiveled slowly, and just as slowly his lazy eyes swept Edward from head to toe. His perusal aroused no discernible alarm in him.

"You were speaking to me, fellow?" he asked.

Edward in his turn looked slowly about the room.

"I must have been," he said. "I see no one else present except the two of us and the lady, and I am not in the habit of speaking to myself."

Slight amusement showed in the other man's face.

"Lady," he said. "I take it she is not with you. She is alone, then. I wish she *were* a lady. It might be mildly less of a yawn to frequent London ballrooms and drawing rooms. You would be wise, fellow, to address yourself to what remains of your ale and mind your own business."

And he turned back to regard the woman's derriere again. She had changed position. Her elbows were now on the sill, and her face was cupped in her hands. The effect of the change was to thrust her bosom into more prominence in one direction and her derriere in the other.

If she could only step back and see herself from this position, Edward thought, she would run screaming from the room and never return, even with a dozen chaperons.

"Perhaps this *lady* would care to sit in my lap while I call to the landlord to bring *her* a pasty and ale so that *she* may share with *me*," Windrow said with insolent emphasis. "*Would* you, sweetheart?"

Edward sighed inwardly and moved one degree closer to an unwilling confrontation. It was too late to back off now.

"I really must insist," he said, "that the lady be treated with the respect that any female ought to be accorded as a matter of right by anyone claiming the name of gentleman."

He sounded pompous. *Of course* he sounded pompous. He always did, did he not?

Windrow's head turned, and his amusement was quite unmistakable now.

"Are you looking for a fight, fellow?" he asked.

The lady seemed finally to have realized that she was the subject of the conversation behind her. She straightened up and turned, all wide, dark eyes in a narrow, handsome face, and all tall, shapely height.

Good God, Edward thought, the rest of her person more than lived up to the promise of her derriere. She was a rare beauty. But this was no time to allow himself to be distracted. He had been asked a question.

"I have never felt any burning desire to enforce gentility or simple civility with my fists," he said, his tone mild and amiable. "It seems something of a contradiction in terms."

"I believe," Windrow said, "I have the pleasure of addressing a sniveling coward. And a stuffy windbag. All wrapped in one neat package."

Each charge, even the last, was an insult. But Edward would be damned before he would allow himself to be goaded into adopting swashbuckling tactics just to prove to someone he despised that he was a *man.*

"A man who defends the honor of a lady, and who expects a gentleman to behave like one and confronts him when he does not, is a *coward,* then?" he asked mildly.

The woman's eyes, he was aware, had moved from one to the other of them but were now riveted upon his face. Her hands were clasped to her bosom as though she had been struck by some tender passion. She looked remarkably unalarmed.

"I believe," Windrow said, "the suggestion has been made that I am not a *gentleman.* If I had a glove about my person, I would slap it across your insolent face, fellow, and invite you to follow me out to the inn yard. But a man ought not to be allowed to get away with being a coward *and* a stuffy windbag, gloves or no gloves, ought he? Fellow, you are hereby challenged to fisticuffs outside." He jerked his thumb in the direction of the inn yard and smiled — very unpleasantly indeed.

Once more Edward sighed inwardly.

"And the winner proves himself a gentleman worthy of the name, does he?" he said. "Pardon me if I disagree and decline your generous offer. I will settle for an apology to the lady instead, before you take yourself off."

He glanced at her again. She was still gazing fixedly at him.

He had, as he was fully aware, backed himself into a tight corner from which there was no way out that was not going to prove painful. He was going to end up having to fight Windrow and either give *him* a bloody nose and two black eyes to take to London with him, or suffer his opponent to dish out the like to himself. Or both.

It was all very tedious. Nothing but flash and fists. That was what being a gentleman was, to many of the men who claimed the name. Maurice, unfortunately, had been one of them.

"Apologize to the *lady?*" Windrow laughed softly and with undisguised menace.

That was when the lady decided to enter the fray — without uttering a word.

She seemed to grow three inches. She looked suddenly regal and haughty — and she shifted her gaze to Windrow. She looked him up and down unhurriedly and appeared to find what she saw utterly contemptible.

It was a masterly performance — or perhaps a mistressly one.

Her wordless comment was not without its effect, even though Windrow was half grinning at her. Perhaps it was a *rueful* grin?

"I misjudged you, alas, did I?" he asked her. "Because you were alone in here and leaning nonchalantly on the windowsill and dressed like a bird of paradise, I suppose. I cannot persuade you to share a pasty and a glass of ale with me? Or to sit on my lap? A pity. And it would seem I cannot persuade this sniveling coward to defend your honor or his own with his fists. What a sad day to have encountered when I had such high hopes of it when I awoke this morning. There is nothing for it, I see, but to resume my tedious journey and hope for a brighter tomorrow."

And he pushed himself away from the counter, setting down his empty tankard as he did so, and would have sauntered out of the inn without a word more or a backward glance. He found an obstacle in his path, however. Before he could reach the door, Edward was there ahead of him and standing in front of it, blocking the way.

"You have forgotten something," he said. "You owe the lady an apology."

Windrow's eyebrows rose and amusement suffused his face again. He turned back to the room and made the lady a deep and mocking bow.

"Oh, fair one," he said, "it pains me that I

may have distressed you with my admiration. Accept my humble apologies, I beg you."

She neither accepted nor rejected them. She gazed coldly at him without relaxing her regal demeanor.

Windrow winked at her.

"I shall look forward to making your official acquaintance at some future date," he said. "It is my fervent hope that that will not be far in the future."

He turned to Edward, who stood out of the way of the door.

"And likewise for you, fellow," he said. "It will be a distinct pleasure."

Edward inclined his head curtly to him, and Windrow left the inn and closed the door behind him.

That left Edward and the lady in the taproom together again. But this time she knew he was there and so the impropriety could not be ignored or even silently fumed over. He was freshly annoyed with her — and with himself for having become embroiled in such an undignified episode.

She was gazing at him, the regal demeanor vanished, her hands clasped at her bosom again.

Edward inclined his head curtly to her and made his way outside. He half expected to find Windrow lying in wait for him in the yard and was almost disappointed to see no sign of the man.

Less than five minutes later he was inside his carriage again and on his way toward London. Ten minutes after that, the carriage passed a far smarter one — of course, it would have been difficult to find one shabbier — traveling with reckless speed in the opposite direction. He caught a glimpse of the coat of arms emblazoned on the door: the Duke of Tresham's. He breathed a sigh of relief that at least he had been spared having to encounter that particular gentleman at the Rose and Crown in addition to Windrow. It would have been the final straw.

Tresham was not his favorite person in the world. And, to be fair, he did not doubt that he was not Tresham's either. The duke had been another of Maurice's friends. It was in a curricle race against him that Maurice had overturned his own and killed himself. And then Tresham had had the effrontery to turn up at Maurice's funeral. Edward had made his opinion known to him there.

He wished anew that he could have stayed at Wimsbury Abbey. But duty called in London. And there was consolation, for Eunice was there too. She was staying with

Lady Sanford, her aunt, and he would see her again.

It struck him suddenly that Tresham was driving in the opposite direction from London. Perhaps he was on his way to Acton Park. Perhaps he was going to remain there throughout the spring. It was something to be hoped for.

Who the devil *was* that lady back at the inn? *Someone* needed to take her in hand and teach her a thing or two about what was what.

But devil take it, she was a rare beauty.

He frowned as he shifted position in a vain attempt to get comfortable.

Beauty was no excuse for impropriety. Indeed, beauty called for more than usual discretion.

He still felt entirely out of charity with her, whoever she was. Unlike Windrow, he did *not* look forward to making her official acquaintance. He hoped rather that he would never see her again. He hoped she was traveling away from London rather than toward it.

Preferably to the highlands of Scotland.

CHAPTER 2

Angeline stood staring at the inside of the taproom door, her hands clasped to her bosom.

She did not even know his name. He had gone away before she had a chance to say anything, and he had not spoken to her either. But of course, he was a perfect gentleman. His words and actions had proved that. It would have been improper for him to speak, for they had not been formally introduced and ought not even to have been in a room alone together. She ought not to be here at all.

She did not know who he was. She did not even know whether he was traveling toward London or away from it. It was altogether possible that she would never see him again.

By the time she had noticed the other man striding toward the taproom door earlier, it had been too late to withdraw to her room.

So she had stayed where she was, hoping not to be noticed. There was no reason why she *should* be. None of the stagecoach passengers had noticed her, after all, and she was standing with her back to the room, minding her own business.

When he had spoken — oh, how her heart had leapt with alarm and indignation! — she had pretended not to hear and hoped he would go away. And then another voice had spoken up, and she had realized that there was more than one man in the tap-room, that the other man must have been there even before the new arrival.

How dreadfully mortifying!

But his words . . .

I doubt you know the lady. Calling her sweetheart, then, would be inappropriately impertinent.

So pleasantly, courteously spoken in low, cultured accents.

He had been championing her cause.

Angeline had changed position, cupping her face in her hands in an attempt to keep it hidden from the two gentlemen — she sincerely hoped there *were* only two. And she had gazed intently at the gateway arch leading out to the street, for the first time willing Tresham *not* to come just yet. He would probably punch the teeth of both gentlemen straight down their throats, which would be a simple overreaction in the one case and a gross miscarriage of justice in the other. He would then blister her all over, without using anything more lethal than his tongue. His tongue, when he waxed eloquent, could be *very* lethal.

And then the newcomer had become even more impertinent, and the other one had defended her again. And the newcomer — so *typically* male — had wanted to make a *fight* of it.

Angeline had been unable either to disappear or to make herself invisible. Nor could she pretend any longer that what was happening in the room behind her had nothing to do with her. Besides, she had not *wanted* to ignore the contretemps. Indignation had long ago replaced fright — she did not frighten easily or for long. And besides again, she had wanted to *see* these two men.

And so she had turned. There *were* only two, one at each end of the counter, like bookends. Not identical bookends, though. And before either had spoken a word more, she had identified which was which. It was really quite easy.

The one slouched back with casual elegance against the counter, supported on his forearms, his riding boots crossed nonchalantly at the ankles, was the impertinent one. Every line of his tall, athletic body, every garment he wore, spoke of a man who was confident and arrogant and fearless and contemptuous of all who were beneath him in consequence — a number that would of course include all women. His face, beneath a shock of dark red hair, was handsome enough if one discounted the fact that he affected world-weariness by keeping his eyelids half drooped over his eyes.

He was a type she recognized instantly. Her father had been such a man. Tresham was such a man. So was Ferdinand, her other brother. So were all their friends whom she had met. They were often lovable and essentially harmless despite all the silliness. Angeline could never take such men too seriously. She was quite impervious to their charms. She would never even *dream* of marrying one of them.

The second man was entirely different, even though he was almost as tall as the other and was well and solidly built. He was dressed neatly and fashionably but without any flair or ostentation or any suggestion of dandyism. His brown hair was cut short and neatly styled. His face was neither handsome nor plain. Although he had an elbow on the counter, he was not leaning on it.

He was . . . an ordinary man. Which was by no means an insult or even a dismissal of his claim to be noticed. *Angeline* had noticed him. And she was as sure as she could be that *he* was her defender, while the other was her tormentor.

Her guess was soon proved correct.

I have never felt any burning desire to enforce gentility or simple civility with my fists, he had said. *It seems something of a contradiction in terms.*

And yet he was *not* a coward, though that was what the other man accused him of. He would have fought if he had had to. His actions at the end had proved that. Instead of accepting partial victory when the almost-handsome redhead was leaving, he had stepped over to the door to block the man's exit and insisted quietly and courteously that he apologize.

He *would* have fought. And though common sense told Angeline that he would very soon have been outsized, outclassed, and out cold if the other man had forced him into it, she would not have wagered against him. Quite the contrary.

How could one *not* fall instantly in love with such a man, Angeline asked herself as she stared at the door after they had both left. In a few short minutes he had shown himself to be her ideal of manhood. Of *gentlemanhood.* He seemed perfectly content and comfortable with his ordinariness. He seemed not to feel the need to posture and prove his masculinity at every turn, preferably with his fists, as most men did in Angeline's admittedly rather limited experience.

He was, in fact, more than ordinary. He was an *extraordinary* man.

And she had fallen head over ears in love with him.

Indeed, she was going to marry him — despite the fact that she would probably never see him again.

Love would find a way.

With which decidedly muddled form of logic she returned to reality and the distinct possibility that if she remained in the taproom any longer she might well be assailed by the comings and goings of yet more travelers — all undoubtedly male. The room was not, alas, nearly as deserted and private as it had appeared when she came down here. And if Tresham caught her here . . .

Well . . . it was best not to put the matter to the test. She would return to her room and *listen* for his arrival. *If* he ever came.

The gentleman's eyes were blue, she remembered as she climbed the stairs. She was certain of it, though she had not seen them from close to. They were not that nondescript sort of gray that often passes for blue. They were as clear as the summer sky. They were his most outstanding feature, in fact.

Oh, she *hoped* she would see him again.

How could she possibly marry him if she did not?

Almost as soon as Edward arrived in London, he was besieged by female relatives who adored him and had nothing but his best interests and his future happiness at heart and were determined to have a hand in securing that happiness for him.

They were a plague.

His mother had been staying with her parents, the Marquess and Marchioness of Beckingham, for the past few months while she recovered as best she could from the sudden death of her elder son. Edward's grandparents had now come to town, and his mother, who had traveled with them — in a new carriage that she had found atrociously uncomfortable — had moved into Ailsbury House on Portman Square to be with her younger son, now her *only* son.

Lorraine, Maurice's widow, who had retreated to her father's house in the country following his death, had now returned to town with Susan, her daughter, and had also taken up residence at Ailsbury House, as of course she had every right to do. She still held the title Countess of Heyward, after all, Edward being as yet unmarried. Besides, he had always been fond of Lorraine and sorry for the fact that she had been in an unsatisfactory marriage with his brother. He was more than happy to offer her and his niece the shelter of his own roof for as long as they needed it.

Both of Edward's sisters were in town for the Season. Alma, the elder, was there with her husband, Augustine Lynd, a prominent government minister, and Melissa, their young daughter. Their two boys were away at school. Juliana was there with her husband, Christopher Gilbert, Viscount Overmyer. They also had three children, all below the age of ten, though Edward often thought that in reality Juliana had four, since Christopher was perennially indisposed with some malady or other and it seemed that no one could nurse him back to health — or rather nurse him on to the *next* illness — half as well as his wife.

All five ladies — grandmother, mother,

two sisters, one sister-in-law — had taken upon themselves the identical project to be accomplished during the course of the Season. They had set their collective hearts and energies upon finding Edward a bride. A bride was necessary, of course. If he were to die without a son, the title and property and fortune would pass to Cousin Alfie — never in his life had Edward ever heard him referred to as Alfred — who lived in the far north of England with his mother and who, all were agreed, was more than a little daft in the head.

It was pointless for Edward to put forward the name of Eunice Goddard at this juncture. She was the daughter of a gentleman, it was true — a Cambridge don whom Edward had greatly admired during his years as a student there — and the niece of Lady Sanford, who had had the good fortune to meet and attach the interest of a wealthy baron at the tender age of seventeen. Eunice might have been considered unexceptionable as the bride of Edward Ailsbury, younger brother of the Earl of Heyward, especially if Maurice and Lorraine had produced a son or two. It would be trickier, though, to convince his female relations that she was the ideal wife of that same Edward Ailsbury now that he was himself the earl.

It would be done eventually, he was confident. Edward, who was not particularly excited at the prospect of marrying anyone this early in life, had decided long ago that when he *did* marry, it would be to Eunice, with whom he could talk upon any subject on earth and with whom he felt perfectly comfortable. He had even made the suggestion to her one day, when he was about twenty and she nineteen, that when the time came to consider the sober responsibilities of home and family, perhaps they might consider doing it together. Eunice had told him on an earlier occasion that she hated the thought of marrying and would put off doing so as long as she possibly could, though she must marry eventually as her father could not live forever and she would hate to be a burden to her brother. She had liked his suggestion and had agreed to it. They had even shaken hands on it.

Clearly their relationship was *not* characterized by high romance. Or any romance at all, for that matter. And yet, Edward thought after his arrival in London, he loved Eunice. He loved her more than any other woman he had known, though probably no more than he loved his female relatives, he admitted with incurable honesty.

Dash it, but he was just not a romantic man.

He did not need to be. Eunice was one of his dearest friends, and what better marriage could one make than with one's dear friend?

He did not really *want* to marry at all, of course. Not yet anyway. But he had to marry someone. Duty demanded it. And if he must marry, then he would rather it be Eunice than anyone else. *Far* rather.

He bided his time before mentioning her to his relatives, however. Not that they were unaware of her existence. They knew that both she and her father had been his friends in Cambridge. They knew too that she was in town and that he called upon her within two days of his arrival there.

She greeted him with warm pleasure in her aunt's parlor, and Lady Sanford, who was instantly alert to the possibility of promoting a match for her niece even more brilliant than her own had been, discovered an almost immediate reason to leave the room, with apologies for doing so and instructions to her niece to entertain Lord Heyward while she was gone.

Edward took both Eunice's hands in his own as soon as they were alone and carried them one at a time to his lips — an extravagant gesture for him, but then it had been longer than a year since he last saw her.

"Miss Goddard," he said, "you are in good looks."

"As are you, *Lord Heyward,*" she said with grave emphasis upon his name. "Must we be formal, then, now that you are the earl? And must I be reassured with flatteries? Must you?"

He smiled at her and squeezed her hands before releasing them.

"I am happy to see you again, Eunice," he said. "One frustration of spending the past year at Wimsbury has been my inability to see you and enjoy your conversation."

"I hope," she said, "your duties as earl are not proving too burdensome. But I know you will perform them conscientiously."

"I must take my seat in the House of Lords," he told her. "I will enjoy listening to the debates, even participating in them. The one thing I do *not* look forward to, though, is delivering my maiden speech."

"But you will do brilliantly at it," she assured him, resuming her seat so that he could take his. "You have a superior mind and have cultivated it with discerning reading. Have you chosen a topic?"

"Not yet," he said with a sigh. "But I will soon. I so wish to say something of lasting

42

significance."

"You will," she said. "I trust your mother is well? Losing a son must be the very worst bereavement any woman can be called upon to suffer. Or any man for that matter."

"She was close to collapse for several months," he said, "and still suffers. She has found a new purpose in life, though. She has set herself the task of finding me a suitable bride."

He smiled ruefully at her.

She did not smile back.

"It is commendable in her," she said. "You must marry soon, of course. It is your duty."

Both her facial expression and her posture were unreadable. She appeared relaxed. Her hands, clasped in her lap, were neither white-knuckled nor fidgeting.

"But I have already made my choice," he told her.

She looked steadily at him for a few moments.

"If you are referring to me," she said, "and a *very* informal agreement we made all of four years ago when both of us were minors, then you must not regard it as any sort of obligation whatsoever, Edward. I would not be an eligible bride for an earl."

"Why not?" he asked her.

"Perhaps *eligible* is not the right word,"

she said after giving the matter some thought. "I am a lady. I am fit to be the bride of any gentleman, no matter what his rank and fortune. *Desirable* would be a better word. Or *brilliant*. I would not be a brilliant match for you, Edward."

"I do not ask for brilliance," he said.

"No," she agreed. "You are not so swayed by outer trappings. But you have responsibilities to more than just yourself now. You must marry, and you must marry well. You need more than just *any* bride. You need a *countess*. Your mother and your sisters will know who is most eligible."

"And my grandmother and sister-in-law?" he said.

"Oh, dear," she said with warm sympathy. "Them too? Poor Edward, they must seem like an army. But yes, together they will find just the right bride for you."

"For me?" he asked her. "Or for the Earl of Heyward?"

She regarded him gravely.

"When your brother died," she said, "and you became the Earl of Heyward, you lost the right to think only of yourself and your own comfort, Edward. You *are* the earl. But of course I tell you only what you already know and accept. You are not a man to shirk your responsibilities. It is one thing I have always admired in you. You must *not* now feel obligated by a sort of agreement you made with me long ago when the circumstances of your life were very different from what they are now."

"And you?" he said. "What are *your* feelings in all this, Eunice?"

"If you remember," she said, "I told you four years ago that I had no intention of marrying until age makes my spinsterhood somewhat of a burden to both me and my brother. That time has not come yet. I am only twenty-three. Let us officially release each other from any obligation that agreement laid upon us, then, even if it is only guilt and fear of hurting each other."

"Is that what you really want for yourself?" he asked. "Complete freedom? Even from me?"

"Life," she said, "is not always or even often about getting what we want, Edward. Far more often it is about doing our duty, doing what is right, taking other people into consideration."

He sighed aloud. She had neatly avoided answering his question, he noticed. Or had she? Perhaps she was embarrassed by that long-ago agreement. Perhaps she was glad of the excuse to bring it to an end. And perhaps not. Perhaps she was being noble.

Or merely sensible.

And what about him? How did her willingness to release him make him feel? Disappointed? Relieved? He really was not sure. There was perhaps a bit of both.

"You are released, then," he said. "And so am I, if you insist upon it. But I will not give up our friendship, Eunice. And I will not give up the possibility that at some future time . . . Well, I will not burden you with that."

"Your thoughts, your opinions will never be a burden to me, Edward," she said. "I will always consider you a very dear friend."

He had to leave it at that. But he felt somewhat depressed as he took his leave — depression more than relief. For he had already accepted the necessity of marrying soon, and if he must now give up the comfortable thought that it would be Eunice he would marry, there was a distinctly *un*-comfortable void where she had been. If not Eunice, then *whom?* Was he going to have to meet and woo a stranger and marry her and get her with child? It was a rhetorical question, of course. That was *exactly* what he must do. It was one of his two reasons for leaving behind the peace and safety of Wimsbury Abbey for London. London in the spring was the great marriage mart, and he had come to shop.

Unless Eunice could be persuaded to change her mind. She had avoided his question about her personal feelings on being set free of their agreement. Perhaps she was secretly hoping that he would refuse to be set free.

It did not take long for the family committee to compile an alarmingly long list of marital possibilities for him, though it took even less time for them to whittle it down to a few probabilities and then to one overwhelming and unanimous favorite.

Lady Angeline Dudley.

Everything about her made her supremely eligible.

She was about to make her come-out. Her come-out ball was to be held less than one week hence, in fact — on the evening of the very day appointed for Edward's maiden speech in the Upper House. She was the daughter and sister of a duke, and her fortune was said to be astronomical. She had lived a sheltered life in the country under the tutelage of an assortment of the finest governesses money could buy. She was at the very top of *everyone's* list of eligible hopefuls this Season and would be snapped up within weeks or even days of her first appearance on the marriage mart.

For Edward there was only one impediment — and it was a huge one. Lady Angeline Dudley just happened to be the sister of the Duke of Tresham.

Of course, he admitted to himself, she could hardly be blamed for the wildness and dissipations of her brother. Or for those of her late father. Or for the scandalous reputation her mother had enjoyed before her untimely death a couple of years or so ago.

Indeed, it might be altogether kinder to pity the girl.

Either way, he soon found himself committed to firing at least the opening volley in what his family hoped would be a rapid and successful courtship campaign. Lorraine took it upon herself to speak to Lady Palmer, with whom she had an acquaintance. Lady Palmer was Lady Angeline Dudley's cousin and her sponsor for the all-important come-out Season. The outcome of the meeting was that Edward was engaged to lead Lady Angeline Dudley into the first set of dances at her come-out ball — arguably the most important set of dances in her life.

Lorraine's initiative was accorded the heartfelt approval of the rest of the committee. Indeed, Edward even heard — and carefully ignored — mention being made of

St. George's, Hanover Square, as the only truly proper setting for a marriage of such social magnitude. The comment came in the voice of his maternal grandmother.

Being accepted to dance that opening set with Lady Angeline Dudley was a huge honor for Edward. It was no less an honor for her, of course. He was one of the most eligible bachelors on the market this year — and he did not doubt that the whole of the beau monde was fully aware that he was actively in search of a bride.

It was all deucedly unnerving.

Just a year or so ago he might have attended any and every *ton* ball without anyone's remembering afterward if he had even been there. Being a second son made one blessedly invisible.

He wondered what Lady Angeline Dudley looked like. And what she was like as a person. But it seemed he was destined to find out soon enough. He was forced to go through the excruciatingly embarrassing formality of applying to Tresham himself for that all-important set with his sister — Tresham *was* back in town, alas. And of course permission was granted, even though he had been forced to endure a long, inscrutable stare from Tresham's black eyes before being informed that if Lady Palmer deemed

Heyward an unexceptionable partner for Lady Angeline, then who was *he* to argue?

Lord! What would it be like, Edward could not help wondering, if he ever had to apply to the duke for permission to *marry* the sister? It did not bear thinking of, though he believed he had acquitted himself well enough on this occasion by staring back at Tresham with equal steadiness of eye.

All of Edward's female relatives were fairly twittering with delight when the matter became official. And it was not just the ladies. Augustine Lynd began cracking jokes about leg shackles and braying loudly over his own wit. And Overmyer began hoping that his gout — which was in his head more than it was in his legs, in Edward's inexpert and unkind medical opinion — would allow him to attend the ball at Dudley House so that he could witness the first fateful meeting between his brother-in-law and his future countess.

It was a relief to Edward to discover during a chance meeting on Oxford Street that Lady Sanford and Eunice were also to attend the ball, even though Eunice despised the frivolities of most social entertainments and was going only because she did not want to disappoint her aunt. Perhaps she would dance a set with him, Edward

50

thought, even though he hated to dance. Even though he *could* not dance, in fact. His right leg and foot might *look* like a right leg and foot, but in reality they were a left leg and foot in disguise. Or so it always seemed when he attempted to perform the intricate steps of any dance yet invented.

Perhaps Eunice would sit out a set with him, then, or stroll in the garden outside with him if it was a pleasant evening. She would not mind having to forgo the pleasure of tripping the light fantastic for half an hour.

Meanwhile he hired a secretary to help him with all the work of being an earl in London with an estate in Shropshire still to run in absentia. And he applied all his energies to composing a maiden speech that would render all the other peers of the realm speechless with admiration when it was delivered in the House of Lords.

He started to suffer from insomnia and sudden cold sweats and clammy palms.

CHAPTER 3

When thinking ahead to her removal to London, Angeline had somehow imagined that she would make her curtsy to the queen the moment she arrived in town — well, perhaps not the *very* moment, but certainly within a day or two — and that she would then sweep off into all the dizzying round of entertainments with which the *ton* filled its days and nights during the Season.

She was quite wrong, of course. For one thing, she had come to town rather early in the year, when there was a mere trickle of entertainments and half the *ton* were still in the country packing their trunks and bandboxes in preparation for the move to their town houses.

For another thing, a young lady needed time — and lots of it — to make endless preparations for her presentation and all the balls and parties and concerts and whatnot that would follow it.

Tresham had explained it to her in the carriage on the way to London, sounding rather bored, as if it were just too, too tedious to have a sister to bring out. And he had been sprawled across a corner of the carriage seat, one booted foot propped against the seat opposite, for all the world as though looking alert and elegant for a sister were too great a bore to be contemplated. Of course, he had looked gorgeous anyway with all his tall, dark, harsh beauty, and Angeline had gazed back at him with fond exasperation.

Brothers had positively *no idea* how to treat a sister.

"Cousin Rosalie will bring you up to snuff," he had said. "She will tell you what to wear, what to do, where to go, whose acquaintance to cultivate, how deeply you must curtsy to the queen." He had paused to yawn. "While I have to exert myself to host a come-out ball at Dudley House, which is something I have never done before and never expect to do again, and so I hope you are properly grateful. And then I must interview all your suitors, who are bound to be queued up outside my door as soon as they know you are on the market for a husband."

He had glanced at her then, a hint of lazy

affection in his eyes. But really, if one was not watching closely, one could easily miss such moments.

Cousin Rosalie was Lady Palmer, actually their *second* cousin on their father's side. She had kindly agreed to sponsor Angeline's come-out and chaperon her throughout the Season. She would be glad to do so, she had assured Tresham, since Palmer was on a lengthy diplomatic mission in Vienna and was making rumblings about her joining him there. She had no patience with either Vienna or any other foreign city and would be glad of the excuse to put him off.

Rosalie called promptly at Dudley House the morning after Angeline's arrival there.

"Goodness, you *have* grown tall" was her first observation.

"Yes," Angeline agreed meekly, waiting for a listing of all her other shortcomings.

But Rosalie only nodded briskly.

"Your modiste is going to thoroughly enjoy dressing you," she said. "I suppose you have nothing, Angeline? You have spent all your life in the country, have you not? Your mother never brought you to town. Having nothing is fine. It is better than having stacks of garments of inferior workmanship and unfashionable design. Tresham has given us carte blanche on the amount we may spend on you, which is no less than I would expect of him."

"I wish to choose my own designs and fabrics," Angeline said.

"But of course," Rosalie agreed.

"I like bright colors," Angeline warned her.

"I can see that." Rosalie looked at her sunshine yellow dress with the blue and green stripes about the hem. There was perhaps a suggestion of pain in her expression. "The design and even the color of your court gown will of course be dictated largely by what the queen demands of young ladies being presented to her. It will be archaic and very uncomfortable, but we will have little say in the matter. It would not do to offend Her Majesty. Your ball gowns — *all* of them — will have to be white, I am afraid. It is de rigueur for unmarried young ladies."

"White?" Angeline cried in dismay. White was her least favorite color — or lack of color — especially when it was upon her person.

Rosalie held up one hand.

"All your other dresses and accessories may be as brightly colored as you wish," she said. "You may dress in all the colors of the rainbow at once if you choose. I may advise against it, and I shall certainly express my opinion, but if you are a true Dudley, as I daresay you are, then you will pay no heed anyway."

"I always listen to advice," Angeline said, brightening. She was going to like her cousin, she believed. She had not set eyes upon her since she attended Rosalie's wedding at the age of eight or thereabouts.

"This is going to be a great delight to me, Angeline," Rosalie said. "I was ecstatic when I gave birth to Vincent. I was pleased when I had Emmett — it is always a relief to have a spare as well as an heir, and I knew Palmer had hoped for a second boy. I was somewhat disappointed when I had Colin and really rather depressed when I had Geoffrey. They are all perfect loves, of course, my boys, but I would have *so* liked to have a girl. But *now* I am to bring you out. I was really very gratified when Tresham asked me if I would."

"I hope," Angeline said, "I will not be a disappointment to you, Cousin Rosalie."

"You will not," her cousin said decisively. "And I am so *glad* you are not a small, soft, lisping, blond, blue-eyed creature like your m—"

She was assailed by a sudden fit of coughing.

Like your mother? Was that what she had been about to say? Surely not. Mama had not lisped. And she had been beauty itself. Perfection itself. Everything that Angeline was *not,* in fact.

"Oh, dear," Rosalie said, patting her chest to stop the coughing. "It is time we had some rain. The air is dry. What was I saying? Ah, yes, that we will go out shopping tomorrow bright and early. And the day after. And the day after that. We are going to have a *wonderful* time, Angeline."

And surprisingly they did. Angeline had never been shopping. She soon discovered that it was the most blissful activity in the world. At least, it was for the time being until there were even more exciting things to occupy her time.

The day for her presentation to the queen was set. And her come-out ball was to be the same evening at Dudley House. Tresham had made all the arrangements, and Ferdinand — who had been waiting at the house the day she arrived and had swept her off her feet and swung her about in two complete circles on the pavement outside the front door while she shrieked her protest and delight — had promised to see to it that she did not lack for partners all evening.

"Not that you will even without my vigilance, Angie," he had said. "In fact, I daresay prospective partners will be queued up beyond the ballroom doors and all the way down the stairs and out the door. Tresh will have to extend the duration of the ball for three whole days to accommodate them all and you will have blisters on all ten toes and on both heels and be unable to dance again all Season. Tell me about your journey. Tedious, was it?"

The days rushed by, and Angeline acquired so many new clothes and shoes and slippers and fans and reticules and a hundred and one other items that she wondered where Betty found room to put them all.

And finally, almost before Angeline was ready for it, the great day dawned. The day of The Curtsy — she thought of it in capital letters — and the come-out ball. Ferdinand might yet prove right, or wrong, about the number of prospective partners she would have, but she was to have at least one. The widowed Countess of Heyward had spoken to Rosalie, and Rosalie had spoken to Tresham, and the Earl of Heyward, the countess's brother-in-law, had spoken to Tresham, and it was all settled — the earl was to lead Angeline into the first set.

The very first set of her very first *ton* ball. She *hoped* the earl was tall, dark, and handsome, or at least some acceptable mixture of the three. Tresham, annoying man, had only said when she asked that Heyward was a dry old stick, but Rosalie had said nonsense, the earl was a *young* man, though she did not believe she had ever actually seen him. Which meant, of course, that he might still be a dry stick, whatever *that* was.

Anyway, it was just a dance, albeit the most important, most anticipated one of her life.

She was up ridiculously early in the morning. At just after seven o'clock she was at the open window of her bedchamber, barefoot and still in her nightgown, her forearms resting along the sill, her bosom propped on her forearms, her back arched inward. She gazed out upon gray early morning drizzle, but rather than allow the inclement weather to dampen her spirits, she sighed with contentment.

Today — within the next few hours — her real life would begin.

She was to be presented to the queen. There was a little flutter of excitement, perhaps even of nervousness, deep in her stomach at the prospect. And then she would be *free.* Free to enjoy all the myriad activities of the Season while searching for the man of her dreams.

Angeline sighed again, more wistfully this time.

She had already found him once, of course. Except that she had not set eyes upon him since that day at the Rose and Crown Inn and would probably never do so again. It would be very romantic to pine for him for the rest of her life but not at all practical. She would grow old and be a spinster and an unpaid nanny to all the children Tresham would produce once he had finished sowing his wild oats and taken a wife. And eventually she would shrivel up like a dried prune and be nothing but a burden to all her nephews and nieces and great-nephews and great-nieces and on down the generations while she relived the ever-dimming memory of the one meeting she had had with the love of her life when she was nineteen.

It all sounded ridiculously pathetic. And ridiculously . . . well, ridiculous.

She was going to put him right out of her mind from this moment on. There, it was already done. Tonight she would meet other gentlemen — hordes of them, if Ferdinand was to be believed. Tonight she would begin to fall in love again.

But her thoughts were distracted at that

60

moment by the sounds of a small commotion in Grosvenor Square below her window. She leaned forward on her forearms and peered downward.

Marsh, Tresham's head groom, was standing down there holding onto the bridle of a horse that was literally chomping at the bit in its eagerness to be off on its morning gallop. And Tresham, all black and long-legged in form-fitting riding clothes, was hurrying down the steps, pulling on his riding gloves as he went. He swung himself up into the saddle, and even as Angeline watched, he assumed instant command of his restless mount and rode off without further ado.

Angeline was assailed by a wave of envy bordering on jealousy.

He must be going for an early morning ride in Hyde Park. She would give anything in the world to be going with him. It was chilly and windy and ever so slightly drizzly, all weather conditions that would make almost any delicately nurtured female shudder with distaste and cling tenaciously to the indoors until the sun deigned to make an appearance.

But she was not a delicate female.

Cousin Rosalie had not said exactly when she would arrive to supervise while Betty got Angeline all decked out in her court

61

finery, but it would probably be ten o'clock at the very earliest. That gave her almost three hours to kick her heels. Or to . . .

Her hair would get damp.

Not if she wore her oldest — and still her favorite — riding hat. Besides, damp hair dried quickly.

Her complexion would turn rosy.

She would look vibrantly healthy among all the wilting lilies who would also be making their come-out. It never hurt to stand out from the crowd. And the worst of the shine would have faded from her nose and cheeks before she needed to leave the house again.

Marsh would refuse to saddle a horse for her without Tresham's consent. No, he would not. Not if she behaved as if it had all been planned yesterday, and — *what?* Had his grace not *informed* Marsh about it and instructed him to have a mount ready for her? How very odd!

No harm would be done. What could she be expected to do alone for three whole hours, after all — *at least* three? She would only get more nervous thinking about her curtsy and the tricky maneuver of backing out of the queen's presence without tripping over the train of her gown. Not that the possibility had struck her until this very moment. But now that it *had,* it would consume her mind and her nerves for every idle moment until she was safely out of the royal presence.

What better way to distract her mind and her nerves than to go for a morning ride? She would take a groom with her. She was not so lost to all conduct that she would go tearing in pursuit of Tresham without proper chaperonage. Besides, Marsh would never allow her to set one horse's hoof beyond the stable doors unless there was someone trustworthy with her.

Tresham would not mind if she joined him on his ride.

Well, he probably would, but he was not her *father.* He was only her guardian, and he had not exerted himself greatly so far to be a vigilant one — except that he had surrounded her with governesses and servants from the moment he became duke at the age of seventeen. And except that he had given vent to a minor volcanic eruption when he had discovered at that inn that the Reverend Coombes had abandoned her and that none of the four grooms or footmen from Acton had been in sight when she rushed downstairs to greet him and that Betty had still been half asleep up in her room. Now he had imposed Rosalie on her.

Not that Rosalie was a great imposition.

He would not scold her today, would he? Not in public, anyway. Or in private. Not today. This was her very special day, perhaps *the* most special of her whole life, and he would not wish to upset her.

And if she stood here any longer holding this rather garrulous mental debate with herself, she thought, straightening up and closing the window, it would be too late to go, and now that she had conceived the idea of taking a morning ride in order to relax her nerves, she could not possibly do without it.

Well, perhaps she *could.* But she *would* not.

She strode off in the direction of her dressing room.

This was the day, Edward thought as he woke up — and wished he could simply fall back to sleep.

There was his maiden speech to deliver in the Upper House. It had been written and rewritten and then written again. It had been practiced and repracticed and practiced again. And just last night — and every night for the last two weeks — he had been assailed by terror at the conviction that it was utter rubbish and he would be laughed out of the House and expelled from the ranks of the nobility.

He was not usually given to vivid, ridiculous imaginings.

And then tonight there was the Tresham ball and the set he was to dance with Lady Angeline Dudley. It was only a *dance*, he had tried to convince himself. But it was the opening set of her come-out ball, and every eye in the ballroom — virtually every eye in the *ton*, in other words — would be fixed upon them. His only hope, a faint one, was that most of those eyes would be directed exclusively at *her*. She was, after all, the most eligible young lady on the market this year and most people would be getting their first look at her.

However, he would think of the ball and that particular dance later.

He went out for an early morning ride in the park despite the inclemency of the weather — it was cloudy and chilly, and a light but persistent drizzle kept everything and everyone uncomfortably damp. If one waited for clement weather in England, though, one might find oneself riding for brief spells once or twice a fortnight if one were fortunate. Besides, he had made arrangements to meet two of his oldest and closest friends and he would not let them down, supposing that *they* braved the drizzle and the chill, that was.

They both did.

Edward's stomach was feeling rather queasy, and he was tired after a night of what he might have thought had been sleepless if there were not the memory of bizarre dreams, all of which had proceeded along the same general lines. In one he had begun his speech in the House of Lords with a flourish until he had faltered at the realization that he had forgotten to put on any clothes before leaving home. In another, he had got up to speak, opened his mouth, noted the respectful attention with which all his fellow peers were regarding him, and realized that he had forgotten to bring either his notes or his memory with him.

"Damnation," Sir George Headley said as they rode through the park together. "I counted upon the Row being deserted this morning. I need a good gallop to blow away the fumes of too much imbibing last night. It is a good thing my brother can turn twenty-one only once in his life."

Rotten Row was indeed surprisingly crowded with riders, some of them ambling along on their mounts, others moving at a brisker canter, some few flying along at a more reckless gallop — reckless because the grass was slippery with moisture and any bare patches of earth were slick with mud.

"We might as well take a turn up and down anyway," Ambrose Paulson said from Edward's other side. He grinned as they rode onto the Row. "Ed is looking rather green about the gills and in dire need of air and exercise, even though *you* were the one doing the drinking, George. But he has a maiden speech to deliver. I wish we might hear it."

"No, you do not," Edward assured them both. "Doubtless everyone in the House will be snoring before I reach the second paragraph."

"They will all thank you afterward for providing them with a good chance to rest," George said, and all three of them chuckled.

Edward breathed in lungfuls of fresh air and ignored the discomfort of water droplets clinging to his face. He began to relax a little, and they rode in companionable silence for several minutes while he mentally rehearsed his speech yet again.

It was George who broke the silence.

"Good Lord," he said suddenly, bringing his horse to a near halt and forcing his two friends to prance about on either side of him while they slowed their own mounts, "what the devil is *that?*"

That, Edward saw when he followed the

direction of his friend's gaze down the Row, was a woman. At first, though only for the merest moment, he thought she was surely a courtesan. She was cantering toward a group of young men, all sunny smiles, while a groom shadowed her a little distance behind. What other sort of lady would be out alone at this hour and in weather like this, after all?

The answer to his unspoken question came to him during that merest moment.

The *same* sort of lady as one who would stand alone in a public taproom, posed provocatively in a clinging bright pink muslin dress as she gazed through a window, oblivious to the effect she was having upon two males standing behind her.

Not just the same *sort* of lady, of course.

The very same one, in fact.

Edward watched, appalled, as she rode into the midst of the group of young men, none of whom he knew, talking volubly as she went. He did not hear the first few words, but then her voice became more audible.

". . . must have decided to go somewhere else, the provoking man. I was about to turn about and go back home when I spotted *you*. I was never so glad of anything in my life. But you must absolutely *promise* not to say a word, Ferdie. He would doubtless cut up nasty though it would be grossly unfair. How was I to know he was not coming here? This is where *everyone* comes to ride. I will ride with you and your friends instead. You will not mind, will you?"

She bestowed the dazzle of her smile upon the group at large. As Edward and his friends rode on by, Edward with his face averted lest she see and recognize him, there was a chorus of enthusiastic assent from the young men.

It would seem, then, that her indiscreet behavior at the Rose and Crown was nothing unusual. How well did she know any of those men? She certainly had not arrived with any of them. And *someone,* it seemed, would be annoyed if he knew she was here alone. As well he might be, whoever he was, poor devil.

Well, *this* time, Edward decided firmly, he was not going to get involved. If she did not know how to behave, and clearly she did not, it was not his concern — even if she did look slender and lithe and very much as though she might have been born in a saddle. And even if when she smiled she made one forget that it was not a bright, sunny morning.

He felt rather hot and ruffled, he realized.

What if she had seen him? She might have recognized him and hailed him. It would have been a ghastly breach of etiquette.

"That," Ambrose said, having refrained from answering George's question until they had moved past and out of earshot, "is a riding hat. At least, I assume it is since it is on the lady's head. And if it were a bird's nest, it would be infinitely more tidy, would it not?"

He and George snorted with mirth.

"A hat," George said. "I do believe you are right, Ambie. Perhaps it would not be such a monstrosity if it were dry."

Edward had hardly noticed the hat the lady wore. But he was about to be given a second chance to observe it. There was the sudden thunder of hooves from behind them, and before they could move to one side or take any other defensive action, five horses and riders went galloping past at full tilt, spraying water and mud indiscriminately in all directions, except over themselves. And then a sixth a decent interval behind the others — the groom.

Second in line was the only lady who had braved the weather this morning, whooping with joyful abandon and laughing with wild glee, just as if she had never in her life heard of feminine decorum — as perhaps she had not.

Her hat, glorious in its profusion of multicolored feathers culled from birds long deceased, bounced on her head in time with her movements and somehow stayed on.

It was perhaps the hat, Edward thought belatedly, that had caused him to mistake her at first for a courtesan.

He glanced down at his mud-spattered buff riding breeches and black boots — both new just last week and immaculately clean this morning. He flicked one gloved finger over his cheek to dislodge something wet that clung there.

"Who is she?" he asked, though he was not sure he wanted to know.

But neither of his friends had seen her before.

Edward really did not want to risk coming face-to-face with her, whoever she was.

"It is time I returned home to get ready for the House," he said.

His stomach answered with a return of the slight queasiness. He turned his mount to leave Rotten Row.

A whooping laugh blew past behind him together with a flying horse and rider. She was galloping back up the Row, Edward presumed without looking around to confirm his guess. It sounded as if she was leading the pack this time.

He felt more spatters of mud pelting against the back of his coat.

And then he sensed something and was unwise enough to turn his head.

She had stopped her horse. She had done it so abruptly, it seemed, that it was rearing up. But she brought it under control with an ease that could only have been born of long practice. Her companions were thundering off into the distance, apart from the groom, who was altogether more vigilant.

Her eyes were fixed upon Edward, wide with recognition. Her lips were parting in a smile.

Oh, Lord!

At any moment now she was going to hail him, and there was enough of a distance between them that at least a dozen other riders, *including his friends,* were bound to hear.

Edward inclined his head curtly to her, touched his whip to the brim of his hat, and rode away.

She did not call after him.

Devil take it, she was in London. He was bound to run into her again, he supposed. Perhaps even this evening. Perhaps she would be at that infernal Tresham ball.

He frowned. This was *not* a day destined to bring him any pleasure. It had already started badly.

CHAPTER 4

Angeline's presentation to the queen had passed without incident. There had been no embarrassing encounters with the train of her gown, and she had met and chatted with other young ladies who were also making their come-out this year. She had high hopes of making friends of some of them.

She had never had a close friend, which seemed like an abject admission to make, even to herself, though she had never felt dreadfully deprived. Her two brothers had been her playmates — and her adored heroes — when she was a child. When she was a girl, she had known all her neighbors at Acton, including those of her own age, and had been on amiable terms with all of them. But of course they all stood slightly in awe of her because she was the daughter and later the sister of the Duke of Tresham, with the result that she had never had a bosom bow, someone with whom to chat and giggle and in whom to confide all the deepest, darkest secrets of her young heart.

Now, among her peers, perhaps she would find such young friends.

And beaux.

All the men in the vicinity of Acton, from the age of fifteen to eighty, were *far* too much in awe of her. Perhaps they all knew Tresham's reputation too well and chose to safeguard their teeth rather than appear too friendly toward his sister.

Oh, she was glad, glad, *glad* that she was here in London at last, that she had made her curtsy to the queen, and that she was dressing for her come-out ball. She could hardly contain her exuberance.

She was already dressed, in fact, and Betty had just put the finishing touches to her very elaborate coiffure. She would not have thought it possible to arrange so many curls and ringlets on her head in such a pleasing arrangement. And she was confident that they would remain where they were. She shook her head gingerly and experimentally, but they did not cascade down about her shoulders. There was, of course, a whole arsenal of pins hidden away under them.

Angeline got to her feet and looked at herself critically in the pier glass. She looked, she supposed, as well as she possibly could look considering two massive and unavoidable facts: first that she was compelled to wear white, and second that she was a great dark beanpole of a girl. She had had the misfortune to take after her father rather than her mother in looks, as had both her brothers. But that fact was fine for them. They were *men*.

Nothing was going to dampen her spirits tonight, though.

Nothing.

She took the ivory fan Betty was holding out to her, opened it, and fluttered it before her face.

"Will I do?" she asked.

"You look ever so lovely, my lady," Betty said. She was not being obsequious. She was just as likely to say the opposite if that was what she thought. Betty often did not approve of what her mistress chose to wear.

Angeline gazed into her own reflected eyes.

Who *was* he?

Her heart had performed a triple somersault when she had spotted him this morning as she went thundering past him up Rotten Row.

There he was.

At last.

Looking neat and lithe in the saddle, and

just a little mud-spattered.

She had been about to call out to him. But, just as he had done at that inn, he had inclined his head to her, showing that *at least* he recognized her, and had ridden away without a word.

His behavior had been perfectly correct, of course. They still had not been formally presented. He had saved her from the horrible faux pas of calling out to a stranger in a very public place. Tresham would have had her head if he had ever heard about it. Even Ferdinand would have been annoyed, though by that time Ferdie was almost at the other end of the Row in a race with his friends. None of them were close enough to answer the question that had burned in her mind.

Who was he?

Angeline fanned her face a little faster before snapping the fan shut.

Would she see him again?

Would he be here tonight?

She turned from the pier glass as a brisk knock sounded at the door. Betty answered it. Tresham and Ferdinand were standing out there, both tall and gorgeous in their black evening clothes with crisp white linen.

Ferdinand was grinning.

"We argued over who should come up for

77

you, Angie," he said, "and we ended up *both* coming. You look as fine as fivepence."

His eyes swept over her in what looked like genuine appreciation.

"Thank you, Ferdie," she said. "So do you."

He was twenty-one, one year down from Oxford, and well on his way to being as dedicated a rakehell as their brother — or so rumor had it, and Angeline did not doubt it. Neither did she doubt that he was wildly attractive to every female who set eyes upon him, and that he knew it.

Tresham looked his habitual bored, handsome self.

"Is this really our sister, Ferdinand," he asked, probably rhetorically, "looking quite tame and civilized and, yes, very fine indeed?"

One might wait a decade in vain for a compliment from Tresham. One ought to cherish one when it did come one's way, then. But Angeline bristled instead.

"Tame?" she said. *"Civilized?* Does that imply that I am usually wild and *un*civilized? What do you know about me, Tresham? Before I came to town, I saw you on precisely two occasions after you were sixteen and I was eleven. And I would hardly misbehave during either Papa's funeral or

78

Mama's, would I? You abandoned me when you left home so suddenly. All you knew about me afterward, presumably, was what you learned in the reports sent you by the various governesses you imposed upon me. And they *all* disapproved of me because I was not a perfect mouse of a young lady. What did they expect? What did *you* expect? I am a Dudley, after all. But I am not *wild* for all that. Or *uncivilized*."

Tresham regarded her steadily from his very dark, unreadable eyes.

"That is better," he said. "Now you have some color in your cheeks, Angeline, and are not unrelieved white from head to toe. Are you ready to go down? Or do you plan to make an entrance to your own ball after everyone else has arrived?"

Ferdinand grinned and winked and offered his arm.

Oh, she adored both brothers, Angeline thought as she took an arm of each and descended the staircase for the all-important duty of greeting the ball guests in the receiving line. She adored them even though she was constantly exasperated by them. She had *heard* much about them even though she had not seen a great deal of them during the past seven years — though Ferdinand had come home almost every school or university holiday, even if only for a few days. She had heard about the dangerous, reckless races, the fistfights, the mistresses, the duels, though that last applied only to Tresham. She had heard of two separate duels fought with pistols, in both of which Tresham's opponent had shot first and missed before Tresham shot contemptuously in the air. And both duels had been over the other man's wife, with whom Tresham was dallying. Fortunately, both duels were long over before Angeline heard about them. She was *very* disapproving of the cause, *very* proud that her brother had shot into the air rather than directly at a wronged husband, and *very* convinced that every nerve in her body had been shattered by the news and would never function properly again.

Cousin Rosalie was waiting in the hall below and smiled at Angeline with approval and encouragement.

"You really do look very distinguished, Angeline," she said. "Other girls are swallowed up by white. You . . . command it."

Whatever that meant, Angeline thought ruefully. And she had noticed that Rosalie called her *distinguished* rather than *pretty*.

She wondered suddenly how her mother would have described her tonight. Would she have called her *fine,* as Tresham and Ferdinand had done? Or *distinguished,* as Rosalie had done? Or *lovely,* as Betty had done? Or *pretty?* Or would she have frowned, as she had done in the past, at her daughter's gangly height or at the extreme darkness of her hair and the indelicacy of her complexion? Or, as she had done once when Angeline was thirteen, at the fact that her eyebrows did not arch elegantly above her eyes?

She had been in the middle of one of her increasingly rare stays at Acton Park at the time, even though Papa was already dead and therefore no longer to be avoided. Angeline had spent the whole of the subsequent week peering into mirrors, trying to arch her eyebrows the way Mama did. But when she had tried the new expression on her mother, Mama had told her she looked like a startled hare and warned her that she would have furrows in her brow before she was thirty if she was not careful.

Perhaps her mother would have approved of her in white, Angeline thought. It was what she had almost always worn herself. Or perhaps not. Perhaps she would have seen more clearly than ever that Angeline in no way resembled herself and would have been unable to disguise her disappointment and her conviction that Angeline would never be the daughter she must have dreamed of. Although Angeline was no longer gangly, she was even taller than she had been at the age of thirteen. And her eyebrows would still not arch.

But she was *not* going to grow maudlin over the hopelessness of her looks on this of all nights. She smiled dazzlingly at Rosalie without releasing her brothers' arms, and they all made their way to the ballroom together.

Its long length looked like an indoor garden, a luscious indoor garden, laden down as it was with white flowers — lilies, roses, daisies, chrysanthemums, among others — and green leaves and ferns. They were in banks about the perimeter of the room and circling the pillars. They hung in exuberant profusion from baskets on the walls. They were reflected in mirrors. The room was filled with their combined scents.

The three large chandeliers had been on the floor for the past several days while every piece of silver and crystal had been polished and shined and dozens of new candles had been fitted in place. The candles had been lit now and the chandeliers hoisted up close to the gilded ceiling, which was painted with scenes from Greek mythology.

The wall sconces had been filled with candles, which were also alight.

The wood floor gleamed. The French windows along one long wall had been opened back so that guests could stroll on the lamp-lit terrace beyond. The orchestra members had already arranged their instruments on the dais at one end of the room. At the other end, the doors to the adjoining salon were open so that guests could help themselves to drinks and other refreshments from tables covered with crisp white cloths.

It was all . . . overwhelming.

Angeline had only ever attended informal dances in the drawing rooms of the more prosperous of her neighbors at home and a couple of assemblies at the village inn.

She stepped alone into the ballroom and stood there, her hands clasped to her bosom, trying with all her might to resist the urge to weep.

This was *it*. This was what she had longed for throughout the lonely years of her girlhood.

Suddenly she felt lonelier than she had ever felt.

And so excited she could scarcely breathe.

Tresham stepped up beside her, drew her arm through his again, set his free hand lightly over hers, and said not a word.

She had never loved him more.

No one had cheered wildly over Edward's maiden speech in the House of Lords, but no one had jeered either. And he had not noticed anyone nodding off to sleep during its delivery. Several members had even shaken his hand afterward. One elderly duke, who carried a hearing trumpet with him but had not used it all afternoon as far as Edward had noticed, had even commented that the speech had been a fine piece of oratory. At which a younger peer had slapped him on the shoulder, winked at Edward, and observed that His Grace had said the same thing of every maiden speech that had been delivered during the past fifty years.

Edward had joined in a general burst of laughter. It had been, actually, the best moment. He had felt accepted.

Anyway, it was a huge relief to have that ordeal behind him.

It would have been pleasant to relax at home for the rest of the day or else to have gone to the theater or White's Club or somewhere else where he could be a passive observer rather than an active doer. But there was this infernal ball of Tresham's to attend. And, if that was not bad enough,

84

there was the opening set to dance with Tresham's sister.

At least Eunice would be there. He would reserve the second set with her and hope she was content to sit it out with him. Then at last he would be comfortable and could relax in the knowledge that this long-dreaded day was effectively at an end.

He arrived at Dudley House with his mother and Lorraine. He was happy to see them both in higher spirits than they had been for a long time. They were both out of mourning. His mother had become reacquainted with some of her numerous friends in the *ton* and seemed determined to put memories of her elder son to rest and concentrate her attentions upon her second son. Lorraine had put on some weight and looked the better for it. The color was back in her cheeks and the gloss in her hair. The weight, the color, and the gloss had disappeared even before Maurice's death. Now she looked her age again. She was still only twenty-three, one year younger than Edward himself. She was a vivid beauty once more.

Edward wished her well. He had always been fond of her and she of him. She had sometimes, though not often, confided her misery to him while Maurice lived. A few times he had tried to talk to his brother but had merely ended up being called a pompous ass for his pains.

Edward made his way up the staircase inside Dudley House, a lady on each arm. This was one of the first grand balls of the Season. He doubted there was a person invited who was not here already or else in the long line of carriages outside the doors. The staircase was crowded as guests awaited their turn to pass along the receiving line.

It still felt strange, Edward thought as they reached the doorway to the ballroom and the majordomo announced their names, to be treated with such deference. Mr. Edward Ailsbury had been able to slip into — and out of — any social event he chose without anyone particularly noticing. The Earl of Heyward was *someone,* even if he was also just an ordinary man or a pompous ass, depending upon who was describing him.

"There is Lady Palmer," Lorraine said, smiling. "She informed me that her brother will be here this evening — Lord Fenner, that is. I wonder if he has arrived yet."

Edward looked down at her with interest. He wondered if there was any significance in her mentioning Fenner, whom he knew as a pleasant enough man, a few years his senior.

"It may take you an hour or two to find

out even after passing along the receiving line," he said. "It looks as if this ball is going to be a squeeze to end squeezes."

"Well, of course it is," she said. "Who could resist an invitation to a ball at Dudley House? The Duke of Tresham *never* hosts balls."

Except tonight, Edward thought ruefully, for his sister, with whom Edward was going to have to dance. He wished suddenly that he had thought of persuading his mother to sit at the pianoforte in the drawing room at home while he practiced steps with Lorraine or one of his sisters. But being rusty on the steps of all the most common dances was not his problem. Having two left feet was, and no amount of practice could rectify that.

The receiving line was short. Lady Palmer was at the near side of it with Tresham next to her. The young lady beyond him was presumably Lady Angeline Dudley, but Edward could not see her clearly, partly because Tresham stood in the way, and partly because almost every lady ahead of him had nodding plumes in her hair.

He bowed to Lady Palmer and agreed that yes, indeed, they were fortunate to have such a fine evening for the ball considering the rain that had fallen fitfully all morning.

His mother smiled and nodded and made a few polite comments of her own, and Lorraine smiled warmly and congratulated Lady Palmer on what already showed the unmistakable promise of being a grand success of an evening.

Edward inclined his head more stiffly to Tresham, who returned the gesture and spoke briefly and courteously to the two ladies. Amazingly, neither Edward's mother nor Lorraine seemed to harbor any particular grudge against the man with whom Maurice had been racing when he died. And perhaps they were right. If it had not been Tresham, it would have been someone else. And Tresham had not directly caused the upset. He had overtaken Maurice just before a sharp bend in the road a moment or two earlier and had been safely around the bend and the obstacle beyond it before that obstacle — a large hay cart — and Maurice's curricle met right on the blindest part of the curve.

Tresham turned to his right, and Edward and the two ladies turned to their left and an avenue of sight opened up.

"May I present my sister, Lady Angeline Dudley?" Tresham said.

Oh, good Lord!

Edward's eyes had alit upon her and hers

upon him long before her brother had completed the brief introductions.

She was looking perfectly respectable tonight. She was dressed in a white gown of simple, modest design, which nevertheless hugged her tall, shapely frame in a thoroughly becoming manner. She was standing upright, with perfectly correct posture. She was smiling politely — and then with heightened color in her cheeks and an extra sparkle in her dark eyes.

She looked more beautiful than ever, though there was nothing delicate about either her features or her coloring.

Edward was appalled.

He bowed to her, and she curtsied to all three of them, though she was looking at him — quite fixedly.

"Lady Angeline," he murmured.

Do not say it, he implored her silently.

Perhaps she needed no urging, though she had definitely been about to speak to him both at the Rose and Crown and in Hyde Park this morning.

"Lord Heyward."

But of course, he thought. He had passed Tresham ten minutes away from that inn. Tresham in a *carriage,* which must be rare indeed. Tresham headed away from London just when everyone else was headed toward it. Tresham on the way to meet his sister at the Rose and Crown. The evidence had been there staring him in the face, including the fact that brother and sister looked remarkably alike. He had not made the connection.

Now he was doomed to dance with her, a lady who did not know how to behave. A Dudley, in fact.

She was smiling at his mother now and talking with her. The line was stalling behind them. It was time to move into the ballroom.

"I shall look forward to leading you into the first set, Lady Angeline," he said.

Her smile was dazzling. She had perfect teeth.

"Oh," she said, "and I shall look forward to it too, Lord Heyward."

"It is a pity," his mother said as they stepped into the ballroom, "that she favors her father's side of the family rather than her mother's."

"Maybe not, Mother," Lorraine said. "Looking as she does, she is less likely to find herself compared with the late Duchess of Tresham. That can only be to her advantage, even if the duchess *was* a rare beauty. And she is not unhandsome. What do you think, Edward?"

"I think she is the most beautiful creature I have ever set eyes upon," he said and then felt remarkably foolish and chagrined. He had not meant the words the way they had sounded. He did not feel any admiration for the girl. Quite the contrary. It had been a quite objective remark, which had come out making him sound like a lovestruck mooncalf.

Both ladies were looking at him with interest.

"She certainly is striking," his mother said. "And charming. She has a vitality not always apparent in girls new to the *ton.* And she was obviously pleased to meet *you,* Edward. She could scarcely keep her eyes off you. You are looking remarkably distinguished this evening. Is he not, Lorraine?"

"Edward *always* looks distinguished," Lorraine said, smiling fondly at him.

Edward sighed inwardly. One hour. One hour from now the ball would have begun and the first set would be over. Then he could relax.

Why did one hour seem like an eternity?

The next half hour, Angeline thought as the long line of guests gradually became a trickle and finally stopped altogether. The orchestra members on the dais were beginning to tune their instruments as though they fully intended to use them soon. The next half hour was going to be the most fateful, the most wonderful of her entire life. It was, in fact, going to be the beginning of the rest of her life.

The blissful beginning.

When Tresham had turned sideways in the line and the two ladies had done likewise and Angeline had been able to see the gentleman who was with them . . .

Well. There were simply no words.

And when she had heard the echo of the names the majordomo had recited a moment before and she had realized that *this* was the Earl of Heyward, with whom she was to dance the opening set . . .

Well.

There were simply no *thoughts*.

Except that suddenly she had had one — a thought, that was — and had almost suffered a heart attack as a result.

"The *Countess* of Heyward?" she had asked Tresham, a hint of a squeak in her voice just before he turned back to greet the next guests in line. "I am to dance the opening set of my come-out ball with a *married man?*"

The possibility that he was *married* had never once crossed her mind.

"The countess is his sister-in-law," he had explained. "She was married to his brother, the late Heyward and one devil of a fine fellow."

Of course. She had *known* that. Rosalie had arranged the opening set with *the widowed Countess of Heyward.*

Then another thought had struck her.

A dry old stick?

But Tresham was greeting someone else and was about to introduce her. Oh, goodness, there were *so* many new faces to memorize and so many names to put with those faces. She stopped even trying.

He was the Earl of Heyward.

Single.

And she was going to dance off into the rest of her life with him.

Into happily-ever-after, even though she had never believed in such a ridiculous notion.

Suddenly she did.

And the next half hour was to be all hers.

All theirs.

He came striding toward her as soon as she stepped inside the ballroom, Tresham on her right, Cousin Rosalie on her left, a look of firm purpose on his face as though this was a very serious moment. As though it was something that *mattered* to him.

As perhaps it was.

Angeline stopped herself only just in time from clasping her hands to her bosom. It had not escaped her attention, focused though she was on the Earl of Heyward, that simply *everyone* in the ballroom was looking at her. Of course everyone was. It was not even conceited to believe so. This was her ball, and she would lead off the first set. Besides, she was the most eligible young lady in London this year. She was the sister of the Duke of Tresham.

The Earl of Heyward stopped in front of her, inclined his head to both Rosalie and Tresham, and then fixed his eyes upon her. His beautifully *blue* eyes.

"This is my set, I believe, Lady Angeline," he said.

He was holding out a hand toward her, palm down.

She felt as though she must just have run five miles against a stiff wind. She smiled and decided not to open her fan. The last thing she needed was *more* breeze.

"Yes," she said. "Thank you, my lord."

And she placed her hand on the back of his — it was firm and warm — and stepped out onto the empty dance floor with him.

Their very first touch.

There was a sigh of something from the

spectators, and the orchestra ceased its tuning.

Angeline's stomach felt as though it was suddenly inhabited by a whole swarm of fluttering butterflies. Of nervousness? Of excitement? Both?

He led her to a spot close to the orchestra dais and left her there while he took his place a short distance away.

It was the signal for other couples to come and join them, to form the long lines of dancers for the first set, the ladies on one side, the gentlemen on the other.

Angeline gazed across at Lord Heyward, and he looked steadily back.

He was neatly, fashionably dressed. But there was no excess — no high shirt points threatening to pierce his eyeballs, no creaking corsets, no profusion of fobs and chains, no elaborately embroidered waistcoat, no haircut with its own name, like a Brutus, for example.

And no smile.

Meeting her, dancing with her, *was* serious business to him, then.

He was not a frivolous man.

He was probably the polar opposite of Tresham. And of Ferdinand. And her father. All of whom she loved, or had loved, to distraction. But none of them would ever be her husband. Neither would any man remotely like them. She had *some* sense of self-preservation.

She was going to marry someone like the Earl of Heyward.

No, correction.

She was going to marry the Earl of Heyward.

He might not know it yet, but he would.

They were a little too far apart to converse comfortably. And she did not wish to shout inanities across at him, though several couples beyond them were doing just that.

He held his peace too.

And then the orchestra played a decisive chord and the chatter died. The butterflies in her stomach did not, but fluttered to renewed life. She curtsied in the line of ladies. He bowed in the line of gentlemen. And the music began and they were off, performing the intricate steps of a lively country dance. Before she knew it, Angeline found that it was their turn — they were the lead couple, after all — to twirl down the set between the lines of clapping dancers.

The butterflies had disappeared without a trace.

She was so happy she thought she might well burst.

But awareness returned soon enough. And with it came a realization that first amazed her and then touched her.

Lord Heyward danced with careful precision and rather wooden grace. Actually, the grace was quite minimal. Even nonexistent. His timing was a little off, as though he waited to see what everyone else was doing before he did it himself. And occasionally there was a definite hesitation.

The poor man could not dance. Or rather, he *could,* but dancing was not something that came naturally to him or gave him any enjoyment whatsoever. His face was blank of expression, but there was a certain tension behind the blankness, and Angeline guessed that he was concentrating hard upon not disgracing himself.

And yet as the lead couple they were the ones most on display to the many guests who were not themselves dancing but were only watching — and storing tidbits of gossip to share in tomorrow's drawing rooms.

Oh, poor Lord Heyward. He was not enjoying himself at all.

This was *not* the way to begin their . . . Their *what?* Relationship? Courtship? Happily-ever-after?

It was not the way to begin it, anyway, whatever it was.

The first dance of the set came to an end, and there was a brief pause before the second began. As soon as it did, Angeline realized that the rhythm was even faster than it had been before. Lord Heyward looked like a man who had been climbing the steps to the gallows until now but had suddenly emerged onto the flat platform and the trapdoor and noose itself.

There was really nothing else she could do, Angeline decided, except what she proceeded to do.

She turned her ankle and stumbled awkwardly.

CHAPTER 5

Angeline had always been impulsive. She had always had a tendency to act before she thought, usually with less than desirable results. Her governesses had habitually, and unsuccessfully, attempted to teach her the wisdom of a lady's always pausing to consider what she was about to say or do before actually saying or doing whatever it was.

She had done it again. *Acted,* that was, before thinking of the consequences of what she was about to do.

Her ankle was not damaged. It was a little sore, perhaps, but only with the sort of pain that diminished to nothing at all within minutes and was really not worth the bother of fussing over. But . . .

Well, this was her come-out ball. Worse, this was the opening set of her come-out ball. All eyes were upon her. That seemed to include even the eyes of her fellow dancers. *And* of the orchestra members. She had turned her ankle, though *not* the ankle belonging to the leg she had broken last year, and she had stumbled awkwardly, and she had gasped with pain, and . . .

Well, and the world gasped with her and converged upon her from all corners of the globe. The music stopped abruptly, and dancers and spectators came dashing, all presumably in the hope of catching her before she hit the floor.

The Earl of Heyward reached her first and wrapped an arm about her waist and held her firmly upright so that she could not possibly tumble to the floor even if that had been her intention, which it had not.

It was a distracting moment, or fraction of a moment. For he was all firm, muscled masculinity, and Angeline would have liked nothing better than to revel for at least a short while in the unfamiliar delight of being held in a man's arms — well, almost in his arms, anyway. And not just any man's arms. And what was that absolutely *wonderful* cologne that clung about his person?

But voices all about her were raised in alarm or concern or puzzlement.

"Lady Angeline!"

"You have hurt yourself."

"She has hurt herself."

"Set her down on the floor. Don't try

moving her."

"Carry her over to the French windows for some air."

"What happened?"

"Hand me my vinaigrette."

"Send a servant to fetch a physician."

"Did she faint?"

"The music was too fast. I *said* it was, did I not?"

"The floor is too highly polished."

"Have you sprained your ankle?"

"Has she broken her ankle?"

"How dreadfully unfortunate."

"Oh, the poor dear."

"What *happened?*"

"Trip over your own toes, did you, Angie?" This last in the cheerful voice of Ferdinand.

And those were only a sampling of the myriad exclamations and comments Angeline heard. This, she thought, had *not* been one of the best ideas she had ever conceived.

"Oh, dear," she said, feeling the heat of a very genuine blush rise in her cheeks, "how very clumsy of me."

"Not at all. Are you hurt?" Lord Heyward asked her with flattering concern.

"Hardly at all," she said, laughing lightly.

But *that* was no answer, especially for a large audience, all of whose members were now hushed in an attempt to hear what she had to say. She winced as she set her foot back on the floor, and the guests winced with her.

"Well, perhaps just a little," she said. "We had better sit out what remains of this set so that I will be able to dance for the rest of the evening. I am so sorry for causing such a fuss. Please ignore me."

She smiled about at the gathered masses and rather wished it were possible to be sucked at will into a great hole.

"Thank you, Heyward. I shall take Angeline to a withdrawing room to rest for a while. The dancing may resume."

It was Tresham, cool and black-eyed. In control. Taking charge.

Lord Heyward's arm loosened about her waist but did not entirely drop away.

"Lady Angeline is my partner," he said, sounding as cool as Tresham. "I shall help her to that love seat over there and sit with her, as is her wish. She may then decide if she is fit to dance the next set or if she would prefer to withdraw for a spell."

It was an exchange that did not even *nearly* qualify as a confrontation, Angeline thought, looking with interest from her brother's face to Lord Heyward's. And yet . . . And yet there was *something* there, some ever so minor clash of wills. And, just as he had at the Rose and Crown, the earl won the day with quiet courtesy. Tresham stared back at him for a fraction of a second longer than was strictly necessary, raised his eyebrows, and turned to nod at the leader of the orchestra.

The whole incident had lasted for a maximum of two minutes, probably less. The earl offered his arm this time rather than just the back of his hand, Angeline linked hers through it and leaned upon him with just enough of her weight to look convincing, and he led her to the love seat he had indicated, which was wedged in next to the orchestra dais and was therefore somewhat isolated from the other seats in the ballroom.

The orchestra struck up its lively tune again and the dancers danced. Angeline glanced at them a little wistfully while Lord Heyward rescued a brocaded stool from half under the dais and set it before her to support her injured foot. She rested it on the stool and sighed.

"Ah," she said, "that is better. Thank you, my lord."

He inclined his head to her and seated himself beside her. *Close* beside her since the seat was narrow. Even so, he kept a very correct sliver of air between their two bodies.

"I adore dancing," she said as she opened her fan and plied it slowly before her face. "I daresay you do too. I do apologize for depriving you of the pleasure of participating any further until the next set."

"Not at all," he said. "Besides, I do *not* enjoy dancing."

She could feel the heat from his body and smell that very enticing cologne again. She would not mind at all, she thought quite scandalously, if he accidentally touched her arm or kissed her hand. Or her lips, for that matter. She had never been kissed. She had *wanted* to be for some time now. And who better . . .

The ballroom was surely exceedingly warm.

"I suppose," she said because she did not want him to suspect that she had guessed the truth, poor man, "you have been dancing for so many years that you have become quite jaded."

"Not at all," he said again. "I have always been clumsy at it. I have been able to avoid dancing until this year. I was insignificantly positioned as the younger brother of an earl who was married and beginning to set up his nursery. When he died last year, my life changed."

Ah, an honest man. One who was willing to admit that he was a clumsy dancer. There were not many honest people in this world, Angeline suspected, especially on the subject of their own defects.

"And now you are expected to dance all the time," she said, smiling at him. "You were forced to dance with *me*."

"I was not *forced*, Lady Angeline." His eyebrows rose, and she noticed that they arched very nicely indeed above his eyes without unduly creasing his brow. "It was my pleasure."

Ah, not always honest. Her smile deepened.

"You were in mourning all last year, then, were you?" she asked him. "I have been in mourning too, though not last year. It was the year before. For my mother. I ought to have made my come-out last year. Is that not strange? If I *had*, I would not have encountered you at that inn outside Reading or in Hyde Park this morning. And I would have had a different partner with whom to dance the opening set of my come-out ball. You would have been away somewhere mourning for your brother. How random a thing fate is."

Perhaps he did not see their meetings as

105

fate. Or not as a happy one, anyway. If he did, he had nothing to say on the subject. And when she glanced at him, she could see that his lips were rather tightly set.

It really was a fast and vigorous dance, she thought as her eyes strayed beyond his shoulder. Tresham was dancing with the widowed Countess of Heyward and Ferdinand with the small, blond-haired, very pretty Lady Martha Hamelin, with whom Angeline had chatted at great length at St. James's Palace this morning. Trust Ferdie to single out the loveliest girl in the room.

She really hoped Lady Martha would be one of those close friends she craved.

"I *ought* to have made my come-out last year," she said again, resuming her story, "but I broke my leg."

She glanced down at it. Her foot was reclining on the brocaded stool. Her *left* foot. It was the right foot she had turned on the dance floor a short while ago. Oh, dear. It was too late now, though, to make the correction. He would surely notice. So, perhaps, would half of those gathered in the ballroom. She was not unaware of the fact that many eyes were turned their way.

"You are accident prone, Lady Angeline?" he asked.

"I fell out of a tree," she said. "I was crossing the bull's meadow because I was late and needed to return home quickly and because there was no sign of the bull. I *did* look, for one does not wish to come face-to-face with two tons of annoyed bull in the middle of a meadow, does one? I still do not know where he could possibly have been hiding, but he was there right enough. He was hiding deliberately, I daresay, lying in wait for just such an opportunity as that with which I presented him. I went up the tree like a monkey when he came charging after me, and I sat up there for what seemed like an hour, though I daresay it was no longer than ten minutes or so, while he prowled about down below trying to devise a way of getting at me. I have never been more thankful for the limited attention of bulls. I might have been up there for a *week*. He lost interest eventually and wandered away, and I was so relieved and so frantic to get away before he returned *and* because I had invited visitors and it was becoming more and more probable that they would be at the house before me, that I did not pay the descent of the tree my full attention and missed my footing on a lower branch and fell to the ground. I landed on my left leg and actually heard it crack. I was very vexed with myself, but it might have been worse. I might have landed on my head. And by some miracle the bull did not return while I moved to the fence and scrambled beneath it as quickly as I could on my bot— Well." She fanned her face briskly.

He was looking fully at her and it struck her foolishly that she could well drown in his blue eyes if she gazed into them for long enough.

"I hope," he said, "you learned to be more punctual for appointments, Lady Angeline, so that in future you need not be tempted to cross forbidden and dangerous meadows."

She tipped her head to one side and regarded him thoughtfully.

"I told the story to make you smile," she said. "Other men slap their thighs when I tell it and roar with mirth. Ladies titter behind their fans and look merry."

"I wonder," he said, "if they would all laugh so hard if it were Tresham telling the story about his *deceased* sister."

"Lord Heyward," she said, "are you perhaps just a little bit stuffy?"

And there, she had done it again. Words before thought. But it was too late to recall them.

His nostrils flared slightly. She had annoyed him, which was really hardly surprising.

But she had not meant her observation to be an insult or even a criticism. She did not mind in the least if he was a little stuffy. Not under the circumstances. It had probably never occurred to anyone else whose ears she had regaled with that particular story that it might just as easily have been a *tragic* one.

Perhaps she ought to have used the words *serious-minded* rather than *stuffy*. They had a more positive connotation.

"According to your definition of the word, Lady Angeline," he said, "no doubt I am. I do not find stories of charging bulls amusing. Or stories of unescorted ladies being accosted by impudent fellows in inn taprooms, though I daresay such incidents could be made to sound uproariously amusing. Or stories of daredevils racing their curricles along a narrow road used by other innocent and unsuspecting travelers, though I daresay such incidents have entertained many a gathering of men who admire sheer daredevilry. I make no apology for being *stuffy*. Life is too serious a business for idle persons to endanger themselves and others by being hoydens or rakehells."

Angeline gazed at him.

And had a thought.

Had his brother died in a curricle race? Had he been a daredevil?

Did he blame *her* for what had happened at the Rose and Crown, even though he had defended her so gallantly? Because she ought to have been chaperoned or not there at all?

He certainly blamed her for the bull incident. Because she had been *late* for an appointment.

She might have bristled with anger at the implied criticism, as she undoubtedly would have done if it had been Tresham delivering the scold, or Ferdinand. Or Miss Pratt.

But she stopped to think — a rare occurrence — and plied her fan slowly as she did so.

She might indeed have died if that tree had not been in that particular spot in the meadow or if she had indeed fallen on her head instead of her left leg. Or if the bull had come back. That handsome red-haired gentleman might have done her considerable harm in the inn taproom if there had been no one there to speak up for her — though she did not *think* she would have been in any real danger. Or, if the man had refused to apologize to her, Lord Heyward might have been beaten to a pulp out in the yard — though she did not *think* so. But even if he had sustained just a black eye, it would have been at least partly her fault. She ought not to have been where she was.

She must seem like a careless, unladylike, frivolous chatterbox to Lord Heyward. And a hoyden to boot.

Was he wrong?

Miss Pratt would agree wholeheartedly with him.

But even if he was right, was that *all* that could be said of her? Surely not. There was all that part of herself that was . . . Well, that was *herself*. All those things about her that were too muddled or confusing or, well, simply too *deep* to be put into words. She was not even sure she knew them all herself. Sometimes she believed she did not know herself at all. But she did know that she was not *just* a thoughtless, garrulous hoyden.

And then, of course, there was her appearance. How could she possibly compete with the likes of Martha Hamelin? She could not. She could only be herself.

Oh, goodness, she could not think of all this *now*.

And her fan was whipping up a veritable hurricane.

"You do not approve of me," she said, which was probably a gross understatement.

It was also a depressing realization when she was head over ears in love with him. And then she had a sudden thought, which came from nowhere, a sudden memory of the way he had looked in Hyde Park. "Did I splash you with mud in the park this morning? I went there for a gallop because I have done nothing but shop for *weeks* before today and had simply *oceans* of energy pent up inside. And I was feeling really quite nervous at the thought of meeting the queen and perhaps tripping over the train of my court gown. Even now I turn cold at the very thought, though fortunately it did not happen. I went to the park to find Tresham, but he had gone somewhere else to ride, provoking man. It was very fortunate indeed that Ferdinand was there. I would have been obliged to ride directly home if he had not been, and Marsh would have known that Tresham had not really arranged to meet me. He would have looked reproachfully at me, and I would have felt three inches high. *Did* I splash you?"

"It was of no moment," he said, which, of course, was merely a polite, roundabout way of saying yes. "Mud brushes off clothes once it has dried. And I hope I have not been ill-mannered enough to give the impression that I dislike you, Lady Angeline. I would not presume to pass judgment upon any lady."

She fanned her face and smiled ruefully at him.

"If you did *not* dislike me," she said, "you would have denied doing so quite vehemently instead of merely saying *I would not presume to pass judgment on a lady.* I shall persuade you to alter your opinion of me. I am out now. My hoydenish youth is over, and today I have become a lady — elegant, refined, discreet, quiet, and everything else a lady ought to be. I shall be the *perfect* lady for the rest of the spring — indeed, for the rest of my life. Beginning this evening. Well, at this moment of this evening, anyway."

He looked at her, and suddenly his lips curved upward slightly at the corners and his eyes twinkled with amusement — and a small dimple made its appearance in his right cheek, close to his mouth. It was an absolutely devastating smile — or *almost* smile. If Angeline had not already been seated, her knees would surely have buckled under her.

"Well," she said, "perhaps I ought not to be *too* rash. I shall be *almost* perfect, and you will be forced to admit that you misjudged me at the start."

"I hope, Lady Angeline," he said, "I will

never misjudge you or, indeed, judge you at all."

"How wretchedly unsporting of you," she said. "That would mean you do not care at all."

The almost smile was gone without a trace.

There had been a suggested intimacy in her words. And why should he wish for any sort of intimacy with her? She looked like a dark beanpole, she had been rashly alone in that taproom, she had splashed him with mud this morning while galloping and whooping along Rotten Row, she had made a spectacle of herself on the dance floor just now, and she had told him the story of the bull and her own foolish behavior. And she looked like a swarthy beanpole. Had she already listed that one? And, if she might add something else, he was doubtless wealthy enough and well placed enough socially — good heavens, he was an *earl* — not to care a tuppenny toss that she was the enormously rich daughter of a duke.

Her prospects suddenly looked rather gloomy.

No, they looked *challenging*.

But at the moment she was horribly embarrassed, for he did not respond to her unwary words. Neither did he look away from her.

She was saved by a flicker of movement over by the ballroom doors, to one side of the line of dancers. New arrivals. Apparently there were always people who arrived hopelessly late for a ball. The receiving line had broken up ages ago.

The new arrivals were three gentlemen, all of them quite young and quite presentable. There would be three more partners for all the young ladies present, then, Angeline thought. It had not escaped her notice that there were more young ladies here than there were young gentlemen. It was always thus, Cousin Rosalie had told her when she had remarked upon it earlier, though the situation would probably improve as the evening went along. This is what Rosalie must have meant.

And then Angeline's eyes widened, and her closed fan came down with a thump on the Earl of Heyward's sleeve. One of the three gentlemen, the tallest and most handsome, had dark red hair and — though he was not close enough for her to see them clearly from where she sat — eyes that were hooded beneath slightly drooped eyelids.

"Well, will you look at *that,*" she said. "The *nerve* of the man."

He turned his head to look in the direction of the ballroom doors.

"Windrow?" he said. "I daresay he does not know who you are, Lady Angeline, any more than I did until an hour ago. Perhaps he will be embarrassed when he *does* know. Though perhaps not."

"Windrow?" she said.

"*Lord* Windrow," he said. "I believe you will discover that he is one of your brother's friends."

"*Which* brother?" she asked.

"The Duke of Tresham," he said, turning back to her. "But friends are required to treat one's sister with the proper respect. If you wish to see him punished, I daresay a word in Tresham's ear will secure your wishes."

She lifted her fan from his arm and focused her attention back on him.

"Punished?" she said. "He was very effectively punished at the time, I believe. He would have enjoyed a fight, even if he had lost, which I daresay he might have done as he surely made a grave error in judging you a weakling and a coward. He would still have felt like a *man.* But you challenged him as a *gentleman,* and you forced him to *apologize.* I daresay he felt thoroughly humiliated by the time he left despite the bravado of his final words."

116

And his wink.

The set was drawing to an end. So was Angeline's precious half hour with the Earl of Heyward. She did not doubt that it would be the last with him for this evening anyway. What a shame. How sad.

Except that the whole of the rest of the most exciting evening of her life stretched ahead. And she had the rest of her life to secure the earl's interest and his courtship and his proposal of marriage.

"I shall return you to Lady Palmer's side," he said, getting to his feet and extending a hand for hers — a hand rather than an arm this time. "You will wish to be at her side for your next partner to claim you. I daresay you are eager to dance again — with someone who *can* dance, that is. You may set your *left* foot back on the floor if you wish. I suppose it is well rested by now. One hopes your *right* foot is feeling better."

Oh, he *had* noticed. How mortifying! And he knew what she had done. But had he misunderstood her motive? Did he believe she had feigned a stumble in order to avoid having to dance with such a clumsy, wooden fellow? She could hardly ask him, could she?

"I will surely dance all evening," she told him as she got to her feet and took his offered arm. "I shall do so because a number

117

of gentlemen have already expressed an interest in dancing with me. And because I adore dancing, of course. But I can assure you, Lord Heyward, that I will not enjoy any other set even half as much as I have enjoyed this one."

And how was *that* for blatant flirtation?

"I am delighted to have been of service to you, Lady Angeline," he said, a hint of sarcasm in his voice.

Ah, he *had* misunderstood. And now he thought she was lying.

His hand was warm and steady beneath hers.

His cologne wrapped about her senses.

Being in love was an altogether pleasant sensation, she thought, even if bringing it to a happy conclusion was going to be the biggest challenge of her life.

Was something worth having, though, if it did *not* present a challenge?

CHAPTER 6

"I do hope Lady Angeline did not seriously hurt her ankle," Edward's mother said after their set was over. "But she was very brave and dignified about it and very eager to remove herself from the floor so that the dancing could resume. Most young ladies would have made much of the moment and wailed and swooned and made quite a fuss before demanding to be carried off the dance floor."

"And she is not silent and insipid as so many girls are these days, is she?" Alma added. "She engaged you in what appeared to be a lively conversation, Edward. It is important for the wife of an important man to be able to converse sensibly."

Sensibly?

"She is beautifully tall," Lorraine said with a sigh. "I am envious to the point of jealousy. She is actually prettier than I thought at first. I think it is in the expression more than in the features alone. She fairly sparkles. She is going to be besieged by suitors and not *just* because she is the sister of the Duke of Tresham."

"Edward," Juliana said, tapping his arm with her fan, "Mrs. Smith-Benn is making her way toward us with her daughter. The mother is the daughter of Lord Blacklock, you know."

His life had indeed changed, Edward realized before the ball was even an hour old. Freedom and relaxation did *not* come as he had hoped once the opening set was at an end. For of course, he was now very eligible indeed, and this was the great marriage mart. And anyone who did not make a move *now,* when it was early in the Season, might find later that all the best prizes had already been snapped up. Or so he had been warned. And it worked in both directions, of course. Men were not the only ones seeking spouses.

His mother and sisters and sister-in-law did not even have to make any effort to seek other partners for him. He did not have to look dutifully about him to choose some for himself. He did not have a chance to find Eunice. Or to slink off to the card room. Young ladies, escorted by their mamas, came to court *him.* They came usually and apparently to speak to his female relatives, who then introduced them to him, and he did what was expected of him — he asked the young lady to dance. It was all rather alarmingly easy.

He danced the second set with Miss Smith-Benn, who was a blond, blue-eyed, delicate little beauty, the third with Miss Cartwright, a handsome brunette with slightly protruding teeth, and the fourth with Lady Fiona Robson, who smiled a great deal and was passably pretty despite the fact that she had freckles. He acquitted himself well enough on the dance floor, even if that meant only that he did not make an utter idiot of himself. And each of the three was polite enough not to feign injury in order to avoid dancing with him. None of them chattered on about charging bulls or called him *stuffy* when he failed to be amused at irresponsible stupidity.

Really . . . *stuffy.*

Lord Heyward, are you perhaps just a little bit stuffy?

The fact that she was *right* did not excuse her breach of good manners. Especially when she had preceded it with a fake injury that she could not even disguise well enough to remember *which* ankle she was supposed to have sprained.

It was, then, the supper dance before Edward could maneuver matters more to his own liking and find time to seek out Eunice. He did it by returning Lady Fiona to her mother's side and then neglecting to return immediately to his family's side. He had done his duty for long enough. He needed a break. And no one would be able to fault him. He was still in the ballroom. He was still taking a partner.

He had seen Eunice dance once. But she had spent most of the evening sitting with her aunt and conversing with a group of older ladies, all gorgeously decked out and plumed and sparkling with jewels. They all turned identical gratified expressions toward him when he approached.

"What a fine evening this is, Lord Heyward," Lady Sanford said. "It is quite a triumph for the Duke of Tresham, who has never been known to host a ball here before, you know, despite the splendor of his ballroom. Such a waste! And Lady Angeline Dudley appears to be taking very well indeed even though she is unfortunately tall, poor lady."

"And with a complexion one can describe only as swarthy," Mrs. Cooper added. "Her looks would have been a severe trial to her poor dear mama had she lived."

"We will be offending Lord Heyward," a lady whom Edward did not know said, smiling archly at him. "He danced the opening set with Lady Angeline and perhaps has a particular interest in her."

"I do find her quite remarkably beautiful," he said. "However, she is not the only beautiful lady in the room. Miss Goddard, would you do me the honor of dancing the next set with me?"

Eunice got to her feet while her aunt looked at her with triumph and the other ladies looked with interest. She set her hand along the top of his.

"Poor Edward," she said as they walked away. "I will not hold you to your offer. I will not expect you actually to *dance* with me. It is quite unbearably stuffy in here, is it not?"

"You will stroll with me on the terrace?" he asked hopefully. "I cannot tell you how grateful I would be."

She chuckled softly.

"And were you implying back there," she asked, "that I was one of the *other* beautiful ladies in the room? Being the Earl of Heyward has given you a flattering tongue."

She was wearing a light blue gown that was neither fashionable nor unfashionable, neither new nor old, neither pretty nor ugly.

It was the kind of gown one purchased, he thought, when one did not intend to buy a dozen and did not want the chosen one to be so distinctive that it would be recognized wherever she went. It was not inexpensive — her father, though not extraordinarily wealthy, did not lack for funds either. She wore no jewelry or other adornments. Her brown hair was dressed in a knot high on the back of her head with a few ringlets curling over her temples and along her neck to soften any suggestion of severity. She was of medium height and slender, pleasing figure. She had a pretty face made more so by the bright intelligence of her gray eyes.

"I was not just implying," he said. "I was *stating*."

"Then thank you," she said as they stepped through one set of open French windows onto the terrace beyond. "You were quite right about Lady Angeline Dudley, though. She is indeed beautiful, even though I suppose it is possible to list all sorts of defects if one considers her person piecemeal. As is true of everyone. There is no such thing as pure beauty. *Her* beauty comes more from within than from without. I see her only through a woman's eyes, of course, but it seems to me that she is the sort of lady who is far more attractive to men than to other women. Am I right?"

He looked down at her as they began to stroll. With almost any other lady he would suspect an ulterior motive in her question, a plea to be assured that indeed he did not find Lady Angeline attractive at all, but that he found *her* irresistibly so. Eunice, he knew, had no such motive.

"I do consider her lovely to look at," he said. "But she is oh so frivolous, Eunice. She turned her ankle deliberately so that she would not have to dance with such a clumsy fellow as I. I wonder how many people noticed that she rested the wrong foot on the stool I fetched for her."

"Oh," she said, and when she looked back at him there was a hint of amusement in her eyes. "*I* did not. But how very careless of her."

"And then she proceeded to regale my ears," he said, "with a tale of how she broke her leg last year after climbing a tree to avoid the attack of an angry bull. She had been knowingly crossing his meadow because she was late for some visitors who were coming. She expected me to *laugh* at the story."

"You must admit," she said, "that it *is* rather droll."

He had a sudden mental image of Lady

125

Angeline Dudley dashing across a meadow and straight up the trunk of a tree with a bull in hot pursuit. It *was* rather funny, he supposed, when translated into pictures rather than just words. And he had to admit one thing in the woman's favor. She did not mind laughing at herself. It was the very last thing most people were inclined to do.

"Oh, I suppose so," he said, "if one ignores the fact that she might have been killed, either by the bull or by her subsequent fall from the tree."

"But then she would not have been telling the story to you or to anyone else," she said very sensibly, "and the question of its humor or lack thereof would not have arisen."

"I suppose not," he said. "She was in Hyde Park this morning, Eunice, when I was riding there early with Headley and Paulson. She arrived there alone, or with only a groom to accompany her, anyway, and met her brother quite by accident — the other brother, Lord Ferdinand Dudley, not Tresham. He was there with some other men, and she proceeded to gallop along Rotten Row with them despite the mud, whooping as she went. And she was wearing the most garish hat I have ever seen. If there was a color yet invented that was *not* in it, I would be surprised."

126

"At least she did take a groom," she said as they came to a stop against the stone balustrade and turned to gaze down into the garden, which was dimly lit by a few lamps swaying from tree branches.

Did it take Eunice to convince him that he really was stuffy? But really, a young lady who had not even been officially *out* at the time ought not to have made such a public exhibition of herself. Had she even *known* any of those men apart from her brother? But it was just like Eunice always to see the best in another person. She was quite unlike those tabbies with whom she had just been sitting. Poor Eunice. It was no wonder she did not enjoy social events.

"Edward," she said, "I think you really ought to pursue a courtship with her."

"What?" he said, jerking his head sideways to stare at her.

"She has enormous consequence," she said. "You have only to look about you. I doubt there are many members of the *ton* who are not here this evening. And the reason is that this is Dudley House and the host is the Duke of Tresham and the ball is in honor of his sister, who has just made her come-out and is now ready to take a husband."

"But, Eunice —"

127

She did not let him finish.

"And she is rather lovely and full of life and fun," she said. "She has qualities that are perhaps missing from your life."

For a moment he was stunned into silence.

"They are qualities I can do very well without," he said firmly when he found his voice again. "She is a *Dudley,* Eunice. Tresham is her *brother.* He was one of Maurice's closest friends, if you will remember. They were every bit as wild and irresponsible as each other. It was Tresham Maurice was racing against when he died."

"Lady Angeline Dudley is not the Duke of Tresham any more than you are Maurice," she pointed out. "And to be fair, Edward, the duke is still a single man, and he is still young, probably no older than you are. Who knows how he will behave when he is married? He may change completely. Many men do, you know, particularly if they have a fondness for their wives. Your brother unfortunately seemed *not* to be reformed by marriage. But we ought not to judge him, not having walked in his shoes. Though I suppose you have more of a right to judge than I do. But *he* changed *you,* Edward, or at least had a powerful influence upon you. The wilder he grew, it seemed, the more you moved to the opposite extreme. Perhaps it is not the best place for you to be. Extremes usually are not. I know you are determined not to be the husband he was, but perhaps . . ."

She stopped. Was she saying he was *wrong?* That he ought to be less concerned about duty and good sense and . . . and plain *decency?* Surely not. Not Eunice!

"Perhaps?" he prompted.

"Oh, never mind," she said. "But I do think you should seriously consider marrying her, Edward."

He drew a deep breath and released it slowly.

"I still want to marry *you,*" he said. And suddenly he really did, very much indeed. Without further delay. By special license. Then he would be comfortable and safe.

She sighed.

"It did seem a good idea at the time," she said softly, "and it still would be . . . *comforting* to lean upon it. One feels a little bereft to be entirely free. But I do believe, Edward, that everything happens for a reason. The fact that you are now the Earl of Heyward makes a great deal of difference to both of us. It has shaken us out of our complacency. But perhaps it was meant to."

"You think," he said stiffly, "that I consider myself too important now to marry you?"

"I think no such thing," she said, smiling into the darkness of the garden. "Oh, Edward, I *know* you are not so fickle. But perhaps I think you too important for me. Though *important* is probably not quite the right word."

"I have not changed," he protested.

"Yes, you have," she said sadly. "Not in yourself, maybe, but in . . . in who you are. You are the *Earl of Heyward,* Edward, and the title has forced you to change. As it ought. You have never shirked duty."

He turned and looked with unseeing eyes through an open French window into the ballroom, where the final dance of their set was in progress. He was feeling remarkably unhappy. How was he to persuade her that she was the only one he had ever considered marrying, that she was the only one he could contemplate marrying with any confidence of finding peace and companionship and comfort?

Peace and companionship and comfort?

From a marriage?

Was there nothing else to be hoped for, then?

And safety. That word too had leapt to mind just a few minutes ago.

Safety?

Yes, a marriage ought to be safe, ought it not?

His train of thought was suddenly broken as his unseeing eyes focused. Sharply.

"Oh, I say," he said.

"What?" Eunice turned too to look into the ballroom.

"Of all the gall," he said. "*Windrow* is dancing with her."

"Windrow?" she said. "Dancing with — ?"

And he told her the whole story of the episode on the road to London, with the exception of a few unnecessary details. In this version, for example, Lady Angeline Dudley had merely been standing at the window of the taproom.

"How typical of you," Eunice said when he had finished, "to have risked your own safety in order to defend a lady who was behaving so badly from a gentleman who was behaving worse. Especially when you did not even know her. But he did apologize. I daresay there was *some* decency left in him, then, though that does not entirely excuse him from behavior that was not becoming in a gentleman."

"And now he is *dancing* with her," he said. "And *ogling* her. And no one but me knows how outrageous it all is. She does not look happy."

131

Or perhaps he was imagining that. She *was* smiling.

"Which is very much to her credit," Eunice agreed. "Lady Palmer is her chaperon. She is a very proper lady. However, without the pertinent information, she would not have known to refuse him the nod of approval when he came to solicit Lady Angeline's hand for the set."

"And Tresham," he said through his teeth, "is his *friend*. He has a whole army of such ramshackle friends."

"But to be fair, Edward," she said, "he would doubtless not feel very friendly at all to Lord Windrow if he knew the man had accosted and insulted his sister at an inn."

Edward's nostrils flared. But he could *not,* of course, stride into the ballroom to demand that Windrow step away from Lady Angeline Dudley and quit Dudley House without further ado. Or ride in there on a white steed, brandishing a flashing blade in one hand while with the other he scooped the lady up to the saddle before him and bore her off to safety. This was none of his business. And she was doubtless safe from harm tonight, though heaven knew what Windrow was saying to her. He was saying *something*.

"The set is almost at an end," he said,

"but it is the *supper dance.* He will be leading her in to supper, Eunice."

"It is altogether possible," she said, "that he has apologized abjectly again tonight, now that he knows who she is, and that she has forgiven him, though I certainly would not have done so in her place. Not easily, anyway. He certainly ought to have been made to grovel. Perhaps she is enjoying both the dance and the prospect of sitting beside him at supper."

It was indeed possible, Edward conceded. She was no delicate flower, after all. Quite the opposite. She was really quite as ramshackle as her brothers, though perhaps that was a little uncharitable. Perhaps she was delighted to see Windrow again. Though she *had* been outraged when she first set eyes upon him at the ballroom doors, he remembered.

"And perhaps not," Eunice said as the music came to an end and the sound of voices from within the ballroom rose and the guests turned almost as one in the direction of the doors and the supper room beyond. "And she ought not to be compelled to go undefended just because she is too polite to make a fuss. Come along, Edward. We will follow them out and secure a place at their table if we are able. He will not dare be impertinent in *your* hearing. Indeed, I expect he will be quite ashamed of himself."

Windrow would doubtless shake in his dancing shoes as soon as his eyes alit upon the sniveling coward from the Rose and Crown, Edward thought ruefully. And this really *was not* his business. Or Eunice's. He did not want her within fifty feet of Windrow.

But she had taken his arm and was drawing him purposefully along with her in the direction of the supper room.

After the first set Angeline danced with two young gentlemen and one older one — a marquess, no less — before it came time for the supper dance. She had enjoyed every moment, even the labored and florid compliments the marquess had seemed to feel obliged to press upon her while his breath came in increasingly audible gasps and his corsets creaked. She had enjoyed too the brief intervals between sets when she had been able to speak with other guests. She had spent a few animated minutes with Lady Martha Hamelin and Maria Smith-Benn, the outcome of which was that they were to visit Hookham's Library together the next day.

She had two new friends.

She hoped — oh, *how* she hoped — that the Earl of Heyward would ask her for the supper dance. She knew it was unexceptionable for a gentleman to dance with a lady twice in one evening — Cousin Rosalie had told her so. It must be rare, though, at a girl's come-out ball, when everyone wished to dance with her, especially if she was rich and well connected. And she knew that Lord Heyward did not approve of her. Good heavens, could she blame him? She had called him *stuffy,* albeit in an affectionate way. He may not have detected the affection, however, which was perhaps just as well. And he knew that her accident had been deliberate. He believed she had done it because she was embarrassed to be seen dancing with him.

Anyway, she *hoped.* It would be the loveliest ending to the loveliest day of her life if she could dance — no, stroll on the terrace with him and then sit with him at supper. Perhaps she would have a chance to redeem herself somewhat in his eyes. She must think in advance of some sensible subject upon which she could converse with him. Had she read any good books lately? At all? She *could* tell him that she was going to take out a subscription at the library tomorrow because she was feeling *starved* of good reading material and could he recommend anything that she might not already have read?

And then a double disappointment set in, though actually one of them was more in the way of being an outrage than a disappointment. First she watched Lord Heyward return his last partner to her mama's side and then begin his journey about the perimeter of the ballroom in her direction. He stopped along the way, though, to talk to a group of ladies, and when he moved away from them a minute or so later, he had one of them — the youngest — on his arm and proceeded to lead *her* out onto the terrace.

Angeline did not know the lady, though she did remember greeting her in the receiving line. It was impossible to remember every name that had been announced, or even most. Or even *some,* for that matter. She had remembered Maria Smith-Benn's name and Lady Martha Hamelin's because she had met and liked both at the palace earlier. And she had remembered the names of the Earl of Heyward, of course, and the Countess of Heyward and the dowager. And Cousin Leonard, Lord Fenner, because he was Rosalie's brother and Angeline must have met him at Rosalie's wedding all those years ago. And there were a couple of Ferdinand's friends who had been riding with him this morning and whose names she had recalled this evening without prompting. And that was about it. She must make more of an effort in the coming days. She must try to memorize one name each day. No, better make that ten names.

Was it possible?

And then came the other great disappointment hot on the heels of the first — or, rather, the *outrage*. It came sauntering along in company with Tresham and stopped before her, and there was Lord Windrow, smiling warmly as if he had never in his life set eyes upon her until this evening and had *never* suggested that she sit on his lap and share a meat pasty and a glass of ale with him.

He had the impressive physique she remembered and the dark red hair, which now gleamed like copper in the candlelight, and the handsome face and, yes, the green eyes that were slightly hooded beneath lazy eyelids. Someone had once mentioned in Angeline's hearing the evocative term *bedroom eyes.* This is what that person, whoever it was, must have meant.

Lord Windrow had bedroom eyes. Doubtless he thought of them as lady-killer eyes. Men could be very silly.

"Rosalie, Angeline," Tresham said, "may I present Lord Windrow, who has asked for the introduction? My cousin, Lady Palmer, Windrow, and my sister, Lady Angeline Dudley."

Angeline would have burst with indignation if she could while he fawned over Rosalie and kissed her hand. And then he turned to Angeline and bowed very correctly and smiled again with just the right amount of deference a man ought to show to the young sister of his friend. He made no attempt to kiss *her* hand.

"With your permission, ma'am, and if I am not already too late," he said, addressing Rosalie oh so correctly, "I shall lead Lady Angeline Dudley into the next set. I will consider it a great honor. Tresham is a particular friend of mine."

Which was hardly surprising, Angeline thought nastily. It did not take a great stretch of the imagination to picture her brother offering to take a lady onto his lap to share refreshments if he were ever to encounter one standing alone in an inn taproom. She contemplated an outright refusal to Lord Windrow. Except that he had not addressed the offer to her. He had talked *of* her as though she did not exist in her own right.

Rosalie had been growing increasingly agitated. The dancing was about to resume, and Angeline had been steadfastly refusing all evening to reserve the supper dance for anyone who had asked for it. By this time, Rosalie had just been saying, most gentlemen would assume that she already had a prospective partner, and she was in grave danger of being a wallflower at her own come-out ball. At the supper dance, no less. There could, apparently, be no worse social disaster for any young lady. Angeline, of course, had been hoping desperately that the Earl of Heyward would come along to request the set.

"I am certain Lady Angeline will be delighted," Rosalie said with a nod of approval and no doubt a huge inward sigh of relief.

Tresham wandered off to seek his own partner. He had danced every set so far, a strict attention to duty that must be simply *killing* him while at the same time sending his chosen partners and their mamas into transports of joy.

Angeline was not delighted at all. But what was she to do short of making a scene? She had already done that once this evening when she had turned her ankle. She would be the talk of London drawing rooms for the next *decade* instead of just the next week if she snubbed Lord Windrow in front of all her brother's gathered guests.

She set her hand on his sleeve and contented herself for the moment with assuming a cold, haughty demeanor, similar to the one she had turned on him at that inn.

"Ah, fair one," he murmured to her as he led her onto the floor, and he had the effrontery to move his head a little closer to hers. "I said it would be a pleasure to renew my acquaintance with you, but I had no idea just how great a pleasure it would be. Tresham's *sister.*"

"He would flatten your nose and knock all your teeth down your throat and blacken both your eyes if he knew what you said to me at that inn," she said.

"Oh, goodness me, yes," he agreed. "*And* shatter every rib in my body. *If* he succeeded in hobbling both my legs and securing both my hands behind my back and tethering me to a post before he commenced, that is. And if he blindfolded me."

Men and their silly boasts!

"I did not know," he said abjectly. "I mistook you for a lesser mortal."

She looked at him with cold hauteur, and

he chuckled.

"I must," he said, "have been blind in both eyes. Which perhaps makes it just as well that that sniveling coward was there to apprise me of my error."

"Lord Heyward is *not* a coward," she said. "Nothing compelled him to confront you or to defend me. He did not know my identity any more than you did. And when you would have left, nothing compelled him to block your way and insist that you apologize."

He grinned at her.

"Perhaps he is an idiot," he said, "as well as a sniveling coward."

She pursed her lips as though she had just swallowed a particularly sour grape. She was *not* going to engage in any argument with him. She had said her piece.

"You were sitting with him when I entered the ballroom, regrettably late," he said. "I was told that you sprained your ankle partway into the opening set and were forced to sit out the rest of it. I am delighted that you have recovered so soon and so completely. Or was the injury, ah, *convenient?* I have noticed that the fellow dances rather as though he has two wooden legs."

"I was *sitting* with Lord Heyward because I *wished* to do so," she told him.

141

The music rescued her from even more severe annoyance, and they moved off into the set. Fortunately, the figures of the dance kept them apart for much of the time and there was little chance of conversation. When he *was* able to talk to her without being overheard, he larded her with extravagant compliments, though they were far more deliberately amusing than the Marquess of Exwich's had been earlier.

He was trying to make her laugh. He could not try to make her smile because she was already doing it by the time the dance began. It would not do for the spectators to notice that there was something wrong. The rumor mill would jump at the opportunity to concoct some suitably ghastly story to explain her sudden moroseness.

The Earl of Heyward was still out on the terrace, she noticed with an inward sigh. He was still with the lady in blue. The two of them were standing against the stone balustrade, talking earnestly, as though they had known each other all their lives.

Angeline felt a wave of envy.

If only . . .

And then she remembered again that this was the *supper* dance and that she would be expected to sit with Lord Windrow and be polite to him. And *smile* at him.

Life could be very trying at times.

She could positively *weep*.

Except that this was still the most exciting day of her life. And actually, if she ignored her indignation, she would have to admit that her partner was quite amusing in an entirely silly sort of way. And he was a graceful dancer.

He was very like Tresham, of course. And Ferdinand. And most of Ferdinand's friends who had been riding with him this morning. There was a whole breed of such men — careless, shallow, amusing. And really quite, quite unthreatening.

She was not at all afraid of Lord Windrow. Indeed, she never had been. She just had no interest in his flatteries and was still indignant that he had had the effrontery to solicit a dance with her — in the hearing of both Cousin Rosalie and Tresham. That was low. *Very* low.

Who *was* that lady in blue?

CHAPTER 7

This was *not* a good idea, Edward thought. It was absolutely none of his business whom Lady Angeline Dudley danced with — *in the presence of both her guardian and her chaperon.* And no possible harm could come to her. The setting could scarcely be more public, and she was still very much the focus of everyone's attention.

He did not want to be seen anywhere near her again this evening. He did not want anyone to get the wrong idea. And it would be wrong. His mother and the committee of female relatives were going to have to shift their attention to the alternate list. Better yet, they were going to have to stand back and let him choose for himself.

Eunice had just admitted that she felt a little bereft at the fact that they had released each other from that informal agreement they had made four years ago. She had been acting nobly when she released him, then, doing what she felt she *ought* to do. She thought he should marry someone closer to him in rank, and she thought that someone should be Lady Angeline Dudley. But even Eunice, with all her intelligent good sense, could be wrongheaded at times. *She* was suited to his rank. She was a lady by birth and upbringing. More important, she was suited to *him.* They were very similar in many ways.

The more he thought about it, the more determined he was that it was Eunice he would marry after all. He would bring her around to his way of thinking. His family might be a little disappointed, but they would not make any great fuss. They loved him. They wanted his happiness.

Inside the supper room Windrow was seating Lady Angeline at a small table. It was not well done of him. The ball was in her honor, and she surely ought to be seated at the long table. On the other hand, of course, the whole purpose of her come-out was that she find a suitably eligible husband, and everyone knew that Windrow was of an ancient, respected family and as rich as Croesus to boot.

Perhaps her relatives were all holding their collective breath and hoping no one else would join the two of them at their table.

Eunice drew him inexorably onward. They wove their way past tables beginning to fill up with chattering guests.

"Oh, here, Edward," she said at last. "There are two empty places at *this* table. May we join you?"

The last words were addressed to Windrow and Lady Angeline.

It seemed to Edward that Windrow was not at all pleased — until his eyes moved past Eunice and alit upon Edward himself, that was. Then he looked deeply amused. He jumped to his feet to draw back a chair for Eunice.

"Heyward," he said, "present me to this lovely lady, if you would be so good."

"This is Lord Windrow, Eunice," Edward said as she seated herself. "Miss Goddard, Windrow, Lady Sanford's niece."

"And now," Lady Angeline said, smiling brightly, "I will not suffer the embarrassment of having to cover the fact that I do not remember your name, Miss Goddard. I was introduced to dozens of people this evening, almost all of them strangers, and their names went in one ear and out the other, I am afraid. *Not* that I am deliberately careless of other people's identities. Miss Pratt, the last of my governesses — I had six in all — taught me that one of the essential attributes of a true lady is that she never forget a face or the name that goes with it. Even the faces and names of servants. She stressed that last point, perhaps because she was in the nature of being a servant herself and knew how often people looked at her without really seeing her at all. Her words were very wise, I am sure. But I am equally certain she never attended a ball of this size and found herself expected to remember everyone and greet them all by name the next time she saw them. So do forgive me for not remembering your name at first. I will know it now for all time."

The woman could certainly talk, Edward thought as he seated himself. Her silence at the Rose and Crown Inn obviously had not been typical of her at all.

"Your governess's advice was sound, Lady Angeline," Eunice said. "But of course it is impossible to know everyone in the *ton* after a single brief introduction, and no one would realistically expect it of you. The important thing is always to do one's best. It is all that is required of one in this life."

Windrow had glanced from Eunice's face to Edward's and back again while she spoke. The gleam of amusement in his eyes had deepened if that were possible.

"But not in the next, Miss Goddard?" he asked.

"I beg your pardon?" She looked at him with raised eyebrows.

"In the next life," he said, "we may relax and do somewhat less than our best?"

"In the next life, Lord Windrow," she said, "if there *is* a next life, which I seriously doubt, we are presumably rewarded for having done our best here."

"Or not," he said. "For not having done it."

"I beg your pardon?" she said again.

"Or we are *not* rewarded," he said, "because we have not done our best. We are sent to the other place."

"Hell?" she said. "I have *very* serious doubts about *its* existence."

"Nevertheless," he said, "doubts are not certainties, are they? I believe, Lady Angeline, you must continue earnestly memorizing names during the coming days so that you may avoid the risk of ending up in hell when you die."

Lady Angeline laughed.

"How utterly absurd," she said. "But I thank you, Miss Goddard, and I shall remember your wise words — *the important thing is always to do one's best*. My best was never good enough for Miss Pratt — or any of my other governesses — with the result that I often quite deliberately did considerably less than my best. I suppose I was not an ideal pupil."

"And they were not ideal governesses," Eunice said. "The primary goal of any governess ought to be to encourage and inspire her pupil, not to discourage and dishearten her. Expecting and even demanding perfection is quite dangerously *wrong.* None of us is capable of perfection."

"Hence the need for heaven," Windrow said. "To reward those who at least do their best."

"Exactly," Eunice said, looking steadily into his mocking eyes with their drooped eyelids and refusing to be cowed by them. "Though it is all perhaps wishful thinking on our part."

"If you could but prove that to me, Miss Goddard," he said, "I should never again feel the need to try my best."

Plates laden with appetizing foods of all descriptions, some savory, some sweet, were brought to the table at that point. And another servant came to pour their tea.

Edward looked around quickly and met his sister Alma's eyes. She nodded approvingly at him.

Then he looked at Lady Angeline. She was

gazing back at him, her eyes bright with laughter.

"And what about *you,* Lord Heyward?" she asked as she took a lobster patty from the plate he offered. "Is it important to you always to do your best?"

She had called him stuffy. Did she want further evidence that she was correct?

"It would depend," he said, "upon what I was doing. If it were something I knew I ought to do, then of course I would do it to the best of my ability. If it were not, then even my best might not be good enough. If, for example, someone at a social gathering asked me to sing, I might agree and try my very best. But I would succeed only in murdering the ears of a roomful of unsuspecting guests. It would be far better in that case, then, *not* to try my best. Not to try at all, in fact."

"Oh, dear," she said. "Are you that bad?"

"Utterly tone-deaf," he said.

She laughed.

"But Lord Heyward was devoted to his studies at Cambridge, where my father is a don," Eunice said. "And he has been devoted to his position as Earl of Heyward during the past year. Duty always comes first with him. He will never fritter away his time and resources in rakish pursuits, which many gentlemen in his position deem almost obligatory, I believe."

Oh, Lord, Edward thought, she was trying to court Lady Angeline for him and scold Windrow all at the same time. He picked up the plate of cakes and handed it around.

"Rakish pursuits?" Windrow said with a shudder. "*Are* there such gentlemen? Point out one to me, Miss Goddard, and I shall challenge him to pistols at dawn."

"Rakish pursuits," she said, looking steadily at him, "*and* the frivolous pursuit of violence. When duty and courtesy and kindness could be embraced instead."

"Miss Goddard," Lady Angeline said, "you and I think very much alike. Men can be so *silly,* can they not? Perhaps they impress each other when their first reaction to anything even remotely suggestive of an insult is to issue a challenge. But they do not impress *us.*"

Edward met Windrow's eyes across the table, and the man lofted one eyebrow.

Edward was feeling like a very dull dog indeed, since he obviously did not fit into the category of those who indulged in rakish pursuits — or of those who pursued frivolous violence as an answer to insult.

Eunice and Lady Angeline Dudley, he thought, were as different from each other as day and night. Lady Angeline was gorgeously dressed and coiffed, her face vividly alive with smiles and sparkling dark eyes. She was a chatterbox. She was bold and indiscreet. She often dressed in garish colors. She was frivolous. Eunice was neatly dressed and coiffed, her manner restrained and refined, her conversation intelligent. She was serious-minded. Yet strangely the two had found common ground upon which to converse.

"Miss Goddard," Windrow was saying, "I am crushed by your disapproval of my offer to rid your world of at least one rakish gentleman. And stunned by your superior insight into the essential difference between the sexes. You simply must grant me an opportunity to redeem myself in your eyes. You must dance the next set with me."

Eunice looked coolly at him.

"Must I, my lord?" she asked.

He sighed, one hand over his heart.

"Ah, Heyward," he said, "we have much to learn of the fair sex. Miss Goddard, would you do me the great honor of allowing me to lead you into the next set? Or ought I to apply to Lady Sanford?"

"I am of age, my lord," she said. "And thank you. That would be pleasant. Edward, would you please pass the plate of savories?

The shrimp tarts are quite delicious."

Well, Edward thought. Poor Eunice. She had come here in order to rescue Lady Angeline from the clutches of a rake only to find herself caught up in those clutches instead. But she might have said no. And she was perfectly capable of looking after herself.

"I saw that you were out on the terrace during the last set, Lord Heyward," Lady Angeline said. "I was quite envious. The ballroom is really quite stuffy, is it not? So is the dining room. It is because there are so many people here, I suppose. Was it pleasant outdoors?"

He could not quite understand this lady, Edward thought. She had made it perfectly clear earlier that she disapproved of him, that she found him *stuffy,* and she had gone to great lengths not to have to dance with him, yet at the end of the set she had told him that she would not enjoy any other set even half as much as she had enjoyed theirs. And now she was blatantly hinting . . .

"Very," he said. "Would you care to stroll there before your next partner comes to claim you?"

"There is no next partner," she said. "Not yet, anyway, though I suppose there *will* be if I am still free when the dancing resumes."

"Then perhaps," he said, "you would care to grant the set to me and stroll with me for a full half hour."

"That sounds like heaven," she said. "You are kind. I must first go and tell Cousin Rosalie, though. Not that she will mind. Indeed, she will be delighted. You see? She is sitting with Lady Heyward, your sister-in-law, and Lord Fenner, Cousin Leonard, Rosalie's brother. And they are all nodding in this direction as if they are feeling very satisfied indeed with life."

"Allow me to go instead," he said, getting to his feet and directing an apologetic glance in Eunice's direction.

Lady Palmer did indeed express her delight at his offer to escort Lady Angeline out onto the terrace, and Lorraine beamed her approval.

This was *not* good, Edward thought a couple of minutes later as he led Lady Angeline out of the supper room. He had danced the opening set of her come-out ball with her. He had sat with her at a small table for supper. Now he was leading her out before many people had even returned to the ballroom and it would soon become obvious to anyone who was interested — almost everyone, in other words — that he had taken her outside and was keeping her there through the upcoming set.

And both his sister-in-law and her chaperon looked thoroughly delighted, as though everything was proceeding according to some preordained plan.

It all seemed very much like the beginning of a courtship, he thought uneasily. And how easy it would be to get caught in a trap and find himself unable to extricate himself.

The lady in blue was Miss Goddard. The Earl of Heyward called her *Eunice*. She called him *Edward*. And she looked like — and talked like — a very sensible lady. She was also rather pretty.

Angeline had expected to dislike her heartily. But she did not.

"I hope," Lord Heyward said as they walked across the empty ballroom floor in the direction of the French windows, "Windrow did not insult you again, Lady Angeline."

"Oh," she said, "he was just being silly. Though I do think he ought to have stayed away from me this evening and then sought me out more privately to offer a proper apology. I suppose it would have been worth very little, however, for he would not apologize if I were not who I am and if I were not Tresham's sister, would he? Not that he apologized anyway. Though he *did* after a fashion at that inn when you blocked the doorway. That was very brave of you."

His arm was as solid and warm as it had been earlier. He was a few inches taller than she was. He had a handsome profile. His very straight nose showed to advantage from a side view. She could smell his musky cologne again.

The air out on the terrace was deliciously cool, though not at all cold.

He had not really wanted to bring her out here, she thought. Who would have expected that she would turn out to be *flirtatious?* She had never had any chance to practice flirtation, or even to *think* of it. It was not one of the lessons Miss Pratt had taught, after all. Yet she had all but asked him to bring her here, and then, when he would have brought her just for five minutes or so until Cousin Rosalie had accepted another partner for her, she had wheedled him into offering to keep her out here for the whole of the next set — plus the five minutes or so before it started.

Oh, dear. Conscience smote her.

"You did not wish to bring me out here, did you?" she asked.

He turned his head to look at her as they

156

began to stroll along the length of the terrace. The lighting out here was dimmer than it was in the ballroom. More romantic. It also hid her blushes. It did not hide his slight frown.

"How can I possibly answer that question?" he asked.

"You might have said a resounding *of course I did*," she said. "But you would not have meant it and I would have known."

"I am delighted to have rescued you from Windrow, at least," he said.

"Perhaps," she said, "it is your destiny in life to save me from Lord Windrow. Someone can write it on your tomb after you die, among all the other accolades: *He repeatedly saved Lady Angeline Dudley from the evil clutches of a rake.*"

Oh, and it happened again. He looked sidelong at her and his dimple appeared. Though it was more a slight crease in his cheek than a dimple. It was more *manly* than a dimple. And the corner of his mouth lifted.

Angeline laughed.

"I think it is a little unfair to describe Lord Windrow as *evil*, however," she said. "Most rakes are not, are they? They are just overgrown boys who have not yet grown up. And yet they think themselves *so* manly and *so* irresistible to the ladies. They are silly but harmless, and one cannot help feeling rather fond of them. *Not* that I am fond of Lord Windrow, though I suppose I would be if he were my brother or my cousin. I adore my own brothers, but I have no illusions about them. Tresham is particularly wild, but of course he was the eldest of us, and he left home when he was sixteen after a quarrel with Papa, though neither of them would ever tell us what it was all about. He has fought two duels that I know of, both over ladies, and both times he shot into the air after being shot at. That was very noble of him, since he was almost certainly in the wrong. I was very proud of him when I heard, though it was a good thing I was far away when both duels were fought. I would have *killed* him if my nerves had held together long enough."

Oh, dear, she thought, listening to her voice rattling on at a rapidly accelerating pace as though it were someone else's, she was actually feeling *nervous* in an excited sort of way.

Whatever had happened to her plan to *talk about books?*

The orchestra members were tuning their instruments inside the ballroom again. There was a swell of voices as people returned and took their partners for the next set. Angeline would dearly have liked to be dancing it too, but given the choice she would far prefer to be where she was. More particularly, she preferred being with whom she was, even if he was making her feel nervously excited.

And even if he *was* silent. He had not been silent when he was out here earlier with Miss Goddard. She would wager they had been talking about some deeply intellectual subject. The trouble was that Angeline did not know of any such subjects, deep or otherwise.

"Are you going to marry Miss Goddard?" she asked abruptly.

"Marry her?" he said in astonishment. "Whatever gave you that idea?"

"You call her *Eunice,*" she said. "She calls you *Edward.* I do not call you that. You do not call me *Angeline.*"

"I have known her for a number of years," he said. "Her father tutored me and befriended me at Cambridge. I spent many hours at their house. She is a . . . a dear friend."

A *dear friend.* What on earth did that mean? What would it feel like to be a man's dear friend? To be *Lord Heyward's* dear friend? To call him *Edward?*

She really ought to dislike Miss Goddard after all, Angeline thought.

The music began in earnest, the dancing began, and a few other couples appeared on the terrace.

"Tresham has had lamps strung from some of the trees in the garden," she said. "It is lovely down there. Would you like to see?"

He hesitated.

"Are you sure you ought to go so far away from your chaperon?" he asked.

She almost laughed out loud.

"You brought me out here with her blessing," she reminded him. "This is my own *home*."

Perhaps he was wondering what Miss Goddard would say. But he made no further objection, and they descended the stone steps to the garden with its lawns and trees and winding paths and ornamental pool and fountain. It was not a large garden. The house was in the middle of London, after all. But it had been carefully and pleasingly set out to give the impression of space and rural quiet.

She had brushed off his bereavement earlier in order to talk about her own and what had happened to her the year after her mother died. But the loss of his brother must have had a huge impact on his life even apart from the fact that he was now obliged to attend balls and actually dance. She knew almost nothing about him.

"What happened to your brother?" she asked.

He remained silent for a moment. Perhaps he did not want to talk about it. But he did.

"He was in a curricle race," he said. "Such sports are always inadvisable, but when they *are* engaged in, then all proper caution should be exercised. Maurice raced around a bend in the road with reckless *incaution* because Tr— , because his opponent had just overtaken him and he was determined to gain back the advantage. At least, this is what I presume was his thinking. I do not *know.* He died before I could ask. He collided with a large hay cart coming in the opposite direction. It is fortunate that the carter escaped without injury, considering the fact that he was entirely innocent. Maurice's curricle was overturned and he was tossed from it. He broke his neck."

"Oh," she said. Ferdinand had been boasting just last week about a curricle race that he had won, even though Tresham described him as one of the world's worst whips. Angeline had almost had a fit of the vapors, even though she had been *very* proud of her

brother for winning. She had not understood quite how dangerous such races were,
however. "I am so sorry."

"So am I," he said. "He had no business
behaving so recklessly. He had duties to his
position. More important, he had a wife and
a young daughter."

"Perhaps," she said, "he succumbed to a
momentary temptation to return to the
wildness of his youth. Perhaps he was not
always so irresponsible."

"He was," he said curtly.

Angeline said nothing as they wound their
way along a path in the direction of the
pond.

"I loved him," he said just as curtly.

And she realized something. He was a
man in pain. Still. It was perhaps even more
painful to mourn for someone who in many
ways did not deserve your grief than it was
to mourn for someone who did. No, there
was no *perhaps* about it. There was still a
deep, unresolved pain somewhere in the pit
of her stomach whenever she thought about
her mother.

"And so you feel," she said, "that you
must do better than he did."

There was a rather lengthy silence this
time as they stopped by the pond and gazed
onto its dark surface, which was lit in part

by one of the lamps in a nearby tree. The fountain bubbled softly in contrast with the sound of lively music coming from the ballroom.

"Not really," he said. "I was always more serious-minded than Maurice. I always felt that I should do what I ought to do and that I should consider the effect my behavior would have on other people, particularly on those close to me, if I did not. I was always a dull fellow, and I compounded my dullness by criticizing the way Maurice neglected Wimsbury Abbey and the other estates. I criticized him for his wild, reckless behavior, especially after his marriage. But —"

"But — ?" she prompted when he stopped.

"But everyone loved him despite it all," he said. "Everyone adored him, in fact."

"Even the Countess of Heyward?" she asked softly.

"Lorraine." He spoke just as softly. "I believe she did at the start. She had a difficult confinement with Susan. He was there when it started. Then he went out. He returned three days later, in the same clothes, unshaven, red-eyed, still foxed. He had been celebrating with his friends, he told us."

"Perhaps," she suggested, "pain frightened him."

"But Lorraine could not have run away if *she* was frightened," he said. "I believe her love died during those three days. Or perhaps it was nothing so sudden and dramatic. Perhaps her eyes were gradually opened both before and after the birth. It must be hard to be married to a rake."

"Yes," she agreed.

One solution, of course, was to become as rakish as one's husband. As her mother had done. If *rakish* was the right word to apply to a woman, that was.

"There is a seat just behind us," she said. "Shall we sit for a while?"

He looked back and then led her toward it. It was set just below the branch from which the lamp swung in the slight breeze. Dim light flickered over their heads and then reflected in the water. There was the smell of water and greenery, Angeline noticed. It was more enticing than the heavier scent of all the flowers in the ballroom.

They sat in silence for a few moments and she sensed his growing discomfort.

"I do beg your pardon," he said abruptly at last. "I ought not to have spoken of such personal matters."

164

It was the darkness and relative seclusion, she guessed, that had loosened his tongue. She was glad it had happened, though. She felt that she had learned a great deal about him in just a few minutes, when perhaps he had spoken incautiously of private concerns. But she did not want them to become maudlin.

"What ought we to be talking about, then?" she asked him. "The weather? Our health? *Bonnets?* I can talk of bonnets forever if you have enough time to listen. I have bought thirteen of them since coming to London. *Thirteen.* Can you imagine? But every time I buy one, you see, and think it is the prettiest thing I have ever seen in my life, I see another the very next time I am out shopping that is even prettier, and what am I to do? I must buy the other one as well, of course, since it would not be kind to return the first and I cannot possibly live without the second. Someone at the shop *made* the first, after all, and would be hurt if I returned it for the reason that I had found something I liked better. And then, of course, I find one even prettier than the one that was prettier than the first, and I must have *it.* And . . . Well, and so on. Am I incorrigible?"

He did not smile, but she sensed that his

discomfort had left him and that he was more relaxed. Perhaps he was even smiling. She could not see his face clearly enough to know for sure. Perhaps he *needed* someone to talk about bonnets with him occasionally rather than books.

"What answer am I to give to that?" he asked her. "I suspect you are exaggerating."

"Not at all," she said. "*Thirteen*. Ask Cousin Rosalie. Ask *Tresham*. He has started to look pained, poor man, every time a new bill appears on his desk. But he gave us carte blanche to shop for my come-out and has no grounds now upon which to complain, has he? And they were all irresistible bonnets. Though I have always had a weakness for hats. Did you like the one I was wearing in the park this morning?"

"Your hat?" he said a little too quickly. "I did not notice it."

"Liar." She laughed. "Ferdinand told me it was quite atrocious, that it made him almost ashamed to be seen with me. But my brothers are always blunt to the point of rudeness. They used to play horrid tricks on me when we were children. Sometimes they allowed me to play with them, particularly if their game called for them to rescue a lady in distress or to win a lady's favor with some deed of great derring-do. But sometimes they did not want me, and then they would tell me to meet them in a certain place at a certain time and sneak away a different way and at a different time. And then they would always ask me with a show of great innocence why I had not shown up and would take great pleasure in giving me the details of all I had missed."

She smiled at him and reached out to cover his hand with her own.

Oh, goodness me. Action before thought — again.

She knew immediately that she had committed a dreadful wrong. For one thing, he stiffened instantly though he did not move his hand. For another, she felt immediately heated and breathless and flustered — and quite unable to snatch back her hand or, better yet, to tap his lightly and withdraw her own as though nothing untoward had happened at all.

Instead, she left her hand where it was and gazed at him with wide eyes.

Oh, goodness gracious me, she could *feel* the touch all the way up through her breasts into her throat and her cheeks and all the way down to her toenails.

It was not the first time she had set her hand on the back of his. She had done it when he led out into the opening set of dances. She had done it again when they had left the supper room. But somehow this was altogether different.

He turned his hand beneath hers so that they were palm to palm. And then he closed his fingers about her hand.

She swallowed hard and loudly enough to drown out all other sounds for a half-mile radius.

"Have you been told," he asked her, "that I am to be your primary suitor, Lady Angeline? Have you been instructed to allow me to court you?"

She almost froze with horror. He *did* think she was flirting with him.

She was not really. *Was* she?

Flirting was such a *trivial* thing.

"No," she said. "No. Absolutely not. I was told that you had requested the opening set with me. I could have said no, but I had no reason whatsoever to do so even though I did not know at the time who the Earl of Heyward *was*. Nothing was said about courtship. In fact, Tresham —"

But she could hardly tell him that Tresham had called him a dry old stick, could she?

"I am sorry," he said. "I have embarrassed you."

"No, you have not," she lied, and she

closed her eyes briefly so that she could concentrate upon the sensation of having her hand enclosed in his.

Cool night air. Warm, steady, very male hand. The most delicious contrast in the whole wide world.

And then she felt her hand being raised until it was against his lips.

Angeline, eyes still closed, thought she might well die. Of happiness.

"I must return you to the ballroom," he said.

Must you?

But she did not say the words aloud. Thank heaven! She had been quite forward enough tonight as it was. She got to her feet and drew her hand from his to straighten her skirt.

"This has been a memorable day," she said brightly as she looked up to find him standing only a few inches away from her. "Has it been as happy a one for you as it has for me? Despite the fact that you have had to dance? I will never forget a single moment of it."

"It has been a happy day," he said.

She tipped her head to one side. He had spoken with a remarkable lack of enthusiasm.

"But the happiest part is that it is almost

over?" she said, smiling ruefully.

"You are pleased to put words in my mouth," he said. "I would not be so ill-mannered as to suggest any such thing, Lady Angeline."

But he had not denied it.

"I hope," she said, and her voice sounded breathless in her own ears, "it will be a happier day in retrospect than it has been in the living. I *do* hope so."

And she whisked herself about and strode back along the path in the direction of the terrace and the ballroom beyond, her hands clutching the sides of her gown. She could almost *hear* Miss Pratt calling after her to *stop striding like a man* and remember that she was a *lady.*

She did not want him to catch up to her and offer his arm. She did not want to touch him again.

Not yet.

She would *suffocate.*

Tresham and Ferdinand had both used to tell her that she never did anything by halves — whether it was galloping her pony hell-bent for leather, diving into the lake at the deepest part as though she meant to dive right down to China, or climbing the highest tree as though to reach the clouds. It had always been said with a certain degree of affectionate admiration.

They would not admire her now.

For she did not fall in love by halves either.

She was an absolutely hopeless case, in fact.

No, *not* hopeless.

One day he would love her too.

Passionately.

If one was going to dream, one might as well dream big.

CHAPTER 8

Edward enjoyed more than half a day of relative freedom. He rode early in Hyde Park again with a group of friends — there were five of them this time — and encountered no one he did not wish to see. No one with the last name of Dudley, in other words. He spent an hour or so in the study with his secretary, looking over some important papers, dictating a few letters, deciding which of a flood of invitations he ought to accept and which he would decline, with regrets. He attended the House and even spoke up during one of the debates that interested him. He was to meet Headley and another friend later at White's, where they were to dine together. They would probably linger there over their wine and their port until it was time to return home to bed.

It was only a relative freedom, of course, for his mind would not remain focused just upon the day's business.

He must find time to call upon Eunice soon. He could not help feeling that he had abandoned her last evening when Windrow had asked her to dance. He ought to have objected, to have put a firm stop to the man's insolence. Not that he owned Eunice, of course, or had any claim upon her at all, in fact. She would undoubtedly have been vexed with him if he had interfered. And she was still insisting that he marry someone more suited to his station, even though she *had* admitted that the ending of their agreement had left her feeling unsettled.

Dancing with Windrow had actually had a positive effect upon her fortunes. She had had partners for each set afterward. It was true that she professed to despise dancing and all the frivolities of *ton* entertainments, but even so, she surely did not enjoy being a wallflower either.

Anyway, he must call upon her.

But even apart from that obligation his sense of freedom was only a very temporary one. For he must still marry. He must still choose a bride. Perhaps Eunice. Definitely not Lady Angeline Dudley.

He could not simply dismiss the latter from his mind, however. She kept popping into it at any odd moment of the day. It was usually in a thoroughly negative way. She was bold, talkative, frivolous. Good Lord, she had talked with great enthusiasm about her thirteen new bonnets. But he was forced to admit — grudgingly — that she could also be amusing, especially on the subject of her own shortcomings and foibles. And he had had the feeling with the hat story that her chosen topic had not been an idle one. He had suspected that she was trying to cheer him up, that she was deliberately trying to coax a smile out of him.

Which only meant, of course, that she saw him as an old sobersides, to quote Maurice's habitual description of him.

Why had she persuaded him to take her outside, then, first onto the terrace and then down into the garden? She had denied being instructed to court his favor. And why would Tresham give such instructions anyway — or countenance Lady Palmer's giving them? Tresham despised him.

He tried not to think about her. He tried to enjoy the illusion of freedom offered by the day.

But he kept remembering, more than anything else, that moment when she had set her hand upon his. Or rather, he remembered the moment immediately following that one, when he had been assailed by a powerful and totally unexpected tidal wave of lust. He ought not to have been surprised. He had experienced it before — in the taproom of the Rose and Crown Inn. And he had acted without even a trace of his usual caution and discretion. He had first turned his hand beneath hers, then closed his fingers about it, and then raised it to his mouth.

It was a dashed good thing she was an innocent, albeit a flirtatious one. She could not otherwise have failed to notice . . .

Fortunately — *very* fortunately — his mind had got a grip on his body soon enough for him to be struck by the oddity of her flirting with him. He was not the sort of man with whom women flirted. Not women like Lady Angeline Dudley, anyway. Actually, not *any* kind of woman. Even Eunice had never flirted with him. And he had realized that Lady Angeline could have only one possible motive for flirting.

He still believed it to have been her motive, even though she had denied it quite vehemently, and it made no real sense anyway. But for very pride's sake she had been forced to deny it.

Every time Lady Angeline Dudley popped into his head — and it was far too often — he firmly quelled the thought. It was too deuced uncomfortable, and she was too deuced . . . Well, if he tried to think of a type of lady he most definitely did *not* want to marry, she would be at the very top of the list. Head and shoulders above every other type.

He would meet someone else even if Eunice would not have him. There were already a few distinct possibilities, in fact — Miss Smith-Benn, Lady Fiona Robson, Miss Marvell, for example.

He enjoyed his day of freedom as far as he was able, then — his *partial* day, that was.

He arrived home late in the afternoon and was informed by his butler that his grandmother was taking tea in the drawing room. Edward went up there to see her. She was with his mother and Lorraine. Susan was sitting on her lap. The child wriggled down, though, when the door opened and came flying across the room, arms spread wide, face alight with welcome.

"Uncle Edward!" she cried in her very precise three-year-old voice.

Edward scooped her up, and she cupped his cheeks with her hands, puckered her lips, and kissed him on the mouth.

"You said you would take me for an ice the first nice day," she said.

Ah. Cupboard love.

"And so I did." He grinned at her.

"It is a nice day," she said. "Your whiskers are rough."

"So what should I do?" he asked her. "Take you for an ice or ring for my valet to come and shave me?"

"Ice," she said.

"Five minutes, then," he told her. "Give me a moment to greet your mama and your grandmama and great-grandmama."

He set her on the floor and bent to kiss his grandmother's cheek.

"You grow more handsome every day, Edward," she said. "Your grandfather and I would have attended the Tresham ball last evening, but doubtless we would both have fallen asleep within the first hour. I am delighted to hear that you danced both the opening and the after-supper sets with Lady Angeline Dudley, though apparently you did not *dance* either one. That is all to the good as you had more opportunity to engage her in conversation and get to know her. Adelaide tells me she is a handsome girl, and Lorraine tells me you think her the most beautiful creature you have ever seen."

Edward winced. An exact quote, if he was not mistaken.

"I enjoyed the evening, Grandmama," he said. "I did have other partners too, though."

She waved a dismissive hand.

"I have already invited Lady Palmer to take tea with your grandpapa and me tomorrow afternoon," she said, "and Lord Fenner, her brother, at Lorraine's suggestion. I used to know their grandmother on their mother's side, you know, though she was older than I. Lady Palmer is to bring Lady Angeline Dudley."

Edward knew what was coming with a dull certainty.

"Your mother and Lorraine will be there," his grandmother said. "And you must come too, Edward. You will wish to take Lady Angeline for a drive in the park afterward if the weather is fine, as I daresay it will be. A courtship must be pursued vigorously, especially when the lady is so very eligible."

Edward opened his mouth to explain that there *was* no courtship and closed it again. His mother was smiling. So was Lorraine. And Susan was tugging at one tail of his coat.

"Come on, Uncle Edward," she said.

"Susan," Lorraine said reproachfully, but he held up a staying hand.

"It seems that immediate action is what most ladies expect and demand," he said. "We will go, Susan. Immediately, or as soon as you are fit for the outdoors."

Lorraine got to her feet to fetch outdoor clothes for her daughter, who was now clinging to Edward's hand and bouncing up and down in her eagerness.

And it struck Edward unexpectedly and for the first time ever that it might be great fun to have children of his own.

But his sense of freedom had fled all too quickly and too soon. He had not put his grandmother right on her misconception when he had had the opportunity, and somehow it seemed that it was already too late to do so.

Well, a tea, followed by a brief drive in the park, was not exactly a declaration of an intent to marry the girl, was it?

But it felt as if the noose was tightening.

The day following Angeline's come-out ball was really rather an exciting one even if it *was* somewhat anticlimactic. But, as Cousin Rosalie had explained when she left the ball at some ridiculously late hour — or early, depending upon which end one looked at it from — Angeline would need a quiet day in which to recover from all the excitement and exertion, and so would she.

Enough bouquets arrived to fill the ballroom over again if she had felt inclined, Angeline thought. But, disappointingly, there

179

were no flowers from Lord Heyward. And no visit from him either, though she did have one from the Marquess of Exwich, who came in the afternoon to offer her marriage.

It was excruciatingly embarrassing to be forced to go down to the library, as Tresham insisted she do after he had been closeted with the marquess for all of half an hour while Angeline sat upstairs, all unsuspecting, reading one of her new library books. She had to listen to the proposal in person and refuse it in person. Tresham had flatly refused to do it for her.

She had better get used to it, he told her afterward, having the nerve to sound *bored*. It was likely to become a frequent occurrence until she put a stop to it by accepting one of her suitors. And he would be damned before he would gain a reputation as a tyrant by refusing the serious offers of perfectly eligible gentlemen on behalf of his sister.

She would put a stop to it when the right man came along, she told him. But she did not tell him that she already knew who the right man was. He would merely fix her with one of his looks and pass a remark of the dry old stick variety. When Cousin Rosalie had commented at the end of last evening upon the gratifying fact that only the Earl of Heyward had requested and been granted two sets with her charge, Tresham had fixed *her* with his stare and then spoken his mind.

"Devil take it, Rosalie," he had said. "I hope a sister of mine can do considerably better than Heyward. Is she to yawn her way through the rest of her life? Lockjaw might set in after the first fortnight or so."

Which he really had no right to say. Did he even *know* the Earl of Heyward? Besides, it was *her* life, was it not? No one was asking *him* to marry Lord Heyward.

The morning was exciting even apart from all the bouquets from last evening's admirers — or admirers of her fortune anyway. For she went to Hookham's Library with Maria and Martha, and all three of them took out a subscription and borrowed books, a lengthy process that involved a great deal of talking and laughing. And then they rounded the corner of one high bookcase and came face-to-face with Miss Goddard, who appeared to be making her choice of books with considerably more serious intent. But she smiled warmly at Angeline and consented to be introduced to Maria and Martha, and then, at Angeline's suggestion, the four of them proceeded farther along the street to a tearoom, where they spent a whole hour drinking tea and talking.

Perhaps she ought not to have chosen Martha and Maria as friends, she thought ruefully during that hour as she looked from one to the other of them. Although they did not really look alike, both were small and fair and dainty and exquisitely pretty. She must look like a gypsy in contrast. Not that she had anything against gypsies. Indeed, there had been a time when she almost seriously considered running away to join a group of them who settled for a while a mile or two from Acton in their gaily painted caravans with their brightly colored clothes and their lively, toe-tapping music. But her papa would have come in hot pursuit if she had done so, and though he had never once lifted a hand to her, she was wary of provoking his wrath. His tongue was as lethal as Tresham's was now.

Anyway, she *liked* her two new friends, their looks notwithstanding, and they appeared to like her. They had mulled over yesterday's triumphs while at the library together and discussed the merits and demerits of their various dancing partners. Maria thought Lord Heyward a little on the dull side, though perfectly well bred. Angeline thought Mr. Griddles would be rather handsome if he did not appear to have twice as many teeth as he was supposed to have. Martha could talk only of Mr. Griddles, whose teeth as far as she was concerned were his finest asset, and Angeline had to admit that they were at least white.

They had shared information about how many bouquets they had received this morning. Angeline had received the most, but she was quite willing to concede — even to be the first to suggest — that the reason was that it had been *her* come-out ball.

Now with Miss Goddard their conversation was altogether less giddy. They talked about books. Angeline and her friends favored novels, but only if they had happy endings. They were all agreed upon that.

"I can tolerate soaking a dozen handkerchiefs while I am reading a book," Maria said on behalf of them all, "but I absolutely cannot *abide* weeping at the end unless it is with happiness. What is the *point* of sad stories? They ought not to be allowed. Or there ought at least to be a warning on the covers, and then no one would bother reading them and getting depressed by them."

Miss Goddard also read novels, but not often. When she did, she also preferred a happy ending provided it was a believable one and not of the happily-ever-after variety. She preferred reading that was instructional and educational, however, on a subject that made her think, that stretched her mind, that told her something interesting about life and the world that she had not known before.

She ought to have been an utter bore, Angeline thought. And she ought to be detestable for other reasons — not least the fact that she was Lord Heyward's *friend* and that he called her *Eunice.* Her father was a Cambridge *don,* for heaven's sake. She spoke quietly and with very precise diction. She never giggled, and when she smiled, it was with quiet warmth rather than with a bright sparkle.

Angeline actually *liked* her. And she hung upon her every word, encouraging her to talk more and more about the books she read. She would wager that *Miss Goddard* talked to Lord Heyward about books. It was no wonder he liked her so much.

Did he do more than like her?

Did he *love* her? It would not be at all surprising.

"You were very kind last evening," she said, "to converse with Lord Windrow at the supper table and then to dance with him. He is very silly. I daresay Lord Heyward told you what happened on the road

to London a few weeks ago. He was obliging enough to insist that Lord Windrow
behave like a gentleman after he had started
to behave more like a rake."

Martha and Maria, both of whom knew
the story, giggled.

"Kindness had nothing to do with my
behavior last night," Miss Goddard assured
her. "I could see as soon as we joined you
that you were perfectly capable of handling
Lord Windrow's sort of gallantry. He *is* silly.
It is a good word to describe him. He is also
mildly amusing. Must I confess that I rather
enjoyed dancing with him and matching
wits with him? I had only ever been able to
observe rakish gentlemen from afar before
last evening."

"I have two of them for brothers," Angeline said. "They are very exasperating. I love
them to pieces."

"Lord Ferdinand Dudley is *very* handsome," Maria said with what seemed to be
a barely suppressed sigh.

Miss Goddard smiled warmly.

"I *have* enjoyed this," she said. "Thank
you so much for including me in your outing. But I must return home now. My aunt
will be wondering what has become of me."

And that was the end of that. She left and
it was time for them all to gather up their

respective maids and make their way home.

"Is she a *bluestocking,* do you suppose?" Maria asked after Miss Goddard was well out of earshot.

"I would not be surprised," Angeline said. "I rather like her even so."

"But poor lady," Martha said, "feeling obliged to read those dreadfully dull books instead of the novels from the Minerva Press."

Angeline held her peace, but secretly she thought that she might try one of those books for herself the next time she went to the library.

The excitement of her day was not over after she had sent the Marquess of Exwich on his way later in the afternoon. Half an hour after that a note arrived from Cousin Rosalie to inform her that they had been invited to take tea the following afternoon with the Marquess and Marchioness of Beckingham. They were the Earl of Heyward's maternal grandparents, the note explained. Lord Heyward was to be there too, and Angeline must be prepared to drive in the park with him afterward, weather permitting. It would be a positive step forward in a possible courtship, Rosalie had also added, for Hyde Park was where everyone of any consequence went during the afternoon to see and be seen.

Whose idea had all this been, Angeline wondered. His? His grandmother's? She would wager it had not been his. But did it matter? She would see him again regardless. She would drive with him in the park, converse with him. Everyone would see them together.

Oh, she could scarcely wait.

She could make him fall in love with her, even if she did look like a swarthy gypsy.

Of course she could.

If *only* it did not rain.

It did not rain. And it would not. There had been scarcely a cloud in the sky all day.

The Earl of Heyward was the last to arrive for tea, but Angeline did not mind, as long as he *did* come. And he surely would. Half his family was there.

The Marchioness of Beckingham was a small, slender lady with regal bearing, very white hair, and a long-handled lorgnette, which she used more as a baton to be waved about than as something to see through. She settled into conversation with Cousin Rosalie and Mrs. Lynd, the earl's sister, but not before looking Angeline over from head to toe and nodding.

"You look nothing like your mother," she

said almost as though it were a compliment. "Your face has character. And I have always envied tall ladies. I envy them even more now that I have started to sink in the opposite direction."

She had not called Angeline either pretty or beautiful, but her words had felt like approval.

The marquess was tall and thin and slightly stooped and white-haired like his wife. After greeting Angeline and Rosalie, he returned to what appeared to be an engrossing discussion of politics with Mr. Lynd, who apparently was a government minister.

The widowed Countess of Heyward, Angeline noticed with interest, sat a little apart with Cousin Leonard. They had been something of an item five years ago when the countess had made her come-out, Rosalie had told her during the carriage ride here. Then the late Lord Heyward had come along to sweep her off her feet, and Leonard had not looked at a lady since. Not in the way of marriage, anyway, even though he was now close to thirty.

For five years Rosalie had not looked kindly upon the countess. But so many foolish young ladies fell for handsome rakes, she explained, married them, doubtless with the conviction that they could reform them, and then regretted it for the rest of their lives.

"I do hope, Angeline," she had said, "you will prove to have better sense than to allow that to happen to you. I am very pleased that the Earl of Heyward has shown an interest in you, despite what Tresham says."

The dowager countess and Viscount and Lady Overmyer, also Lord Heyward's sister, engaged Angeline in conversation after the greetings were over, even though the viscount sat a little distance from them, having explained that he had a slight cold and did not wish to pass it on to either Lady Angeline or his mother-in-law. All three of them were flatteringly attentive to what she had to say, and all three of them complimented her on the success of her ball. The viscount expressed a hope that she had taken no permanent harm to her ankle and suggested that even now it might be wise if she kept her foot elevated whenever she was not forced to use it.

Lord Heyward had asked her last evening if she had been prodded into encouraging his courtship, Angeline remembered. Was *he* being pressured by three generations of his own family into courting *her?* It would hardly be surprising. He was in need of a bride, Rosalie had explained to her, as there was no heir of the direct line remaining, his brother having fathered only a daughter before his untimely death. And Angeline was perhaps the most eligible young lady on the market this year.

And then he arrived, looking wonderfully . . . *neat* in a form-fitting coat of dark green superfine, buff pantaloons, and high-topped Hessian boots, his short hair slightly tousled from his hat.

Angeline beamed at him as he bowed to all of them, and waited impatiently while he spoke to his sister-in-law and Cousin Leonard and then to his grandmother and Cousin Rosalie and — at slightly greater length — to his grandfather and Mr. Lynd. But finally he came toward her group and actually took a seat next to his sister.

"Communing with your own thoughts over there, are you, Christopher?" he asked the viscount.

"I am attempting to keep my cold to myself, Edward," his brother-in-law explained. "Ill health is my cross to bear in this life, as you know, but I try to bear it with patience and protect my fellow humans, the ladies in particular, from having to share it with me."

"That is admirable of you," Lord Heyward

said good-naturedly while Lady Overmyer poured him a cup of tea. "Thank you, Juliana."

He scarcely looked Angeline's way for the next half hour, though he participated in the general conversation. But she did not mind. There were still no clouds in the sky.

Finally the countess got to her feet, swiftly followed by Cousin Leonard.

"Mother," she said, addressing the dowager, "Lord Fenner has brought an open barouche and has invited me to drive in the park with him. Will you mind dreadfully returning home in the carriage alone?"

"Unless you would care to come with us, ma'am?" Cousin Leonard asked politely.

"One can be exposed to too much sunshine in an open carriage," the dowager said, smiling graciously from one to the other of them, "and I did not bring a parasol with me. Thank you, Lord Fenner, but I will return home in the comfort of my own carriage. Edward was kind enough to bring it to London for me from Wimsbury Abbey. You go and enjoy yourself, Lorraine."

It was the Earl of Heyward's cue, it seemed.

"Lady Angeline," he said, getting to his feet and looking directly at her at last, "would you give me the pleasure of driving you too in the park? I have the curricle with me."

A curricle. Angeline had never ridden in one, since they were not vehicles much used in the country. But she thought them quite the most dashing of vehicles even if they could kill people who did not drive them with the proper care and attention. She would wager Lord Heyward was far from being a careless or inattentive driver.

She smiled brightly.

"What a splendid idea," she said. "Thank you, Lord Heyward. I would like it of all things. May I, Cousin Rosalie?"

Rosalie inclined her head.

"You must be careful not to drive too fast, Edward," Viscount Overmyer said, "even if the air does appear to be warm today. It is *not* warm when one is traveling at any speed. And you would not wish to cause Lady Angeline a chill."

"Thank you, Christopher," Lord Heyward said. "I shall keep that advice in mind if I should feel the sudden urge to spring the horses."

Angeline almost laughed aloud. But she might hurt the feelings of the viscount, who had spoken in earnest and was concerned for her health.

"Thank you, Lord Overmyer," she said,

smiling at him. "But I trust Lord Heyward to keep my best interests at heart at every moment."

"It is one of Edward's most admirable traits," his sister said. "He is utterly trust-worthy, Lady Angeline."

"We will leave now," Lord Heyward said, "before I am elevated to sainthood."

And he bent to kiss his grandmother's cheek.

CHAPTER 9

He felt that he was making a grand public statement, Edward thought uneasily.

Engage a lady for two sets at her come-out ball, including the first, sit with her at supper, and then, two days later, on a perfect spring afternoon when absolutely *everyone* would be out, drive her in the park — on the high seat of a spanking new curricle.

Add a large, wide-brimmed bonnet in varying shades of green and orange — and not subtle shades at that — laden with artificial fruit and flowers and ribbons and bows and Lord knew what other bells and whistles, and a dazzlingly smiling face below it, and a mobile mouth, and a hand that waved to everyone and his dog — yes, she did indeed wave to a little fluff of a mutt, which was prancing along the pedestrian path with its mistress, its stub of a tail adorned with a blue ribbon bow.

He might as well be done with the whole business and put an engagement notice in tomorrow's papers. He might as well get the wedding invitations made up and sent out. He might as well book St. George's on Hanover Square for the ceremony and plan the wedding breakfast. He might as well start fitting out his nursery.

"Is this not all absolutely *wonderful?*" Lady Angeline Dudley said as he drove through the crowd of carriages and horses that made the fashionable afternoon loop in Hyde Park.

Or drove *with* the crowd would be a more accurate description. It was impossible to move at a faster pace than the slowest of the vehicles ahead of him, and that was very slow indeed. Speed was not the purpose of an afternoon drive in the park, of course. Neither was getting somewhere — hence the circular nature of the drive. One came to be sociable, to mingle with one's peers, to hear the newest gossip, to pass along something even newer if one was fortunate enough to have heard anything suitably salacious. One came to see who was with whom and, sometimes, who was *not* with whom.

One came, sometimes, to make a statement. Sometimes one made a statement even when one did not wish to do anything of the kind, when one wished, in fact, to do the absolute opposite.

Sometimes one could wish one's female relatives in perdition.

"It is your first drive in the park?" he asked.

She had ridden on Rotten Row, of course, at least once, but that was a different matter entirely.

"Oh, yes," she said. "Neither Tresham nor Rosalie would allow me to come here before I was out, and yesterday Rosalie insisted that I *rest*. I went to Hookham's Library, though. Oh, I met Miss Goddard there, and we went to a tearoom together and talked for a whole hour. And the Marquess of Exwich called at Dudley House in the afternoon. He came to offer me marriage, the silly man. Oh, there is . . . *what* is his name? He was my third partner last evening. Sir Timothy Bixby, that is it. The lady with him danced once with Ferdinand. I cannot — How do you do?" She had raised her voice.

They stopped for a few moments to exchange pleasantries with Bixby and Miss Coleman.

Exwich, Edward thought. He must be fifty if he was a day. He had been married how many times? Two? Three? And he had how many children? Six? Eight? Eighteen? All girls, apparently.

"Did you accept?" he asked as they drove on.

She looked blankly at him for a moment and then smiled broadly.

"Lord Exwich?" she said. "Oh, no. He wears *corsets*."

Which was, apparently, reason enough to refuse his marriage offer. And perhaps it was too.

She had taken tea with *Eunice?* He still had not called on her himself.

It took them an hour to make the circuit. Virtually everyone there, of course, had also been at Tresham's ball, so everyone must be greeted and everyone's health must be inquired after, and everyone must be reminded of what a beautiful day it was in case they had not noticed for themselves.

And everyone looked with open speculation from Edward to Lady Angeline and back again. *Two* men of his acquaintance actually winked at him.

"You must be ready to return home," he said at last. "I will —"

"Oh, no." She turned a dismayed face his way. "It cannot be time to leave already. We have seen scarcely anything of the park."

Did she not know that one was not meant to? Hyde Park was vast. The fashionable oval was not.

"You would like to drive for a little longer?" he asked.

"Oh, yes, please," she said. "But can we find a less crowded area?"

"But certainly," he said, drawing his curricle free of the crowds and turning down a quiet avenue *away* from the park gates rather than *toward* them.

In full view of half the *ton.*

This was becoming a statement with full fanfare.

He might as well send out invitations to the first christening party.

She raised a parasol above her head — it was an apricot color to match her muslin dress — though what function it could possibly serve given the size of her bonnet he did not know.

"Lord Heyward," she asked him, "are you being coerced into courting me?"

He turned his head to frown down at her.

"Coerced?" he said.

"I suppose it is the wrong word," she said. "No one could coerce you into doing anything you did not wish to do. But are you being . . . persuaded, *pressured* into courting me?"

He had asked her a similar question two evenings ago and she had denied it. Now he understood why. Good Lord, it was *not* a question he wished to answer.

"You refer to my grandmother and my mother and sisters?" he said. "They are like female relatives everywhere, I suppose. They wish to see me happily settled. They wish to see the *succession* happily settled. They are eager to pick out all the most eligible young ladies for me, on the assumption that I am quite incapable of doing it for myself."

"And I am an eligible young lady?" she asked.

"Of course," he said. "Probably *the* most eligible."

Two children were chasing after a ball on the wide lawn to one side of the path. A lady sat on the grass some distance away from them. Apart from them there was no one in sight.

"And if you had the choosing," she said, "without any necessity of pleasing your relatives, would you choose someone *ineligible?* Or *less* eligible?"

Oh, Lord.

"Lady Angeline," he said, "I consider this a quite inappropriate topic of conversation."

She twirled her parasol and laughed.

"You would never choose anyone *ineligible*," she said. "You are a very proper gentleman. You are devoted to doing your

199

duty. You would never follow your heart rather than your head. You would never do anything impulsive. No one would ever find *you* up a tree while an angry bull prowled about the trunk below."

"I am, yes, a dull dog," he said, hearing with dismay the irritation in his voice. "It is time I took you home."

"But it is not dull," she said, "to be proper and dutiful and to act with considered judgment. It is not dull to be a *gentleman*. And *must* we go home? When everything about us is so lovely and I am having my first ever ride in a curricle and *loving* it? How do you like my bonnet?"

She lowered her parasol as he turned to look at it.

"It is one of the thirteen?" he asked.

"Number eight," she said. "And actually it is *fourteen*. I counted them yesterday and there was one more than I remembered."

"I thought," he said, "that you bought each new bonnet because it was prettier than the one before. Why, then, are you wearing number eight instead of number fourteen?"

She grinned at him.

"I said it for something to say," she said. "I often do that. I love all my bonnets — except perhaps the pink one. I bought it because I loved the shade of pink and still do. But it is virtually unadorned. It is boring. I shall have to do something about it if I am ever to wear it. And it would be a horrid waste of money if I never did wear it after all, would it not? You have not answered my question. I suppose you are too polite to tell me the bonnet is atrocious. My brothers are not so tactful."

"Is my good opinion so important to you, then?" he asked her.

She considered.

"No," she said. "I have always had dreadful taste in clothes. I concentrate most of it upon my bonnets. Sometimes I take advice with dresses and other garments. And sometimes not. But I always choose my own hats."

"Who told you you have dreadful taste?" he asked her.

"Apart from my brothers? Oh, everyone. My governesses — every one of them." She looked for one moment as if she would raise her parasol again, but she changed her mind and rested it across her lap. "My mother."

And he understood something about her in a flash — something he did not really want to know. Somewhere beneath the bright, noisy dazzle that was Lady Angeline Dudley there was a vulnerability. Perhaps even a massive one.

When she had said *my mother,* she had almost whispered the words.

Her *mother* had told her she had bad taste? Her mother, who had been so exquisitely beautiful herself and who had had exquisite taste in dress? Edward remembered her. But how could anyone *not* remember her once he had set eyes upon her?

"Your hats are distinctive, Lady Angeline," he said. "This one is. The one you wore when you rode on Rotten Row the other morning was. Was that one of the fourteen?"

"*That* one?" she said. "Oh, no. That was just an old thing I wore because I needed to keep my hair dry for my presentation to the queen. It is an old favorite."

"It drew comments," he said. "This one will be talked about after today. I daresay the other thirteen will be too as you wear them, even the pink one, if the shade is anything similar to that of the dress you wore on the way to London."

"It is almost an exact match," she said. She laughed. "Everyone will talk about what ghastly taste I have in hats. But I do not care. I like them."

He turned the curricle along a path that ran parallel to the waters of the Serpentine.

"And that, ultimately," he said, "is all that

matters. *You* like them. And a strange thing will happen in time. Gradually your hats will come to be associated with you, and people will look eagerly for new ones. And some people will begin to admire them. Some will even envy them and emulate them because they will assume that it is the bonnets that give you the bright sparkle that characterizes you. They will be quite wrong, of course. The bonnet will lend nothing to their character. You must not retreat into what others deem fashionable and tasteful if you prefer something else. It is sometimes better to be a leader of fashion rather than an habitual follower."

Good Lord, did he really believe that? Or was he giving her appalling advice?

"Even if no one follows my lead?" she asked, looking across at him with brightly smiling eyes.

"Even then," he said. "When the parade goes by, there will be no one to look at but you. But everyone will look. Everyone loves a parade."

Her smile had softened and she turned her face rather sharply to face front again. He had to keep his eyes on his horses and the path ahead — there was more traffic here. Even so, he had the distinct impression that the brightness of her eyes as she looked away did not have everything to do with laughter. And indeed, there was no laughter in her voice when she spoke again.

"I shall remember what you have said all the rest of my life," she said. "I shall *lead* fashion, even if no one follows behind me."

"Someone always will," he said, and he knew he was right. It was the nature of leadership.

They turned their heads at the same moment, and their eyes met. It was definitely tears that were in hers. They were not swimming there and they were not spilling over onto her cheeks, but they were there.

And then, just before he looked back to the path ahead, there was a spark of mischief there too to brighten the tears.

"You *still* have not answered my question," she said. "Do you or do you not like my bonnet, Lord Heyward?"

"I think it quite the most ghastly thing I have ever seen," he said, "with the possible exception of the riding hat you wore the other morning."

She went off into peals of bright laughter, turning heads their way and causing him to smile.

Good God, was he in danger of *liking* her?

She was a walking, talking disaster. She was the very *last* woman that old sobersides, the Earl of Heyward, needed to become entangled with.

His thoughts flashed to Eunice.

Well, he *did* like her sense of humor — Lady Angeline's, that was. He had to admit it yet again. There was really very little humor in his life. There had never seemed much room for it.

He turned the curricle in the direction of Grosvenor Square and Dudley House. He had the uneasy feeling that he was getting into something he was going to find it very difficult to get himself out of.

Even impossible?

And did he mean *was getting?* Or did he mean *had got?*

"I just hope," Cousin Rosalie said, "that she has learned her lesson *this* time. I am convinced her marriage was not a happy one."

"I believe," Angeline said, "she is genuinely fond of him. She sat apart with him at Lady Beckingham's this afternoon, and she appeared very happy when she drove with him in the park afterward."

They were talking about the Countess of Heyward, who had apparently broken Cousin Leonard's heart five years ago by marrying the earl and was now being offered a second chance to get it right, according to Rosalie.

"I dread to imagine," she said, "what will become of him if she breaks his heart again."

Cousin Leonard was almost completely bald. He also had a nose that went on forever. Even so, he was a kindly, pleasant-looking gentleman, and Angeline thought that even the beautiful Countess of Heyward would be fortunate to have him. There was such a thing as family bias, of course.

"I daresay she will not," Angeline said.

They were in the carriage returning from an evening at the theater, where Cousin Leonard had invited them to join him in his box. It had been a thoroughly pleasant evening, even apart from the novelty of seeing a play acted out live upon a stage instead of just being read from the pages of a book, which Angeline had always found remarkably tedious and Miss Pratt had always insisted was the *only* way to appreciate good drama.

The theater was packed with people, and Angeline was able to gaze her fill — and be gazed upon. Several people had come to the box during the interval to pay their compliments to one or another of them. Lord Windrow had cocked one mobile eyebrow at her from across the theater and inclined his head in an exaggeratedly deferential bow. The Earl of Heyward was not present. Martha Hamelin was, and they were able to flutter their fans at each other from a distance and smile brightly.

What had made the evening particularly special, though, was the fact that Cousin Leonard had issued yet another invitation before they left. He was organizing a party to spend an evening at Vauxhall Gardens, and he hoped they would be his guests there. The idea had occurred to him while he was driving in Hyde Park earlier in the afternoon and Lady Heyward had informed him that it must be three years at the very least since she was last there but she longed to go again.

Vauxhall Gardens!

The thought of going there was sufficient to send Angeline into transports of delight. It was the most famous pleasure grounds in the world. Well, in Britain anyway. She was not sure about the *world*. There was a pavilion and there were private boxes and sumptuous food. There were music and dancing and fireworks and broad avenues and shadier paths. There were lanterns in the trees and a boat to take one across the river.

But the fact that she was going there was not all.

The evening was being arranged for Lady Heyward's benefit. But Lady Heyward had apparently shown some unease over any impression of carelessness or heartlessness she was giving her late husband's family, so Leonard was going to make it a family party — or a two-family party, to be more accurate. Perhaps, he said, Tresham and Ferdinand would come.

The Earl of Heyward was sure to be there too, then, Angeline thought while she stared dreamily into the darkness beyond the carriage windows as they drove home. The earl and Vauxhall all in one evening.

"I daresay," Rosalie said from the seat beside her, just as if she had read Angeline's thoughts, "the Earl of Heyward will accept Leonard's invitation to Vauxhall. Do you like him, Angeline? Did you enjoy your drive in the park with him this afternoon?"

He had given her permission to continue wearing the bonnets she liked. *Not* that she needed his permission or anyone else's. But he had made her feel that it was the right thing to continue wearing them, that it would be the *wrong* thing to bow to popular opinion.

He had said something else too. Angeline

thought a moment, bringing the exact words to mind again in his own voice.

Some will even envy them and emulate them because they will assume that it is the bonnets that give you the bright sparkle that characterizes you.

. . . the bright sparkle that characterizes you.

No one else had ever said anything even half as lovely to her.

And he had advised her to set fashion rather than follow it — even if no one followed her.

But the loveliest memory of all from this afternoon — oh, by far the loveliest — had come when he had *joked* with her. And it *had been* a joke, not an insult as it was when Tresham or Ferdinand said similar things.

I think it quite the most ghastly thing I have ever seen, he had said when she had pressed him for an opinion on her gorgeous green and orange bonnet, *with the possible exception of the riding hat you wore the other morning.*

And then, while she had laughed with genuine amusement because the words were so unexpected, he had *smiled*. He really had. A full-on smile that had set his blue eyes dancing and had shown his teeth and creased his cheek on the right side.

"Oh, I did," she said in answer to Rosalie's question. "It is the loveliest place in the world to be on a sunny afternoon. Though I daresay Vauxhall at night will be even lovelier."

She gazed out at a streetlamp that broke up the darkness for a moment.

"And yes," she said. "I like the Earl of Heyward well enough."

"I am delighted to hear it," Rosalie said briskly. "Though there are plenty of other gentlemen worthy of your consideration if it turns out on further acquaintance that you do not like him *quite* well enough. I am not the sort of chaperon, I hope, who expects her charge to marry the first gentleman presented for her inspection."

"I know," Angeline said. "I am very fortunate to have you, Cousin Rosalie. More than fortunate. I am *happy.*"

Happier than she would be if it were her own mother presenting her to society and the marriage mart? But she made no attempt to answer the question, which was pointless anyway. Mama was dead.

Cousin Rosalie reached out and patted her hand.

I think it quite the most ghastly thing I have ever seen, with the possible exception of the riding hat you wore the other morning.

Angeline smiled secretly into the darkness.

■ ■ ■ ■

Damnation, Edward thought the following morning when he opened the invitation Lorraine had warned him would be coming.

Vauxhall!

It was famous for its glitter, its vulgarity, its artificiality. He had never been there. He had never wanted to go. He still did not. He could not think of many places he would less like to go.

But go he must.

Lorraine had been close to tears in the drawing room before dinner last evening when she had spoken of the planned visit to Vauxhall. Both he and his mother had been present as well as Alma and Augustine.

"It has been only a little over a year since Maurice's passing," she had said. "I would not offend any of you or appear uncaring or . . . or *fast* by engaging in too many social pleasures too soon or giving the appearance that perhaps I have a . . . a *beau.* Will you all please come too to Vauxhall, and persuade Juliana and Christopher to come, so that it will be in the nature of a *family* outing?"

"I doubt if Christopher will risk the

dangers of night air and the smoke of fireworks clogging his lungs," Augustine had said, looking at Edward with a twinkle in his eye. "Unless Juliana persuades him that it is safe, of course, or that going to Vauxhall is essential for *her* good health. That would do it. He is soft in the head where she is concerned."

Edward's mother had got to her feet and hugged Lorraine tightly.

"Lorraine," she had said, "no one could have been a better wife to my son, and no one could be a better mother to my granddaughter. But Maurice is dead and you are alive. You must not be ruled by guilt or the fear that we will think you somehow unfaithful to his memory. I assure you we will not. But Vauxhall? My dear! It is for young people. I will certainly not go there with you. But Alma and Augustine surely will, and I daresay Juliana and Christopher will too. And Edward, of course."

Of course. Of course he would and of course he must. *Not* just because his mother had given him little choice, but because he was fond of his sister-in-law and could see that she already had a genuine regard for Fenner — and he for her. And Fenner was a steady character. He was not just another Maurice.

Duty called, then. Oh, and affection too. Duty did not preclude love. Indeed, it could hardly exist *without* love to impel it onward.

So he would go. To Vauxhall of all the undesirable places. With the near certainty that Lady Angeline Dudley would be a fellow guest. If Fenner was inviting all of Lorraine's family, it stood to reason that he would invite all of his too. And devil take it, that included the Duke of Tresham as well as his sister.

"Send an acceptance of this one," he told his secretary, waving the invitation in one hand before setting it down on the desk.

She would *love* Vauxhall. She would bubble over with exuberance. He could picture it already in his mind. Lady Angeline Dudley, that was, not Lorraine. Lorraine's enjoyment would be altogether quieter, more dignified, more decorous.

CHAPTER 10

Angeline was sitting very upright in a small boat on the River Thames, wishing that somehow she could open up her senses even wider than they already were and will them to take in every sensation of sight, sound, smell, and touch and commit them to memory for all time.

Not that she would have trouble remembering anyway.

It was evening and darkness had fallen. But the world — *her* world — had not been deprived of light. Rather, the darkness enhanced the glory of dozens of colored lanterns at Vauxhall on the opposite bank and their long reflections shivering across the water. The water lapped the sides of the boat in time with the boatmen's oars. There were the sounds of water and distant voices. She was on her way to Vauxhall — at last. The hours of the day had seemed to drag by. The air was cool on her arms. It was a little shivery cool actually, but it was more shivers of excitement she felt than of cold. She held her shawl about her shoulders with both hands.

Tresham had insisted upon the boat, though there was a bridge close by that would have taken the carriage across in perfect comfort. Angeline was very glad he had insisted. And she was still surprised he had accepted his invitation from Cousin Leonard. She *knew* he had been about to refuse it, but then he had heard that Belinda, Lady Eagan, Leonard and Rosalie's cousin on their mother's side, having arrived unexpectedly in town just last week, was also to be of the party. Lady Eagan's husband had run off to America with her maid a year or so ago, and Angeline could hardly wait to meet her. She hoped she was not gaunt and abjectly grieving, however. That would be distressing.

Tresham was reclining indolently beside Angeline, one long-fingered hand trailing in the water alongside the boat. He was looking at her rather than at the lights.

"You do not have a fashionable air, Angeline," he said. "You are fairly bursting with enthusiasm. Have you not heard of ennui? *Fashionable* ennui? Of looking bored and jaded as though you were a hundred years old and had already seen and experienced all there is to be seen and experienced?"

Of course she had heard of it — and seen it in action. Many people, both men and women, seemed to believe that behaving with languid world-weariness lent them an air of maturity and sophistication, whereas in reality it merely made them look silly. Tresham did it to a certain extent, but he was saved from silliness by the air of dark danger that always seemed to lurk about him.

"I have no interest in following fashion," she said. "I would prefer to *set* it."

"Even if no one follows your lead?" he asked her.

"Even then," she said.

"Good girl," he said, a rare note of approval in his voice. "Dudleys never follow the crowd, Angeline. They let the crowd follow *them* if it chooses. Or not, as the case may be."

Remarkable, she thought. Absolutely remarkable. Tresham and the Earl of Heyward agreed upon something. Tresham would expire of horror if she told him.

"You know why you have been invited this evening, I suppose," he said.

"Because Leonard is our cousin?" she asked, keeping her eyes on the lights, which were becoming more dazzling and more magical by the minute. They looked even more glorious if she squinted her eyes.

"Because Lady Heyward and her family have singled you out as the most eligible bride for Heyward," he said. "And for some reason that eludes my understanding, Rosalie seems just as eager to promote the match. I was always under the impression that she was a sensible woman, but matchmaking does have a tendency to distort female judgment quite atrociously. You had better watch your step, Angeline, or it will be the earl himself who will be turning up at Dudley House next to petition for your hand. And you know how much you love having to confront and reject unwanted suitors."

There had been two more since the Marquess of Exwich. And the embarrassing thing with the second of the two had been that when Tresham had come to the drawing room to inform her that Sir Dunstan Lang was waiting in the library to propose marriage to her, she had been unable even to put a face to the name. And when she had gone down and had a faint memory of dancing the evening before with the young gentleman standing there looking as though his neckcloth had been tied by a ruthlessly sadistic valet, she had no longer been able to recall his name.

Embarrassed was not a strong enough word for how she had felt.

"I will be careful," she promised.

"It would be an almighty yawn to have the man as a brother-in-law," he said. "I can only imagine what it would be like to have him for a husband. No, actually, I cannot imagine it and have no intention of trying."

"Why do you dislike him so much?" she asked.

"Dislike?" he said. "There is nothing either to like or to dislike in the man. He is just a giant bore. You ought to have known his brother, Angeline. Now, *there* was a man worth knowing. Though I daresay I would not have wanted you to know him — not before his marriage anyway. He might have been the devil of a fine fellow, but he was not the sort to whom one would want to expose one's sister."

It was odd, Angeline thought, that he did not want her to marry anyone like himself, and yet at the same time he did not want her to marry someone altogether more worthy, like Lord Heyward. She wondered if she would feel similarly when it came time for him to choose a bride. Would no lady be good enough for him in her eyes?

Or would she be warning every lady in sight away from him?

Would he ever be in love? She doubted it. But the thought saddened her, and the very last thing she wanted to feel tonight was sadness. Besides, the boat was drawing into the bank, and Tresham was vaulting out even before it was quite there and offering her his hand, and excitement bubbled up in her again until she thought she might well be sick.

Then they were inside the gardens and completely wrapped about in magic. They walked along a wide avenue already half crowded with revelers, all of them in high spirits — there was no ennui here. There was conversation and laughter, and there were trees on either side, their branches laden with more of the colored lamps. And though the breeze was a little cool, Angeline was thankful for it, for it set the lamps to swaying slightly, and the colored arc of their lights moved with them and danced among the branches and across the path. And far above, if one tipped back one's head, there was the blackness of the sky dotted with stars. She could smell the trees — and food. An orchestra was playing somewhere ahead.

And then they came to the pavilion with

its tiers of open boxes and its semicircular set of more boxes about an open area used, surely, for dancing. And Rosalie was waving from one of the boxes, and Cousin Leonard was standing to greet them and show them to their seats, and there was everyone else to greet. Angeline and Tresham were, of course, the last of the party to arrive. Her come-out ball was perhaps the only event for which Tresham had been early his entire life. The Countess of Heyward was there and Mr. and Mrs. Lynd, Viscount and Viscountess Overmyer, Ferdinand, Cousin Belinda — though she was not actually *their* cousin, it was true.

And the Earl of Heyward.

Suddenly the excited anticipation Angeline had felt all day, the wonder and delight of the river crossing, and the sheer glory of her first impressions of Vauxhall all came together to be focused upon the person of one man, the quietest, least fussily dressed of any of them, as he bowed politely and wordlessly to them. It did not matter. She did not see him objectively. Perhaps she never had. She saw him with her heart, and her heart sang with happiness.

But it was a momentary rush of feelings. She would not embarrass herself by wearing her heart upon her sleeve. She was a member of a party. She smiled brightly about at everyone.

She had not seen Lady Eagan for years — probably not since Rosalie's wedding. She was blond and slightly on the buxom side — though perhaps *voluptuous* would be a more accurate word. She was also beautiful in a languid sort of way, with full, pouting lips and eyes — or rather eyelids — rather like Lord Windrow's. *Bedroom* eyes. If she felt either humiliated or grieved by Lord Eagan's defection, she was doing an admirable job of disguising it.

Why had Lord Eagan run off with her maid? Now that Angeline had seen his wife, it would seem more believable if *she* was the one who had run off with *his* valet. Though looks could be deceptive. However it was, it was all very shocking and therefore vastly intriguing.

Angeline found herself seated, without any maneuvering at all on her part, between Mr. Lynd and the Earl of Heyward, and suddenly the evening air no longer felt uncomfortably cool. In fact, it felt decidedly warm and charged with energy all down her right side, which was, coincidentally, the side upon which the earl sat. She made no attempt to converse exclusively with him, though, or he with her. Conversation was general, and it was vigorous and covered a whole host of topics that included politics, both domestic and foreign, music, art, and gossip. It had none of the insipidity of conversation in the country. Angeline was exhilarated by it. How wonderful good conversation was, and how much there was to learn from it, far more than one ever learned in the schoolroom — a fact that seemed to be a contradiction in terms.

"I do believe," she said, "that I have learned more in the month since I came to London than I did in all the years I spent with my governesses."

"Book learning often does seem to be a useless waste of youth," Mr. Lynd said. "But it gives us the basic knowledge and tools with which to deal with life once we have left it behind."

"If we *do* leave it behind," Ferdinand said. "We can learn a great deal from our daily lives and from our interaction with the minds and opinions of others, but there is no surer way of expanding our knowledge and experience than by reading."

Ferdinand, Angeline remembered, had done rather well both in school and at Oxford. She tended to forget that and assume that he was *only* a very handsome but rather shallow rakehell. How dreadful to do one's own brother an injustice. She stared curiously at him. She really did not know him well at all, did she? They were brother and sister and yet they had lived so much of their lives apart. How sad it was.

"School often seems dull and irrelevant to life," Lord Heyward said. "But what we learn there gives us the grounding for a richer appreciation of life when we grow up. You are quite right about that, Augustine. How could we appreciate a poem or a play, for example, if we had not learned what to look for as we read? We could hope to be entertained, I suppose, but our minds, our understanding, our *souls* would remain untouched."

"Oh," Angeline said, "then all those tedious, *tedious* lessons in which Miss Pratt dissected a poem or play line by line and explained the meaning and significance of every word help me to appreciate poetry and drama *now,* do they? And is pure enjoyment to be despised?"

"Oh, bravo, Lady Angeline," Lady Overmyer said. "Why read a poem or watch a play if one is not entertained by it? What do you have to say to *that,* Edward?"

"It sounds to me," he said, "as though those lessons of yours were merely tedious, Lady Angeline, and were in grave danger of killing your interest in literature for all time. But there is a way of teaching that informs and guides and leads and encourages and *excites* the pupil at the same time. I was fortunate enough to know a few such teachers."

"I had such a governess when I was a girl," Cousin Rosalie said. "But she was a rarity. I have realized that since."

"Learning was painful enough when I was a girl," Cousin Belinda said, fanning her face. "Must we now *talk* about it?"

There was general laughter, and the conversation swept on to something else.

Their supper was brought to the box soon after, and they feasted upon a variety of sumptuous foods, including the wafer-thin slices of ham for which Vauxhall Gardens was famous, as well as the strawberries with clotted cream.

"Why does food always taste so much more appetizing out of doors?" Angeline asked.

The question led to a lively discussion.

"All I know," Mrs. Lynd said to end it, "is that you are quite right, Lady Angeline, and it must be the reason why most of our eating is done *indoors*. We would all weigh a ton in no time at all otherwise."

Everyone laughed. Everyone appeared to

be having a wonderful time. Angeline looked happily about her and glanced at Lord Heyward. He was smiling at his sister. *This,* she thought, was the happiest night of her life.

And then the orchestra, which had been playing quietly all evening, struck up a more lively tune to signal the beginning of the dancing.

They played a waltz tune, and Angeline gazed wistfully on as Tresham led Cousin Belinda onto the floor, and Cousin Leonard followed with Lady Heyward, Mr. Lynd with Rosalie, and Ferdinand with Lady Overmyer. Angeline had been granted permission to waltz at Almack's within the past week and could now officially dance it anywhere. And it was the most divine dance ever invented. Dancing it in the outdoors would surely be simply . . . heavenly.

"Well, Edward," Mrs. Lynd said, "it would be too lowering for you to waltz with your sister. You must dance with Lady Angeline instead, then, and I shall twist Christopher's arm and he will waltz with me. A certain amount of exercise is good when one is out of doors, I have heard. It fills the lungs with good, clean air and counteracts the effects of stale air breathed in when one sits in a box doing nothing. And it aids the digestion."

She winked at her brother as Lord Over-myer got to his feet.

"I was about to ask you anyway, Alma," he said. "You are looking very fine this evening."

"Why, thank you," she said as he led her away. "Flattery will win you a dancing partner any evening of the week."

Lord Heyward was also on his feet, and for one moment Angeline was assailed by an almost irresistible longing. But only for a moment.

"Oh," she said, "you look like a drowning man who has been up for air twice and is about to descend for the third and final time. I shall save your life. I do not wish to waltz."

He sat down again.

"I do know the steps," he assured her.

"I know all the keys on a pianoforte and every note on a sheet of music," she told him. "But somewhere between my eyes and my head at the one extreme and my fingers on the other, the message gets lost. Or scrambled anyway. I was the despair of my governesses. It seems I can never ever be a proper lady if I am not an accomplished musician."

"You are kind," he said.

"And you can never be a proper gentleman," she said, "because when you dance your legs turn to wood."

"It is that noticeable?" he asked. "But it must be. You feigned a sprained ankle rather than have to continue dancing with me at your come-out ball."

"I turned my ankle," she said, "to save you from the embarrassment of having to dance on. But you danced with other partners afterward, and so my sacrifice was in vain. Can there be anything more romantic than the waltz, do you suppose? Unless it is a waltz beneath the stars and colored lamps?"

Cousin Leonard and the Countess of Heyward were gazing into each other's eyes as they danced. They were probably quite unaware of anyone else around them — or even of the stars and lamps.

A waltzing couple must *always* maintain a proper distance from each other even though their hands must touch throughout and indeed the gentleman must keep one hand on the lady's waist and she must keep one hand on his shoulder. Those hands must *never* move after being properly placed, even by as much as half an inch.

Angeline could hear the rules listed in the severe voice of Miss Pratt, who had taught her the waltz even though she very strongly disapproved of it.

There was not even a sliver of air between Tresham and Lady Eagan as they waltzed. And not only his hand was resting on her waist. His whole *arm* was. Her hand was not on his shoulder at all, but against the back of his neck. There were only a few slivers of air between their faces.

Angeline sighed inwardly and fanned her face. And she wondered if Tresham had accepted his invitation only because Cousin Belinda was to be here. Was it possible that he *had* seen her since Rosalie's wedding?

"Romantic?" Lord Heyward said in answer to her question. "It is just a dance."

She looked at him sidelong.

"Do you not believe in romance, Lord Heyward?" she asked.

He hesitated.

"I believe in love," he said, "and commitment and affection and fidelity and . . . comfort. I believe in happy marital relationships. I know a few, though not as many as I could wish. But *romance?* It sounds altogether too giddy to me, the sort of thing that leads people into falling in love, whatever that means, and acting without considered judgment and often ensuring an unhappy life for themselves trapped in a lifelong connection that quickly reveals romance and falling in love to be just a sad illusion. I have known a few of those connections."

Oh, dear.

Angeline fanned her face again.

"Perhaps," she said, "it is possible to be happy *and* in love, Lord Heyward. Perhaps romance can lead to love and affection and commitment and . . . What else did you list? Ah, yes, and to comfort. In a rare case. Do you not think?"

"I have no evidence of that," he said. "But I suppose it is human nature to wish that you were right. To *hope* that you *are* right. It is perhaps wiser always to try to think and speak and act with good sense and judgment."

"But wishes, hopes, and dreams are what give us the will and the courage to go on," she said. "I would not want to go on without dreams."

He was looking directly at her, she found when she turned her head toward him, having just witnessed Tresham for the merest moment denying even those few slivers of air space between his face and Belinda's.

"Dreams can only lead one astray and cause ultimate despair, Lady Angeline," he said. "But you are young. You have just made your debut into society, and the whole of a possibly glittering future is ahead of you. I would not wish to deny you your dreams. But have a care. They can be dashed in one impulsive moment."

Oh, she thought as she gazed into his eyes, what had he dreamed? And what had happened to dash those dreams? He spoke as though he were *not* young.

But he believed in love. And she had seen that it was true. He loved his family.

He just did not believe in romantic love. How foolish of him.

She smiled brightly at him.

"I will not force you to *waltz,* Lord Heyward," she said, "but I will sigh and look thoroughly forlorn if you do not at least offer to take me walking. We are in the loveliest place in the whole wide world, and I have scarcely seen any of it."

He got to his feet again and offered his arm.

"Neither have I," he said. "This is my first visit here too."

"Then we will explore together," she said, rising and taking his arm and glancing Rosalie's way. Over Mr. Lynd's shoulder, Rosalie met her glance and nodded her approval. Mrs. Lynd was also smiling their way.

Tresham was whispering something in

Cousin Belinda's ear. At least, Angeline assumed he was whispering. He would not need to speak aloud when his mouth was one inch away from her ear.

What happened next was entirely his fault, Edward admitted to himself later. He acted with uncharacteristic impulsiveness, and he reaped the consequences.

They strolled up the main avenue along with dozens of other revelers. Vauxhall Gardens was really not half as bad as he had expected. Perhaps it would look tawdry, or just very ordinary, in the daylight, but at night it had its appeal, he had to admit. The colored lamps were a particular inspiration. And the straight, wide avenue and the trees that bordered it were impressive and well kept. Everyone appeared to be in high spirits, but there was no obvious vulgarity. No one was noticeably foxed. The music formed a pleasant background to conversation.

It seemed to be a place intended purely for innocent enjoyment. There was nothing really wrong with that, was there? Sometimes life was to be simply enjoyed. *He* was enjoying himself. It was a surprising admission, but when he tested it in his mind, he found it was true.

Lady Angeline Dudley chattered on about everything in sight. Edward found that he did not mind. He even enjoyed listening to her enthusiasm. Sheer innocent exuberance was all too rare a commodity, he thought. Most people of his acquaintance were, to a greater or lesser degree, jaded. Including, perhaps, himself.

There must be something very pleasant about being able to go even beyond enjoyment to see all this as magical, as she clearly did, to be filled to the brim with unalloyed happiness. He almost wished he could be like her. It felt strangely . . . what was the word? *Comforting?* It felt strangely comforting to be within her aura, to have all that chatter, all that exuberance, all that sparkle directed at him — dull old sobersides that he was.

He had been feeling rather down for a few days and consequently had alarmed his family by neglecting to attend either a ball or a soiree they had particularly wanted him to attend. Though they *had* consoled themselves with the fact that Lady Angeline Dudley would be here tonight in the most romantic of settings London had to offer. He had called upon Eunice and had taken her out walking. And, after listing all the reasons he could think of — it had seemed like an impressive list to him — why it made perfect sense for him to marry her and her to marry him, he had made her a formal proposal.

She had said no.

She had listed reasons of her own, none of which had sounded nearly as convincing as the items on *his* list. But the depressing fact was that she had refused him, and that she had told him he must not ask her again, that he must forget her and do what he knew very well he *ought* to do and choose someone more eligible. Someone like Lady Angeline Dudley, whom she found herself liking very well indeed, even if the girl was no intellectual giant.

"She is good-natured, Edward," she had said, "and certainly not unintelligent. And she has a quality of — Oh, what is the word I am searching for? Of *light* or *joy* or *something*. Whatever it is, it is enchanting. It makes me smile. *She* makes me smile."

Eunice was not usually lost for words. And she was not, generally speaking, a person to throw around words such as *enchanting* and *joy.*

So he was going to have to turn his mind to the serious business of selecting a bride. Someone who was not Eunice. Or Lady Angeline Dudley either. Of that he was determined. Lord, she found even the *waltz* romantic. He would kill that sparkle inside her within a fortnight if he married her.

After the first few minutes she was alternately chatting and silent beside him. But it was an eloquent silence on her part and surprisingly companionable on his. He felt no need to rush in to fill it each time. She gazed about them with wide eyes and parted lips, drinking in all the sights and sounds.

And then, looking ahead, he saw three men in the middle distance heading their way, and even from this far away he could tell that they had been drinking rather more than was good for them. And even from this far away it was clear that they were ogling the ladies they passed and making remarks that were annoying a few of the gentlemen with those ladies. They were clearly trouble waiting to happen.

And one of them happened to be Windrow.

Edward contemplated turning abruptly back before Lady Angeline saw them. He considered moving inexorably onward and dealing with trouble if it came. That, though, might involve drawing unwelcome attention their way, since he certainly would not countenance any of those three men looking at her or speaking to her with disrespect.

For himself he would not mind a bit of trouble, but he *would* mind for any lady who was under his escort.

He took neither of the two courses he considered. He took a third and did something he did not consider at all.

"Perhaps," he said, "you would like to get away from the crowds for a few minutes, Lady Angeline, and stroll along one of the side paths among the trees."

He had just spotted one of those paths coming up on their left, and he moved them onto it almost before she could turn her head to smile at him. He was unfamiliar with those side paths, of course. He had never been to Vauxhall before.

He knew almost immediately that he had made a mistake. The path was narrow and dark. There were no lamps strung in the tree branches here. The only light came from the main path and, when the canopy of branches overhead was not too thick, from the moon above. The path was also winding and deserted.

"Oh," Lady Angeline said, her voice warm with delight, "what a very good idea, Lord Heyward. This is heavenly, is it not?"

They could have walked single file in some comfort, but that would have been somehow ridiculous. They walked side by side, her

arm through his and clamped to his side —
he had no choice. They brushed together a
number of times either at the shoulder or at
the hip or at the thigh or, once or twice, at
all three simultaneously. Again, he had no
choice.

Even the music sounded more distant
from in here. The voices and laughter of
revelers sounded a million miles away.

And what had happened to the cool night
air?

"I do beg your pardon," he said. "The
path is far narrower than it looked. And it is
very dark. Perhaps I ought to take you back
to the main avenue, Lady Angeline."

Windrow and his companions would
surely have gone past by now.

"Ah, but it is lovely here," she said. "Can
you hear the wind in the trees? And the
birds?"

He stopped to listen. Her ears were keener
than his. All he had heard, with growing
unease, were receding voices and distant
music. But they were surrounded by nature
and the sounds and smells of nature, and
she was right — it really *was* rather lovely.
And the moon was almost, if not quite, at
the full. There must be a million stars up
there. And indeed, if one tipped one's head
right back, one could see a surprising

number of them.

They were as lovely as the lanterns. No, lovelier.

He felt the tension seep from his body and drew a deep, fragrant breath.

"Look at the *stars,*" she said almost in a whisper. Her voice sounded somehow awed.

They were in a small clearing, he realized, and there was an almost clear view upward. Turning his head, he could see that her face was bathed in moonlight. Her eyes shone with the wonder of it. And she turned her face to share the wonder with him. She smiled, but not with her usual bright smile. This was more dreamy, more . . . intimate.

As if they shared some very precious secret.

"I *am* looking," he said. Though it was not at the stars he was gazing any longer, but into her eyes. And why was he whispering?

Her lips parted, and the moonlight gleamed on them. She must have moistened them with her tongue.

He kissed her.

And immediately lifted his head. He felt rather as if lightning had zigzagged its way right through the center of his body.

She did not move.

And the lightning or the moonlight or

something had killed his brain.

He kissed her again, turning her as he did so with one arm about her shoulders so that he could twine the other about her waist. And he opened his mouth, parting her lips as he did so, and plunged his tongue deep into her mouth. It was all heat and moisture and soft, smooth surfaces.

Someone moaned — he sensed it was not he — and one of her arms twined about his neck while the other circled his waist and she kissed him back with fierce enthusiasm.

If there was any modicum of common sense left to rattle about inside his head, it deserted him at that point, and his one hand slid hard down her back until it spread over that very shapely derriere that had so disturbed him a month ago on the road to London. And the tip of his tongue traced the ridge along the roof of her mouth while his other hand moved downward and forward to cup one of her breasts. It was warm and soft and full.

He felt himself harden into arousal.

Someone had a furnace going full blast and both doors open wide — and there was only one way to put out the fire. His hand tightened over her bottom and pressed her closer.

And then, while the rest of his body was

only *feeling* an intense desire for the woman in his arms, his eyes suddenly *saw* against the insides of his closed eyelids.

They saw *Lady Angeline Dudley.*

And his mind spoke two very clear, very stern words to him.

Good Lord!

The admonition came too late, of course. Far too late.

Impulsiveness and lust had been his downfall.

He returned his tongue to his own mouth, moved his hands to cup her shoulders, and took a step back. A very firm step.

Her face, heavy-lidded and moist-lipped, open and vulnerable, was achingly beautiful in the moonlight.

But it was the face of *Lady Angeline Dudley.*

"I do beg your pardon," he said, his voice sounding almost ridiculously steady and normal.

They were useless words, of course. There could *be* no pardon.

"Why?" she asked, all wide, dark eyes.

"I ought not to have brought you here," he said. "I have done the very thing I ought to have been protecting you from."

"I have never been kissed before," she said.

He felt ten times worse, if that was possible.

"It was *wonderful*," she said with dreamy emphasis.

She was indeed a dangerous innocent. One kiss and she was like clay in the kisser's hands. In unscrupulous hands that could spell disaster. What would have happened if he had not come to his senses? Would she have stopped him? He doubted it.

"I have compromised you horribly," he said.

She smiled and looked more herself.

"Of course you have not," she said. "What is more natural than for a man and a woman to kiss when they find themselves alone in the moonlight?"

Which was *precisely* his point.

"I will take you back to the box and your chaperon and your brothers," he said.

Her *brothers.* Good Lord. Tresham was not exactly a spotless role model. He had been behaving scandalously on the dance floor back there with his mistress — or one of them. It was common knowledge that he had been carrying on with Lady Eagan even before Eagan left her. Perhaps he was even *why* Eagan had gone. It had perhaps been less honorable but safer than challenging Tresham to a duel. Even so, *Tresham* would not think it was the most natural thing in the world for any man to kiss his *sister* while walking in the moonlight with her. Tresham would take him apart limb from limb.

"If you must," Lady Angeline said with a sigh. "You must not worry, though, Lord Heyward. I kissed you just as much as you kissed me. And no one saw. No one will ever know."

Except the two of them. That was two people too many.

She took his arm and snuggled up to his side as they stepped onto the narrower part of the path again.

"Tell me you are not *really* sorry," she said. "I want to remember tonight as one of the loveliest of my life, perhaps even *the* loveliest, but I will not be able to if I am to believe that you regret having kissed me."

He sighed — with mingled exasperation and relief — as they stepped back onto the main avenue. And there was indeed no further sign of Windrow.

"It has been a lovely evening," he lied.

"And the fireworks are still to come," she said happily.

Yes, indeed.

CHAPTER 11

Angeline woke up smiling.

She gazed up at the elaborately pleated canopy over her bed and stretched until her toes cracked and her fingers curled over the top of the headboard. She laced her fingers behind her head.

She could tell that it was raining even though the curtains were still drawn. She could hear a pattering against the window-panes. But it *felt* as if the sun were shining.

Was it possible for life to be brighter?

Vauxhall Gardens must be the most wonderful, most magical place on earth. Everything about it was perfect. And the company had been the best possible. Conversation had been lively and conducted on a variety of subjects, all of which she had found interesting. Mr. Lynd had danced with her. So had Viscount Overmyer and Cousin Leonard. The music had been divine, the food scrumptious.

The fireworks had been breathtaking, awe-inspiring. They had been beyond the power of superlatives to describe, in fact. The only disappointing thing about them, as she had said at the time, was that the display had come to an end far too soon. As had the evening, of course.

But it had been by far the most wonderful evening of her life.

Oh, *by far.*

Angeline bent her legs at the knee and rested her feet flat on the mattress, the blankets tented over them.

Her mind had been skirting around the very best part of it all. She had allowed the memories to crowd into her mind the moment she awoke, but she had very deliberately kept the best for last so that she could give it her undivided attention. And even now she would think of that very best memory a bit at a time, keeping the very, *very* best, the very most glorious until last.

The Earl of Heyward.

Even his name was lovely. So much lovelier than any other she knew. Poor Martha was smitten by Mr. Griddles. And if that name were not bad enough in itself, there was his first name. What parents would inflict the name *Gregory* upon a poor baby when his last name was *Griddles?* But that was precisely what his parents had done.

The Earl of Heyward was *Edward.* Edward Ailsbury.

His conversation was sensible. He had participated in every topic of discussion without trying to dominate any, and he had expressed his opinions even when they had conflicted with someone else's — and yet he had listened courteously to those other opinions. He was obviously fond of his family. He had taken Lady Heyward for a stroll while Angeline danced with Cousin Leonard. And he had looked a little sheepish when Mrs. Lynd, while talking briefly about her children, had said that her youngest, as well as Lady Heyward's daughter and Lady Overymyer's three, would grow fat before summer came if her brother kept taking them to Gunter's for ices.

"But what are uncles for, Alma," he had asked, "if not to spoil their nieces and nephews horribly before taking them home to their parents?"

"And you have promised to take all five of them to the Tower of London next week, Edward," Lady Overmyer had added. "Is that not a little rash of you?"

"Probably," he had agreed. "I shall enforce good behavior by threatening to forgo the ices on the way home."

They had all laughed, and Angeline had stored in her heart the image of Lord Heyward as a doting uncle.

But the very best part could be postponed no longer. Her memory was fairly bursting with it. She wiggled her toes against the mattress and closed her eyes.

He had kissed her.

She had kissed him.

Her very first kiss.

He had taken her off the main avenue, where everyone else was walking, and had found a quiet, enchanted little clearing into which moonlight poured — so much more romantic after all than the lamps — and he had kissed her once, then drawn her right into his arms and kissed her again.

Oh, it had been *nothing* like anything she had ever expected a kiss to be. She had always wondered what her lips would feel like when being kissed and what the man's would feel like. She had wondered how she would breathe. She could not remember breathing *at all,* but she supposed she must have done so or she would be dead.

She could not even remember clearly what her lips had felt like, or his. For a kiss had proved to be far more than just a touching of lips. Their whole bodies had been involved, their whole *beings.* Oh, goodness, as soon as his lips had touched hers for the second time, his mouth had opened and so had hers — and he had pressed his tongue into her mouth. It sounded shocking if it was put into words. But she was thinking more in remembered sensations than in words.

Her insides had turned to a sort of aching jelly. Her legs had felt weak. She had been throbbing in a place to which she could not put a name. And their bodies had been pressed together. He had been all hard-muscled, solid, unfamiliar masculinity and familiar cologne, and she had clasped him to her with arms that strained to draw him even closer. But how much closer could he have got short of removing a few layers of clothes? The very thought of *that* reminded Angeline of how hot that clearing had seemed for the few minutes of their embrace. As though someone had lit a fire and piled on a forest of kindling and a ton of coal.

His one hand had been spread — oh, dear — over her bottom. The other had come beneath one of her breasts and closed about it.

It was surely the most startlingly glorious first kiss anyone had ever experienced. Not that she was interested in anyone else for the moment.

It had been the very best experience of her life. She could not imagine that anything in her life could exceed it. Ever. Except that she had wanted it to go on and on forever, and of course it had not.

And the dear man had apologized afterward.

As if he had somehow taken advantage of her. As if he had somehow *compromised* her. He had even said so. A lady's honor could not be compromised if there was no one there to see, could it?

Indeed it could, said Miss Pratt's voice in her head, at its most severe. *A lady must always be a perfect lady, even in the privacy of her own boudoir.*

Which was about the most stupid of many stupid pronouncements Miss Pratt had made.

She had told him it was her first kiss. She had told him it was wonderful. Perhaps she ought not to have said either thing. She must have sounded very naive. But why not? Why pretend to be worldly-wise and jaded when one was not? She had begged him to tell her he was not really sorry, and he had admitted it was a lovely evening.

Lovely was an understatement. For she had made perhaps the most wonderful discovery of all last night. Lord Heyward was a very proper, serious-minded gentleman to whom courtesy and reason and good sense were more important than posturing and violence. But it could always be said that such men were dull. Tresham called him a dry old stick.

But *it was not so.*

She now knew *from personal experience* that such a man could also be passionate in his private dealings with the woman he loved. Very passionate indeed.

With the woman he loved.

Angeline's eyes were still closed. She wiggled her toes and opened her eyes at last. Was that who she was? *The woman he loved?* She must be. He could not possibly have kissed her like that if she was not. Could he?

She would see him again this evening. At least, she hoped she would. There was Lady Hicks's ball to attend, and apparently it was always one of the great squeezes of the Season.

Oh, surely he would be there too.

She threw back the bedcovers and swung her legs over the side of the bed to the floor. She had planned to walk in the park this morning with Martha and Maria — she had *so* much to tell them. It was still raining, of course, so that idea must be abandoned. But there were always shops just waiting to be shopped at, and there were tearooms where one might sit and talk with friends. She had far too much energy to remain at home merely waiting for this evening to come.

When Edward arrived at Dudley House later the same afternoon, he was shown into the library on the main floor while the butler went off to see if the Duke of Tresham was at home. Edward could not even allow himself the luxury of hoping he was not. Besides, he was almost sure Tresham would be here. He had been at the House earlier, as had Edward himself. He would certainly have returned home before going out for the evening.

Edward looked around at the shelves of books that lined the walls and wondered if Tresham ever as much as opened the cover of any of them. The large oak desk was clear apart from an inkpot and some quill pens on a blotter. Comfortable-looking leather winged chairs flanked the fireplace. A chaise longue was set at the other side of the room. One could not imagine Tresham spending much of his time in a library of all places.

He walked closer to the fireplace for the

simple reason that he did not want to be found hovering just inside the door, looking as uncomfortable as he felt. But a man stood in front of his own hearth, not someone else's. He changed direction and crossed to the window instead. He stood looking out.

He did not believe he had ever felt more depressed in his life. Or more purely embarrassed. He wished he were anywhere else on earth but where he actually was. On the opposite side of Grosvenor Square he could see a maid cleaning off the boot scraper outside one door and found himself envying her her quiet, uncomplicated existence. Which was nonsense, of course. No one's life was all quietness or lack of complications. It just seemed sometimes that someone else's life — *everyone* else's in this case — was preferable to one's own.

As luck would have it, his mother and Lorraine had just been returning from a visit as he was leaving the house, bringing with them both his grandmother and Juliana, and they had all, of course, wanted to know where he was going all spruced up and freshly shaven.

"Oh, out," he had said vaguely, kissing his mother and grandmother on the cheek.

"Take my word for it, Adelaide," his

grandmother had said, "there is a lady involved. Lady Angeline Dudley, I trust."

"She was at Vauxhall with us last evening," Juliana had said, smiling. Just as if his mother and grandmother had not already known that.

"I do hope you are not planning to take her driving in the park, though, Edward," his mother had said, glancing out the hall window. "It is not actually raining again, but it is going to be at any moment. I do not at all like the look of those clouds. What a gloomy day it has been."

"Perhaps," his grandmother had said, waving her lorgnette in his direction as though conducting a symphony, "he is going to Dudley House to propose marriage to her, Adelaide. Did he dance with her at Vauxhall, Lorraine? Did he steal a kiss from her? Vauxhall is the very best place in London for stolen kisses. I still remember that. Ah, the memories."

They had all laughed, and Lorraine's face had turned an interesting shade of pink.

And they had forgotten to demand an answer to the question. Or had there been a question? Edward had escaped before any of them could remember it — or remember to ask it.

They would know soon enough.

251

He was dreading hearing the library door open behind him. He would hate it even more, though, if it were the *butler* who opened it with the news that His Grace was indeed from home. He would not have been shown into the library, though, if that were the case, would he?

Did the man always keep guests waiting so long? How long *had* he been waiting? It felt like an hour. It was probably no more than five or ten minutes. And then the door opened and he turned.

Tresham was looking very black-eyed. Why was it his eyes that one always noticed first? His eyebrows were also raised. His long fingers were curled about the handle of a quizzing glass. If he had the effrontery to lift it to his eyes . . .

He did not.

"Heyward," he said, the hint of a sigh in his voice. "For a moment I was propelled back in time when my butler handed me your card. But then I remembered, alas, that *that* Heyward is no more. To what do I owe the pleasure? I hope my guess is not correct."

Of course it was correct. And he could hardly have been more insolent if he had tried.

"I have come to ask for the hand of Lady

Angeline Dudley," he said.

This time the sigh was not hinted at. It was quite explicit. And it was not immediately accompanied by words.

"Have you?" Tresham said. "In marriage, I presume you mean. How very tedious of you. She will say no, you know."

"Perhaps," Edward said stiffly, "we may allow *her* to say it, Tresham. Or yes, as the case may be. I merely need your permission to pay my addresses to her. I would imagine my eligibility is self-evident, but I am quite prepared to give you details should you feel obliged to hear them."

Tresham regarded him silently for a few moments before dropping his quizzing glass on its ribbon and making his way across the room to sit behind the empty desk.

"I do indeed insist that Lady Angeline say no for herself on such occasions," he said. "One would not wish to develop a reputation for being a tyrant of a brother, would one? But you would not have had the experience. Both your sisters were married before you inherited your title."

He was not the first to offer for her, then, Edward thought. Of course, she had mentioned Exwich proposing to her, had she not? It was a great pity she had not accepted one of her other suitors, even if he could not in all conscience wish Exwich upon her. But such a thought was pointless.

"Do take a seat," Tresham said, indicating a chair across the desk from his own with one indolent hand. "You will indeed convince me that you are an eligible suitor for Lady Angeline's hand before I allow you to speak to her, Heyward."

He was quite within his rights, of course. But surely almost any father or brother but Tresham would have left details of a marriage settlement to be worked out *after* the lady had said yes. Very well. Marriage settlements worked both ways. She must bring an acceptable dowry to the marriage. They would discuss that too.

Edward seated himself, quite determined not to appear an abject supplicant.

He looked the Duke of Tresham in the eye and raised his own eyebrows.

Angeline had read the same page of the same book half a dozen times in the last half hour, and she *still* had not absorbed a word of it. It was Mr. Milton's *Paradise Lost* and needed her full attention. It was a work of literature of which she believed Miss Goddard would approve. Not that she had seen that lady at all since her first visit to the library. If she had a chance to talk to the Earl of Heyward this evening — *if?* — she would mention it to him. She had already read six of the twelve books that comprised the work and had enjoyed them immensely. Miss Pratt had never let her read it because someone had once said in the governess's hearing that Mr. Milton had made Satan far more attractive than God. Angeline had been relieved at the time for it was a *very* long poem and she had never enjoyed reading poetry. But it was turning out to be fascinating.

She could not to save her life read this page today, though.

She could not *wait* for this evening to come. Would he somehow contrive to kiss her again? Could she somehow maneuver matters —

The drawing room door opened, and she looked up to smile at Tresham. He was not smiling back. He was looking horridly bored. It was a growingly familiar look.

Oh, no, she thought with an inward sigh. Who was it this time?

"You had better go down to the library, Angeline," he said. "Another eligible hopeful anxiously awaits his fate."

She closed her book after placing her bookmark to mark her page.

"Must I?" she said. But it was a pointless

question. Yes, of course she must. "Who is it this time?"

He almost grinned. Certainly he looked amused.

"The dry old stick," he said.

"The Earl of Heyward?" Her voice rose to a squeak.

"None other," he said, and now he definitely was grinning. "Contain your passion, Angeline, and go on down there. The man is desperate for a wife, I hear, but he might at least be realistic in his choice. I almost said no on your behalf, but I could not deny you the pleasure."

She was already on her feet, she realized when she went to get up. She stared at him, speechless.

The *Earl of Heyward* had come to offer her *marriage?*

Already?

She did a panicked mental review of her appearance. She had changed into a day dress after returning home from shopping with her friends, though she had not had Betty redo her hair. What was the point when it would have to be done yet again this evening and she was not going anywhere or seeing anyone before then? And it had not looked too badly flattened from her bonnet, not after she had fluffed it up with her hands, anyway. Her dress was the old sunshine yellow one with the colored stripes about the hem that she so liked. It was just the thing for such a gloomy day, she had thought.

Was she looking good enough to face a *marriage proposal from the Earl of Heyward?* But if she suggested going up to her room to change and have her hair done first, Tresham would look at her as if she had suddenly sprouted an extra head.

"I shall go down," she said meekly, though she thought her heart might well beat its way through either her chest or her eardrums or both at any moment.

"There is no need to look so tragic," her brother said, holding the door open for her. "It will all be over in five minutes. And tomorrow it will be someone else."

She made her way downstairs, wondering if her legs would hold her up. How could one body, even if it *was* unnaturally tall, contain such happiness?

The butler himself was waiting outside the library to open the door for her. He closed it behind her after she had stepped inside.

He was standing in front of the desk, all neat and smart and unostentatious in his dark green coat with buff-colored pantaloons and immaculately shining Hessian boots and white linen. His hair was neatly combed. She could tell he was freshly shaved. He had probably used that lovely cologne again, though she could not smell it from here.

He had had the advantage of her. He had known about this proposal and had been able to dress and groom himself accordingly.

She felt almost suffocated with love for him.

He was not smiling. Of course, he would not be. This was a solemn occasion. He would not smile at their wedding either. She would wager on it, though of course she had been told innumerable times that a lady *never* wagered. Everyone was agreed, though, that the few coins a lady bet at card games did *not* constitute wagering.

She smiled at him even though she knew he would not smile back.

And she remembered last night and that kiss. Was it possible that this was the same man? That passion in private moments could so transform a person?

"Lord Heyward," she said.

He came hurrying across the room toward her, all earnest attention.

"Lady Angeline," he said, reaching out a hand for hers and closing his fingers warmly about it when she put it in his.

And then — oh, *and then.*

He went down on one knee before her in a gesture that was absolutely unnecessary and did not at all suit his character but was nonetheless hopelessly romantic.

She gazed down at him with parted lips and shining eyes.

"Lady Angeline," he said, "will you do me the great honor of marrying me?"

Yes, yes, yes. Oh, yes, yes, Y-E-S!

But something happened in the moment before the words could spill past her lips. Or perhaps in a fraction of that moment.

It was something that took her forever to put into words in her head when she looked back later, but took the merest fraction of a second to dash into her consciousness now and drown the words that were about to be spoken.

He had said nothing about love or happiness or her making him the happiest of men. It was as if he were down on one knee because he had been told by someone that that was the way a marriage proposal was done.

He had *never* said anything about love — not about loving her, anyway. Quite the contrary, in fact. He had said *just last evening* that he believed in marital fidelity but not in romance or *falling* in love.

When she had told him later, after their kiss, that it had been the loveliest evening of her life, he had replied that it had been a lovely evening — and that was *after* she had said her memories would be ruined if he regretted kissing her. Really it had been the most lukewarm of responses after the volcanic eruption of their embrace.

And volcanic eruptions of that nature did not *have* to proceed from love, did they, despite what she had thought at the time. Not for men, especially. Men were always taking mistresses, and presumably it was not so that they could sit beside them on couches and hold their hands and kiss them chastely on the cheek once in a while and be comfortable.

Passion could mean lust as easily as it could mean love.

Lord Heyward could not possibly *love* her anyway. She had done nothing but embarrass and disgust him from the moment of their first encounter. She was not at all the sort of woman with whom he must dream of spending the rest of his life. If there was such a woman, she was surely Miss Goddard. She was serious and dignified and intelligent and pretty, and they were already such close friends that they used each

260

other's given name. Indeed, probably the only reason he was not at Lady Sanford's now proposing marriage to Miss Goddard was that according to his strict code of gentlemanly conduct he had compromised *her* last night and so was here instead. And his family probably disapproved of Miss Goddard because she was not as dazzlingly eligible as Angeline was.

But eligible was not the same thing as *suitable.* Miss Goddard was far more suited to him. *She,* on the other hand, was as unsuitable as she could be. She was tall and dark and ugly. She could not even arch her eyebrows without wrinkling her forehead horribly and looking like a startled hare. She was loud and stupid and indiscreet. She prattled on about trivialities just as though there was nothing between her ears except fluff. She had no dress sense whatsoever — just consider her *hats,* which everyone thought so hideous. Just consider *this dress.* All she had ever read were lurid Gothic novels and six and a half books of *Paradise Lost* — not even quite a half. And she could not even read *that* intelligently. She too thought Satan a splendid character and God a great yawn. *And* her mind could be distracted merely at the thought of another ball to attend.

She was hopeless.

She was unlovable.

Their developing romance had been *entirely* in her own head.

"Lord Heyward," she said, gazing into his eyes, willing him to assure her that every bad thing she had ever been told about herself — even though she *knew* every one of them was true — was so much nonsense, and that even if it was not he did not care a tuppenny toss for any of it because he loved her to distraction, "is this because you kissed me last night?"

And the horrible thing was that he stared back at her and did not immediately rush to deny it.

"I compromised you," he said. "I have come to make amends."

Oh, Tresham had been right all along, she thought. He was a dry, dry stick that had been baking out in the desert for a hundred years. Except that he had every right to feel reluctant to marry her. Any man would. Men only flocked here to propose to her because she was the *Duke of Tresham's* sister and had an almost indecently large dowry. No man could have any other reason.

"You do not love me?"

And why had she whispered the words? Perhaps because she ought not to have uttered them at all. She could not possibly have sounded more abject if she had tried.

He got to his feet though he still retained hold of her hand — in both his own.

"I am fond of you," he said, "and I do not doubt affection will deepen between us as time goes on. I hope I did not give the impression I have come here today *only* because I kissed you last evening. I —"

He seemed lost for further words.

"I am the most eligible of prospective brides," she said. "And you need a bride. I need a husband, and you are the most eligible of prospective grooms. It *does* rather sound like a match made in heaven, does it not?"

He was frowning.

"It is not quite like that," he said. "I-I *want* to marry you. Dash it all, Lady Angeline, this is the first marriage proposal I have ever made. I hope it will be the last. I have made a mess of it, have I not? Do forgive me. What can I say to put it right?"

But there was nothing. She had asked him right out if he loved her, and he had answered — *I am fond of you, and I do not doubt affection will deepen between us as time goes on.*

She would have been far more cheered if he had said a definite no, he did not love her at all, in fact he hated her.

There was *passion* in hatred.

There was none whatsoever in *I am fond of you, and . . . affection will deepen between us.*

Angeline slid her hand out from between his and looked down at it, forlorn and cold and on its own again.

"I do thank you for your flattering offer, Lord Heyward," she said, "and for your concern to make all right after last evening. But there was no need to be concerned, you see. No one knew and no one will ever know. Not unless *you* tell. I let you kiss me, and I kissed you back because I *wanted* to, because I had never been kissed before and I am nineteen years old and it is a little ridiculous and pathetic never to have been kissed. Now I have been, and I thank you for the experience. It was really very pleasant, and next time I will know far better what to expect and how to behave. And I will not expect everyone whom I will allow to kiss me to rush here the next day to offer me the respectability of marriage. Not that I will allow *everyone,* or even many men, to kiss me. I'll probably allow very few, in fact. Of course, you are a gentleman, which not many men are despite what their birth and upbringing may lead them to call themselves. I am sure you do not make a habit of slinking off into the bushes with every girl who has never been kissed just so that you can show them how it is done. That would not be at all honorable, and you are always unfailingly honorable. Besides, you would be forever dashing off to propose marriage the day after, and *one* of them might say yes and you would be miserable forever after. Unless you *loved* that particular one, of course, except that —"

I am babbling.

She stopped doing it and turned her hand over so that she could examine her palm with as much attention as she had been giving the back of her hand.

There was a short silence.

"I am sorry," he said then.

His voice was quiet, flat.

And that was all. There was another silence, a rather lengthy one this time, and then she was aware of him bowing rather abruptly to her. He left without another word. She heard the door open quietly and then close just as quietly. There was no passion even in his exit.

The long line that curved around her palm from just below her forefinger and disappeared into the folds of her wrist was her lifeline, was it not? It looked as if she was going to live at least a hundred years. That meant she still had eighty-one left.

Eighty-one years of heartbreak. Would it fade by about the seventieth of those years? The seventy-fifth?

The door opened again, much more forcefully.

"Well?" Tresham asked.

"Oh." She looked up. "I said no and sent him on his way."

"Good girl," he said briskly. "Am I supposed to escort you to the Hicks ball tonight, or is Rosalie coming by here?"

You, she was going to say. But she was not sure she could get even the one more word past her lips without its wobbling all out of control and making her feel like a prize idiot.

She yanked the door open and fled out into the hall and up the stairs, leaving someone else to close the door behind her.

The Duke of Tresham stared after her, his brows almost meeting above his nose.

"What the devil?" he asked of the empty room. "All I asked was whether I am to escort her to this infernal ball tonight."

And then he scratched his chin and looked thoughtful.

CHAPTER 12

Edward considered passing the drawing room doors and going straight up to his room. It would have been easy to do — the doors were closed. But he knew they were in there, all of them. He had asked the butler. His grandmother was late going home today — of all days. Juliana too.

He stopped outside the room, sighed, and went in. There was no real point in postponing the inevitable, was there?

"Edward." His mother smiled at him.

"I'll pour you a cup of tea," his sister-in-law said. "Though it may be only lukewarm by now. I shall ring for another pot."

"Don't bother," he said. "I am not thirsty." He was actually, but not for tea.

"It is no bother," she assured him.

"Well?" His grandmother raised her lorgnette, but not all the way to her eye. She very rarely looked through it, having been blessed with exceptionally good eyesight for an elderly lady. "*Was* it a marriage proposal you were making, Edward? What did she say?"

"It was," he said. "And the answer was no. And so that is that for the time being."

"Lady Angeline Dudley?" his mother said, both looking and sounding shocked. "You offered her marriage, Edward, and she said *no?*"

"Oh, but, Edward," Lorraine said as she pulled on the bell rope, "from the way she was looking at you last evening, I thought she was quite taken with you."

"I am convinced of it," Juliana said. "And Christopher agreed with me."

"Apparently she was not," he said, clasping his hands behind his back and forcing a smile.

"The girl is playing hard to get," his grandmother said, pointing the lorgnette in the direction of his heart. "She cannot do better than you and she knows it and fully intends to have you, Edward, mark my words. She wants to be *wooed*. Girls do, you know, especially the most marriageable ones. They do not want to feel that they are nothing but commodities, and who can blame them? *Every* girl wants to be wooed. *I* did, and I was. Oh, your grandfather was a one, my boy. I could tell you tales to make your hair stand on end."

"Edward," Juliana asked after a short pause while the fresh tray of tea was carried in, "did you tell her you *loved* her?"

Dash it all, no, he had not. He supposed he ought to have. It was clearly what she had wanted to hear. She had asked him if he loved her, in fact, and even then he had missed his cue. He had attempted honesty instead.

"What does that *mean?*" he asked, taking a seat since obviously he was about to be plied with tea whether he wanted it or not. "I fully intend to cherish any lady I marry, to cultivate a friendship with her, to grow fond of her, to protect and defend her, to give her my time and attention whenever I am able, to remain faithful to the vows I make to her. Is that not what love is?"

"Oh, Edward," his mother said, "you will make the best of husbands."

"But every lady likes to be told that she is *loved* when a man asks her to marry him," Lorraine said as she handed him a cup of hot tea. "She needs to be made to feel that she is special, that she is the one. The *only* one."

Did Maurice make you feel that way?

But fortunately he stopped himself just in time from asking the question aloud. He was in no doubt that Maurice *did*. He would have. That was the kind of person he had been. He had certainly known what women wanted and expected. Perhaps there was something in the old adage, though, that actions spoke louder than words.

Except that words seemed to be important to a woman being proposed to.

"We are expected to mouth a great many platitudes and hypocrisies and out-and-out lies," he grumbled. "It is how society seems to function. Sometimes, I believe, people ought to be told the truth, especially about the important things in life. Why should I pretend to feel this romantic thing called love when I do not? Is it kind to the lady concerned to pretend?"

She had been about to say yes, he thought. Her eyes had been shining, her lips had been parted, she had leaned slightly toward him as he kneeled on one knee before her — feeling like a prize idiot. She had looked as she had looked last evening just before he kissed her and just after, when she had told him it was the loveliest evening of her life.

Good Lord, she had behaved as if *she* was in love with *him*. How could anyone love *him?* In the romantic sense, that was. He could almost *hear* Maurice snickering with incredulity.

She could not possibly entertain romantic feelings for him. It must be just that she was eager to marry someone eligible. And as she herself had pointed out, he was one of the most eligible bachelors in town this year. And because she had fixed her choice on him, she had to convince herself that she also *loved* him. It seemed so typical of women. They thought with their emotions, or their imagined emotions. If she had agreed to marry him, she would have discovered soon enough that she was marrying nothing but a dull and very ordinary man.

"Why do you have to *pretend*, Edward?" his mother asked in response to what he had just said. "I am not sure I have ever known a more loving man. You have a way of always putting the needs of others before your own. You *are* allowed to reach for some happiness of your own too, you know. You are allowed to love in a way that will engage all your emotions. Your whole being, in fact. You do not owe us all so much that there is nothing left for yourself."

He looked at her, his cup suspended halfway to his mouth. He had never heard her talk this way before. And her voice was shaking. *I am not sure I have ever known a more loving man.* Yet she had adored his

271

father, who had treated her with careless affection. And she had adored Maurice.

You are *allowed to reach for some happiness of your own too . . .*

He *was* happy. Well, he would be once he was back at Wimsbury Abbey for the summer. And once this business of choosing a wife and setting up his nursery was over with and he could settle into the life of a married man and father.

He would be happy if that wife was Eunice.

Perhaps now was the time to mention her. The time to make a stand, to reach for his own happiness.

But just three days ago, she had refused him — quite firmly and irrevocably. She had told him not to ask her again.

Two proposals and *two* refusals in three days. He had told an untruth to Lady Angeline. His proposal to her had *not* been his first, just the first formal one.

He was not a virgin. He had had a few women, though he had never kept a mistress. He had enjoyed all of them. He found sex exhilarating and satisfying — and necessary, though he had not had a woman since Maurice's death.

He had never wanted any of them as he had wanted Lady Angeline Dudley last night. *Why* had he wanted her? Pure lust did not explain it entirely. He had met many beautiful women in his time. He had met some of them this year. A few of them were exquisitely lovely. He could look at them with great appreciation, but he did not feel any overpowering urge to bed any of them.

Only Lady Angeline Dudley.

Whom he did not even like.

Though that was not strictly true. He liked her humor. He liked the way she did not laugh at others but only at herself. He liked her bright sparkle, her unabashed enjoyment of life. And he did suspect that there was more to her than met the eye. A few times he had had a fleeting glimpse at a certain insecurity in her. It puzzled him. Why should she of all people feel *vulnerable?* She was beautiful, and she surely had everything any young lady could want as she made her debut in society. She had already had a few marriage proposals if Tresham was to be believed. And why would he lie?

He had never wanted to bed Eunice. He had wanted to *marry* her — at some future date. He still did. She would suit him perfectly, and the urge was strong at this very moment to rush back out of the house and over to Lady Sanford's to beg her —

on his knees in earnest this time — to put him out of his misery and betroth herself to him.

Which was not very flattering to her, was it?

He could not really imagine being in bed with Eunice. It was somehow an embarrassing thought.

Whereas with Lady Angeline Dudley . . .

She had said no. They had *both* said no. There was no more to be said.

"I *am* happy, Mama," he said with a little laugh that sounded false even to his own ears. "We will not make a tragedy out of this. If I remember correctly, you had other names on your list than just Lady Angeline Dudley's. And I am not entirely helpless on my own account. I am quite capable of looking about me for my own bride. Lady Hicks's ball is this evening, is it not?"

The very *last* thing he felt like doing this evening was attending a ball and actually *dancing*. But duty was already reasserting itself, and there was no point in curling up under his bedcovers, his eyes tightly closed, willing the world to go away, as he might have done when he was five years old.

"It is indeed," his mother said with a sigh. "Oh, Edward, I *so* want you to be happy."

He set down his cup, which was still

almost full, he noticed, and got to his feet.

"Grandmama," he said, "are you ready to go home? I'll have the carriage brought around and take you there if you wish. You too, Juliana."

"That would be good of you, Edward," his grandmother said. "Your grandpapa is supposed to come this way from his club to take us home, but he is probably deep in conversation setting the world to rights and forgetting all about clocks and the passing of time and Juliana and me sitting here listening for carriage wheels."

Edward strode from the room, glad of something to do.

Lady Angeline, will you do me the great honor of marrying me?

Good Lord, talk about platitudes! And on one knee, no less. He winced. He had been a walking — or kneeling — cliché.

Lord Heyward, is this because you kissed me last night?

I compromised you. I have come to make amends.

Deuce take it, had he really said that? Could he not have denied it, told her that last night's kiss was only the thing that had convinced him he did not want to wait any longer before asking her to marry him? Surely a little lie could be excused in such

275

circumstances. She had needed *reassuring,* for God's sake.

You do not love me?

And the question had been whispered and phrased in the negative. Dash it, but there had been definite vulnerability there. He really ought to have lied. After all, he had fully intended to treat her for the rest of her life as though he loved her. Indeed, he *would* have loved her, in his own way. How could he *not* love his own wife, after all?

Instead he had spoken the most heartlessly asinine words that had ever passed his lips. He had spoken the strict truth and made it sound as dry as dust. Drier.

I am fond of you, and I do not doubt affection will deepen between us as time goes on. And then, far too inadequate, and far, far too late — *I hope I did not give the impression I have come here today only because I kissed you last evening.*

He had gone to offer her marriage because he had compromised her — even if no one knew it except the two of them — and he had ended up insulting her quite horribly. Perhaps even hurting her.

He was a horrible man. His mother must be quite wrong about him.

Had he hurt her?

Could he possibly make amends?

But no, he could not. She had said no, and he must respect her decision.

Except that . . .

Oh, good Lord, she *had looked hurt.*

Despite all the prattling on she had done about getting experience at kissing, with the implication that kissing *him* had meant nothing else but that to her — well, despite it all he had the strong suspicion that he had hurt her.

She prattled to cover her insecurities.

Now *there* was a disturbing revelation, if it was true.

Lady Angeline Dudley prattled all the time.

Dash it all.

He strode off to order his carriage brought around only to come face-to-face with his grandfather in the hall.

"Ah, my boy," he said, clapping Edward on the shoulder with one large hand, "you are still here, then. I feared you might be taking your grandmother home by now, and I would never have heard the end of it. Women, my boy. There is no living with them, and no living without them."

He winked and smiled broadly as though he had said something of unique originality.

Angeline was having a frantically good time

at the Hicks ball. She had never been so merry before in her life.

She linked arms with Martha and Maria before the dancing started. She had to be in the middle, of course, because she was so much taller than either of them, as well as being darker and built really on a larger scale altogether. The two of them must look like dainty ribbons dancing about a maypole, in fact. They promenaded about the perimeter of the ballroom, the three of them, chatting and laughing — even out-and-out giggling once or twice.

She danced three sets in a row and smiled dazzlingly and chattered incessantly to her partners, even when the figures of the dance took them so far apart they would have needed ear trumpets to hear every word. She smiled at all the other dancers in passing, ladies and gentlemen alike — except that she conveniently failed to notice the Earl of Heyward when he lumbered past ten feet away from her with his partner and so did not smile at him. It was the same moment anyway as that in which she almost tripped over her own slipper, though she recovered well enough that no one noticed except Ferdinand, who grinned at her.

She chattered between sets to all who wandered her way. A flattering number of those who came were gentlemen, some to ask for dances, some just to be amiable. There were a few notorious fortune hunters among them, according to Cousin Rosalie. But poor men must marry rich wives. It was only good sense. Angeline did not hold their poverty against them. She smiled as brightly upon them as she did upon all the rest.

Ferdinand wandered over to her when there was a lull in the crowd gathered about her and congratulated her upon rejecting yet another suitor for her hand.

"For they have all been nonsensical so far, Angie," he said. "But none more so than Heyward. I suppose the best that can be said of him, poor man, is that he is *worthy*. He is undoubtedly that. But the fellow cannot *dance*."

"Tresh calls him a dry old stick," she said, smiling until she felt her lips might crack.

He gave a short bark of laughter.

"It is a good one," he said. "I must remember it."

She fanned her tightly smiling lips and turned to greet her next partner.

It was only as she was dancing with him that Angeline realized that Miss Goddard was at the ball. She was tucked into a shady, crowded corner of the ballroom with a group of older ladies, wearing the same blue gown she had worn at Angeline's own ball. Oh, goodness, she must not have danced at all or Angeline would have seen her sooner. Was one of those ladies her chaperon? Why had she not made some effort to find partners for Miss Goddard?

Angeline had been looking out for her since that day in the library but had not seen her anywhere.

Her partner — goodness, she could not even remember his *name,* which was shockingly careless of her and not at all fair to him — returned her to Cousin Rosalie's side when the set was at an end. Angeline spoke quickly before another crowd could gather.

"I am going to speak with Miss Goddard for a moment," she said to Rosalie. "She is sitting over there."

"Miss who?" Rosalie asked, but Angeline was already on her way.

She fanned her face and smiled brightly as she approached, and Miss Goddard, seeing her coming, smiled back.

"Lady Angeline," she said in her quiet, serious voice. "How do you do?"

"I have borrowed Mr. Milton's *Paradise Lost* from the library," Angeline said. "I have read six of the books and have started the seventh. I am loving it. I cannot wait to find out what happens."

"Oh." Miss Goddard looked a little taken aback. "Well done. I read it when I was a girl. I have always meant to read *Paradise Regained* but have not yet brought myself around to it."

"The Earl of Heyward called at Dudley House this afternoon," Angeline said. "He offered me marriage, but I said no."

There was a short silence, during which Miss Goddard stared at her without expression.

"I am surprised," she said. "And sorry. Surprised and sorry that you said no, that is."

"He does not love me," Angeline said. "I asked and he said no. Well, he did not say an out-and-out no. That would have been ungentlemanly, and Lord Heyward is always a gentleman. He talked about fondness and affection and other things that all meant the same thing. But he could not say he *loved* me."

"No," Miss Goddard said quietly, "he would not. He ought to have lied because he would have been devoted to you for the rest of his life, you know. He could not possibly *not* be. It is not in his nature. But he finds it difficult, if not impossible, to lie, even if only for the sake of diplomacy."

"He once said that my riding hat was the most atrocious thing he had ever seen in his life," Angeline said.

Miss Goddard was startled into laughter.

"No!" she said. "*Edward* said that?"

"But he smiled as he said it," Angeline said, "and I laughed too. He has a lovely smile."

"Yes." Miss Goddard looked arrested. "Pardon me, how very rude I am being. Lady Angeline, may I present my aunt, Lady Sanford? Lady Angeline Dudley, Aunt Charlotte."

Angeline sat on an empty chair facing the ladies, her back to the dance floor, and chatted for a while. She looked around again only when Miss Goddard fixed her eyes upon something or someone beyond and above Angeline's shoulder and opened her fan, though she held it in her lap.

Lord Windrow was approaching, all lazy smiles and mocking charm.

Angeline jumped to her feet and smiled brightly again. She fluttered her fan before her face. He was *just* what she needed this evening — or *whom* she needed, perhaps. He must have just arrived, which would be typical of him. Certainly she had not seen him before this moment, and she surely would have done if he had arrived earlier.

282

He feigned a look of surprise.

"Ah, fair one," he said, bowing elegantly. "And the delectable Miss Goddard, whose stimulating conversation I have sought but not found, alas, since a certain memorable evening that is regrettably long in the past."

Angeline set her closed fan on his sleeve. The next dance was to be a waltz, was it not? *And* it was the supper dance. This was perfect. And she actually *liked* Lord Windrow, she realized, in much the way she liked her own brothers. He was a rake and a rogue, but at least he was an interesting one. An *amusing* one. And she was not in any danger whatsoever of being taken in by his charm. She would be able to relax and enjoy herself thoroughly with him. No matter that he had made some very improper advances to her at that inn and never apologized adequately for them. What gentleman would not have tried to take advantage of her under similar circumstances?

The Earl of Heyward would not, Miss Pratt's voice answered very clearly and promptly in her head. Angeline ignored it.

"This is to be a waltz," she said, "and I am happy to be able to say that I am allowed to dance it. *And* I am free." She smiled at him with deliberately exaggerated coquetry.

"My heart would have been smitten with dreadfully negative emotions if you had not been either or both," he said, his eyelids drooped over his eyes in their customary way — though his eyes were keen enough beneath them. *And* they were laughing. "I would have felt obliged to challenge every patroness of Almack's to . . . ah, not pistols at dawn. That would have been unsporting. *Fans* at dawn? I hear they can do dreadful damage when slapped across a man's wrist, and the ladies would have an advantage over me in that I have never practiced dueling with a fan. However, it is now unnecessary for me to put my life and wrists at risk. You will waltz with me, Lady Angeline?"

"Oh, I will," she said. "It is my favorite dance in the whole world, you know."

"And Miss Goddard," he said, looking beyond Angeline as he offered his hand. "May I prevail upon you to reserve the first set after supper for me? I shall be devastated beyond all hope of resuscitation if I must return home tonight without having danced with the two loveliest ladies in the room."

Angeline turned her head and smiled with genuine amusement at Miss Goddard. Would she say yes? Angeline hoped so, absurd as Lord Windrow was. It was really too, too bad that she had sat here all evening without partners. Did gentlemen not have *eyes* in their heads? Even if the blue of her gown would be far more effective if it were brighter?

"Thank you, Lord Windrow," Miss Goddard said. "That would be delightful."

She spoke with cool courtesy. It was impossible to know if she really was delighted or not. Perhaps she *liked* being a spectator at a ball rather than a participant, though it was hard to imagine.

Oh, Angeline thought as she was led away onto the floor, she had wanted to have a good talk with Miss Goddard. She had wanted to pour her heart out to her. She wanted to be Miss Goddard's *friend,* though she had no idea why. They were as different as night and day. Miss Goddard must think her horribly giddy and empty-headed. She wanted to prove her wrong if she could. She wanted to learn from her. She wanted . . .

She wanted actually to find some dark, remote corner and bawl her eyes out. But that would be pure foolishness and would make her all red-eyed and ugly.

There was no sign of the Earl of Heyward. Yes, there was. He was sitting on a love seat close to the supper room doors in conversation with Lady Winifred Wragge, who had the brightest red hair Angeline had ever seen, together with green eyes that slanted upward slightly at the outer corners and a complexion that reminded one of peaches and cream. She was also — of course — small and dainty. He was bending slightly toward her, giving her the whole of his attention, as he always did with a partner, and she was giving him all of hers in return.

Well.

Angeline turned the full force of her very happiest smile upon Lord Windrow, who was looking lazily back, apparently more amused than ever.

"Is this not an absolutely *wonderful* evening?" she asked.

"It is so wonderful, my fair one," he said, "that I am lost for a word that is more wonderful than wonderful."

She laughed.

"I *do* tend to exaggerate," she admitted.

"I do not," he assured her, giving her the full benefit of his bedroom eyes. Well, perhaps not the *full* effect. They were still filled with amusement.

She laughed again.

He waltzed divinely. And *that* was no exaggeration at all.

She could not have been happier.

CHAPTER 13

Betty arrived in Angeline's dressing room the following morning with watery eyes, a reddened nose, and a voice that a baritone might have envied if only there had been some volume to it. And she admitted when asked — it was self-evident really — that her head was pounding and she felt wretched.

Angeline promptly sent her back to bed with the command that she stay there all day and not even *dream* of getting up even tomorrow unless she was feeling well again. And then she sent a direction to the kitchen that her maid be dosed and coddled with anything and everything the cook could devise that might soothe a head cold and all its attendant ills.

Then she was left with a bit of a problem, for Rosalie was not coming until the afternoon, yet Angeline wanted to go out this morning. She could have taken one of the other maids, of course, but the housekeeper would look at her with long-suffering reproach if she suggested it. And she was certainly not going to ask Tresham himself to escort her, even supposing he was still at home. It would take too long to send for Ferdinand, even supposing *he* was home.

She would go out alone, then. She was not going far. No harm would come to her, and it was unlikely anyone she knew would see her and report the indiscretion to her brother.

She walked alone to Lady Sanford's, then, and found to her great delight that that lady was from home but Miss Goddard was able to receive her. It was Miss Goddard she had come to see. She had conceived an idea during a night of restless, fitful sleep, and it had restored her spirits considerably.

"This is an unexpected pleasure," Miss Goddard said, getting to her feet as Angeline was shown into a small parlor.

"I hope it *is* a pleasure and not an imposition," Angeline said, taking the seat Miss Goddard indicated and removing her gloves. "It is just that I realized last evening when I saw you hidden in the shadows of the ballroom that I had been hoping ever since first meeting you that we could be friends. Which is absurd, I know, when you are an intelligent, well-educated, well-read lady while I —"

She stopped abruptly.

"While you — ?" Miss Goddard raised her eyebrows.

"I chatter," Angeline said. "Constantly. About nothing at all. I cannot seem to help it. My governesses — *all* of them — told me I had nothing but fluff in my head and that it revealed itself whenever I opened my mouth. And I never made any particular effort to learn from them. I would sometimes try, but my mind would wander after a few moments. I hated poetry and drama in particular. Miss Pratt used to read a poem or a play out loud, giving very deliberate emphasis to every word, and she would stop after every few lines in order to point out all the literary and intellectual merits contained in them. By the time she got to the end of a poem or speech, I had *no* idea how it had started and was almost *screaming* with boredom."

"So would I have been," Miss Goddard surprised her by saying. "What a perfectly dreadful way to teach. I really do not believe I would have liked your Miss Pratt. I suppose she was a very worthy lady."

There was a twinkle in her eye.

"Oh, very," Angeline said. "There was not

289

a fault to be found in her. Which made my behavior toward her that much more reprehensible. I played the most awful tricks on her. I put a huge daddy longlegs of a spider between her sheets one evening, and her screams when she went to bed must have woken everyone in the village a mile away. I felt ashamed of that one afterward, though, for I knew she had an unnatural fear of spiders."

"It was probably not your finest moment," Miss Goddard said. "But it does sound as if you were severely provoked. Learning ought to be exciting. *Reading* ought to be. How can one possibly enjoy it, though, when one is forced to stop every few lines to listen to someone else's interpretation of what has been written? Especially the interpretation of someone *worthy*."

Angeline laughed, and so did Miss Goddard. But she had expressed very similar ideas about learning to those Lord Heyward had expressed at Vauxhall. *Could* learning ever be exciting?

"Did you want to discuss *Paradise Lost?*" Miss Goddard asked. "It is some time since I read it, but it left a lasting impression upon me and I would be happy to share my thoughts with you."

She would like it of all things, Angeline

thought. She would really love to have a friend with whom she could talk about sensible, intelligent things. But it was not why she had made a point of coming here today. Today she had something else to say — something noble. Today she would do something for someone else, she would be unselfish, and then she would feel better. She needed to feel better. She had spent so many wakeful hours last night telling herself that she had enjoyed herself at the Hicks ball more than she had enjoyed herself on any other occasion in her life that her head had ached with all the happiness, and so had her heart. After this visit she could feel truly happy.

"I really came to talk about the Earl of Heyward," she said, leaning slightly forward in her chair.

"Oh." Miss Goddard sat slightly *back* in hers. "Are you regretting that you refused him?"

"No, not at all," Angeline said, her heart plummeting nevertheless to take up residence in the soles of her shoes. "I want to ask you a question. You must not feel obliged to answer, for of course it is impertinent of me and absolutely none of my concern. But all this business of *ton* alliances and marriages is horridly complicated, you know. Everyone wants to marry well, which means choosing and setting one's cap at the most eligible . . . *other.* I will not say *man,* because it works both ways, though that did not really occur to me until after I had come to town and made my come-out. I had always thought that it was only we ladies who would be hoping to find the perfect husband, but of course that was shortsighted of me because men have to marry too, for a variety of reasons, and they also want to marry the very best candidate. And the very best, for both men and women, is not necessarily the person they like best. It is often whom their *family* likes best, or who society suggests is best, or who has the most illustrious title and lineage or the most money, provided it has not been acquired in business or commerce, of course, for then it is tainted by vulgarity, just as if money were not simply money. No one even thinks about *love* or the fact that the two people have to *live* together after they marry and make the best of what often turns out to be not a very great bargain at all even if it pleases all the rest of the world. People can be terribly *foolish,* can they not?"

"Far too frequently," Miss Goddard agreed. "What is your question, Lady Angeline?"

"Well, it is *very* impertinent," Angeline said. "But I shall ask it anyway since it is what I came here to do. Do you love Lord Heyward, Miss Goddard? I mean, do you *love* him in a way that makes you ache *here* when you think that perhaps you will never have him?" She tapped a closed fist over her heart.

Miss Goddard sat farther back in her chair and set her arms along the armrests. She looked perfectly relaxed — except that the fore- and middle fingers of her right hand were beating out a fast little tattoo.

"Why would you ask such a question?" she asked. "We are friends. We have been for years."

"But would you *marry* him if he asked?" Angeline asked her.

Miss Goddard opened her mouth once to speak but closed it again. She started once more after a short silence.

"We once had an agreement," she said, "that we would marry each other at some time in the distant future if nothing happened in the meanwhile to change our minds. Neither of us felt drawn to marriage at the time, though we both recognized that eventually we might see the advisability or the necessity of entering the marital state rather than remaining single. We were seekers of knowledge at the time, two earnest young people who had not yet felt the pull of the world beyond the pages of a book or the learned confines of Cambridge or the exciting workings of our own minds. Something did happen to change our minds, of course. Edward's brother died and he became the earl in his place. It made all the difference, you know. Not to *who* he is, but to *what*. And the what *is* important in the real world."

"But why?" Angeline asked her. "He does not *need* to marry money. At least, I do not *believe* he does, or Tresham would not even have allowed him to speak to me yesterday. He does not need to marry position. All society really demands of him is that he marry respectably. You are eminently respectable, Miss Goddard. You are a lady, and you are refined and sensible and intelligent. And you are his *friend*."

Miss Goddard smiled.

"Lady Angeline," she said, "you refused Edward yesterday. Are you trying to *matchmake* for him today?"

Angeline looked down at her hands. It was precisely what she was doing. Though not so much for him as for her new friend, whom she liked exceedingly well. She dearly loved Martha and Maria and hoped they would remain her close friends for the rest of her life, but Miss Goddard was the friend she had always yearned to have. She could not understand quite why it was so. It just *was*. And it hurt her heart to see her friend a wallflower at balls, unseen and unappreciated when she was the equal of anyone and the superior of most. She was *Angeline's* superior.

"It just struck me," she said, "that in all likelihood you love him and he loves you and yet he was forced into offering for me. Not *literally* forced, I suppose, but definitely maneuvered by what society expects of him. And by his family too, even though they are very pleasant people. I believe they actually *like* me and genuinely believed that I would be the best possible wife for him. But it is *you* he ought to marry. It is you he *must* marry. When he strolled about the ballroom with you last evening after supper — after you danced with Lord Windrow — you looked very *right* together. As if you belonged with each other."

"He certainly thought *you* looked very happy," Miss Goddard said.

"Oh," Angeline said. "I *was* happy. Quite blissfully so. I have never enjoyed an evening so well in my life."

She looked down at her hands again. And

instead of picking up the conversation, Miss Goddard let it rest. The silence stretched. Angeline looked up again after what must have been a full minute.

"I just want to be your friend," she said, "if that does not strike you as being too utterly absurd. I thought we might walk together in the park occasionally or go to the library together or spend a little while in each other's company if we are attending the same entertainment. But I also want you to know that I will not find it awkward if you wish to encourage Lord Heyward's suit. I will not feel you are somehow betraying me — if you accept my friendship, that is. Indeed, I would be very happy for you. I — Oh, dear, I have no right to be saying any of this. And the very idea that you would wish to be my friend —"

"Lady Angeline." Miss Goddard leaned forward suddenly and reached out a hand in Angeline's direction. "I grew up in Cambridge with my father and my brother — my mother died when I was six. I grew up surrounded by men. In many ways it was a wonderful upbringing. I was allowed to read anything I wanted and to listen to endlessly stimulating conversations and drink in knowledge to my heart's content. I knew no girls of my own age — I never went to school. Now I am here with my aunt, too old to mingle easily with girls of your age, too young to settle into a resigned spinsterhood. I am not poor or of lowly birth, but neither am I really a member of the *ton* except as the niece of Lady Sanford. I have never had a come-out. I do not have a bright and sparkling personality to be noticed when I *do* mingle in society. I do not wish to paint an abject picture of myself. I have always been very content with my lot in life. I have been privileged in many ways. Although I did not have governesses or go to school, I believe my own education to have been an excellent one. It was certainly one that always excited me. But Lady Angeline, I believe I have *always* longed for a female friend."

"Even one with a head full of fluff?" Angeline asked her.

"Your governesses ought to have been boiled in oil," Miss Goddard said.

They both laughed.

"I like you exceedingly well," Miss Goddard said. "If I wish to consort with intellectual giants I will return to my father's home and consort to my heart's content. I would like to have a *friend,* even if we must discuss *Paradise Lost.*"

And they both laughed again — at just

the moment the parlor door opened and the Earl of Heyward was ushered in by a servant careless enough not to have come first to see if Miss Goddard was home.

He stood arrested in the doorway.

Angeline's heart leapt up into her throat and then dived again for the soles of her shoes. It was a most disconcerting feeling. She stood up — as did Miss Goddard, who crossed the room toward him, both hands extended.

"Edward," she said, "I have been enjoying a conversation with Lady Angeline Dudley, as you can see. We have both been agreeing that the Hicks ball last evening was a splendid event. Indeed, Lady Angeline believes that she has never enjoyed herself more in her life."

Angeline smiled brightly.

"It was indeed a fine squeeze," he said stiffly, keeping his eyes upon Miss Goddard. "I am sorry, Eunice. If I had known you had company, I would have gone away. I will do so now and come back another time."

"No," Angeline said, "I was just leaving. You must sit down, Lord Heyward. Not that it is my place to offer you a seat in Miss Goddard's house — well, Lady Sanford's house, but she is from home at the moment and so it is Miss Goddard's place to tell guests where they may sit and *if* they may sit. But you must not feel obliged to curtail your visit just because I am here. I have stayed far too long already, and I daresay Miss Goddard is wishing me to perdition. I shall . . . go."

"Lady Angeline came alone," Miss Goddard said, looking only at the earl. "Her maid is indisposed. I shall send my own maid with her."

"Oh, no —" Angeline began.

Lord Heyward fixed her with his very blue gaze. It looked ever so slightly hostile.

"Lady Angeline," he said, "it will be my pleasure to escort you home. I am surprised that the Duke of Tresham and Lady Palmer allowed you to leave Dudley House alone."

"Oh, they did not know," she said, "and I have no intention of telling them. They would scold for a fortnight. I am quite capable of walking alone, however. I have not noticed footpads lurking on every corner, have you?"

His stare became icy.

"I will escort you home, Lady Angeline," he said.

He had no business. He had absolutely no business. He was not her father or her brother or her husband or . . . or her betrothed. He was nothing whatsoever. And it was not even an offer this time. It was a categorical statement, and his glance did not even waver as she gave him the full force of her haughty glare.

"I do think that would be good of you, Edward," Miss Goddard said.

And Angeline was the first to look away — in order to glance reproachfully at her new friend, who could have used this visit, her aunt being absent, to further her own courtship with the Earl of Heyward. *And* to save her new friend from a blatant instance of male domineering.

"Very well, Lord Heyward," she said, looking back at him. But she would . . . Yes, she would. She would be *damned* before she would thank him.

There! She felt marginally better at the shocking language even if it did not find its way past her lips.

Miss Goddard smiled placidly at her.

Traitor! Judas!

Edward was *not* in a good mood.

He had not been even before he arrived at Lady Sanford's, but at least he had expected a nice quiet, sensible conversation with Eunice. He had expected his visit to feel like balm to the soul. Perhaps she would even consent to take a short walk with him again since it was a sunny, pleasantly warm day.

Instead, here he was out walking with *Lady Angeline Dudley* of all people the day after she had refused his formal marriage offer. She had refused to take his arm, which made walking really quite awkward. And she had dared to give him that same haughty, regal look she had given *Windrow* during that infamous scene just outside Reading. As if *he* was the one behaving with deliberate lack of discretion. *No* proper young lady set foot outdoors without a chaperon or trustworthy companion.

I have not noticed footpads lurking on every corner, have you? As if they advertised the fact upon large boards carried about their necks. And as if footpads were the only danger. Had she learned *nothing* from her experience at the Rose and Crown?

He was feeling downright irritable. And somehow, grossly unfairly, in the wrong, as though he owed her some sort of apology. He had not told her he loved her — as if those words *meant* anything. Why should one feel guilty for telling the truth? The world had turned all topsy-turvy. It had been a far simpler place when he was merely Mr. Edward Ailsbury.

"Does Tresham employ no other servants than your own personal maid?" he said, breaking the silence between them even though he had sworn to himself that he would not. "And is this the same personal maid who was conspicuously absent from the taproom at the Rose and Crown Inn a month or so ago? Is she often indisposed?"

His voice sounded as irritated as he felt.

"If this is a veiled comment upon my behavior, Lord Heyward," she said, "I must inform you that it is none of your business. *I* am none of your business."

"For which I am very thankful indeed."

"For which I will always be eternally grateful."

They spoke simultaneously.

"At least we are agreed upon something," he said.

"We are," she said as they crossed a main road and he tossed a coin to the young crossing sweeper who had cleared a steaming pile of manure out of their path.

"I am delighted," he said, "that you had such a very happy evening. It was obvious at the time, of course, without Eunice's having to tell me so."

"What is *that* supposed to mean?" she asked.

"Nothing," he said. "I was merely being civil."

"You sounded spiteful," she said. "I had a *wonderful* time. I had wonderful partners."

"Including Windrow, I suppose," he said. "You looked as if you were enjoying his company."

"I was," she said. "*Enormously.* He is charming and amusing."

"If I remember correctly," he said, "you told me just two nights ago at Vauxhall that it was the most wonderful evening of your life. Must every evening exceed the one before it in the pleasure it brings you? Will you not soon run out of superlatives? Or will *wonderful* suffice for all?"

"I was merely being civil at Vauxhall," she said. "I thought you might be offended, even hurt, if I did not say I had enjoyed what happened there."

Good God, he thought, they were scrapping like a couple of petulant children.

Why?

He had offered her marriage yesterday because he considered that he had compromised her at Vauxhall and because everyone seemed agreed that she was the most eligible candidate to be his countess. She had refused. Everything was in order. The story was at an end.

Much to his relief.

She was not at all the sort of woman of whom he could ever approve. She had *no idea* how to behave.

What the devil had she been doing calling upon Eunice? Poor Eunice!

"Do you like my bonnet?" she asked.

It was striped, the two colors being red and orange. Actually, garish as it was, it was also rather attractive. Its small, stiff brim framed her face becomingly, and its tall crown gave it a slightly military air. Certainly she was not trying to downplay her height.

"Must you always maneuver people into being either rude or untruthful?" he asked, his irritation returning — if it had ever left.

When he turned his head, it was to discover that she was smiling.

"You told the truth once," she said, "and I laughed and you smiled. It was a good moment."

"Then it is overbright and those colors should never be seen together upon the same person, not to mention the same *garment*," he said. "And it actually suits you perfectly. It suits your character."

Her smile deepened though she kept her gaze on the pavement ahead.

"I shall lie awake tonight," she said, "trying to decide if that was a compliment or an insult, Lord Heyward."

"It was a bit of both," he said curtly. And *he* would lie awake tonight wondering why his manners seemed to desert him when he was with Lady Angeline Dudley. But she would try the patience of a saint.

She laughed. One could not help but like her laugh. It was not a ladylike titter or an *un*ladylike bellow. It always sounded purely merry. And it was infectious, though he did *not* laugh with her.

They were nearing Dudley House, he was happy to see. They walked the remaining distance in silence and he came to a stop at the bottom of the steps in order to watch her safely inside. She stopped too and turned to look up at him.

"I am *not* going to thank you," she said. "I am not grateful."

"I do not expect you to be," he told her. "I did not insist upon escorting you in order to incur your gratitude. I did it because it was the right thing to do."

Good Lord, he thought, he had kissed those lips just two evenings ago and held that body close to his own. He had burned with desire for her.

Had he been *insane?*

And then she smiled again, and there was

a flutter of something dashed uncomfortable somewhere in his chest area.

"That is precisely what I so liked about you the first time I met you," she said. "Now you are becoming a little tiresome."

"If you would learn to behave with greater discretion," he said stiffly, "you would be given no opportunity to find me tiresome or otherwise, Lady Angeline, and I am sure we would both be happier for it."

The smile remained on her face as she tipped her head a little to one side, though it looked almost wistful now.

"Yes," she said. "We would. Good day, Lord Heyward."

And she whisked about and half ran up the steps and through the door, which a footman was already holding open. The door closed behind her.

And now the morning had been ruined.

It was ruined even further when he returned to Lady Sanford's and was shown again into the small parlor where Eunice sat alone.

"Ah," she said, "I wondered if you would come back. You look like thunder. Poor Edward, were you *very* annoyed with her?"

"She has no *idea* how to go on," he said. "I offered her marriage yesterday, you know. I did not mention it to you last evening, but

I did. She refused. I have never been more relieved in my life. Did she come here to tell you? To gloat?"

"Why would she do that?" she asked him, indicating the same chair Lady Angeline had been sitting on when he entered the parlor earlier. "It would suggest a meanness of spirit of which I think her quite incapable."

Yes, he agreed with that at least. It was his own comment that had been mean. Lady Angeline Dudley did *not* bring out the best in him.

"She came," Eunice said, "to ask me to be her friend and to assure me that she would not mind in the least if I married you, since it is obvious to her that you and I love each other dearly."

"She *what?*" he asked, frowning.

"There is something just a little . . . sad about her," she said, "though I am not at all sure that is the right word. *Wistful* would perhaps be better. And of course she is wrong about us. Not wrong in believing that we love each other dearly. I believe we do. But wrong in assuming that it is a *romantic* love that we share."

He was still frowning.

"I wish you would change your mind about marrying me, Eunice," he said. "Life would suddenly become so tranquil."

"And dull," she said softly.

He looked keenly at her.

"Am I too dull a dog even for you, then?" he asked.

"Oh, no." She sighed. "You are not a dull dog at all, Edward, though you often behave like one and actually seem to believe you *are* one. You are not. You just have not . . . oh, learned who you are yet."

His brows snapped together again.

"At the age of twenty-four I do not know who I am?" he said. "I would say that I, more than most men, have self-knowledge."

"Then you are wrong," she said. "But I will not belabor the point. Edward, she loves you quite passionately, you know."

"*Lady Angeline Dudley?*" he exclaimed. "Nonsense, Eunice. And talk about someone who does not know herself!"

"Oh," she said, "I agree that there is much confusion in her mind. She has had a sheltered, rather restrictive, and loveless upbringing, and now she has been thrown upon the *ton* to cope with a Season and the flood of admirers who wish to court her and marry her. She is excited by it all and repelled by it and really quite . . . well, confused. But she has seen someone who is a rock of stability in a sea of just the op-

308

posite, and she wants it very badly and very passionately."

"*Me?*" he said. "If you will remember, Eunice, she *refused* me just yesterday."

"You could not assure her that you love her," she said.

"She told you that, I suppose?" he asked, wrath replacing amazement. "Was I expected to *lie?*"

"No, not at all," she said. "You were probably quite right to say what you did, since it was the truth. And she was quite right to refuse you, though I believe she broke her own heart when she did so."

"She was having a *rollicking* good time last evening," he said.

"Oh, Edward," she said, "*of course* she was."

In some ways, he thought, Eunice was no different from other women after all. She spoke in riddles.

"I think you would be wise," she said, "to look upon yesterday, Edward, not as the end of the courtship, but simply as the closing lines of the opening act. The rest of the drama is yet to be written. There is nothing more unsatisfactory than an unfinished drama."

He would have liked to let loose with a string of profanities. But he could not do so, of course. Not until he was alone, anyway.

"I take it, then," he said, "that I really must let go of my hopes with regard to you, Eunice?"

"Oh, you really must," she said gently. "We would not suit, Edward, believe me. One day, I trust that you will know the truth of that as well as I do. We were meant to be friends, not lovers."

He swallowed and got to his feet.

"I will not keep you any longer, then," he said.

"Oh, and now you have pokered up," she said. "We have had disagreements before, you know, and you have always assured me that you have been stimulated by them rather than annoyed. Don't be annoyed with me now. And write the rest of that drama."

Drama be damned, he thought as he bowed to her and left the room, the final dregs of his hopes dashed.

A few minutes later he was striding down the street, muttering some of those profanities — a string of them actually — though he did check first to make sure that no one was within earshot.

He did not feel a whole lot better when he was finished.

CHAPTER 14

During the two weeks following his disastrous proposals to both Eunice and Lady Angeline Dudley, Edward was so mortally depressed that more than once he was on the verge of announcing that he was going to return to Wimsbury Abbey until next spring. Why should he not postpone marrying, after all? He was only twenty-four, he felt perfectly healthy, and he was neither a reckless driver nor a dueler. He did not indulge in any activities, in fact, that might put a sudden period to his existence. Barring some unforeseen accident, it would be quite safe to wait another year or so before settling down. Though all accidents were unforeseen, he supposed, or they would not *be* accidents. And really, what was the point of waiting? The deed must be done eventually, and why not now so that he could put the whole business behind him and start

making the best of married life and father-
hood?

At the end of the two weeks there was a
distraction. Fenner came to call late one
afternoon, but instead of asking for Lorraine
as he often did in order to drive her in the
park, he asked to speak privately with Edward.

This was mystifying, Edward thought. He
was neither Lorraine's father nor her
brother. He was no blood relation at all, in
fact.

"The Countess of Heyward's father is not
in town," Fenner explained when the two of
them were alone in a downstairs salon. "I
shall be writing to him, of course. But the
countess has requested that I speak with
you, Heyward. She feels responsible to the
family of her late husband, especially so
soon after his passing. She is exceedingly
fond of you all and claims to have received
nothing but kindness and affection from you
since her marriage. Indeed, she feels as
though you *are* her family, and of course
you really are her daughter's family. You
share the guardianship with the countess, I
believe. The countess is very afraid of offending you, even hurting you."

It had been perfectly clear, of course, that
a serious romance was brewing between

Fenner and Lorraine. Edward had not realized it had reached such a critical stage already, but it was not really surprising, was it? They were both mature adults and both were free. It was a perfectly eligible connection. With his head Edward could even be happy for them — Maurice had not been a good husband. But with his heart? Well, Maurice had been his brother. Now it felt as though he were being consigned to the grave all over again. His mother would feel it too. So would Alma and Juliana. But theirs had been a blood connection with Maurice. Lorraine's had not. And there *was* a difference. And they had all taken Lorraine to their hearts when she married into their family. She felt in many ways more like a sister than a sister-in-law.

"Lorraine's happiness is important to us," he said. More important under the circumstances than their grief, which was a private, ongoing thing.

"I wish to marry the countess," Fenner said. "I loved her five years ago and I have not stopped loving her since. She wishes to marry me. I am confident that she loves me. However, neither of us wants to do anything that will appear distasteful to your family. If it appears to you that we are acting with indecent haste, then we will wait a year. No longer, I hope. But we *will* wait a year if we must. I hope we do not need to."

He paused and looked inquiringly at Edward.

Love, Edward thought broodingly. What the devil did it mean? It meant all the euphoria of romance and all the underlying but unspoken power of lust, obviously. Perhaps it had only to be believed in to be experienced. But was there any real substance to it? Did it last? Somehow one had the feeling that with Lorraine and Fenner it would, perhaps because they had taken the wrong path five years ago — at least, *she* had — and now had a second chance to take the right one. Second chances were very rare. If Maurice had not agreed to — or suggested — that curricle race, if he and the driver of the hay cart had not met exactly on the blind part of that bend, if — Well, if any of a thousand little, seemingly insignificant details of life had been in the smallest way different from the way they actually had been, then the whole of life would be different.

There was absolutely no point to such thoughts. Lorraine and Fenner had been given their second chance, and they were embracing it with firm resolve. As they ought. Maurice was dead, and life went on.

"I cannot speak for my mother and sisters, Fenner," he said, "though I believe they will agree with me wholeheartedly. Lorraine was the best of wives to my brother and she was and is a good mother to my niece. Her happiness is as important to me as if she were my sister. If she can find that happiness with you — and I do believe she can — then I see no reason why the two of you should be made to wait a year or even a day longer than you choose. The mourning period is at an end. Life must continue for all of us. I wish you well."

He offered his hand, and Fenner grasped it warmly.

"Thank you," he said. "You are kind."

And Edward found himself, quite unreasonably, feeling more depressed than ever. Because Maurice was dead and Lorraine was moving on? Because other people seemed to believe in love and sometimes it could lead them to happiness? Or because of something else?

It did not take long for it to strike him that Fenner was Lady Palmer's brother and Tresham's cousin — or *second* cousin, anyway. He was Lady Angeline Dudley's second cousin. And Lady Palmer was her sponsor for her come-out Season. This betrothal was sure to bring the two families together, even if only for the wedding. If he never saw a single member of the Dudley family again, he would be entirely happy. But Fenner was a member of that family even if only in the capacity of second cousin.

His forebodings were well founded, he discovered less than a week later, just after he had read the official announcement of the betrothal in the morning paper. Actually, the situation was even worse than he had anticipated, for it was not just the wedding that was to bring the families together.

Lady Palmer had decided to celebrate the betrothal with a brief house party at Hallings in Sussex, her husband's country estate. Edward and his family were invited to attend, of course, and he did not need to be told that Fenner's family would be there too. The party was to last five whole days.

Nothing could be more conducive to further depression. Five days of trying to avoid Lady Angeline Dudley in the intimacy of a country setting. If he had known what was facing him when he left Wimsbury Abbey less than two months ago, he would *never* have left. The duty of taking his place in the House of Lords be damned. And he would have chosen a bride from the ranks of the local gentry.

But it was too late now.

The rest of the drama is yet to be written, Eunice had said to him a few weeks ago. It was utter nonsense, of course. There was *nothing* still to be written. It was unlike Eunice to be so very wrong.

He had not set eyes upon her since the morning she had said it. He missed her.

Angeline was desperately gay during the three weeks following her rejection of the Earl of Heyward. She spent almost every morning out riding with Ferdinand and his friends or walking in the park with Maria or Martha, sometimes both together, or shopping on Oxford Street and Bond Street. She bought three new bonnets as well as feathers and ribbons and fans and reticules that she did not need but could not resist. She visited the library twice and borrowed books each time, though there was really little point as there was absolutely no time to read — there was too much fun to be had doing other things. She called upon Miss Goddard twice, careful to take a recovered Betty with her, and they sat and talked all morning both times, since both times it was raining and they could not go out for a walk. She could not remember afterward what they had talked about except that it was *not* bonnets and beaux and *not* Lord Heyward.

They had each talked an equal amount, though, and really had not stopped for a moment.

She spent the afternoons paying calls with Cousin Rosalie or attending garden parties or Venetian breakfasts or picnics or driving in Hyde Park with one or another of her many admirers. There was not an idle afternoon.

And there were always more evening entertainments to choose among than there were evenings. There were balls, soirees, concerts, the theater, the opera, dinners. Sometimes it was possible to attend both a dinner *and* a concert or the theater.

Everywhere she went there were people she knew, and she was gradually learning to put names with faces without making too many errors. And there were always new people with whom to become acquainted. There were ladies who were friendly — younger ones who would link arms with her and stroll at a party, older ladies who remembered her mother or her father and loved to talk to her about them, elderly ladies who remembered her grandparents. And of course, there were her particular friends, Martha and Maria, who had also taken well with the *ton* and were always abuzz with excitement about various beaux or would-be beaux. There was Miss Goddard, by whom she sat at one concert and with whom she felt free to be quiet and actually enjoy the music.

And there were the gentlemen. There were the older ones, who tended to be courtly and who occasionally paid her the compliment of actually *conversing* with her. There were Tresham's friends — Sir Conan Brougham and the blond and handsome Viscount Kimble in particular — who treated her in an avuncular manner, though they were not many years older than she. And Ferdinand's friends, who tended to treat her as a regular one of the fellows, especially as she saw most of them only when they were all out riding. And there was a whole army of younger men, as well as a few older ones, who flocked about her wherever she went and paid court to her and flirted with her and flattered her and danced with her and walked and drove with her and occasionally proposed marriage to her.

There was Lord Windrow, who always pursed his lips and regarded her with laughing bedroom eyes whenever they were at the same social event, but generally kept his distance from her. She found him amusing and would have flirted outrageously with him if he had given her the chance since he clearly understood the game and would not take her seriously.

And there was, of course, the Earl of Heyward, who was at many of the same events that Angeline attended. It was unavoidable. The *ton* was not huge in number. Everyone tended to get invited everywhere, and everyone usually accepted the invitations. Angeline became quite adept at never being closer than half a room away from him and never looking his way and never *ever* meeting his eye. It was not difficult, of course, for he was clearly just as intent upon not seeing *her.* And he always *was* intent upon some other young lady, always a pretty, *dainty* young lady.

She would have been quite indifferent to him, would have forgotten him entirely, if it had not been for one fact. She *still* believed Miss Goddard was in love with him and he with her and that they would surely marry if only society was not so silly about such things. She found herself wishing that she could do something to bring them together. It would somehow soothe her sore heart if she could do that and be noble and selfless about the whole thing. She would be *perfectly happy* if the two of them married, and then she could get on with the business of falling in love and marrying and living happily ever after. No, forget the *ever after* part, for there was no such thing, of course, and it would not be desirable even if there were. It would be *tedious.* Quarreling would be fun when one knew one would kiss and make up and be happy all over again. Sometimes she thought wistfully of that sort-of quarrel she had had with Lord Heyward when he escorted her home from Lady Sanford's, but she put the memory firmly from her mind. She was going to be *noble* from now on.

Besides, she was too busy enjoying herself to brood upon quarrels or almost-quarrels, too busy smiling, laughing, chattering, dancing, doing whatever exuberantly happy people did, having the time of her life.

And then came the day when she realized that she was not going to be able to avoid closer contact with the Earl of Heyward forever. Cousin Leonard had proposed marriage to Lady Heyward and been accepted, and Angeline was as overjoyed about it as Cousin Rosalie was. But Rosalie was planning a special celebration of their betrothal by having them at Hallings in the country over a long weekend and making a house party of it. *They* were all to go — Leonard's family, that was — and so were the countess's in-laws, even though they *were* only in-laws and she was about to marry out of their family. But she had only a reclusive father, Rosalie explained, and looked upon her late husband's family as her own. They had been exceedingly kind to her.

Angeline must suggest any other guests she wished to be invited, Rosalie told her, since the intention was not to make it *just* a family gathering. For her part there were a few neighbors she would ask to come to stay.

At first Angeline could feel only a sick sort of dread and excitement — a horrid and bewildering mix — at the knowledge that she and Lord Heyward were doomed to spend five days in the same house with the same smallish group of people. But it was unavoidable. She had no choice but to go — both Tresham and Ferdinand were going and Rosalie, of course, was the hostess.

And then she had a grand flash of inspiration. Though perhaps *flash* was the wrong word, suggesting as it did that the idea came to her instantly and full blown. It actually took a little longer than that to come to full fruition, but it certainly was inspired when it did.

She was attending Lady Loverall's garden party in Richmond one afternoon with Cousin Rosalie. The grand mansion in which Lord and Lady Loverall lived had a back garden that ended with the River Thames, actually jutting out into it in the form of two jetties. Angeline thought it might well be the loveliest place on earth to live. Certainly it was a perfect setting for an outdoor party on a perfect summer afternoon. Even though clouds occasionally covered the sun, they were actually welcome as a break from the heat.

As she was looking about for a group of acquaintances she might join, her eyes alit upon Miss Goddard standing, as she usually did at the few entertainments she attended, with her aunt and a group of older ladies. They were on the terrace close to the refreshment tables. Angeline's face lit up with delight. Miss Goddard was *just* the person she most wanted to see. She had been intending to call upon her tomorrow morning, in fact.

"Miss Goddard," she said, as she approached her, "how *lovely* that you are here. Do come strolling down by the water. Would you not give everything in the world to live here?"

"Perhaps not everything," Miss Goddard said, laughing. "But it is certainly a pleasure to visit. I will come, thank you. Perhaps we may stop along the way to look at the flowers. They are a feast for the eyes, are they not? And probably for the nose too."

Angeline linked an arm through hers and drew her away from the other ladies after exchanging greetings and pleasantries with them all.

"Did you receive your invitation?" she asked. "Have you replied to it yet? I *do* hope your answer is yes. I shall be vastly disappointed if it is not."

"I did indeed," Miss Goddard said, "and was greatly surprised by it as well as gratified. Why would Lady Palmer invite me to spend a few days at her country estate in Sussex? I scarcely know her."

"But I do," Angeline said. "She is my sponsor, and she specifically asked me if there was anyone I wished her to invite. I daresay she thought I might be embarrassed by some of the guests. Well, one in particular."

"Embarrassed?" Miss Goddard said.

"Cousin Leonard," Angeline said, "Lord Fenner, Rosalie's brother, that is, has recently become betrothed to the widowed Countess of Heyward. You may have seen the announcement in the papers. We are enormously pleased by the news. She broke his heart a number of years ago, you know, during her come-out Season when she was dazzled by the Earl of Heyward — the *then* earl, I mean, of course — and married him, but now she loves Cousin Leonard as dearly as he loves her — *that* is clear for everyone to see — and all is going to be well that ends well. That is a quotation from Mr. Shakespeare, is it not? The actual title of one of his plays, in fact? Well, *close* to the title. Anyway, the house party is actually to be a *betrothal* party, and so of course all of the countess's family will be there. Or her in-laws, anyway. There is no one of her own family in town. The countess's family — her *in-law* family — were all very attentive to me during that short time when everyone seemed to imagine that the Earl of Heyward and I might make a match of it, though they must all have had windmills in their heads to think such a thing. Anyway, they will all be at Hallings as well as Lord Heyward himself. Rosalie is probably afraid I will be embarrassed, since he proposed marriage to me and I said no. And so she wishes to invite a few other people to come for my sake. It is very good of her. I suggested you, as I would particularly like to have a few days to spend in your company."

That was all perfectly true. But it was not the whole truth, for it had not taken long for Angeline to realize that the house party would provide the ideal setting for a proper courtship between Miss Goddard and the earl, and that *she* might be the one to bring it about. It would have the added attraction that his mother and his sisters would also be there to observe how very genteel Miss Goddard was and how very much she and the earl adored each other and how well suited she was to being his countess even if she *was* merely the daughter of a Cambridge don. Not many ladies had that distinction, after all.

"Please come," Angeline said, squeezing her arm.

"I have never attended a house party," Miss Goddard said.

"Oh," Angeline said, "neither have I. But I have *always* wanted to. They must be enormous fun. You will come?"

"I will be pleased to," Miss Goddard said. "I think."

Miss Goddard bent to smell one of the delicate pink roses they had been examining, though truth to tell Angeline had not been paying them a great deal of attention. She had been too busy noticing that the Earl of Heyward was at the garden party too, and that he had that red-haired lady on his arm again — Angeline never could remember her name. She was very careful not to look directly at them and hoped Miss Goddard would not notice and become depressed at seeing him with someone else.

They strolled down to the riverbank and watched eight of the other guests out on the water in the four small rowing boats, two to a boat. The boats looked very small and unsteady to Angeline. She would not mind too, too much if she were riding in one of them and got tipped in. The water might be cold, but once in and over the first gasp of shock, one would soon become accustomed to it and would actually feel quite warm — until it was time to come out again. However, she did not believe she would wish to fall in today. She was wearing a new dress of fine sprigged muslin, which she loved despite its delicate colors. It would look like a dishrag if it got dunked in the river. Worse, her new hat would look like a dead duck, except that a dead duck would not necessarily be garlanded with multicolored bedraggled flowers and drooping ribbons.

"How lovely it must be out on the water," Miss Goddard said with a sigh.

But as Angeline drew breath to reply, someone else did so before her.

"It would be all the lovelier for having the delectable Miss Goddard riding upon it," the voice said, and they both turned in astonishment to find Lord Windrow about to step between them, almost forcing them to drop each other's arms and take one each of his instead. "And so ride upon it you will. And, oh fair one, you must go out there also but not *with* Miss Goddard, alas. Those boats were made for two. If three were to try to cram into one, it would sink like a rock and leave nothing but three bubbles to be lamented over by spectators on the bank."

"Assuming," Miss Goddard said, "that none of the three could swim."

"Or one — but that one would have all the bother of deciding which of the other two he would save," he said. "Nothing but trouble could come of it, whichever one he chose."

"Assuming," she said again, "that the swimmer was the man. If it was one of the ladies, she would not hesitate to save the other lady. If she were to save the man, he would feel humiliated and he would be ridiculed for the rest of his life. His life would not be worth living. It would be more merciful to leave him to die tragically beneath his bubble."

"Alas," he said, one hand over his heart, "you would abandon me to a watery death, Miss Goddard."

"I daresay you swim, though," she said. "Do you?"

"But of course," he said.

Angeline laughed at the absurdity of the exchange and twirled her parasol. And when one of the boats came in a mere minute or two later, Lord Windrow seized it even though there were two other couples very obviously waiting for it too. He handed Miss Goddard in with exaggerated care and turned to bow over Angeline's hand.

"It is always said," he murmured, "that the wise man saves the best until last."

Angeline laughed again.

"But alas," he called to her as he hopped into the boat and pushed it away from the jetty, "no one has ever yet called me a wise man."

The rogue! She gave her parasol another spirited twirl just as the Earl of Heyward appeared upon the scene — alone and looking like thunder. There was not a redhead in sight — except Lord Windrow, whose hair was actually more copper than red.

"Lady Angeline," he asked, "has Windrow been bothering you again?"

His eyes were upon the boat, which was now well out in the river. Miss Goddard, her back to Angeline, was reclining in her seat and trailing one hand in the water. Lord

Windrow was smiling lazily at her and saying something as he pulled on the oars.

"He is not quite the black-hearted villain you take him for," Angeline said, feeling suddenly breathless. "Even at that inn he was just being silly. It is in his nature to be silly." Though perhaps that was an unfair word to use. He *was* silly, but really in a rather witty and charming way. Angeline believed that he rather *liked* her. Nothing more. His flirtation was far too light to be either serious or menacing. "I am quite safe with him. Besides, Miss Goddard always seems to be present to save me from him."

She turned her face to smile at him and was jolted to discover how close he was. For three weeks now there had always been at least half a room's distance between them. She had not looked into his eyes since that day he insisted upon escorting her home from Lady Sanford's. And despite all the flowers and trees offering their myriad scents for her pleasure, not to mention the river, it was his light and subtle cologne that enticed her senses. His eyes were bluer than the water.

"But who is to save *Eunice?*" he asked curtly, those blue eyes squinting as they followed the boat along the river.

Angeline was about to make a tart remark

about that tiny rowboat on the wide river for all the world to see *not* being the likely scene of any wicked seduction. But the breath she had drawn remained unused, and her mouth remained half open. Her parasol stopped twirling.

Inspiration had hit her like a flash of lightning.

But of course!

She would persuade Rosalie to invite *Lord Windrow* to Hallings too. Rosalie would not mind. On the contrary, she would be pleased. She had been growing concerned over the fact that Angeline did not seem to favor any one of her suitors over the others. Lord Windrow was handsome and charming and elegant. He was eligible even if he had never given any indication that he was in search of a bride. He was one of Tresham's friends, which was perhaps not a great recommendation in itself except that Tresham did not befriend just *anyone.* No, Rosalie would be *delighted.*

And when they were all at Hallings, Angeline would maneuver him and Miss Goddard into more situations just like this one and drive poor Lord Heyward insane with fear for her safety and perhaps with jealousy too, for Lord Windrow really was handsome and he seemed to enjoy flirting with Miss

Goddard, who could match his wit. Lord Heyward would realize that he could not live without Miss Goddard, and she would realize she could not live without him, and their great love for each other would be clear to everyone else at Hallings, including his family, and because they loved him and would come to love her, they would give their blessing to the match and the two of them would be betrothed before the end of the house party and married in St. George's, Hanover Square, as soon as the banns had been called, and they would live happily ever after.

And Angeline would have been the mastermind behind it all. She would have done a noble thing. True love would have triumphed over adversity.

Angeline's parasol was twirling again and setting the flowers on her bonnet fluttering in the sudden wind.

Lord Heyward drew his attention away from the boat and turned to look directly into her eyes. Neither of them spoke for endless moments.

"I beg your pardon," he said abruptly at last. "Your safety is not my concern. I must appear like an interfering busybody."

"But perhaps Miss Goddard's safety *is*

your concern," she said. "You are fond of her."

"Yes," he agreed, looking suddenly bleak.

Oh, it would work. *Of course* it would work.

But why did her heart feel broken in two and her spirit as though it were crawling along the bottom of the river on its belly?

"You will wish to wait here for the boat," she said, "so that you may rescue Miss Goddard from the evil clutches of a rake. I see Maria Smith-Benn strolling up there with Mr. Stebbins and Sir Anthony Folke. Maria is my particular friend, you know. I shall go and join them."

And she smiled brightly and waved an arm in their direction. They stopped to wait for her, all of them smiling a welcome. Sir Anthony, despite the fair curls that spilled all over his hat brim no matter how often he pressed them ruthlessly beneath it, was really rather good-looking in a boyish sort of way. And Mr. Stebbins had had his eye on Maria for the past week or two — to Maria's delight.

Within moments Angeline was laughing and happy again.

And she could not wait to talk with Rosalie, to suggest one more guest for Hallings.

Her idea was quite, quite brilliant and could surely not fail.

CHAPTER 15

Hallings was a solidly built, no-nonsense gray stone square of a mansion set at the end of a long, winding driveway that meandered through a spacious, well-landscaped park. The house was fronted by rather old-fashioned formal gardens consisting mainly of box hedges and gravel walks and some statuary. It looked a pleasant enough place in which to spend a few days if the weather held. It would at least provide a welcome break from all the busy hurry of London. At least, that was the consensus of opinion among the occupants of the carriage in which Edward traveled — his grandfather's rather than the old one from Wimsbury, which everyone but his mother thought a monstrosity of discomfort.

Edward wished he was anyplace else on earth.

It was bad enough that he was going to be spending a few days in close proximity with

Tresham and his sister. Worse was the fact that the family committee had ruled just yesterday that the search for a bride was not going well enough, despite the fact that Edward had been halfheartedly courting no fewer than six young ladies during the past month and that all six were offering well-bred encouragement. And the committee had come up with the thoroughly alarming conclusion that he should return his attentions to Lady Angeline Dudley.

It had been pointless to remind them that he had already courted her once, proposed marriage to her, and been rejected. That meant *nothing,* according to his grandmother and her dismissively waving lorgnette. No girl worth her salt was going to accept a man's first proposal.

"Especially when he cannot assure her that he *loves* her," Juliana had added pointedly.

"And you will be spending five days in company with her," Alma had said. "You will have the ideal opportunity, Edward, to try again and to get it right this time."

"I like her very well indeed," Lorraine had said. "She has spirit."

"I even like her hats," his grandmother had said, "and wish I dared wear ones like them myself. At least then people would look at *them* instead of at my wrinkles."

"And she has not looked happy since she refused you," his mother had said.

What? *What?*

Was she talking about the same Lady Angeline Dudley as the one he knew? Had she *seen* her lately, as he had — or, rather, as he had tried not to do? She flirted with simply everything that happened to be male, and everything that was male flirted right back. A new regiment could be made up out of her admirers to swell the ranks of the British army. And she was always simply spilling over with exuberance. Every host could save a fortune in candles if he so wished when she was at a ball — her smile could light up even the largest ballroom.

She had not been *happy?*

"You have not looked happy in the last few weeks either," his mother had added.

He frowned. Not happy? Had she not seen him constantly dancing attendance upon some lady or other — and sometimes even literally dancing? Did she not *know* that he had attended dinners and theater parties and garden parties and who knew what else every single day?

He was shown to his room soon after his arrival, as were all the other guests, but he could not skulk there forever, even if he would dearly like to do just that for the next five days. Having changed and shaved afresh, he dismissed his valet and went down to the drawing room for tea.

Fortunately there were a few more guests than just family. Lady Eagan was here, though she *was* family, of course. She was Fenner's cousin. There were also a few strangers. There was a tall, cadaverous man with a kindly face, bushy gray eyebrows, and sparse gray hair that looked untamable by comb, brush, or water. Lady Palmer introduced him as the Reverend Joseph Martin, the newly retired vicar, who had always been a particular friend of Lord Palmer's. She also introduced Mr. Briden, a neighbor who had come to stay for the duration of the house party, and his two young daughters, Miss Briden and Miss Marianne Briden. Fenner's close friend Sir Webster Jordan was also present.

And there were two other guests, who took Edward totally by surprise. Eunice was here. He could think of no reason why she would have been invited apart from the strange friendship that seemed to have developed between her and Lady Angeline Dudley. He was, nonetheless, delighted to see her. He had not spoken with her since the day of that garden party, when she had looked actually annoyed to see him waiting for her on the bank of the river. Though she *had* taken his arm after Windrow had strolled away, and they had spent a pleasant half hour together.

He was even more surprised — and far less pleased — to discover that Windrow himself was also among the guests. But, as Lady Palmer explained, he was a neighbor, his country seat being a mere ten miles away.

And so the house party began with tea and conversation and laughter. It continued later with dinner and cards in the drawing room afterward and some music. The Misses Briden both entertained the company on the pianoforte. Then Lady Eagan accompanied Lord Ferdinand Dudley as he sang a series of folk songs in a surprisingly pleasant tenor voice.

Edward was relieved to discover that Lady Palmer was more tactful than his female relatives — or perhaps she had no wish to encourage a resumption of his attentions to her charge. She seated him at some distance from Lady Angeline Dudley at the dinner table and placed him at a different card table afterward.

By the time he went to bed, he was cautiously optimistic. He had enjoyed conversing with the Reverend Martin and Miss Briden at dinner, and he had enjoyed being partnered by Lady Palmer herself at cards. Keeping half a room's distance between Lady Angeline and himself had proved really no more difficult than it had in any of the ballrooms and drawing rooms he had frequented for the past month.

Though it struck him as he got ready for bed that his reluctance to be any closer to her was odd. They were both adult members of the *ton,* after all. Their courtship, if it could be called that, had been brief and had ended with very little fuss — he had offered, she had refused. Why should they not meet now without any embarrassment or other discomfort?

But they *had* met, very briefly, on the banks of the River Thames, when he had rushed quite thoughtlessly to her rescue after seeing Windrow step between her and Eunice and offer her his arm. Why *had* he felt it necessary to be her protector yet again when she was absolutely *none* of his business? He had felt like an utter idiot afterward, especially when it had turned out that it was Eunice Windrow had taken out in a boat, not Lady Angeline. But he had made the mistake of looking directly into Lady Angeline's eyes on that occasion, and he *had* felt a quite alarming discomfort. Her huge dark eyes had looked far more likely to cause drowning than all the waters of the river.

No, it was safer to keep his distance.

Safer?

He doused the candle, climbed into bed, and addressed himself to sleep. He was *not* going to let his mind wander along that particular path.

It took him only two or three hours to drop off.

By the following morning Angeline had decided that she needed an accomplice if her grand scheme was to have any chance at all of succeeding. There was no point in maneuvering matters so that Miss Goddard and Lord Windrow were thrown together in Lord Heyward's sight if Miss Goddard simply wandered away or allowed someone else to join them.

Both things had happened last evening. When Angeline had used great skill to bring the two of them together at tea and had moved away herself as if she had heard someone call to her from across the room, Miss Goddard had done nothing whatsoever to discourage the Reverend Martin from joining them. She had even directed most of her conversation his way and had given Lord Windrow no chance at all to do anything that might alarm Lord Heyward and bring him dashing to the rescue. And when Angeline had gone to great lengths again after the card games were over to suggest, when Miss Goddard and Lord Windrow were close to each other, that it might be pleasant to stroll outside on the terrace, both agreed with her — but Miss Goddard had turned and linked her arm through the very shy Miss Marianne Briden's, and Lord Windrow had been left to stroll between Lady Overmyer and Mrs. Lynd, causing them a great deal of laughter as he did so. It had all been very exasperating. If one was going to make the effort to matchmake, the least one could expect was that the lady concerned would cooperate. But how could she if she did not know what Angeline was trying to do?

The only thing for it was to let her know, to enlist her active support.

They were both up in time for breakfast — Angeline because she had arranged the night before to go out riding early with her brothers and Cousin Leonard and Sir Webster Jordan, Miss Goddard because Angeline suspected she always rose early. Angeline invited her to go walking afterward before everyone else was up, and they strolled arm in arm along the paths of the formal gardens.

"It was very obliging of you," Miss Goddard said, "to persuade Lady Palmer to invite me here. I am enjoying myself very much indeed even though the house party has scarcely begun yet. We have interesting fellow guests. Did you know that the Reverend Martin has actually been to the Holy Land?"

"I did not," Angeline said, but though she felt a stirring of interest, she was not to be distracted. "I arranged to have you invited here for one main reason, you know, even though I hope I would have thought of inviting you anyway, as I value your friendship a great deal."

"Oh?" Miss Goddard turned an inquiring face toward her.

"I thought it was high time," Angeline said, "that you and the Earl of Heyward were brought together in the same house for a few days — with his family present."

"But for what purpose?" Miss Goddard asked, all amazement.

"I know," Angeline said, "that you are a pair of star-crossed lovers. Just like Romeo and Juliet, though they were ridiculously young, of course, and their families were feuding quite viciously because they were Italian and that is what Italians *do,* though I suppose families of other nationalities can be just as bad and I do not suppose *all* Italian families feud with one another or it would be a very uncomfortable place to live. Really, the two of them were *nothing* like you and Lord Heyward except that they were star-crossed. It is as plain as the nose on my face that you love him and he loves you and that you would make a perfect couple. A *married* couple, that is."

Miss Goddard's eyes fixed disconcertingly upon Angeline's nose for a moment, but she said nothing.

"And it is perfectly absurd," Angeline continued, "that you cannot marry just because he is an earl and you are the daughter of an academic gentleman. I daresay his family assumes that you must be inferior or even vulgar. During the next few days they will see just how wrong they are, and they will see how he loves you and how you love him, and because *they* love him too, they will . . . They will give their blessing to your marrying, and . . ."

She could have sworn before they started walking that the garden was flat. But it must be sloping quite steeply upward and they must be walking much faster than she had thought. She could hardly catch her breath. And where was the wind coming from to make her eyes water so? She could not *feel* any wind.

"Lady Angeline," Miss Goddard said quietly and gently, "Edward and I are friends."

"Of course you are," Angeline said, blinking her eyes and realizing that they had come to a stop before a fat little stone cherub whose sightless eyes seemed to be gazing skyward. "That is the whole beauty of it. When he briefly courted me, entirely because I was the bride his family picked out for him because I am so eligible, they did not *know* me. They had not even met me. When he briefly courted me, he kissed me, just once and just briefly, you understand, because we were at Vauxhall and the path was secluded and the moon was almost full and one *does* tend to do silly things under such circumstances, I — What was I saying?" She ought not to have told Miss Goddard the earl had kissed her.

"When Edward briefly courted you," Miss Goddard said, reaching out a hand to touch the sculpted curls of the cherub.

"Well," Angeline said, "we were not *friends* at all, you see. He said he was *fond* of me, which really means nothing at all, does it?

For I had asked him if he *loved* me, and he could hardly just say no, could he? At least, he *could* have, but he *would* not because he is a gentleman and he would not wish to hurt my feelings. And I daresay if I had said yes and married him, he *would* have been fond of me for the rest of my life. He would not have allowed himself to do any less. But we would never have been *friends.* I think a husband and wife really ought to be friends, don't you?"

"Yes, I do," Miss Goddard said as they strolled onward.

"But he was playing cards last evening with Cousin Rosalie as a partner," Angeline said, "and you with Sir Webster Jordan. And so it might go on for five days. I do have a plan, but I need to tell you about it so that you can do your part. It is not *wrong,* you know, actively to pursue what you want. And it is not wrong for you to want the Earl of Heyward. It is not *his* fault he had to inherit the title."

"What is your plan?" Miss Goddard asked after a short silence.

"Lord Windrow," Angeline said.

"Lord Windrow?"

They had stopped walking again, but not to look at anything in particular. Just at each other. Miss Goddard's eyebrows were

arched above her eyes, and she looked nothing like a startled hare. Only like someone
who did not understand what was being
said to her.

"At the garden party," Angeline said,
"Lord Heyward came rushing up just as
Lord Windrow rowed you out onto the river.
He asked if Lord Windrow had been bothering me, but it was *you* he was concerned
about. When I said I was quite safe and that
you always seemed to be there to save me,
he asked who would save *you*. And he did
not take his eyes off you."

"He was there waiting when we returned,"
Miss Goddard said. "I was really rather annoyed, for I do not need Edward or any
other man to rush to my defense every time
another man pays me some attention —
which is not often, you know. He took me
up to the terrace for refreshments and we
enjoyed half an hour of each other's company."

"I saw," Angeline said. "When we were
going home from the party I asked Cousin
Rosalie to invite Lord Windrow here so that
we can do it again. And again if necessary.
Lure him into your company, that is, so that
Lord Heyward will go wild with worry for
your safety, though you will not be in any
real danger, you know, as you will never be

far from everyone else, and besides, I do not believe Lord Windrow is a real rogue. He likes to tease and he likes to flirt. But deep down he is a gentleman — not as honorable a one as Lord Heyward himself, perhaps, and he *does* have a tendency to want to settle arguments with his fists, but men are brought up to think that is a manly way to behave and so one cannot entirely blame them, can one? My brothers are just the same. We will . . . Will you do it?"

"Lure Lord Windrow into my lair and flirt with him?" Miss Goddard asked.

"Oh, not *flirt,*" Angeline said. "But appear to be . . . trapped in his company. Appear . . . oh, not unsafe exactly, but uncomfortable and a little anxious. Lord Heyward will then rush to your rescue as he did at the garden party, and he will realize, if he is not already realizing it, that the only way to keep you permanently safe is to marry you. And his family will see how he cares for you, and . . . Well."

Miss Goddard looked gravely at her until a smile grew deep down in her eyes. It never arrived full-blown in the rest of her face, but it was definitely there.

"Lady Angeline," she said softly. She tipped her head to one side. "Oh, Lady Angeline."

And absurdly Angeline wanted to cry. Fortunately she did not do so.

"*Will* you?" she asked.

Miss Goddard nodded slowly.

"I will," she said.

Experiencing contradictory feelings was nothing new to Angeline. She could feel pride and triumph over any of her brothers' mad exploits at the same moment as she felt that every nerve in her body was vibrating with terror at what might have happened and fury that they would subject themselves so foolishly to such danger. But nothing compared with what she felt now.

Elation, yes, certainly.

And such a terrible despair that she bit her upper lip hard enough to draw blood.

Edward had fallen asleep late and woken up early. It was not a great combination, leaving him tired as it did. However, he had used the early morning hours to think a few things through and to make a few decisions, and he found himself facing the new day in a better frame of mind than he had been in yesterday.

For one thing he had made up his mind that he was going to forget about his antagonism toward Windrow. The man had behaved badly on the road to London, it was true, and Edward could not regret that he had called him to account for it. He would do the same if it happened again. But the man was no monster of depravity. He was something of a rake, that was all. At that inn he had mistaken Lady Angeline, not for a maid — there was really no way he could have done that since she had looked nothing like a servant — but for a woman traveler of careless enough behavior that perhaps she was also of loose morals. The bright, bold color of her dress had probably contributed to the impression. If she had taken him up on his offer of a shared meal and a shared chair, he doubtless would have pushed his advantage and tumbled her somewhere upstairs before going on his way.

But she would have had to be willing. He would not have forced her. Rakes were not necessarily rapists. They were very rarely so, in fact. They had no need to be. There were always enough willing women to give them satisfaction for a price — or sometimes even for no price but their own gratification.

When Windrow had realized his mistake, he had gone on his way after a careless apology and the suggestion of a threat to Edward in order to save face, all of which had appeared to amuse him. He would doubtless have enjoyed a bout of fisticuffs if his challenge had been accepted. He would certainly have enjoyed a tumble upstairs. But since neither had been forthcoming, he had probably forgotten the incident within the first few miles of his journey, as well as the two persons involved — until he encountered them again at the Tresham ball. Then he had chosen to behave with a certain impudent amusement at the colossal nature of the error he had made.

He had chosen to beg a set of dances from both Lady Angeline and Eunice. He had done the same thing at the Hicks ball. He had taken Eunice boating on the river at the Loverall garden party and would probably have taken Lady Angeline out too if *he* had not intervened and driven her away.

It was not admirable behavior. Neither was it dangerous. It had all been very public and very harmless.

And here he was a guest at a house party with Lady Angeline's family, including his friend Tresham. His hostess was Lady Angeline's chaperon. All the guests were highly respectable people. They even included a clergyman. Windrow had been invited because he was Lady Palmer's neighbor and was in almost every way perfectly respectable.

It was true that he liked to flirt with Lady

Angeline. But who did not? She seemed to attract men like moths to a flame. And it was true that Eunice appeared to have taken to heart what he had told her about Windrow and had, bless her heart, done all in her power to divert his attentions onto herself. He was not worried about Eunice. Windrow would have no lascivious intentions toward *her*. She was far too intelligent and sensible for his tastes. And though spending time with him must be tedious indeed for her, she was quite capable of extricating herself from his company whenever she wished.

Anyway, Edward was happy that she had been invited to this house party. He had feared a few times in the course of the Season that life must be rather dull for her. Dullness had not been an issue in the quiet, scholarly setting of Cambridge. In London it was more so. Lady Sanford did not take her to many *ton* entertainments, and even when she did, she made no effort to seek out young company for her. Although she seemed fond of Eunice, she did tend to treat her more like a companion than a young niece in need of friends and at least some form of amusement.

Edward made another decision during the early morning hours, as he lay on his back in bed, his hands laced behind his head. He was going to relax and let the house party unfold as it would. That meant ignoring Windrow, or at least ignoring him as a possible danger to Lady Angeline Dudley. It also meant making no deliberate effort to avoid Lady Angeline herself. For a whole month, if he was honest with himself, he had been irritated over the fact that he thought of her far more often than he thought of any of the six young ladies he had been halfheartedly courting. He had been irritated over the fact that he both disliked and disapproved of her and yet . . . did not.

His feelings toward other people were not usually ambivalent. With her they were. He needed to sort them out if he was ever to have any peace of mind again.

His family wanted him to resume courting her. So did Eunice. Eunice had even told him a month ago, the day after Lady Angeline refused his marriage offer, that he ought to consider the refusal merely the first act of a drama, that he should write the rest of the play.

Very well, then. Oh, he would not actively court her. But he would not avoid her either. He would let events unfold as they would. If he was fortunate, events would conspire to keep them apart. Though that, of course, would do nothing to help him sort out his feelings.

But Lord, he thought just before he got up to face the day, both Eunice and his female family members were about as wrong as they could possibly be. He and Lady Angeline Dudley were about as suited to each other as day is to night.

It was a poor comparison, of course. For night and day were two sides of the same coin. One could not exist without the other. They were the perfect balance of opposites, the perfect harmony of nature taking its course.

Night and day worked perfectly together, in fact.

Damnation!

Chapter 16

Angeline's chance came that same afternoon.

A number of the guests went out walking, since the sun was shining down from an unusually cloudless sky and all were agreed that the good weather was not to be missed despite a breeze that was brisk at times.

It was not a formal walk. Rosalie had explained the day before that she had deliberately refrained from trying to organize every minute of her guests' stay. Most of them needed a rest from the hectic pace of the London scene, and at Hallings they must relax and amuse themselves in any way they wished, even if that merely meant nothing more strenuous than reading or chatting or dozing in the drawing room or conservatory.

Although they all started out more or less together, then, smaller groups of them went off in different directions soon afterward.

The dowager countess confessed herself quite content to stroll in the formal garden and leave the more strenuous walking to the younger people. Mr. Briden commended her good sense and asked if he might join her. Tresham and Cousin Belinda turned determinedly east as soon as they were on the terrace when the rest of the group was already drifting west. Cousin Leonard and the Countess of Heyward bent their heads together in private conversation and walked across a wide lawn in no particular direction at all and at a speed that did a fair imitation of a tortoise. Mr. and Mrs. Lynd strode off arm in arm in the direction of a largish lake at the foot of a long, sloping lawn, taking the Reverend Martin with them. Viscount Overmyer and his wife were going into the village to look at the church, which had stained-glass windows worth looking at.

The Misses Briden were in a group that included Ferdinand, Sir Webster Jordan, the Earl of Heyward, and Lord Windrow. Angeline and Miss Goddard were also a part of it, and a chattering, merry, noisy group it was too. It also appeared to have the lake as its destination, though no one had actually said that was where they were going and no one seemed in any hurry to get there. Angeline might have enjoyed herself enormously if it had not been for her plan. But this was the perfect opportunity to put it into effect, though she had no clear idea of how exactly it was to be done. It must *be* done, though. They were already halfway through the first full day of their stay.

She linked her arm through Miss Goddard's and walked more briskly with her for a few moments until they were ahead of the main group. But first she slanted a smiling glance at Lord Windrow — and felt as if her heart were suddenly beating at twice its normal speed. Had that been too flirtatious a glance? Not flirtatious enough? Had he noticed? Had anyone else? Had *Lord Heyward* noticed? Oh, dear. She had never before ventured into the world of intrigue.

And perhaps her effort had all been for naught. It seemed that they strolled alone together forever while the merry voices of the larger group grew more distant by the second. But forever was actually no longer than a minute or so. Then the hoped-for voice spoke from close behind them.

"Ah, cruel fair ones," Lord Windrow said on a sigh, "your burst of energy left behind four gentlemen to escort two ladies, a dismal ratio when one happens to be one of those men. At the same time, we were deprived of the company of surely the two loveliest ladies in the land. Perhaps you will accuse me of exaggerating, but if there are any lovelier, I have not yet seen them."

"But now," Miss Goddard said as he moved between them and offered an arm to each, "you have transferred the same dismal ratio of two to one to *us*, Lord Windrow."

"Walking together as you were, then, two ladies with no gentlemen at all as an escort, was preferable to having at least one?" he asked. "You have wounded me to the heart, Miss Goddard. Indeed, I believe you have crushed that organ beyond repair."

"Oh, what a bother," Angeline said, removing her hand from his arm and coming to a sudden stop. "I have a stone in my shoe and will have to stop and remove it."

"Allow me to be of service," Lord Windrow said, turning to her, all concern, but she fluttered a hand in his direction.

"Oh, no, no, no," she said. "I should be mortally embarrassed. It will take no more than a moment to do it myself. Do walk on, the two of you. I shall catch up in no time at all."

He would have argued. He opened his mouth to do so, but Miss Goddard spoke first. Thank *heaven* she understood what was happening and had agreed to collaborate, Angeline thought.

"We certainly would not wish to embarrass you, Lady Angeline," Miss Goddard said. "I know just how you feel. Come, Lord Windrow."

And off they went. Angeline glanced back at the rest of the group and directly at the Earl of Heyward, who increased his pace and came directly toward her, just as she had planned.

"Oh, there is no need to be concerned," she said when he drew close. "He was merely being silly again. Miss Goddard kindly went ahead with him. She is in absolutely no danger, I do assure you, though no doubt she will be relieved if you hurry to her rescue. It would be very good of you."

"Lady Angeline," he said while the rest of the group moved on past, chattering and laughing, "you were favoring your right foot when you stopped. Have you hurt yourself?"

"Oh, no, no," she said. "I have a stone in my shoe, that is all. It will take me just a moment to remove it and catch up to the group. Do please hurry and rescue Miss Goddard."

"As you quite correctly remarked," he said, "she is in no danger whatsoever. And she does not suffer fools gladly. She will wait for the others to come up with them when she can endure Windrow's conversation no longer. Allow me."

And he went down on one knee before her, *just* as he had done when he proposed marriage to her, and held out one hand for her foot.

Oh, dear.

It was her *right* foot, was it not? Yes, he had just said so. She raised it and he edged off her shoe. And because she was in danger of losing her balance, she was forced to lean slightly toward him and rest her hand on his shoulder. Oh, such a firm, warm shoulder, a shoulder to depend upon. He turned over the shoe and shook it before setting it on the ground and brushing his hand across the sole of her stockinged foot.

"I could not *see* a stone," he said, "or feel one."

"Sometimes," she said, "they are so small that they are virtually invisible to the eye, but they can be agony on the feet. I daresay you got it."

And he fit the shoe back on her foot and stretched it over her heel. She wriggled her foot in it and set it down on the ground.

"It has gone," she said. "Thank you."

He stood up and looked into her eyes.

"Miss Goddard —" she said.

"She will not thank me for rushing up to her like an overanxious chaperon," he said. "Shall we walk?"

She stared at him for a few moments. *This* was not the way she had planned it. Lord Windrow had acted just as he was supposed to. Why had Lord Heyward not?

He was offering his arm. His eyebrows were raised. Miss Goddard would be so very disappointed. But what was to be done? Nothing *could* be done at present. They would have to try again. Angeline took his arm and sighed inwardly. Why did his arm always seem steadier, more reliable than any other man's? It was just an arm, after all.

They could have caught up with the group with the greatest ease. But Lord Heyward made no attempt to do so. Instead, he took a different direction entirely, taking Angeline with him.

"I wonder if there is a path up that hill beyond the trees," he said. "I believe there must be, for there is a folly at the top of it — some sort of ruined tower. Do you see it?"

She followed the direction of his pointing arm. And she forgot instantly about her failed plan and about the group of young people making their merry way in the direction of the lake.

"Oh, I do," she said. "Shall we find the way up to it? There must be a splendid view from up there."

"If the climb will not be too much for you," he said.

"I am not a wilting violet," she told him.

"I did not believe so," he said. "I have never yet seen a wilting violet tear across a meadow and straight up a tree."

She glanced sidelong at him. Had Lord Heyward just made a *joke?* And about behavior he so despised?

"Of course," he added, "I have never actually *seen* you do it either."

He *had* made a joke.

"That is really too bad," she said, "for I have no intention of performing an encore just for your benefit, you know."

And there it was — that dimple in his cheek. And there went her stomach, doing a tumble toss, and she beamed her delight and laughed out loud. Oh, but she was *over* this. *Long* over it. Except that they were just two young people strolling in a private park during a house party and enjoying a summer afternoon. Why should they not joke and laugh together? It did not *mean* anything.

They found the path with no trouble at all once they had wound their way past the band of trees at the foot of the hill. They toiled up it without wasting breath talking. It was steep and rather overgrown with coarse grass. At one time it must have been used frequently — perhaps when Cousin Rosalie's boys had been younger, before they all went off to school, or perhaps before Lord Palmer went on his diplomatic mission to Vienna. By the time they reached the top Angeline was quite out of breath, and she was sure her face must be horribly flushed and damp with perspiration. But Lord Heyward was panting too.

"Perhaps," he said, "I ought to have asked myself if the climb would be too much for *me*."

She smiled at him. *Another* joke.

"At least it will be all downhill on the way back," she said. And because she was so warm, she untied the ribbons of her bonnet and let them flutter free. Her chin and neck immediately felt cooler.

But goodness. Oh, goodness. They were surrounded by nothing but view. Angeline turned completely about and saw house or park or village or farmland or countryside wherever she gazed.

"Oh, *look*," she said unnecessarily, for of course he was already looking. What else could one do up here but stand and marvel?

"I will wager," he said, "that the view is even more magnificent from up there."

He was pointing at the tower.

"But no one would wager against you," she said. "Besides, a lady never wagers. And I am a perfect lady now that I have made my come-out, remember?"

His eyes came to hers, and she could see that he *did* remember. The first time he had almost smiled at her was during the first set of her come-out ball when she had told him that from then on, now that she was *out,* she would be a perfect lady and there would be no more incidents like being alone in an inn taproom or galloping and whooping along Rotten Row during a rain or dashing across an occupied bull's meadow.

"I'll race you to the top," she said, grasping her skirt at the sides and dashing across the short distance to the tower.

It looked far larger and more imposing from up here. Angeline pushed open the studded wooden door and stepped inside — and instantly forgot the race to the battlements. The walls and the floor were a brightly colored, intricate mosaic of colored stones. Slit arrow windows let in sunlight and would at any time of day — they faced in all directions. There was a wooden bench all about the perimeter, made soft with red leather cushions, though the color was marred somewhat by a layer of dust. A wooden ladder staircase in the middle of the room led upward to a trapdoor.

"What a glorious retreat!" she exclaimed. "If I lived at Hallings, I would come up here every day. I would bring my books and my easel, and I would sit here and read and paint and dream."

She had been alone a great deal at Acton over the years and had made a friend of the hills and woods where she had played with Tresham and Ferdinand as a child. She would have made a retreat out of Dove Cottage by the far lake in the park, since it was beautifully situated, but it was where her father had housed his mistress — one of them, anyway — and she could never erase the wound of that memory from her mind.

Lord Heyward was climbing the ladder and pushing at the trapdoor until it disappeared into space and fell back somewhere up there with a thud. Angeline climbed up after him and took his offered hand to step out onto the battlements. He closed the trapdoor behind them.

"And what was the prize to be if you raced me to the top?" he asked her.

She turned to smile at him.

"You did not accept the wager," she said,

"just as I did not when you said the view would be even more magnificent from up here. I daresay we can see for *miles* in every direction. Oh, this was worth every moment of the climb, was it not?"

The tower was properly battlemented, of course, though there was some crumbling to one side at the front. It had been constructed that way, for this was a folly and was therefore supposed to look like a ruin, like something that had been here for a thousand years. Angeline rested her hands on the higher projections of the battlements and raised her face to the sky.

"It's a little gusty up here," Lord Heyward said, raising a hand to hold on to his hat. "You had better —"

The attempted warning came too late. Even as Angeline lifted both hands to grasp the ribbons of her bonnet and tie them securely beneath her chin again, they whipped free, and her bonnet lifted from her head and sailed off into the sky and down over the slope in the direction of the lake below. All that saved it from a watery grave was the presence of a tree at the foot of the hill that was taller than its fellows. The ribbons caught and tangled in its upper branches and the hat lodged there to end up looking like a particularly exotic bloom.

"Ohhh!" One of Angeline's hands slapped against her mouth while the other reached out foolishly into empty space and Lord Heyward's hand clamped about her upper arm like a vise to prevent her from following the path her bonnet had taken.

They watched it all the way down without saying a word. And then Angeline burst into uncontrollable laughter and, after a moment, Lord Heyward joined her, bellowing with mirth at something that really was not funny at all.

"My poor hat," she wailed between spasms.

Another healthy gust of wind tugged at her hairpins and won the battle with one of them. She turned and slid down the wall until she was sitting against its shelter, her knees drawn up before her. And Lord Heyward slid down beside her, his legs stretched out, and removed his hat.

They were still laughing.

"Did you *s-s-see* it?" she asked when she could catch her breath. "I thought it might fly all the way to America."

"I thought it might cause heart seizures among all the birds inside the park," he said.

"It looked like a demented parrot. It still does."

Which was a horrible insult to her bonnet.

Angeline laughed again. So did he.

"Oh, look at me," she said as she grasped one fallen lock of hair and attempted to twist it up into the rest of her coiffure, which was probably hopelessly flattened anyway. "Just *look* at me."

He turned his head and did so, and somehow their laughter faded. And they were sitting almost shoulder to shoulder, their faces turned toward each other.

Angeline bit her lip.

That was *Lord Heyward* with whom she had been laughing so merrily?

"You look windblown and wind-flushed and very wholesome," he said.

"I shall have to think about that," she said, "to understand whether I have been insulted or not."

"Not," he said softly.

There were beads of perspiration clinging to his brow where his hat had been.

"You are kind," she said. "But goodness, I am not much to look at to begin with."

The lock of hair, pushed firmly and quite securely beneath another, promptly fell down over her ear again as soon as she let go of it.

"Why do you say that?" he asked.

"Well," she said, looking down at her lap, "just consider my mother."

"I knew her," he said. "Not personally, but I saw her more than once. She was extremely beautiful. You look nothing like her."

"You noticed?" She laughed softly.

"Do you wish you did?" he asked.

It was funny. She had never really asked herself that question before. She had lamented the fact that she was not as beautiful as her mother had been, but — did she really wish she looked like her? It would change everything, would it not?

"When I first saw you," he said, "when you turned from the window at the Rose and Crown, I thought you were the most beautiful woman I had ever seen. I thought so again when I saw you at Dudley House."

She laughed.

"I am so *tall*," she said. "A beanpole."

"Perhaps you were at the age of thirteen or so," he said, "but certainly not now."

"And I am so dark."

"*Vividly* dark," he said.

"I cannot even arch my eyebrows properly," she said.

"What?" He looked baffled.

"When I try it," she said, "I look like a startled hare."

"Show me," he said.

And she turned her face obediently toward his again and showed him.

His eyes filled with laughter once more.

"By Jove," he said, "you are quite right. A startled hare. Who was the first to warn you about it?"

"My mother," she said.

The laughter faded.

"She was disappointed in me," she said. "She loved Ferdie. She took him to London with her a number of times, but never me. I daresay she hoped my looks would improve before she had to show me to anyone beyond the neighborhood of Acton. And she had lovers, you know. Of course you know. *Everyone* knew. But it is quite unexceptionable for a married lady, is it not, once she has presented her husband with an heir and a spare, *and* a daughter in her case. And why should she *not* take lovers when Papa had mistresses and even kept one in a cottage on the corner of the estate, saying she was an indigent relative. But she was not. I always knew she was not even before I knew what a *mistress* was. She never *looked* poor, and she never came to the house for a meal, which she would have done at least once in a while if she had been a poor relative, would she not? And of course Tresham has mistresses, even married ones. He has fought two duels I have heard of and perhaps more that I have not. I daresay Ferdie has mistresses too, even though he is only twenty-one. I have sworn and sworn that I will not marry a rake, even if it means marrying a dull man instead. Better to be dull than to be so unhappy that one is forced to take *lovers*. She *was* unhappy, you know, my mother. If she had lived, perhaps she would have thought me improved, and she could have brought me out and helped me find a husband, and we could have become friends and she would have been happy and proud."

She grasped her knees and turned her face from his and shut her eyes tightly.

"I am babbling," she said.

Oh, *where* had all that come from? How absolutely *mortifying*.

"And then Tresham left home abruptly when he was sixteen and never came back," she added for good measure, "and Ferdinand went off to school and sometimes did not even come home during the holidays but went to stay with school friends instead, and Papa died a year after Tresham left, and

Mama stayed most of the time in London after that, even more than before, it seemed, and all I had left was my governesses. They did not like me, and I do not blame them. I made myself unlikable."

There. Oh, *there.* She wished she really had cast herself over the battlements in pursuit of her hat. She brought her forehead down to rest on her knees, and felt after a few moments his hand come to rest against the exposed back of her neck — and then stroke lightly back and forth.

"You were a totally innocent bystander in your family dramas, you know," he said. "Whatever made your parents' marriage an unhappy one had nothing whatsoever to do with you. They had their lives to live and they lived them as they saw fit. Whatever drove your elder brother away so suddenly and kept him away had nothing to do with you — or you would have known it. And your younger brother was a boy learning to spread his wings. He sought out friends of his own, no doubt heedless of the fact that his sister was lonely for his company. As for your governesses, women like them have a hard lot in life. They are often impoverished gentlewomen unable for whatever reason to marry and so have homes and families of their own. They often take out their unhappiness upon their pupils, especially if those pupils are rebelling against life for some reason or other. You are *not* unlovable."

His hand on the back of her neck was hypnotic. She felt *so* embarrassed and *so* close to tears. And if she was so lovable, why did *he* not love her?

"If your mother had lived," he said, "perhaps you would have come to discover that she did not have to grow to love your adult self. Perhaps she always loved you. I never really doubted that I was loved, but I always felt I had to earn love, that I had to work extra hard for it because my brother was so much more easily loved than I was. He was always a charming rogue. Everyone adored him despite all his faults — sometimes even *because* of them, it seemed. And he was selfish. He did not really care when he hurt people's feelings, or even if he did care, gratifying his own desires was more important. It always seemed unfair to me that I tried so hard and yet was loved less. I discovered two things after he died."

"What?" she asked into her knees.

"One was that I *was* loved," he said. "More than I had known, I mean. I never had been loved less, in fact, only differently. And I learned that I tried to do what was right by my family and friends and even strangers because I *wanted* to, that I tried not to hurt other people because I did not *want* to hurt them. I was as selfish in my own way as Maurice was in his, for even if I had had the choice I would not have lived his life."

Angeline swallowed.

"I tried to talk him out of that curricle race," he said. "I reminded him that there was Lorraine to consider. And at the time Susan was ill. She had a fever. Lorraine was beside herself with worry. She needed Maurice to be there with her. He called me a pompous ass. And then I said something that will forever haunt me."

Angeline lifted her head and looked at him. He was staring off across the top of the tower with unseeing eyes. His hand fell away from her neck.

"I told him to go ahead," Lord Heyward said. "I told him to break his neck if he wished. I told him I had everything to gain if he died, that I would be Heyward in his stead."

She set a hand on his thigh and patted it.

"And what you said was provoked," she said. "It had nothing *whatsoever* to do with the accident. Did you *want* him to die?"

"No," he said.

"Did you love him?" she asked.

"I did," he said. "He was my brother."

"Did you *want* to be Earl of Heyward?" she asked.

He closed his eyes and pressed his head back against the wall.

"I did," he said. "I always felt I could do a better job of it than he did. I wanted the title and position for myself. Until I had them — and did not have him. And now I have to watch his wife marry someone else. I am going to have to watch another man bring up my brother's child. And I have to *know* that for Lorraine it is a happily-ever-after. I have to be *happy* for her because I am fond of her and know her life with Maurice was hell. But he was my *brother*."

She gripped his thigh and said nothing. What was there to say? Except that no one is without pain, that pain is part of the human condition. And there was nothing terribly original in *that* thought, was there?

"As Tresham and Ferdinand are my brothers," she said. "Perhaps they will never marry. Perhaps — But I will always love them, no matter what."

He opened his eyes and turned his head toward her.

"It was your brother with whom mine was racing that day, you know," he said.

"Tresham?" She frowned, and her stomach

churned.

"I have always blamed him," he said. "I even did it to his face at Maurice's funeral. I suppose when sudden tragedies occur, we always feel the need to nominate some living scapegoat. But in reality Tresham was no more to blame for what happened than I was. For even if he was the one who suggested the race — and it was just as likely to have been Maurice — my brother did not have to accept. And even if Tresham overtook him just before that bend, he did not force Maurice to take the risk of pursuing him around it at suicidal speed. And Tresham did apparently turn back as soon as he saw the hay cart and realized the danger. He did try to avert the collision. He must have done, else he would not have seen it happen — he would have been another mile farther along the road. And he *did* see it. I have been unfair to your brother, Lady Angeline."

"As you have been unfair to yourself," she said. Oh, it could just as easily have been Tresham who had died in that race. How would she have borne it? Would she have blamed Maurice, Earl of Heyward? She probably would have.

"Yes." He sighed. "Love hurts. And how is *that* for a cliché?"

She sighed. They were growing maudlin.

"I suppose my bonnet is lost for all time," she said. "I liked it particularly well when I bought it last week. The blue and yellow reminded me of a summer sky, and the pink — well, I always have loved pink."

"Last week," he said. "It is number fifteen, then?"

"Seventeen, actually," she said. "And today was the first time I had worn it. Well, perhaps the birds will enjoy it until it fades and rots into shreds."

"Let's go and have a look," he said, getting to his feet and reaching down a hand to help her to hers.

They made their way carefully down the ladder and out of the tower back to the path. They stepped off it a little farther along and looked downward. The slope, covered with long grass that rippled when the wind gusted, was long and far steeper than the one they had climbed. Her bonnet was an impossible distance away, though *impossible* had never figured large in the Dudley vocabulary.

"I can get down there if I go carefully," he said.

"Carefully?" She laughed. "One does not go down a hill like that *carefully,* Lord Hey-ward."

And she grasped his hand in hers and started downward with him — with long strides and at a dead run. She whooped and screeched as they went and felt a few more hairpins part company with her hair. And then they were both laughing again and hurtling along as fast as their feet would carry them — and ultimately, alas, faster even than that. Angeline lost her footing first and then he came tumbling down too and they rolled together until the level ground with its longer grass close to the lake brought them to a halt. By some miracle they had missed colliding with any trees.

They lay still for a few moments, laughing and half winded, side by side, hand in hand. And then he raised himself up on one elbow and gazed down at her, their laughter suddenly gone, their eyes locking.

Her arms came up about his neck at the same moment as his pushed beneath her, and they were kissing in the long grass as though their lives depended upon melding together with no space between them or *in* them or *through* them. As though they could somehow become one person, one whole, and never *ever* be lonely or loveless or unhappy again.

When he lifted his head and gazed down at her, into her eyes and into her very soul,

Angeline gazed back, and knew only that she had been *right*. Oh, she had been right to fall in love with him on sight, to continue to love him, to want more than anything else in life to spend the rest of it loving him. And she had known — oh, she had *known* that he was not a dry old stick at all but capable of extraordinary passion. She had known that he was capable of loving *her* with that forever-after sort of love that sometimes seems not to exist outside the pages of a novel from the Minerva Press but actually, on rare occasions, *does*.

Oh, she had been *right*. She had *known*.

She loved him and he loved her and all was right with the world.

His eyes were bluer than the sky.

And then, in a flash, she remembered something else and could not *believe* she had forgotten. She had resolved to be *noble* and self-sacrificing. For Miss Goddard loved him too, and in his heart of hearts *he* loved *her*. They were suited to each other. They belonged with each other. And not only had Angeline pledged herself to bringing them together, but she had also *told Miss Goddard about her plan and enlisted her collaboration.*

Oh, what had she *done?*

When Lord Heyward opened his mouth

379

to speak, Angeline placed one finger over his lips and then removed it again hastily.

"And *this* time," she said, smiling brightly at him, "you do not owe me a proposal of marriage. You do *not*. I would only refuse again."

He searched her eyes with his own and then moved without another word to sit beside her. He was silent for a while. So was she. She doubted she had ever felt more wretched in her life. For not only was her heart broken, but — worse — she had betrayed a friend.

She was going to have to redouble her efforts.

Lord Heyward was looking up into the tree in which her bonnet was stuck. It was an awfully tall tree, and the bonnet was awfully high up it.

"It can stay there," she said. "I have sixteen others, not counting all the old ones."

"Plus all the ones that will take your fancy before you leave London for the summer," he said. "But that is a particularly, ah, *fancy* one."

He got to his feet, and almost before Angeline could sit up he was climbing the tree with dogged determination. It seemed to her that there were simply not enough foot-

and handholds, but up he went anyway. Her heart was in her mouth long before he was high enough to unhook her bonnet from the branch with which it had become entangled and toss it down to her. Which was strange really because her heart also seemed to be crushed beneath the soles of her shoes. How could it be in both places at once?

And her stomach was churning with terror.

"Oh, do be careful," she called to him as he made his way down again. And she spread her arms, her bonnet clutched in one hand, as if she could catch him and keep him from harm if he fell.

He did not fall. Within minutes he was on the ground beside her again, watching while she tied the ribbons of the bonnet beneath her chin and tucked up all the untidy locks of her hair beneath it.

"Thank you," she said.

"I am sorry," he said simultaneously.

"Do not be," she told him. "Sorry, I mean. You are not responsible for everyone who crosses paths with you."

"Even when I kiss them?" he asked.

"Even then," she said firmly, and turned to make her way along the bank of the lake toward the more cultivated lawn that led in a long slope up toward the house. Now that they had moved clear of the trees, she could see Mr. and Mrs. Lynd and the Reverend Martin on the far bank. They were talking with Ferdinand and Miss Briden. There was no sign of Miss Goddard and Lord Windrow — or of any of the others for that matter.

Lord Heyward fell into step beside her. He did not offer his arm. She made no move to take it. They walked in silence.

How could she, Angeline thought. How *could* she have fallen in love with him again when she had pledged herself to bring him to a happy union with Miss Goddard, who was her *friend?* No, not fallen in love *again,* she thought bitterly. She had never stopped loving him, had she?

Would she *never* make sense to herself?

"I do apologize," he said as they made their way up the long lawn to the house, "if I have offended you."

"You have *not,*" she said crossly, turning to him. "Why must you always worry about *offending* me? Perhaps *I* have offended *you.* If I had not untied the ribbons of my bonnet because I was hot after the climb, it would not have blown off and we would not have run down the hill so that you could put your life in danger to rescue it, and we would not have kissed, and you would not have thought that you owed me a marriage offer again, and I would not have had to tell you that it is unnecessary and that I would refuse it anyway. And do notice that I said *we* would not have kissed, not *you* would not have kissed me. It takes two to kiss, you know, unless it is forced, which it clearly was not either just now or in Vauxhall. *We kissed.* And we do not need to marry just because of it. I will never marry you, so if you are still devising a way to do the gentlemanly thing, forget it. Sometimes I wish you were not such a gentleman, though the fact that you *are* was precisely why I liked you so much the very first time I saw you."

The lawn was sloping. She was fairly gasping for air.

He took her hand in his own and drew it through his arm. He bent his head toward hers and looked into her face.

"Don't cry," he said softly. "I am sorry. Whatever it is I said or did to hurt you, I am sorry. And don't tell me *not* to be. It is not in my nature to hurt others and not be sorry for it. It is who I am, Lady Angeline. Forgive me, if you will, for asking forgiveness."

He smiled at her. A real smile. Except that it looked a little sad.

She was not *crying. Was* she?

Oh, what was she going to *do?*

But it was not a valid question, because it had only one possible answer.

CHAPTER 17

Lord Windrow cast a glance back over his shoulder after he had been walking for a few moments with Eunice.

"Ah," he said, "as I suspected. Lady Angeline Dudley is not to be left to remove the rock from her shoe unassisted after all. Heyward has rushed to her rescue and is on one knee before her. It is an affecting scene and would not be without romantic appeal were he not such a dull fellow."

"Edward is *not* dull," Eunice said. "And of course you were quite right to suspect this would happen. Anyone would have predicted it — except Lady Angeline herself."

"It was not, ah, *planned,* then?" he asked.

"The stone in the shoe?" she said. "Yes, that part was, or some such action anyway. But it was a quite different outcome that Lady Angeline planned. I really must tell you about it, for it is quite mad, and rather touching — and not at all honorable where you are concerned."

"My dear Miss Goddard," he said, touching his fingertips to her hand as it rested in his arm and dipping his head closer to hers — and turning with her so that they veered off the route to the lake and moved in the direction of a grove of trees a short distance away, "I am intrigued. And I am all ears."

"Edward and I have known each other for a number of years," she told him. "We are close friends. We even talked some years ago about marrying each other, but we spoke of it as a possible but by no means certain event comfortably far in the future. We did not consider ourselves betrothed. At the time he was an earnest young student and I was — well, an earnest young woman. If either of us had ever heard the word *romance*, it was in a purely academic context."

"Ah," he said, his fingertips lightly patting her hand. "You were merely a *budding* flower at that time, then, were you? I wish I had known you then, for academic learning ought always to be reinforced with practical action, you know."

She slanted him a glance as they stepped between an ancient oak and a beech tree and walked on into the deeper shade of the grove.

"But when you were a student, Lord Windrow," she said, "did you reinforce practical action with academic learning?"

"Ah, touché," he said. "You make a point. A rather barbed one, it is true, but a point nonetheless."

"After Lady Angeline refused Edward's marriage offer," Eunice said, "she —"

"She did *that?*" he asked, sounding vastly amused. "You astonish me."

"He could not assure her that he loved her," Eunice explained.

"Ah," Lord Windrow said. "*Another* word that has only academic meaning for Heyward? But did he not have sense enough to lie?"

"Afterward," Eunice continued, "she befriended me and then she conceived the idea that Edward and I love each other passionately but are held back from marrying by his sense of duty and his family's expectations that he marry well. She saw us — she *sees* us — as star-crossed lovers who must be helped to our happily-ever-after."

Lord Windrow regarded her with laughing, lazy eyes.

"She is willing to give up the man for whom she pines to her new best friend?" he asked. "I assume she *is* pining. Her partiality for Heyward, mystifying as it is, is also as plain as the nose on your face. Which is a particularly fine specimen of nosehood, I must add."

Eunice gave him a speaking glance.

"Lady Angeline is very sweet," she said, "and very kind and very confused. I like her exceedingly well, you know. If you think to mock her in my hearing, think again."

"Mock a lady?" he said, his free hand over his heart. "You do me an injustice, Miss Goddard. You have wounded me to the soul."

"She gave me her blessing a while ago," Eunice said, "but she believes that circumstances have contrived to keep us apart — Edward and me, that is. And so she has decided that she must lend an active hand. She arranged to have me invited to this house party."

"I must remember," he said, "to thank her."

"And she arranged," she said, "to have *you* invited here."

Their footsteps had already slowed as they progressed deeper among the trees. Now they stopped walking altogether, and he released her arm in order to turn to face her. He regarded her with half-lowered eyelids, beneath which his eyes looked both keen and amused.

"Ah," he said. "But this brain of mine is dense, Miss Goddard. Perhaps I ought to have given more of my attention to academic learning when I was a student after all. We both have Lady Angeline Dudley to thank for bringing us here and, presumably, for throwing us together this afternoon — I never did for a moment believe the boulder-in-the-shoe story — so that we may end up here in this secluded and, ah, *romantic* part of the park. And yet she is intent upon promoting a match between you and *Heyward?*"

Eunice sighed.

"Edward bristles at the mere mention of your name, you know," she said. "You represent for him all that is most depraved in the ranks of bored aristocrats. He considers you a rake of the first order. And his opinion has *some* justification, you must confess. I know what happened at that inn outside Reading, and it was not well done of you."

"Alas," he said, one hand over his heart again, "I was guilty of a colossal error of judgment on that occasion, Miss Goddard. It was *not* my finest moment. Lady Angeline Dudley was alone in the taproom, her back to me, and she was dressed — well, *loudly.* I mistook her for something she most certainly was *not,* and I reacted as almost any red-blooded male would, who had no ties of marriage or like commitments to hold him back."

"*Edward* did not," she said.

His eyes laughed.

"Not all of us can be saints, Miss Goddard," he said. "Some of us are sinners, sad to say. But even sinners are capable of redemption. Be gentle with me."

She shook her head and smiled.

"What was supposed to have happened," she said, "at least, what Lady Angeline expected to happen, was that Edward would come rushing to my rescue as soon as he saw us alone together and wrest me from your evil clutches and bear me off — well, here, I suppose, or somewhere just like it. Somewhere secluded and — *romantic.*"

"And you were a party to this scheme, Miss Goddard?" he asked.

"Since this morning," she admitted. "She feared that all her careful scheming would come to naught if I did not know that I was to lure you off when my cue came, so that Edward could come and rescue me."

"But instead," he said, "he rescued *her.* One only wonders if he is capable of taking advantage of opportunity when it comes knocking at his door."

"Edward is *not* the dull, unimaginative man you take him for," she said. "He grew up in the shadow of a charismatic wastrel of a brother, and he has spent his life trying to compensate for the careless neglect with which the late earl treated those nearest and dearest to him. He takes duty seriously. He takes *life* seriously. But I have always known that he is capable of deep feeling and deep passion. And now he is in love, poor Edward, and thoroughly bewildered, especially over the fact that the object of his love is totally the opposite in every conceivable way of the sort of lady he would expect to choose for a bride. He has not yet understood, of course, that that is what makes her so perfect for him."

"Ah," Lord Windrow said, "what an excellent person you are, Miss Goddard. You are not only intelligent, but you have a female's logic too."

"I *am* female," she said.

He looked her over lazily from head to foot — from her unadorned straw bonnet and the smooth brown hair beneath it, over her plain but serviceable muslin dress of pale green, on down to her sensible brown walking shoes.

"Yes," he said before lifting his eyes to hers, "I had noticed."

"Well," Eunice said after swallowing, "thank goodness for that."

"And so Heyward is supposed to believe that I am having my wicked way with you in the forest, is he?" he asked.

"He is." She smiled at him. "He knows better, though. He trusts my good sense."

"Does he indeed?" His lazy eyes searched her face. "But does he trust *me?*"

"He trusts my ability to handle you," she said.

He took one step forward, and she took a half-step back in order to steady her back against the sturdy trunk of a tree.

"That sounds fascinating," he said. "How *would* you handle me, Miss Goddard?"

"Since I have no experience," she said, "and therefore cannot answer your question directly, Lord Windrow, I can only suggest that I answer it with — how did you phrase it? — with practical action."

"Ah," he said, taking another step forward, so that his body, from shoulders to thighs, brushed against hers, "take your time, Miss Goddard. There is no hurry at all for your answer. And do feel free to handle me to your heart's content."

"Thank you," she said. "I will."

And he brought his mouth down, open, across hers.

"And now," he said several minutes later, his lips still brushing hers, "you have no need to answer my question. Sometimes action speaks far louder than words. And that pearl of wisdom is the academic portion of your lesson for today. Heyward would be shocked at how misplaced his trust in you is." His lips moved down to her throat. "Although if his trust was merely in your ability to handle me, then it could be argued just as forcefully that his trust was *well* placed."

"Yes," she said. "But poor Lady Angeline. She will doubtless believe she has failed and will wish to try again."

"A plan I thoroughly applaud," he said, stepping back and looking with keen approval at her flushed face and rosy, just-kissed lips. "Can you persuade her to try again this evening?"

He grinned.

"Oh," she said, "I will do no such thing. I would not have agreed to this afternoon if I had not felt that Lady Angeline needed a nudge in Edward's direction. I knew he would not come after me, but I hoped he might spend some time with her and that the two of them might come to their senses. Whether it has worked or not, I do not know. But I was not cut out for intrigue. I shall tell her later that I have no romantic interest at all in Edward or he in me and that she must put aside her schemes. I daresay she will be relieved, for of course she loves him herself and must be heartbroken over her conviction that he belongs to me. She really is a *very* sweet girl and my first female friend ever. I value her friendship and will not toy with it any longer."

"I am sorry to hear that," he said. "I *am* cut out for intrigue, you see, and I believe it would be perfectly splendid to play Lady Angeline Dudley at her own game and at the same time accelerate her into the arms of her dull swain, who you insist is *not* dull at all. I have been used, Miss Goddard, and I am deeply offended. I am entitled, it would seem, to revenge in kind."

"Oh." Eunice looked at him with sharp interest. "What did you have in mind?"

He smiled slowly.

Dinner that evening was an elaborate affair in official celebration of Lorraine and Fenner's betrothal. The meal consisted of twelve courses and was followed by speeches and toasts and dancing in the drawing room afterward to music provided by a small group — pianist, violinist, and flautist — from the village nearby.

It was a happy and merry occasion, for which Edward was glad. It might have been rather melancholy for his own family to see Maurice's widow move on in her life with a different partner. But they had all taken her so thoroughly to their hearts from the moment of her marriage to Maurice that she felt like one of their own, and they *were* happy for her, despite the fact that Edward noticed his mother wipe a tear from her eye when she thought herself unobserved.

For himself, he was distracted. The events of the afternoon had shaken him quite considerably, for he had discovered himself quite unexpectedly and not altogether happily in love. Yes, it really was the only term he could use to describe his feelings, but it was not at all the sort of silly, shallow, wishful-thinking feeling he had expected it to be.

He was in love with Lady Angeline Dudley. He was enchanted by her and invigorated by her. And it was not just a sexual feeling, though it certainly was that too. It was more a longing for . . . well, he did not have the language for a sensation he had always despised and distrusted and really not believed in at all as a serious emotion.

It was a longing for *her*. For her as a part of himself. For . . . No, there was no way of expressing it in words. *Happily-ever-after* was not it at all, though it was the only phrase that came close. It all sounded so very trivial in words.

It was very serious.

Perhaps what he had learned most about himself during the afternoon was that he had surely always wanted simply to have *fun,* to let go and enjoy himself, to *laugh.* To laugh with someone else, to enjoy himself with someone else. He kept reliving that run down the hill. It had been mad — the slope was *far* too long and steep to be negotiated safely — and he never did mad things. It was one of the most wonderfully *free* things he had done in his life — running and falling and rolling and laughing. And kissing. And feeling grass all around them, and smelling it, and seeing blue sky above and the branches of trees and her yellow, blue, and pink bonnet wedged in an upper branch, its ribbons fluttering gaily in the breeze.

Feeling *young.*

Not that the afternoon had been all carefree enjoyment. It had not. She had spilled out her soul to him up on the battlements of that folly. Or that was how it had felt anyway, and he had understood all the loneliness of her girlhood and all the surprising insecurities that had been instilled in her by a vain, insensitive mother and dull, insensitive governesses. She was not at all the sort of woman she appeared to be. Well, she *was.* The exuberance, the boldness often amounting to indiscretion, the sheer zest for life were all real. But there was more than just that aspect of her person. Far more. Even the bold colors she liked to wear and the extravagant, garish hats made more sense now. She could never get her appearance and fashions right, she thought, so why not get them defiantly *wrong?*

He had poured out his heart to her too — almost deliberately, to start with. He had wanted her to feel less embarrassed about her disclosures by sharing some of his own. But real pain had surfaced — and she had understood and comforted him. She had confirmed what he had always known, of course — that he had been *in no way* responsible for Maurice's accident and death.

And yet . . .

And yet she had made it very clear after their kiss that she did not want to marry him. She would refuse if he asked, she had told him. And then she had got definitely upset. She had been cross and crying.

Why?

She had admitted that she had kissed him

as much as he had kissed her. And . . . what else had she said?

Sometimes I wish you were not such a gentleman, though the fact that you are was precisely why I liked you so much the very first time I saw you.

What the devil did *that* mean?

She wished he were not such a gentleman? But he had *kissed* her, had he not? That was not a very gentlemanly thing to do when they were not even betrothed. If he offered for her now, she meant, it would be only because a gentleman offers marriage to the woman whose virtue he compromises. Just as he had done last time.

Did that mean she did not love him?

Or did it mean that she loved him too much to accept an offer from him only because he felt duty-bound to make it?

Was that why she had refused him last time? Not so much because he had neglected to tell her that he loved her, but because she did love him?

Past tense?

Present tense?

He was *such* a novice at all this. And part of him was still wary. How could he be in love? And how the devil could he be in love with *Lady Angeline Dudley?* He deliberately brought to mind his first two encounters with her — at the Rose and Crown and on Rotten Row — and looked along the dining table to where she was seated between Sir Webster Jordan and Christopher. She was talking with great animation to the former, and he was smiling back at her.

She was a young, warmhearted, exuberant girl, full of dreams and hopes and charm and quite, quite unconscious of her own vivid beauty. Her mother would *still* have disapproved of her, he thought. The competition would have been too stiff.

She lifted her eyes and caught him looking at her. And for a moment — it was so brief that he might have imagined it — she gazed wistfully back. Then she smiled more brightly and lowered her eyes while she listened to what Jordan was saying.

He was not going to take her at her word. He was not going to forget about marrying her. If there was one thing he had learned about women, limited as his experience was, it was that they did not always say what they meant or mean what they said. Dealing with women was *not* an easy thing. But like all skills worth acquiring, it needed to be worked upon.

It was to be an evening of dancing. It was not the best situation in which to begin some determined wooing, but perhaps not the worst either. This was no London squeeze after all, and the musicians were no professionals. He danced an energetic hop with Miss Marianne Briden and a slightly more stately one with Alma. They all watched as Lorraine and Fenner waltzed together.

And then Lady Palmer asked the musicians to play a whole set of waltzes and there was a buzz of approval from the guests.

Edward drew a deep breath, but he dared not hesitate.

"Lady Angeline." He stepped up to where she was standing, talking with Eunice and the Reverend Martin. "Would you care to waltz?"

Her lips formed a soundless O, and she glanced at Eunice and even made a small gesture toward her with one hand. But then she smiled.

"Thank you, Lord Heyward," she said and set her hand on his sleeve as he led her farther onto the floor of the drawing room, from which the Persian carpet had been rolled back earlier in the evening.

His grandmother was beaming at him, Edward could see. Alma, who was with her, was smiling and nodding in his direction. His mother was looking hopefully at him. So, actually, was Lady Palmer. And for the first time he could feel encouraged rather than trapped by their obvious approval of this match. If only it were not a waltz! Or any dance at all for that matter.

"Perhaps," Lady Angeline said, "you would prefer to sit and talk, Lord Heyward. Or perhaps you would like to stroll outside."

The French windows were open though there was no one outside.

"Shall we compromise," he suggested, "and *dance* outside?"

Perhaps his legs would feel more like legs — one left and one right — if he waltzed in the darkness without any critical eyes upon him.

"Oh," she said. "Very well. But I am surprised you did not ask Miss Goddard. She is your friend, and I am sure you would not wish to see her be a wallflower. Your mother and sisters would understand if you danced with her."

"A wallflower?" he said as he led her through the doors and out onto the cool terrace, which was illuminated only by the candles within the drawing room. "Eunice has had a partner for every dance so far. She is going to dance this one with Windrow."

"I do not like that," she said. "And *you* ought not. He is not a man to be trusted."

"Not even in a drawing room full of fellow guests at a house party?" he asked her.

"But if they should venture beyond the sight of everyone else," she said, "I do believe you ought to be concerned."

He had been given the strange impression both yesterday and today that Windrow was actually interested in Eunice — perhaps because she was no easy victim to his charms. Nothing would come of it, of course. Eunice was far too sensible to encourage him, even if she appeared to be enjoying his company right now. She was laughing at something he had said. Eunice should laugh more often. She looked younger and lovelier than he remembered her looking at any time since he had known her.

And then the music began and he forgot about Eunice and Windrow and everyone else in the drawing room. He set a hand behind Lady Angeline's slender waist and took her right hand in his left. He felt her other hand come to rest on his shoulder. Her eyes were large in the darkness. They were looking directly into his.

He even forgot that he could not dance, or, rather, that he did so with extreme awkwardness. And that the musicians were not particularly skilled.

He had been wrong about the candlelight. The sky was clear overhead. The moon was waxing toward the full. A million stars twinkled with varying degrees of brightness. The air was cool but not cold. They moved into the steps of the waltz.

It was the only time ever he had enjoyed dancing. Perhaps because he did not even realize that was what he was doing. They moved as one, in and out of the beams of light cast by the drawing room candles, and they twirled beneath the stars until it seemed that it was they that were whirling in bands of light while the two people beneath them stood still.

Her body was warm and supple, her hand clasped in his. She wore a perfume — or perhaps it was soap — so faint that it seemed more the fragrance of *her*. It wrapped about him like a soft shawl, warming him against the cool of the evening.

They did not speak. It did not occur to him that they might. It did not even occur to him that they were *not* conversing. The silence was eloquent enough with its background of music and voices and laughter.

And when it was over, they stood a foot apart — less — and gazed at each other.

"Lady Angeline —" he said softly.

"Thank you," she said brightly as he

began to speak. She smiled dazzlingly. "That was very pleasant, Lord Heyward. It is chilly out here, is it not? I shall be glad to get back inside."

And the spell was broken.

Was it possible that it had been one-sided, that only he had felt it? Had she been feeling chilly all the time they danced and anxious for the music to end so that she could go back indoors?

He did not believe so.

But she was edgy. She did not trust him, perhaps, to be more than the dull, plodding suitor who had acted out all the platitudes and clichés of a marriage proposal a month ago and had admitted, when pressed, that he was proposing only because he had kissed and compromised her the night before.

What an insufferable ass he had been — as well as an utter simpleton.

It was no wonder she did not trust him now.

The only question was, was it too late to redeem himself? Had his cold manner then killed all her love for him? If she *had* loved him, that was. But she had loved him this afternoon. He had no experience by which to judge such things, but one did not *need* experience. He had felt her kiss and her arms about him. He had gazed into her eyes.

"Yes," he said now and offered her his arm.

Five minutes later she was dancing with Windrow and sparkling and laughing up at him, and Edward felt that he could cheerfully kill the man. But he was dancing with Eunice, and he determinedly gave her his full attention.

"Are you enjoying the house party, Eunice?" he asked.

"Oh, of all things," she said, which seemed an extravagantly girlish thing for Eunice to say. "I have never before been to a house party, you know. And I am *twenty-three* years old."

Ah, he thought as he smiled fondly at her, the butterfly was emerging from the cocoon, was it? The solemn, bookish girl was suddenly realizing that there was life to be lived and that it must be done *now* because time moved inexorably onward. He just hoped she had not pinned all her hopes for happiness upon Windrow, though he did not believe she would be so foolish. He was not about to utter any advice, however. Eunice was quite mature and sensible enough to order her own life.

"And you," she said. "Are you enjoying *yourself,* Edward?"

"I am," he said and smiled.

"You see?" she said softly. "I was quite right, was I not?"

He was not really sure what she meant, though he *thought* he knew.

"Yes," he said. "You were."

She smiled warmly back at him.

CHAPTER 18

By the middle of the following afternoon Angeline was in despair — for more than one reason.

The least important — oh, it was very much the least — was that she had seriously underestimated her leftover feelings for the Earl of Heyward after she had rejected his marriage offer. She had been angry with him at that time and horribly disappointed, so of course she had convinced herself that she did not love him at all and that she *was* loving all the busy activities of the Season and the attentions of numerous other gentlemen. She had even persuaded herself that she was on the brink of falling in love with two or three of them.

It was all nonsense, of course. For she had fallen in love with Lord Heyward the first time she set eyes upon him, and she had not fallen out of love since. It *would be done,* but it had not happened yet. And yesterday had not helped at all. *Why* had he not gone to Miss Goddard's rescue as she had been confident he would, instead of insisting upon helping Angeline get rid of the non-existent stone in her shoe? And why had they not remained with the group afterward? Why had he kissed her? And why had she allowed it? Why had they waltzed on the terrace last evening instead of inside the drawing room? Even that would have been bad enough, but being outside was disastrous. She had never been so deliriously happy as when they were dancing, and never so deeply in the grip of despair as when she came to her senses afterward.

For he had then danced with Miss Goddard, and it had been another waltz because that was what everyone had wanted, and they had talked the whole time, never taking their eyes off each other's. She had glowed with obvious happiness, and his eyes had smiled warmly at her the whole time even if the rest of his face had been in repose.

Oh, they were meant for each other. There was no doubt in Angeline's mind — and surely there could be none in the minds of his mother and sisters either, or in that of his grandmother. And she could not resent the fact, because she liked Miss Goddard exceedingly well and genuinely wished for her happiness.

Why, instead of teaching her poetry and drama and needlework, had her governesses not taught her the most important lesson anyone could learn — that life was really not going to be easy after one was free of the schoolroom?

And there was the second, and more important, reason for Angeline's despair. For she had pledged herself to bring Miss Goddard and the Earl of Heyward together. She had even gone so far as to tell Miss Goddard what she was doing so she could help bring about her own happily-ever-after. She had agreed to do it, had she not? That meant she wanted the Earl of Heyward, that she *loved* him. Angeline was so happy for her that she sank one rung further down the ladder of despair.

And the answer to *that* was to redouble her efforts. Though they were not working nearly as well as she had thought they would. Well, not at all, in fact. Goodness, she had schemed to have both Miss Goddard and Lord Windrow invited here, only to discover that Lord Heyward did not seem unduly alarmed by the attentions Lord Windrow was paying the woman he loved. It was all very frustrating.

Angeline went out riding in the morning with a group of other guests. Miss Goddard was not one of them, however, so there was no chance to implement anything. For some distance she rode between Lord Windrow and Tresham, and the two of them talked of going fishing with some of the other men after breakfast. Lord Windrow also mentioned the fact that it was his mother's birthday and that he really ought to ride over to his home later to dine with her and spend the night before returning tomorrow.

"Will she not come here?" Angeline asked. "I am sure Cousin Rosalie would be delighted to have her, and we could all give her a grand celebration."

It was perhaps not quite the thing to invite someone to Rosalie's house, especially for a birthday party, without first consulting Rosalie herself, but Angeline was sure she would not mind.

"Alas," Lord Windrow said, "my mother is not strong, and she is something of a recluse. If I am to see her on her birthday, I must go to her."

"You will upset the balance of numbers here if you do," Tresham said, "and doubtless throw Rosalie into consternation. Such things matter to the ladies."

"Far be it from me to do anything so

dastardly," Lord Windrow said, smiling at Angeline. "I shall think of some solution. Tell me, Lady Angeline, is there a color *not* represented in your rather splendid riding hat? It would be a shame if there were. It would be sitting all alone on a palette somewhere, feeling rejected and dejected."

Tresham barked with laughter.

"If there is such a color," Angeline said, laughing too, "let it come to me in the form of a feather or a ribbon and I shall add it to the rest."

"Ah," Lord Windrow said, "but how can one improve upon perfection?"

Angeline enjoyed the ride, as she always did. She rode back with Ferdinand, and he gave her a blow-by-blow account of a bareknuckled boxing match he and a group of friends had ridden twenty miles from London to watch a week ago. It had gone fifteen rounds before the champion had finally knocked out the contender, and by that time both their faces had resembled raw meat. It was the best, most enjoyable fight he had seen for ages. Angeline scolded him for going, and begged for every detail he had omitted.

"But don't *you* ever fight anyone like that, Ferdie," she said. "Have *some* regard for my nerves."

But really the morning was wasted, for of course most of the men *did* go fishing after breakfast and did not return until just before a late luncheon. The second day of the house party was already more than half over. And Lord Windrow was indeed going home to Norton Park to see his mother on her birthday — he spoke of it again at the table. Her campaign would have to proceed without him, Angeline thought, at least until tomorrow. *Not* that she was having a great deal of success with him here anyway.

Matchmaking clearly was not as easy as she had expected it to be.

However, something happened after luncheon to cause her to brighten quite considerably. Miss Goddard linked an arm through hers as she was about to wander into the drawing room, where the Misses Briden were settling at the pianoforte to play a duet and a number of the other guests were going to listen to them. Miss Goddard led Angeline to the conservatory instead, where they sat on a wrought-iron seat among the potted plants.

"Edward needs to be jolted out of his complacency," she said. "Yesterday's plan did not work well, did it? He could see, both during the afternoon when I walked alone with Lord Windrow and last evening when I danced in the drawing room with him, that I was in no danger whatsoever. In both cases there were other people within sight or at least hailing distance all the time. And Lord Windrow is a guest here at Hallings and would not behave badly here. He *is* a gentleman, after all."

"Then our plans will not work at all," Angeline said with a sigh. "Not here at least. I *so* thought they would if I could just get you all here, where you are in daily contact with one another. Oh, *what* is the matter with Lord Heyward? I *know* he loves you, and of course you love him. *That* was perfectly clear when you danced together last evening. *Why* does he not simply declare himself?"

"He *is* clearly in love," Miss Goddard agreed. "I do believe he needs only a nudge in the right direction and all will be well. Everyone will live happily ever after."

Angeline felt rather as if someone must have poured lead into the soles of her shoes — or into the base of her heart. He must have said something last evening to make Miss Goddard so confident. She *looked* confident — she was smiling. Perhaps there was no need to do anything else after all. Perhaps matters could just be allowed to take their course. Miss Goddard had strolled in the formal gardens this morning with the Marchioness of Beckingham, the Dowager Lady Heyward, and Lady Overmyer, and they had all looked perfectly happy with one another when they returned to the house.

But Miss Goddard herself felt that he needed a nudge.

"Perhaps we must wait until after we return to London, then," Angeline said, "when Lord Windrow is no longer on Hallings land."

"Ah, but," Miss Goddard reminded her, "he will not be on Hallings land later today, will he — or tomorrow until about noon. And he has already suggested that I accompany him to Norton Park."

"To meet his *mother?*" Angeline was saucer-eyed.

"We have only his word for it that his mother is at Norton Park," Miss Goddard said, "and that today is her birthday. And ten miles is a long way. I daresay there are inns along the route. I am not at all sure I should agree to accompany him. But he explained that his going alone would embarrass Lady Palmer as it would upset the balance of numbers here."

"Oh," Angeline said, her hands clasped to her bosom, "he *does* have dastardly designs upon you, then. Lord Heyward cannot fail to come galloping after you if you go. But you absolutely must not go alone. Oh, good heavens no. I will come with you."

"I made it perfectly clear to Lord Windrow that I would not go *unless* you agreed to come too," Miss Goddard said. "Of course, he pointed out that then the numbers here would be unbalanced again. But he is not correct on that, for of course Edward will follow us."

It was perfect, Angeline thought, ignoring the heaviness of her heart. *Perfect.* Except for one thing.

"There will be a dreadful scandal," she said, "when it is known that we are gone. Tresham will *kill* me. At the very least. Even if he never lays a finger on me."

"Not necessarily," Miss Goddard said. "Not if we explain that we have been invited to meet Lady Windrow and have each other for chaperons — as well as my maid. Aunt Charlotte insisted that I bring one, you know, as she felt it would be inappropriate for me to arrive at such an illustrious house party without. It will not occur to anyone that there is anything remotely improper about our going."

"But why then," Angeline asked, "will it appear improper to Lord Heyward? Can we be quite sure he will come after you?"

"Well," Miss Goddard said, "Edward knows something about Lord Windrow that no one else knows. He will certainly be uneasy, and unease will turn to alarm if you leave a panicked little note for him."

Angeline thought about it. Yes. Oh, yes, she could do that.

"And indeed," Miss Goddard added, "you would not even be lying. For I really do feel uneasy about the whole thing. Why did Lord Windrow suddenly remember *now,* after flirting outrageously with me yesterday afternoon, that today is his mother's birthday? Would it not have made more sense, if that really were the case, for him to have refused the invitation to stay here altogether?"

"You mean," Angeline asked, saucer-eyed again, "that he really is intending to *abduct* you?"

"Well," Miss Goddard said, "I do not believe he would stoop quite so low, but I must admit to feeling some anxiety. Perhaps it is because I know what Lord Windrow did when he met you on the road to London. Though I must confess that apart from flirting with me, he has never given me any personal cause for alarm."

"We will do it," Angeline said. "I shall go

416

and write the note now and leave instructions with cousin Rosalie's butler or a footman to deliver it to Lord Heyward half an hour after we leave."

She got determinedly to her feet.

"Give the note to me," Miss Goddard said, "and I shall make the arrangements."

By this time tomorrow, Angeline thought as she hurried up to her room, Lord Heyward would have proposed marriage to Miss Goddard, she would have accepted, and *she,* Angeline, would have been put out of her misery.

She could then proceed to enjoy the rest of her life untroubled by an unrequited love. For though he had kissed her yesterday and no doubt would have offered her marriage later, and though he had waltzed in the moonlight with her last evening, Lord Heyward did not *love* her. He had admitted as much a month ago, and nothing had changed since then. How could it? One could not simply fall out of love once one was in, and Lord Heyward loved Miss Goddard.

She sighed as she shut herself up in her room.

Edward had not gone riding during the morning, even though he had seriously considered it when he knew that Lady Angeline was to be of the party. He could have tried to ride beside her, to engage her in conversation, perhaps challenge her to a race. But no, not that. He did not know the terrain in the park at Hallings or in the surrounding countryside. He must never encourage her to be reckless. She did that more than enough on her own initiative. *Twice* he had jumped awake during the night in a cold sweat, imagining what might have happened to her when they hurtled down that hill. She might have broken a leg again — or her neck. Or she might have collided head-on with a tree.

Anyway, he had not gone riding. Instead he had sat in the conservatory with Alma, who was an early riser. And he had asked her advice on something that had been bothering him.

"Would it be in bad taste, Alma," he asked her, "to steal some of the thunder from Lorraine and Fenner while we are here?"

She did not stare at him in blank incomprehension as most people would have done. She *was* his sister, after all.

"Lady Angeline Dudley?" she asked.

He nodded, his eyes upon a pink geranium that had bloomed before its fellows in the same pot.

"Though maybe I should not ask her so soon anyway," he said. "She warned me not to. But it does seem like the ideal time with both our families here."

"She *warned* you not to propose marriage to her again?" she asked him, drawing her shawl more closely about her shoulders against the early morning chill. "After you proposed last month, you mean?"

"Yesterday," he said, noticing that all the other geraniums were red. There was just the one pink bloom. Lady Angeline's favorite color — among about fifty others.

Alma placed a hand on his sleeve and patted it.

"Suddenly, right out of the blue," she said, "she told you not to ask her to marry you? I need a little more context here, Edward. Was this when you waltzed with her outside the drawing room last evening?"

"Yesterday afternoon," he said. "We went up the hill beyond the lake — the one with that tower folly on top. While we were up there, her bonnet blew off in a gust of wind and ended up in a tree down below. We went down to get it, but we lost our footing on the slope and rolled down the last part of it. And I — well, I kissed her. I did not force it upon her. She — well, she kissed me back. And then she told me that *this* time I must not offer for her. She said she would refuse me if I did."

"Oh, Edward," she said, squeezing his arm. "Of course she did. And of course she would."

There it was again — female logic. Quite frankly, it baffled him.

"I had better wait, then?" he asked her. "Perhaps forever?"

"Of course not," she said. "But you must make it very clear to her that you ask because you *love* her, because you cannot contemplate life without her. You *do* love her, do you not?"

"Of course I do, but it makes no sense, Alma," he said. "She is the sort of person . . ." He made circles in the air with one hand. "Well, this is the sort of person she is. Instead of letting me walk down the more gradual slope of the hill and back around the base to the tree where her bonnet was stuck, or at least make my way very carefully straight down the steep part while she remained safely at the top, she grabbed my hand and *ran* down. We might both have broken our necks."

"And you lost your footing and rolled and arrived safely and kissed," she said. "Did you also laugh?"

"How could we not?" he said. "Though it

was not really funny, was it?"

"*Life* is not funny," she said, "except when it is. Except when we *make* it fun. Edward, Lady Angeline Dudley is *perfect* for you. We have all seen it from the start. You are finally seeing it for yourself, though you are still puzzled at the realization. You have always been so afraid that you will lose control of your life if you should ever relax and enjoy it."

"I am not as bad as that," he said. "Am I?"

She leaned toward him and kissed his cheek.

"You are not *bad* at all," she said. "That is sometimes the trouble."

"You would have me be more like Maurice, then?" he asked, frowning.

"I would have you be more like *Edward*," she said. "More like Edward as he can be if he lives to his full potential. If he does more than just love. If he also allows himself to be *in* love — with life and with the woman who was surely created just for him."

"Hmm," he said. He was a little embarrassed. Alma was his sensible, practical elder sister. He did not expect to hear poetic outpourings from her.

"But if you expect her to listen to another marriage proposal," she said, "you must first

421

make it clear to her that you ask from the heart, Edward. You must *do* something very decisive to convince her."

He sighed and turned his head to look into her face.

"All I asked," he said, "was whether you thought it would be in poor taste for me to make an announcement — if there *is* an announcement to make — during Lorraine and Fenner's betrothal party."

She laughed and he grinned.

"Well," she said, "there is a simple answer to that one at least. No. It would *not* be in poor taste. Indeed, I believe Lorraine would be overjoyed. She is exceedingly fond of you, you know, Edward. You were always kind to her — and Susan."

You must do *something very decisive to convince her.*

Right. But what?

He went fishing with most of the other men after breakfast. It was one of his favorite activities when he was in the country. And while he fished, he planned to take Lady Angeline walking again during the afternoon. He would talk with her, *laugh* with her again, *kiss* her again. And tell her he loved her. He might feel like a prize idiot as he did so — undoubtedly he would, in fact — but he would do it anyway. Such

422

things were important to women, it seemed, and it was not as though he would be lying. He *did* love her.

Heaven help him.

The afternoon walk was to be delayed, though, he discovered after luncheon when Eunice bore Lady Angeline off to the conservatory for what looked like a private tête-à-tête. He did not see them again, even though he paced about the house long after everyone else had tired of the music in the drawing room, including the Misses Briden, who had been supplying it, and had gone outside or into the billiard room or to their own rooms for a rest.

Windrow was going home for the night — apparently it was only ten miles away. It was his mother's birthday. A little while ago, Edward would have been delighted. Indeed, he would have hoped that Windrow would fail to return. He had got over that, though — as long as Windrow did nothing to threaten Lady Angeline's safety or peace of mind.

And then, late in the afternoon, that was *just* what happened.

The butler waylaid him as he was passing through the hall, and placed a folded and sealed piece of paper in his hands.

"I was asked to deliver this to you personally at four o'clock, my lord," he said with a bow.

Edward looked down at it. His name was written on one side in a neat, precise feminine hand. Eunice's. He raised his eyebrows. A letter? Rather than a word to him in person?

"Thank you," he said, and he went up to his room to read it in private.

Lord Windrow had invited Lady Angeline Dudley and her to accompany him to Norton Park as a special birthday treat for his mother, Eunice had written. Edward would know about that — he did *not*. It had all been arranged quite properly, of course. Both Lady Palmer and the Duke of Tresham had given their permission.

"But, Edward," Eunice had continued, "I know that I have been invited only because permission would *not* have been granted for Lady Angeline to go alone. I am foolish perhaps to feel anxious. I am not normally given to groundless anxieties, as you know. But I *am* uneasy. How can I be certain that Lady Windrow is at Norton? Perhaps she is not. And how can I be certain that somehow I will not be spirited away somewhere, leaving Lord Windrow and Lady Angeline alone? Oh, these concerns *must* be groundless, must they not? I *must* be doing Lord

Windrow an injustice. He is a gentleman, after all, despite what you witnessed on the road to London. But, Edward, he has mentioned an inn on the way to Norton, where he says we will stop for refreshments and a change of horses. But the whole distance is only ten miles. We ought not to *need* to stop, ought we? Forgive this letter. It is unlike me, I know. But Lady Angeline is such an innocent. I fear for her. And Lord Windrow is such a determined flirt — or maybe worse. Do ignore these meanderings if you will — or come in pursuit. I did mention to Lady Palmer when Lord Windrow was not listening that you might follow us over to Norton, and she even seemed pleased. I believe she still has hopes for you and Lady Angeline. Oh, please — it is time to go. Please come. Your ever devoted friend, Eunice."

Edward had turned cold.

It *was* unlike Eunice to panic. She was the most sensible person, of either gender, that he knew. If she was uneasy, there was something to be uneasy about.

And that villain, Windrow . . .

Edward flexed his hands. His fingers itched to be about the man's throat. His knuckles ached to make contact with his jawbone.

This time, Windrow would not need to waste his breath issuing a challenge. He could save it to defend his life, of all but an inch of which he was going to be deprived before the day was over.

Lady Palmer was in the drawing room with Edward's grandmother and mother, the Reverend Martin, and Mr. Briden. It took all of Edward's willpower to smile and greet everyone and wait for an end to the discussion on the merits of remaining in the country all year as opposed to spending parts of it in London or at one of the spas. It took all of his willpower to speak quietly to Lady Palmer.

"Ma'am," he said, "I will be riding over to Norton Park, if the absence of yet another of your guests will not seem a great discourtesy. I did not want to crowd Windrow's carriage, but I did say I might follow after it."

"Yes," she said. "I know that, Lord Heyward. And I am happy for you young people to have an excursion you will enjoy. I am even secretly happy that you *have* decided to go too, for my numbers are now even again and the dining table this evening will not look sadly lopsided."

She laughed, as did everyone else in the room. His grandmother, Edward noted, waved her lorgnette in his direction and actually winked at him.

"Lady Windrow will be *so* pleased to have company," Lady Palmer said. "She suffers with rather delicate health and rarely leaves Norton. But she loves to have visitors. Let me not delay you, though. It is a longish ride."

So Windrow's mother *was* at Norton, Edward thought as he hurried from the room and upstairs to change into riding clothes. Perhaps Eunice's fears were quite ungrounded, then. But there was still that matter of a stop at an inn on the way, and Edward certainly did not trust Windrow at inns. He was going. And let Windrow just *try* something. Edward almost hoped he would. His long-held conviction that a gentleman did not need to resort to violence to make a point was all very well on occasion, perhaps even on most occasions.

But this was not any occasion, or even most.

This concerned Lady Angeline Dudley. Whom Edward loved. How had Alma phrased it? Without whom he could not contemplate living. That was it, or something very like it. And what else had she said?

You must do *something very decisive to convince her.*

Right.

Right!

Ten minutes later, having saddled a horse himself, he was moving away from the stables at a gallop.

CHAPTER 19

Miss Goddard and Lord Windrow were engaged in a spirited discussion of Mr. Richardson's *Pamela,* which Angeline had never read, partly because it had always looked disconcertingly long and partly because she had never found its subtitle, *Or Virtue Rewarded,* even the smallest little bit enticing. Miss Goddard was of the opinion that the hero was the most worthless villain in all of literature — and that *included* Iago in Shakespeare's *Othello* — while Lord Windrow argued that a reformed rake made the most steadfast and worthy of heroes for the rest of his life.

Since Lord Windrow expressed himself with lazy wit and Miss Goddard's earnest opinions were frequently punctuated with bursts of laughter, Angeline felt she really ought to enjoy just listening. She ought indeed to offer an opinion of her own, even if she had not read the book. After all, she did have something to say on the subject of rakes and the possibility — or impossibility — of their ever being reformed.

But she could not concentrate.

She felt a little sick, if the truth were known. They had been here at the Peacock Inn far longer than they needed to be just to change the horses on Lord Windrow's carriage and partake of tea in the private parlor. They had all had two cups of tea, and what remained in the pot must be cold. They had eaten all the cakes on the plate.

And still Lord Heyward had not come.

Angeline had given her letter — it had turned into something longer than a note after the second paragraph — to Miss Goddard, who had gone off to hand it to the butler with clear instructions to put it into Lord Heyward's hands and no other's at four o'clock. Lord Heyward could not have mistaken the danger she had described. She had felt when she had finished composing it, in fact, that she really ought to write a Gothic novel. She certainly appeared to have the talent for lurid hyperbole. He *must* be consumed with anxiety for Miss Goddard.

But he had not come yet.

She had mentioned the inn in the letter, though she had not known its name at the time. But surely he would not have driven right on past. It was a small inn with a small inn yard. And the gates were open wide. Even if he had not known about the possible stop here, he surely could not have missed seeing the carriage in the yard as he passed.

She just hoped that when he came — *if* he came — Miss Goddard would not be laughing. And if she, Angeline, could only have some advance warning of his arrival, she would slip off to use the necessary so that he would find Miss Goddard and Lord Windrow alone together — Miss Goddard's maid was taking refreshments in the kitchen.

Oh, would he *never* come? This was like waiting for Tresham at the Rose and Crown all over again. Except that then she had been excited and exuberant in anticipation of her come-out and the Season and beaux and marriage and happiness, while now she was mortally depressed. For if he came, it would be because he loved Miss Goddard, and it would be such an extravagant gesture that there would be no going back from it.

Nothing could make Angeline happier.

She felt as if *every part* of her — even her eyelids when she blinked — were made of lead.

Waltzing under the stars ought to be

outlawed. It really ought. And so should rolling down hills. And so should . . . Well, *everything* ought to be outlawed.

"Ah, fair one," Lord Windrow said, addressing her directly, "you simply must speak up in defense of rakes. In *my* defense, that is. I am a man who visits his *mother* on her *birthday*. Would a heartless villain do that?"

Despite herself Angeline laughed. And oh, goodness, she had depicted him as just that — a heartless villain — in the letter she had left behind. Yet she could not help liking him. Conscience smote her, as it ought to have done much sooner. She really ought not to have used him in such a dastardly way to arouse Lord Heyward's jealousy, for his behavior toward Miss Goddard had never been improper. And even to herself it had been improper only that once.

As if she needed *guilt* to be added to all her other burdens.

She hoped Lord Heyward would *not* come. Perhaps Cousin Rosalie's butler had forgotten to deliver the letter. Perhaps he had not read it. Or perhaps he had merely laughed at it and dismissed its contents as the ravings of someone who had read too many Gothic novels.

"I believe the word *rake* needs to be

defined," she said. "Or at least it needs to be established what a rake is *not*. As I understand it from what the two of you have been saying, the hero of *Pamela* is not a rake at all, for it seems he tried on a number of occasions to take Pamela's virtue by force and quite against her will. That man is an out-and-out villain, who ought not to be dignified with the name of *rake*. A rake, though capable of all sorts of wild, debauched, *silly* behavior, is still first and foremost a gentleman. And a gentleman never *ever* deprives a woman — and I speak not just of *ladies* — of her virtue against her will."

"Oh, bravo," Lord Windrow said.

"Wonderfully well expressed," Miss Goddard said.

"A rake may never be reformed," Angeline said, "for most men believe it is a *manly* thing to be and something to which their gender entitles them. But they are not *villainous* for all that. Or, if they are, then they have put themselves beyond the pale of mere rakishness."

Lord Windrow and Miss Goddard both smiled at her — just as the door of the private sitting room crashed back against the wall and then slammed shut again.

Between the two swift, deafening actions

the Earl of Heyward appeared in the room.

Angeline clasped her hands to her bosom. Miss Goddard spread hers on the table. Lord Windrow, who had been sitting with his back to the door, got to his feet and turned.

"Ah, Heyward," he said. "Come to join us, have —"

Lord Heyward punched him right on the point of the chin. His head snapped back and he would have tumbled backward if the table had not been in the way. As it was, his back bounced off the lid of the teapot, sending it rolling across the table and clattering to the floor. The teapot tipped and spilled its contents over the cloth.

"Edward." Miss Goddard clutched two fistfuls of the tablecloth.

"Lord Heyward." Angeline lifted her clasped hands to her mouth and bit into one knuckle.

"You!" Lord Heyward, eyes blazing, grasped the lapels of Lord Windrow's coat and hoisted him upright. "Outside! Now! I have had enough of you."

"I rather thought that might be it, old chap," Lord Windrow said, touching his jaw rather gingerly with his fingertips. "It is one of those occasions when fists have already spoken louder than words."

"Lord Heyward!" Angeline cried, jumping to her feet. "I was *wrong.*"

Oh, she was going to do a terrible disservice to Miss Goddard, whose idea this had been. She was going to have to confess all, Angeline decided. She really had not expected that *fisticuffs* would be the result of her deception.

"Edward, no!" Miss Goddard was also on her feet. "Oh, Lord Windrow, I had no idea *this* would happen. How foolish of me not to have foreseen it. Edward, all is proper, as you can see. I am with Lady Angeline as a chaperon, and my maid is traveling with us too. We are indeed going to Norton Park to dine with Lady Windrow. I really, really ought not to have written that letter. Oh, now I know why deception is so very wrong. I am dreadfully sorry."

What letter?

Lord Windrow flexed his jaw as Lord Heyward's hold on his lapels relaxed slightly.

"I would be delighted to meet you whenever and wherever is convenient to you, Heyward," Lord Windrow said, "but I would really rather it not be today, if it is all the same to you. I may already have a bruise to explain away to my mother, whose health is not of the soundest. She may well have a fit of the vapors if I appear before her with bulbous nose and bloodshot, blackening eye — or perhaps even *eyes* — and a missing tooth or two. Besides, there are ladies present."

"A fact that did not seem to deter you last time," Lord Heyward said from between his teeth. But he dropped his hands to his sides, and some of the fire went out of him. "I will *not* have you bothering Lady Angeline Dudley, Windrow, now or ever. Even if she *is* properly chaperoned. Is that understood?"

Lord Windrow brushed his hands over his lapels.

"I suppose," he said, "you will not take a step back until I say *yes,* Heyward, will you? Yes it will have to be, then. I feel a certain discomfort with my nose a mere inch from yours."

Lord Heyward took a step back and turned his head to glare at Angeline.

What had he meant by saying Lord Windrow must not bother *her?* What about *Miss Goddard?*

"I shall remove myself entirely from the lady's presence," Lord Windrow said. "Miss Goddard will doubtless hold me steady if my legs should decide to wobble. Miss Goddard?" He turned to offer her his arm.

She looked pointedly at him as though there were a thousand things she wished to say. But then she closed her eyes briefly and shook her head slightly, took his arm, and allowed him to lead her from the room.

Angeline swallowed.

"I have a confession to make," she said. "I am so sorry. Not a word of that letter I wrote was true."

"What letter?" Lord Heyward's eyes narrowed.

"The one I left for you," she said. "The one Cousin Rosalie's butler was to give you at four."

"There seems to have been a good deal of letter-writing going on," he said. "Who gave the letter to the butler?"

"Miss Goddard," she said.

"Ah," he said. "I begin to understand that I no longer know Eunice to even the smallest degree."

"But you love her," she said. "And she loves you. This was all her idea, though admittedly it was I who originally suggested that you must be encouraged to acknowledge your feelings and the truth that you cannot live without her. What better way to realize that than through fear for her safety at the hands of a rake? And what better person to make you feel that way than Lord Windrow? I asked Rosalie to invite both him and Miss Goddard to Hallings so that I could arrange something — *and* make your family see that she is not vulgar at all, even if she is not strictly speaking a member of the *ton*. But I found I could not do it alone and so I took Miss Goddard into my confidence. She was both willing and eager to help implement my plan. But the first part did not work. Instead of going to rescue her from Lord Windrow when we were out walking yesterday, you insisted upon helping me get rid of the stone in my shoe instead, even though there was not really a stone in it at all. It was all a *ruse*. Miss Goddard said today that we needed more drastic action, and suggested *this* and the letter I left for you. And I did it, though I realize now I ought not to have, for there have been too many lies, and even apart from those I have been very unfair indeed to Lord Windrow, who has never treated either me or Miss Goddard with disrespect — well, except for that very first time. But no real harm was done then, was it? As soon as you pointed out his error to him, or *almost* as soon, he apologized — after you had insisted — and went on his way. And now I have caused him to get hurt. You hit him *very* hard. And it was all my fault. And nothing has worked as it ought, has it? Here you are talking to me instead of to Miss Goddard.

Or, rather, here I am talking to *you* instead of sending you after her. Oh, *why* does nothing work?"

And when, during her lengthy, muddled speech, had he stepped closer to her — closer even than he had been to Lord Windrow?

"Perhaps," he said softly, "because you have everything wrong, Angeline."

No *Lady* before her name?

She swallowed and gazed into his very blue eyes. She had no choice, really. There was nowhere else to look unless she stepped back, and there was no way of doing that without tripping over her chair.

"Do I?" she said.

"It is not *Eunice* I love," he said.

"Oh?"

She dared not hope. Oh, she *dared* not. Perhaps he only meant that he did not love anyone. Not in *that* way, anyway. Perhaps he had not changed. Perhaps he never would.

She sank her teeth into her lower lip.

"It is *you* I love," he said.

Oh.

Ohhh!

It was precisely at that moment that they both heard the unmistakable clopping of horses' hooves, and the rumbling of carriage wheels over the cobbles of the inn yard and out onto the street and along it until the sounds gradually faded into the distance.

"I am not at all sure," Eunice said from within Lord Windrow's carriage, "that we are doing the right thing. Indeed, I am rather sure we are doing the *wrong* thing. For I did not notice another carriage, did you? Edward must have ridden here, a complication I did not foresee."

Lord Windrow, seated across one corner of the carriage, his foot braced on the seat opposite, his arms crossed over his chest, regarded her with amused eyes from beneath drooped eyelids.

"My dear Miss Goddard," he said, "would a man about to race in pursuit of his lady love, whom he feared was being abducted by a black-hearted villain, stop to call out his carriage?"

"You knew, then," she said, "even when we devised this scheme? But what are they to do now?"

"Ride together on the same horse," he said. "A means of locomotion that is vastly romantic in theory, deucedly uncomfortable in practice. Hire a carriage. I daresay the Peacock has some rickety old thing that would serve the purpose. It would, however, and beyond all doubt, be deucedly uncomfortable in both theory and practice. Stay where they are until we return for them. That option has the potential for all sorts of comfort. They have at least three clear choices, then, as you can see."

"We *will* return for them?" she said. "Soon?"

"Tomorrow morning," he said, "after we have breakfasted at Norton and taken leave of my mother."

"But what if there *is* no carriage for hire?" she asked, frowning.

"Then their choices will be reduced to two," he said. "There will be less cause for dithering."

She turned her head to gaze at him.

"You do not really *believe* they will remain at the Peacock, do you?" she asked. "Edward would be the perfect gentleman, of course, and I daresay there are enough rooms for the two of them. It did not look a crowded place, did it? But even so, Lady Angeline would be *ruined.* We did not even leave her my maid."

He smiled lazily.

"I have distinct hopes for Heyward," he said. "That punch he threw — in front of *ladies* — hurt like Hades. I can *still* feel it. I do believe he may not act the gentleman at all tonight. I would not wager upon it, however. He has never been known to set a foot wrong in all of human history to date, and now he has already done it once today. He will either decide that that is quite enough adventure for the next millennium or two, or he will discover in himself a taste for anarchy. One can only hope. As my favorite groom in all the world liked to remark with great wisdom and no originality whatsoever when I was a child, one may lead a horse to water, but one cannot make him drink. And as for your maid, you have need of her yourself. My mother would have a fit of the vapors if you were to arrive unchaperoned, and she would scold me for a month after regaining consciousness. Besides, it may not have escaped your attention that your maid is quite happy to ride up on the box with my coachman and that he is quite happy to have her there. It would have been cruel to them both to have left her behind at the Peacock."

Eunice sighed.

"I never ought to have agreed to this perfectly mad scheme," she said. "For Lady Angeline *will* be ruined whether she comes to Norton unchaperoned later today or returns to Hallings unchaperoned tonight or — heaven forbid — remains at the

Peacock until our return tomorrow morning. And I will blame myself for the rest of my life. Whatever was I thinking?"

Lord Windrow reached out and took her hand in his.

"*You* were thinking of bringing your two friends together in a match made in heaven," he said, "since they did not seem to possess the good sense to do it for themselves. *I* was thinking of a way to get you to myself again for a while."

She looked down at their hands for a moment before curling her fingers about his and sighing again.

"I ought not to encourage you," she said. "You *are* a rake."

"Ah," he said, "but even Lady Angeline Dudley admits that rakes may sometimes be reformed. It is certainly within the bounds of possibility that I may be one of their number. Not probability, perhaps — she did speak of it rather as if it resembled a Forlorn Hope, did she not? But definitely a *possibility*."

"I am the daughter of a Cambridge don," Eunice said apropos of nothing.

"I daresay," he said, "he is fiendishly intelligent and bookish."

"He is," she agreed.

"Both of which traits he has passed on to

you," he said.

"Yes," she agreed. "Though perhaps not the *fiendishly* part."

He lifted her hand and set the back of it briefly against his lips.

"May intelligent, bookish ladies sometimes be reformed?" he asked her.

She thought about it.

"I suppose it may be within the bounds of possibility," she said, "even if not of probability."

"Under what circumstances might it?" he asked.

"I have discovered within myself in the last while," she said, "a desire to . . ."

"Yes?" he prompted her when she fell silent.

"To *enjoy* life," she said.

"And you cannot enjoy being intelligent and bookish?" he asked.

"I can *appreciate* both," she said. "I always have and always will. I certainly have no wish to renounce either. I just want to . . . to have some *fun.*"

"Ah." He returned their hands to the seat between them. "I like the sound of this."

"Edward and I thought we would suit admirably when we made that agreement four years ago," she said. "We were and are alike in many ways. But when I saw him again earlier this spring in London after not seeing him for well over a year, I knew immediately that it was impossible, and not only because by then he was the Earl of Heyward and more was expected of him than to marry someone like me. I also knew that he needed someone to brighten his life, to lift the load of duty and responsibility that he shouldered without complaint after his brother died. I could not do that. I cannot be . . . merry unless someone draws merriment out of me. I have no experience of my own. And then, at the Tresham ball, when you danced with Lady Angeline and Edward and I came to sit at your table during supper, I could see immediately that she admired him and that he was unaccountably concerned about her safety even while he was irritated by her. And I knew that she was *just* the wife he needed. As I got to know her better, I could see too that he was *just* the husband for her. She needs steadiness and he needs . . . joy. And I knew too that I felt a little depressed at the loss of what for four years I had thought I wanted. But I did not want that dream back, or Edward, dearly as I love him. For I realized that I would like some joy too. Or at least a little fun."

"Have you had fun with me, Eunice?" he

asked softly.

She looked sharply at him but let his use of her given name go.

"I have," she said. "You *are* fun — intelligent and sharp-minded and witty and irreverent."

"I sound like a dreadfully dull dog," he said.

"Oh," she said, "and you are handsome and . . . *attractive* and you kiss well. Not that I have anything with which to compare that kiss, but I would be very surprised if even the most experienced of courtesans would not agree with me. There! Is your vanity satisfied?"

He grinned slowly at her.

"We are here," he said. "Come and meet my mother. We will warn her, by the way, that she may expect two more guests, though they have been unfortunately delayed at the Peacock by carriage troubles and may well decide to return to Hallings once the carriage is roadworthy again."

"Oh," Eunice said with a sigh. "I have told more lies in the last few days than I have in my whole life before. After today there will be no more."

And then he escorted her into the grand house of Norton Park and up the winding staircase to the drawing room, where Lady

Windrow was waiting to greet them, a warm smile on her fragile face.

"Charles," she said as he enclosed her in his arms and kissed her cheek and wished her a happy birthday. "I told you when you went to Hallings that you must not dream of coming all the way back here just for my birthday. Ten miles is a long way."

"How could I *not* come for such an occasion, Mama?" he said. "Have I ever missed being with you on your birthday?"

He turned, one arm about her waist, and her eyes rested upon Eunice, who curtsied.

"Besides," he said, "I had another reason for coming, one that will delight you, I believe, as you have been pestering me for years. I wanted you to meet Miss Goddard, the lady I plan one day soon, when the setting and the atmosphere are quite perfect, to ask to marry me. It is time, you see, to do that most dreaded of all things to men, though suddenly it does not seem so dreadful after all. Indeed, it seems infinitely desirable. It is time to settle down."

He smiled sleepily at Eunice, who gazed briefly and reproachfully back at him, her eyebrows raised, her cheeks pink, before wishing his mother a happy birthday.

CHAPTER 20

"What was *that?*" Angeline asked after they had listened for a few moments.

Edward assumed the question was rhetorical since it would have been obvious even to an imbecile what they had just heard, but she was waiting for his answer, all wide-eyed and pale-faced.

"It was a carriage leaving the inn," he said. "Windrow's, no doubt. He is taking Eunice and probably her maid to Norton Park to dine with Lady Windrow."

"Without waiting for *us?*" Her dark eyes grew larger, if that were possible.

"I daresay," he said, "they hope to dine before midnight and fear that that hope may be dashed if they wait. I daresay they think you and I have a few things to work out between us. And no doubt Windrow does not particularly relish the thought of sharing carriage space with me so soon after I hit him. The fact that he did not hit back or accept my invitation to step outside indicated, of course, that he was a party to Eunice's scheme — even perhaps the instigator. And Eunice will have seen the success of her plan, even though she was alarmed at the flaring of violence, and will have considered it fitting — or perhaps she has been persuaded to consider it fitting — to leave us alone to settle what is between us."

"Miss Goddard's *scheme*," she said, "was that I leave that letter for you, so that you would come hurrying after us to rescue *her* from Lord Windrow's clutches. Yet you have just allowed him to drive off with her."

"I would like to read that letter sometime," he said. "I suppose it is a marvel of Gothic literature. But before I came to rescue *you*, it was a letter from Eunice that I read. It was restrained in tone but really rather clever and quite effective. As you see, here I am."

And he was beginning to feel just a little angry, in a different way than he had been feeling until a few minutes ago. He was everyone's puppet, it seemed, and he had been dancing to everyone's tune. Well, to Eunice's, anyway, and that infernal Windrow's. Lady Angeline's was less effective.

"*What* did you say?" She frowned suddenly.

"When?"

"Just before the carriage left," she said.

"It is *you* I love," he repeated, gazing steadily into her eyes.

And it is you I could shake until your teeth rattle. But he did not say those words aloud. Actually it was all part of the same feeling. She fascinated him and annoyed him. She exhilarated him and infuriated him. He adored her and could cheerfully throttle her, even if only *very* figuratively speaking. Theirs would *not* be a match made in heaven. There would be nothing placidly comfortable about their lifelong relationship. But one thing was certain. He knew he was *alive* when he was with her, whatever the devil that meant.

Whatever the devil it *did* mean, it made all the difference.

And he was not even sure what *that* meant.

"I *love* you," he added since she was uncharacteristically mute.

Her eyes seemed to fill her face. And they were swimming in unshed tears.

"You do not." Her voice was accusing. "You do not believe in love."

"If I ever said anything so asinine," he said, "I must have been lying. I love my

450

mother and my sisters and my grandmother and my nieces and nephews. I even love my grandfather. And I love you — in an *entirely* different way. I am going to ask you again to marry me. I'll do it when we are back at Hallings and when the time seems right. And *this* time I am not going to go down on one knee. Whoever started that ridiculous tradition ought to be horsewhipped, except that I suppose he is long dead."

She was smiling through her tears.

"I will not demand it of you," she said. "But how do you know I will say yes?"

He wagged one finger pendulum fashion before her face.

"No more games," he said. "There have been enough games to last us both a lifetime, Angeline. They are at an end. I am going to offer you marriage because I love you and would be unable to live a happy, fulfilled life without you. And you are going to marry me because you love me."

A wave of uncertainty washed over him, but he mentally shook it off. It was time to take a stand. He had the feeling he would be doing it for the rest of his life — except when she was bowling him over with some madness or he was simply indulging her because he had no desire whatsoever to take a stand.

Devil take it, life was going to be complicated. He was never going to know whether he stood on his feet or on his head.

"You are very sure of yourself," she said.

"I am." He clasped his hands behind his back and resisted the foolish urge to cross his fingers.

The private parlor, indeed the whole inn, was suddenly very quiet. Somewhere in the distance a clock ticked loudly.

"We had better follow Miss Goddard and Lord Windrow in your carriage," she said. "Perhaps we can catch up to them before they reach Norton, and our traveling alone together will not appear too, too improper."

"I do not have a carriage with me," he said. "I rode here."

"Oh." She bit her bottom lip. "Whatever are we going to *do,* then?"

He had known what they were going to do the moment he heard Windrow's carriage drive away. He had known it with a ruthless certainty, just as he knew that Windrow would stop here for them in the morning. He would not wish to arrive back at Hallings alone with Eunice, after all, even if she *did* have a maid with her. Good Lord, he might feel obliged to offer for her, and that would be a disaster of catastrophic proportions for Windrow — not to mention Eunice.

"We are going to stay here," he said.

Her eyes widened again. "Tresham would *kill* me," she said. "So would Ferdie. Do you suppose there are two free rooms?"

He guessed there were as many free rooms as there were rooms at the inn, but it was an academic point.

"I have no doubt there is *one* free room," he said, "which we will take. As Mr. and Mrs. Ailsbury. Have a seat and I will go and see to it."

Her lips parted and color flooded her cheeks. Her mouth formed an O, but no sound came out.

He leaned an inch or two closer to her and searched her eyes with his own.

"The time for games is over, Angeline," he said again. "And the time for misunderstandings. It is time to love."

But not yet in *that* way, surely. Such a thing would have been unthinkable to him just a week ago. Even yesterday. Even an hour ago. What *was* he thinking? But he did not particularly want to know. He had spent his *life* thinking, reasoning, figuring out what was the right and proper thing to do, working out how not to hurt those he loved and those in his care. He *had* loved. All his life. And yet he had never . . . *loved.*

Yes, sometimes thought was pointless. For some things were beyond thought or at least beyond logic.

Love had always been a duty, even if the love had been genuine.

Love had never been . . . freedom.

Freedom to ruin an innocent young lady?

Freedom to *love* her.

"Tell me you love me," he said.

"I love you," she told him.

"Tell me you will stay here with me," he said. "Tell me you *want* to. Or tell me not and I will contrive something. There is probably some carriage or gig here I can hire to take you to Norton."

So much for forceful, masterful behavior. So much for taking a stand.

"I will stay," she said. "I will go to the ends of the earth with you if you ask it of me. I will —" She smiled and bit her lip. "You do not want a speech, do you?"

"Are you quite sure?" he murmured.

She gazed into his eyes and nodded — which was speech enough.

It was a surprisingly large chamber for such an insignificant-looking inn. It was square and neat and light and airy. There were wooden beams overhead, some of them sloping with the shape of the roof down over the head of the bed, which had no canopy. The window looked out on fields and meadows and was framed by pretty, flower-patterned white curtains.

The bed was covered with a counterpane that matched the curtains. There was an upright chair on either side of the bed. There was a washstand with bowl and jug, and a large wooden dresser with a square mirror attached to it.

Angeline could see her image in the mirror even though she was standing some distance from it. She could see her hat, a straw wide-brimmed bonnet trimmed with a whole meadow of flowers of all descriptions and colors. It was definitely her favorite — well, *one* of her favorites, anyway. It was tied beneath her chin with bright green silk ribbons. She pulled the ribbons loose and removed the hat. She hooked it over the uprights of one of the chairs.

Then she felt naked. An unfortunate thought.

Lord Heyward had crossed the room and was opening the window as wide as it would go and then closing the curtains over it. They flapped gently in the breeze. They did not dim the light but only made it softer, somehow more rosy-hued. The air smelled enticingly of country and clover and horse. Somewhere close to the inn a horse whinnied. Much farther away a dog barked. A whole choir of birds was singing.

Angeline's heartbeat was thundering in her ears. She felt slightly sick with fear and excitement.

He was looking at her from over by the window.

"Would you like to dine first?" he asked.

First?

"I just had tea," she said.

He had not, of course. Perhaps he was hungry. Probably he was hungry. He was coming toward her across the room, skirting around the end of the bed as he did so. He stopped in front of her, framed her face with his hands, pushing his fingers into her hair as he did so, and kissed her. She set her hands on either side of his waist beneath his coat.

It had sounded a little silly when she had said it downstairs earlier, but she had meant it. She *still* meant it. She would follow him to the ends of the earth if he asked it of her. And he loved *her,* not Miss Goddard.

He *loved* her. He would be unable to live a happy life without her.

He had lifted his head and was gazing into her eyes. And his fingers, she realized, were working the pins free of her hair. She slid her hands up under the silk of his waistcoat and spread her fingers over his back on top of his shirt. He was very warm. Her hair fell suddenly over his hands, about her shoulders, down her back.

"Edward," she whispered.

"Yes."

She had never spoken his name before, even in her mind. It seemed not quite to belong to him. Except that it belonged to her lover. Her soon-to-be lover. She swallowed.

He lowered his head again to kiss her just beneath one earlobe. His tongue flicked over a tender spot she had not known was there, and a surge of something raw, almost painful, darted down through her body and along her inner thighs to weaken her knees. Her toes curled inside her shoes.

His hands were working at the back of her dress, opening the buttons there. She slid her hands free as his mouth moved beneath her chin and down along her throat, and she moved them to undo the buttons of his waistcoat.

She spread her hands over his chest as her dress parted down the back and his hands crossed inside it to pull her against him. He lifted his head and kissed her mouth again, his own open and hot and demanding, his tongue pressing inside and caressing surfaces until that raw feeling returned and multiplied. Her hands were trapped between them.

And then he raised his head again and looked at her with an intense look in his eyes that she had not seen before — something heavy, something . . . passionate. She dropped her arms to her sides, and he drew her dress off her shoulders and down her arms until it fell about her feet, leaving her clad only in her flimsy undergarments and silk stockings and shoes.

He turned to the bed and drew back the counterpane and the top sheet before drawing off her undergarments.

"Sit down on the edge of the bed," he said then, and she sat after kicking off her shoes.

He kneeled down in front of her, took one of her feet to set on his thigh, and drew off her stocking before moving to the other foot.

He was in no hurry. It was almost as if he savored every moment. But how *could* he? Angeline hummed with . . . something. Something terribly needy. But of course, she was naked — entirely so once her stockings were gone — and he was not.

She was *naked* in a room alone with a man in broad daylight.

She fairly pulsed with . . . whatever it was.

But really there *was* no hurry. *It is time to love,* he had said downstairs. And time was not always just one second long or even one minute or one hour. Those were artificial divisions, imposed by humankind. Time was infinite. And it was time to love.

"Lie down," he said, but she got to her feet instead and reached for his coat. One hand blocked her. "No."

"Yes," she said, and his hand fell away.

She undressed him slowly and terribly inexpertly. His coat, she decided before it was off, must surely have been sewn onto him. It was no wonder valets were often hefty-looking men. His waistcoat, by contrast, its buttons already undone, slid off over his shirt and fell to the floor with no trouble at all. She tugged his shirt free of his breeches, and he lifted his arms while she pulled it off over his head.

She got distracted then. So did he, she suspected. For he was taller than she, and she had to lean into him in order to get the shirt off his arms — he did not lower them or lean forward to make her task easier, of course — and her breasts pressed against his chest and the shock of it, naked flesh to naked flesh, had her closing her eyes and drawing a sharp breath and staying just where she was, her own arms raised along his, his shirt bunched above them like a limp flag.

Their eyes met, and then their lips met, and then his shirt went fluttering over her head and his arms came about her and hers about him and she almost swooned at the sheer masculinity of him. She could smell his cologne and something else — *him*. Perhaps it was sweat, but who would have thought that sweat could smell so gloriously enticing?

"You are still half clothed," she said against his mouth.

"I am," he agreed.

She slid her hands to his waist and fumbled with the buttons there until she had them all undone.

And then terror, embarrassment, maidenly modesty, sheer uncontainable excitement, some instinct for self-preservation and very survival — *something* silly anyway — took over and paralyzed her, and she could go no further.

She wormed away from him and lay down on the bed, her head on one of the pillows. She did not draw up the covers even though the air from the window felt suddenly cool. She shivered, though somehow not from cold, and smiled at him — and watched as he pulled off his boots and his stockings, his breeches and his drawers.

And then he was as naked as she and a hot desert blast had replaced the cool breeze coming through the window.

Oh, goodness. Oh, goodness, oh, goodness.

She had seen her brothers when they were boys. They had all gone swimming and diving together, usually in forbidden deep waters, but while she had always kept her shift on, they had never deemed it necessary to keep their drawers on in front of a mere sister.

She had thought she knew what to expect.

But boys grew into men, and sometimes men felt . . . passionate.

And, oh, goodness.

Had her mind ever described him — even if approvingly — as an *ordinary man?*

He was all solid malehood, beautifully proportioned, well muscled in the places he ought to be muscled, lean elsewhere, and . . . well, modesty prevented her from adding anything else to the mental review of his attributes.

His eyes were roaming over her too, she realized.

"I am too tall," she said.

"I know," he said, "that at one time you

were a beanpole and were described as such."

"Yes," she said. "I was the despair of my mother, whose height I overtook when I was twelve. And at that time I had no shape whatsoever, unless an arrow has shape."

"Angeline," he said, and there was something about his voice — for one thing, it was deeper than usual, huskier, "you are no longer a beanpole."

She knew that. But his words implied more. His eyes implied more. His *voice* did. And suddenly and gloriously she knew that she was beautiful, that she had grown into this tall, dark bloom that was herself, and that she was perfect. Perfectly who she was and who she was meant to be. And perfectly loved by Edward Ailsbury, Earl of Heyward.

She blinked several times and swallowed, and reached up her arms for him.

"It is time for love," she said, and realized that she had spoken aloud.

"Yes," he said and came down onto the bed close beside her and raised himself on one elbow to lean over her.

Terror returned for a moment, but it soon vanished. For of course, she had been right a little while ago. Time was infinite. There was no hurry. *Loving* for now was more important than having loved. His mouth moved over hers and over *her,* and his hands moved and his fingers and his legs. And she was being loved slowly and tenderly and maddeningly until all terror was forgotten and only the need, the loving, remained.

She knew nothing. And that was an understatement. Her mother had told her nothing and Miss Pratt certainly had not — probably because she knew nothing herself. Cousin Rosalie had told her nothing. Why should she? Angeline had rejected every marriage proposal she had had, and Rosalie certainly could not have foreseen *this.*

And yet knowledge, experience, really did not matter at all, she discovered during the minutes or hours or infinity that passed after they had lain down together. Her hands, her mouth roamed where they would, instinct and need and his own deep inhalations and muffled exclamations leading her on. Embarrassment and maidenly modesty fled with the terror, and she touched him everywhere, even — eventually — *there.*

He gasped and she closed her hand about him. He was long and thick and rock hard, and soon he was going to be right inside her — she had not spent her life in and out of farmyards without learning a thing or two. No, not *rock* hard, for he was warm and pulsing and alive.

"Angeline," he said, and his hand came between her thighs and parted folds and probed the most private, secret parts of herself. She could both feel and hear wetness but was embarrassed only fleetingly. It *felt* right and so it must *be* right. His hand felt almost cool against her heat.

"Yes," she said. "Yes."

And one of his arms came about her and under her and turned her fully onto her back, and he came over her and lowered his weight on top of her while his other hand came beneath her too. And he lifted her, tilted her as his knees came between her thighs and pressed them wide apart. She felt him *there,* felt panic, quelled it, and he was pressing inward with a slow, steady thrust until she felt stretched to the limit and felt a return of the panic. He paused for a moment and then thrust hard and deep.

There was a moment when pain was so sharp it was unbearable, and then, before she could either cry out or squirm away from him, it was gone, leaving behind only an almost pleasurable soreness, and he was deep, deep in her. She belonged to him, he belonged to her. And she ached and ached.

She opened her eyes. He had raised himself on his elbows and was gazing into her eyes.

"I am sorry," he whispered.

"I am not." She smiled.

She had never averted her eyes in the farmyard or out in the meadows, even though any modest lady would certainly have looked sharply away *and* suffered heart palpitations. Even so, she had not really expected what followed. When she had watched, she had seen the action only from the outside, with none of the physical sensations that went with the action. Now she felt it from the *inside,* and the sensations were so startlingly different from anything in her experience before them that she could only *feel* them and not even try to convert them into language in her mind.

There was no hurry. There was absolutely no hurry. She did not know how long it lasted in minutes. But it lasted a long, long time while he worked her with steady, deep, hard rhythm, a rhythm accentuated by the wet suction of their coupling, and pleasure hummed through her and only gradually built to something more than pleasure but not quite pain. Even the soreness was not quite painful.

Until it all was. And until his movements told her that he felt it too. His hands went beneath her once more, his full weight came down on her, and the rhythm changed as he worked with greater urgency. And something broke in her just when she felt she could stand it no longer, and at the same moment he held rigid and deep in her and made a sound deep in his throat. And she felt a hot flow inside and he relaxed down onto her and she relaxed beneath him, and for an indeterminate time the world went away and yet floated hazily somewhere above her consciousness. She could hear the curtains fluttering and birds singing.

Even infinity had an end.

They *had loved.* And somehow having loved was quite as beautiful as loving. For of course there was no real end to it.

Infinity might have an end, but love did not.

CHAPTER 21

Edward was lying on his back on the bed, one hand over his eyes, one leg bent at the knee, his foot flat on the mattress. He was listening to the soothing sounds of birds singing and the curtain flapping at the window. The air was cool on his naked body, though not cool enough that he was tempted to pull up the covers. Angeline's hand was in his, her arm against him. Both were warm.

He was relaxed. Utterly, totally relaxed in both body and mind. He had expected, when rational thought returned following the sex, that he would feel guilty. What he had done was reprehensible in every sense of the word. But instead he was relaxed. And happy.

Nothing had ever felt so right in his life.

He could have drifted off to sleep. He had chosen instead to float on the edge of consciousness, to savor the delicious feeling of rightness and happiness. Angeline was sleeping — he could tell from the soft evenness of her breathing. She had murmured sleepily when he disengaged from her and moved to her side, but then she had sighed and gone back to sleep.

Her hair was in a fragrant tangle over his shoulder.

Angeline Dudley. Whoever would have thought?

There was some pinkish dried blood on her inner thigh, he had seen, but no dreadful mess. He would clean it off afterward with water from the basin, if it would not embarrass her horribly to have him do such a thing for her. It struck him suddenly that the small intimacies of marriage, not just the sexual ones, were going to bring him enormous pleasure. It struck him that *marriage* was going to bring him enormous pleasure.

Why had he thought just the opposite even a week ago, even a few days ago? Even when he had looked forward to marriage with Eunice, he had not thought of it in terms of pleasure. But he did not want to think about Eunice. He hoped she really would *not* be disappointed when he announced his betrothal to Angeline. And he hoped she was not becoming infatuated with Windrow.

But, no, surely not. She was far too sensible.

And then Angeline drew a deep, ragged breath through her nose and let it out slowly through her mouth with a sigh — a long, satisfied-sounding sigh. He turned his head to smile at her. He hoped she would not be assaulted with guilt when she came fully awake. She had a great deal more to lose from all this than he did, after all.

Though he had his life to lose if Tresham happened to find out. The thought did nothing to dim his smile.

She did not come awake gradually, however — unless the slow inhale and exhale qualified as gradual. By the time he had finished turning his head, she had abandoned his hand and was scrambling up onto her knees beside him. She leaned over him, one hand on the bed, the other on his chest, and her eyes sparkled into his. Her hair was a tangled cloud all about her.

"Now," she said, "I am your *mistress.*"

As though it were the pinnacle of achievement to which all properly brought-up young ladies ought to aspire.

Good Lord! All his relaxed contentment fled out the window.

"You dashed well are *not,*" he said. Had she misunderstood? She could not *possibly* have. He had talked of marriage. He had told her he was going to make her another offer. "You are going to be my *wife.*"

"After you have asked nicely and I have said yes," she said, "back at Hallings tomorrow or the next day. Today I am your mistress. Your *secret* mistress."

"Mistresses get *paid* for their services," he said. "We are going to be *married,* Angeline. Just don't get any ideas about refusing me. I swear I'll —"

"When we get up later to dine," she said, both hands on his chest now close to his shoulders, her face hovering over his, her hair like a curtain on either side of them, "you will pay me — what is an appropriate sum? But no matter. It is merely a token payment. You will pay me one sovereign, and it will be official. I am your secret mistress. It sounds very wicked. It sounds delicious. Admit it."

Indignation wilted and he laughed.

"Edward," she said softly.

"Angie."

"And that will be another secret," she said. "Your name. I will only ever use it when we are together like this."

"Man and mistress?" he said. "*Employer* and mistress? Is it going to cost me a sovereign every time? It could get expensive."

470

"You can afford it," she said. "You can afford *me.* You have to, do you not, for you cannot live happily without me. You have already admitted it. My price, though, is one sovereign to cover the first eighty years. After that we will negotiate."

"In that case," he said, "I will be generous and make it a guinea."

"I will always call you Heyward when we are not alone together like this," she said, "and no one will *know.* I will be your secret mistress all the rest of our lives and no one will suspect a thing. My brothers will always think you are nothing but a dry old stick and will pity me and wonder how I can stand such a dull marriage."

"That is what they call me?" he asked her. He took her by the elbows and eased her down so that her bosom was against his chest and her face was a mere couple of inches above his own.

"That is it," she said, smiling. "They have *no idea,* and they never will."

Her eyes were bright with warm laughter and love. His own smile faded.

"Angeline," he said, "that is precisely what I am, you know. I cannot countenance any wildness in myself or extravagance or drunkenness or debauchery or gambling or recklessness — apart from today, that is, when I have broken just about every rule I could possibly break. I will never change. I am just an ordinary man, a very proper man, a dull man. There will be very little excitement in your life if — *when* you marry me. *If* is no longer an option for you, I am afraid. But you must not glamorize me. You will only be the more disappointed when the truth becomes apparent to you."

Her smile had softened. She laid her head on his chest, turning her face so that one cheek was against him.

"You still do not quite understand, do you?" she said softly. "I do not *want* you to change. I fell head over ears in love with you the first time I saw you just because you are who you are. You were there behind me at that inn before Lord Windrow came inside, were you not? Yet you uttered not one improper word. When *he* did, you chose to reprimand him rather than ignore him or leave the room. When he would have fought you, you pointed out how illogical violence would be under the circumstances, even though I am sure you could have beaten him and even though you then stood accused of being a coward. When he would have left, you stepped between him and the door and insisted that he apologize to me. And then, rather than speak to me when we had not been formally introduced, you left without a word. I did not know for sure until then that there were gentlemen like you. I had experience only with gentlemen like my father and my brothers and their friends. I did not want to marry anyone like them, for whoever I chose would not remain faithful for long, and how can there be marriage and parenthood and contentment and friendship and happiness and growing old together unless there is fidelity? Maybe my mother would have been different if my father had been. Maybe she would have been happy. Maybe she would have remained at home more. Maybe she would have enjoyed us — *me.* From the moment I saw you, I wanted you. I desperately, desperately wanted you. And not just someone *like* you, though that is what I had hoped to find when I left home, even though I doubted and still doubt that there are many such men. I wanted you just as you were, and I *want* you just as you are. I want you to live your dull, blameless life of duty and responsibility. I want you to be a very proper, perhaps even stern husband. I want you to make me feel you *care.* I want you to be a father who spends more time than is fashionable with his children. And in private, when we are alone together, I want you to be *Edward,* my secret and wonderful lover."

His chest was wet. But he would have known anyway that she was weeping. Her voice had become increasingly unsteady as she spoke. He wrapped his arms about her and pressed his smiling mouth to the top of her head.

"Actually," she said a few minutes later, and her voice was steady again, "it is silly to say I do not want you to change. For we all must change or remain static in life, and *that* would be quite undesirable. We would still think and speak and act at the age of thirty and sixty as we did at the age of fourteen. *Of course* we must change and ought to change. You did not love me at Vauxhall. You only lusted after me, or, if that is too vulgar a notion, then you were simply affected by the seclusion of that clearing among the trees and by the moonlight and the distant music. When you came the next day to offer me marriage, you did not believe in love, not *romantic* love, anyway. Now you do. I thoroughly approve of *that* change in you, though I do not suppose it is a real change, is it? You have always been a loving person, after all. It is just that you had not yet opened your heart to that extra dimension of your being. And I have changed too. I knew that I would have no trouble finding a husband once I had made my come-out, for I am Lady Angeline Dudley and all sorts of men would want to marry me even if I looked like a hyena and had the personality of a toad — not that I know anything about the personality of toads, of course. I may be doing them a dreadful injustice. Perhaps they are the most fascinating of creatures. But you know what I mean. I hoped to find a man worthy of my love, though I really did not believe I could ever be worthy of *his*. I have always thought myself ugly and stupid and unladylike and . . . Well, a whole host of other depressing things. But now I know that I am beautiful and bright and an *original* and . . . Am I being boastful?"

He was laughing softly but with great tenderness too, for there was sudden vulnerability in her voice again. He rolled over with her until their positions were reversed and she was lying flat on the bed with him half over her. He kissed her eyes, her mouth.

"Angie," he said, "never stop talking, my love. You are an eternal delight to me. Or if I may make an instant amendment to what I have just said, *do* stop talking occasionally so that I may snatch a few hours of sleep each night and so that I may concentrate upon making love to my secret mistress whenever the spirit moves one or the other of us or both and so that I may read the morning papers and the morning post and . . . Well, I daresay you know what I am saying. But never cease your chattering. And before you ask, I adore today's bonnet. I assume there is straw beneath all the flowers? You must have a particularly strong neck to hold up all that weight."

And then they were both laughing, their noses brushing together.

"You lie through your teeth," she said. "You think it is hideous."

"Not so," he protested. "On this occasion I speak the solemn truth. When I stepped into the parlor downstairs earlier, I thought for a moment that I had opened the wrong door and had gone into the garden by mistake. A beautiful garden."

She gazed wistfully up at him.

"You punched Lord Windrow on the chin," she said, "because you thought he was abducting me."

"So much," he said ruefully, "for unnecessary violence."

"You were quite, quite splendid," she told him. "But poor Lord Windrow, when really he has eyes for no one but Miss Goddard."

He frowned.

"He had better not hurt or compromise

476

her," he said, "or he is going to meet with more than just a single punch to the jaw."

"But she has eyes for no one but him," she said, wrapping her arms about his neck. "Can you not see, Edward, that they are perfect for each other?"

The logic of women again!

"He really is *not* a committed rake," she said. "I have realized that for some time. He has merely been waiting to fall in love with someone who will hold him steady for the rest of his life. Besides, he loves his mother."

He frowned for a second or two longer, for he really was not convinced. But then he could not help laughing. Perhaps there was room in this life for women's logic as well as for his own far more sensible reasoning skills.

He kissed her, an action that took care of an indeterminate number of minutes — but who was counting? — before he withdrew somewhat reluctantly.

"We must stop there while I still can," he said. "We must not go any further yet, perhaps not even tonight. You must be very sore."

"A little," she admitted. "It feels good."

"It would not," he said, "if I were to try acting the great lover again."

"No, probably not," she agreed.

"Are you hungry?" he asked her.

"Starved," she said.

He rolled away from her and swung his legs over the side of the bed. He got to his feet and crossed the room to the washstand.

"Stay where you are," he said. "I am going to wash you."

"Oh," she said. As he approached the bed again with a wet cloth and the bowl, her eyes moved over his naked body and she smiled. "I love you terribly much, you know, Edward. I just wish there were words."

Perhaps it was just as well there were not. She might *never* stop talking.

"If there were," he said, sitting down on the side of the bed and setting about his task, "I would be the one saying them, Angie."

Eunice was sitting very upright in the carriage, her back straight and barely touching the cushions behind her. Her feet were set neatly side by side on the floor. Her hands were cupped one above the other in her lap. Her eyes were on them.

Lord Windrow was slouched comfortably across the corner beside her, his hat tipped slightly over his half-closed eyes. But beneath the indolent eyelids he was watching her keenly.

They had just taken leave of his mother and were on their way back to Hallings. They would stop at the Peacock Inn so that he could reclaim his own horses and see if Heyward and Lady Angeline Dudley were indeed still there.

Eunice's maid had glanced at the sky before the carriage left Norton, seen with obvious relief that the clouds, though low, did not seem to harbor the intention of raining upon the earth beneath just yet, and hopped up onto the box to renew her acquaintance with the coachman, who made room for her without any apparent resentment.

"Lady Windrow was very kind and very gracious," Eunice said, "considering what you said to her yesterday, which, by the way, you had *no right* saying. She must be dreadfully alarmed."

"What I said," he reminded her, "was that I intend to ask you to marry me when the time seems appropriate. I have every right to express my intentions to whoever is willing to listen. If I choose to tell you that I intend flying to the moon, you may feel justified in calling me a nincompoop or you may merely yawn and nod off to sleep, but you cannot challenge my *right* to express such an intention. If memory serves you correctly, you will be forced to admit that I did not say I was going to marry you, only that I was going to *ask* you. Am I right?"

She would have loved to say no. He could see that. But honesty compelled her to tell the truth — or to avoid it.

"You still had no right to embarrass me and alarm your mother," she said.

He crossed his arms and braced one foot against the seat opposite.

"You are perfectly correct," he said. "I did not have any such right."

Her lips tightened.

"Let me get this right," he said. "I embarrass you. I know that I also excite you, Eunice, but that is for private lustful moments only, is it? In public you are embarrassed to be seen with me. Dear me. I suppose it *is* lowering for an intelligent, bookish female to be seen in the company of a mindless rake."

"That is not what I meant at all," she said, turning her head to look at him. "Oh, you know very well it is not what I meant."

His eyes grew sleepier as she glared at him, and he dipped his head a little lower so that his hat brim shaded them more.

"It must be the opposite, then," he said. "The poor little bluestocking daughter of a university don is consumed by awkward embarrassment at being seen in the company of a rich, titled gentleman of the *ton*. She feels so far out of her depth that she fears drowning."

She gazed mutely at him for a moment and then clucked her tongue.

"What utter drivel," she said.

He sighed.

"I am running out of guesses," he said. "I give in. You win. Tell me why my words to my mother embarrassed you."

"Because . . ." she began. She shook her head. "Well, *look* at me."

Plain, sensible shoes. Plain, sensible high-waisted dress and plain white gloves. Plain, sensible bonnet covering neatly combed brown hair caught in an equally neat knot at her neck. Sensible face — *not* plain. Neat figure, not voluptuous, not its opposite either.

"I know," he said. "There is a wart or a mole hidden under those clothes, is there not? Either one would definitely do it. Confess and I will order the carriage turned around so that I can return and tell my mother that I am not after all going to offer you marriage."

She looked at him with tight-lipped exasperation and then burst out laughing.

"Oh, come now," she said. "Admit it. You

did not mean a word. You could not possibly wish to marry me."

"I would lie to my own mother?" He raised his eyebrows. "What a dastardly thing to suggest. On her birthday too. But let me see. Why would I wish to marry you? Perhaps it is your looks, which utterly charm me. Or your wit, which seduces me. Or your mind, for which I feel a powerful, unbridled lust. Or perhaps it is the simple fact that I like you, that I enjoy talking with you and being with you, that I enjoy kissing you and would love nothing better than to do a great deal more than kiss you. Or perhaps it is that I have a hankering to see what you will look like and to know what you will *be* like at the age of thirty and forty and fifty and on upward until death do us part. Or perhaps I am curious to discover what sort of babies we may create together. Or perhaps it is that I have never, *ever* entertained these thoughts before in connection with any woman or even *not* in connection with any specific woman. I believe I must be in love with you, Eunice. Head over ears. Is that the correct expression? Windrow in love. *I* am the one who should be feeling all the embarrassment, not you."

She was staring fixedly at him.

"But your mother must be *so* upset," she

482

said. "You are her only son, Lord Windrow, her only *child.* She must expect so much more of you."

"She was merely being polite, then," he asked, "when she hugged you and kissed you just now? And when she sat beside you on the love seat in the drawing room all last evening, taking the place I had coveted, her arm drawn through yours? My mother was the enormously wealthy only daughter of an enormously wealthy merchant when she married my father. She married him for love, and he married her for the same reason, even though his own finances were rather strained at the time of their marriage. He died four years ago after thirty-five years of marriage, leaving her brokenhearted, though she told me just last night after you had gone to bed that she would not trade those thirty-five years and her heartbreak now for a lifetime with any other man. For some time she has been hoping I will marry. She wants a daughter-in-law and she wants grandchildren. But most of all she wants to see me happy. She wants me to find the sort of love she and my father had. She fell in love with you on sight. You were very different, she said, from the sort of woman she feared I might choose — and that was *not* an insult. It was the highest praise. The only fear my mother has this morning is that perhaps you will say no. She knows I have not always lived the most exemplary of existences during the years since I left home to go to university."

Her eyes were still steady on his. He took off his tall hat and tossed it onto the seat opposite.

"*Will* you say no?" he asked.

He saw her swallow.

"Are you asking?" she said.

He looked around at the interior of his carriage and through the window to the hedgerow rushing past and the fields just visible beyond. The Peacock was only a mile or two distant.

"I suppose," he said, "there is no such thing as a perfectly romantic setting, is there? Or just the perfect time. Only the time and setting that are right and inevitable. Yes, I am asking, my love."

He reached out both hands and took both of hers. Then, because he was not satisfied, he peeled off her gloves, tossed them, inside out, on top of his hat, and held her hands again.

"Eunice Goddard," he said, all pretense of sleepiness gone from his eyes, "will you marry me? I have no flowery speech prepared and would feel remarkably idiotic delivering it even if I had. Will you just simply marry me, my love? Because I love you? Will you take the risk? I am fully aware that there *is* a risk. I can only urge you to take a chance on me while I promise to do my very best to love and cherish you for the rest of my days and even perhaps beyond them. Who knows? It might be fun playing a harp through all eternity if you were there beside me strumming on one too. Does one strum on a harp?"

He grinned at her.

"I would rather swing on clouds," she said, "and jump from one to another. There would be all the thrill with none of the danger, for we could not fall to our deaths, could we? We would already be immortal. I will marry you, Lord Windrow. I think — I *know* — I would like it of all things."

She bit her upper lip, and tears sprang to her eyes.

He raised her hands one at a time to his lips, his eyes never leaving hers.

"Make that Charles," he said. " 'I will marry you, *Charles.*' "

"I will marry you, Charles," she said softly.

"I suppose," he said, "I am going to have to make a journey to Cambridge, am I, to apply to the formidable don for permission to marry his daughter?"

"You are," she said. "He will probably look mildly surprised to discover that I can possibly be old enough to consider marriage yet, and then mildly gratified to discover that someone wishes to marry me without his having to exert himself in any way to find me a husband."

"Admirable," he said. "And will he approve of me?"

"Yes," she said without hesitation. "Vague as he can be, he loves me too, you see."

He kissed the back of her right hand again and looked past her shoulder.

"Ah," he said, "the infamous Peacock, scene of sin and passion — or so it is to be hoped. Heyward may be a dullard in many ways, but I was vastly impressed by the way he got into the private parlor yesterday afternoon without either opening or closing the door. At least, I did not *see* it open or close, did you? Though there was a great deal of banging and slamming for a moment. He veritably pulsated with passion. So did his fist. And so did his person after we left, I would happily wager. And Lady Angeline Dudley likes him, so he cannot be all dullard. I am really rather fond of her."

"I love them both," Eunice said. "Very dearly. And I still think it was very, very wrong of us to leave them here yesterday."

He leaned forward and kissed her briefly on the lips as the carriage made the turn into the small inn yard.

CHAPTER 22

It seemed like a strange marvel to Angeline to discover when they arrived back at Hallings that the world really had not changed — only *her* world had. The house party was proceeding just as if nothing earth-shattering had happened. Indeed, Cousin Rosalie's guests were setting up for a cricket match when they arrived sometime after noon, and they were hailed eagerly by team captains and team members alike to come and swell the numbers.

All the gentlemen were playing except the marquess and Viscount Overmyer, who had awoken in the morning with a tight chest that had eased after his wife had applied a poultice and after he had breakfasted in his room but nevertheless must not be exposed to the vigors of cricket. The viscountess, however, *was* playing, as was Mrs. Lynd, her sister, and the Countess of Heyward and Miss Marianne Briden. All the nonplayers were gathered about to watch.

And instead of floating on pink clouds for the rest of the afternoon, as she had imagined doing, basking in all the glory of the Great Secret she was harboring, Angeline recaptured the childhood she had lost after her brothers left home and threw her heart and every stitch of her energy into a game of cricket. She was on the opposing team to Edward and cheered wildly for her team when he hit a long shot that would have resulted in several runs if Ferdinand had not picked it out of the air at full stretch. And she refrained from sticking her tongue out at him when *he* cheered as she lunged sideways to catch a ball hit by the Reverend Martin, made a spectacular catch, began to celebrate a moment too soon, and . . . dropped it.

Mrs. Lynd was formidably good as both a batter and a fielder. So were Tresham and Sir Webster. And the Reverend Martin had, he admitted later, been a bowler on the first eleven both at Eton and at Oxford in the dim, distant years of his youth, and it was obvious he had lost none of his skills even if his joints did tend to be creaky at times.

Angeline's team lost ignominiously, a disaster that caused them a great deal of shared laughter and brought them a great deal of sympathy from the spectators. The marquess even gave it as his opinion that they would have won handily if only they had not lost — a comment whose great wit sent him off into a wheezing cough.

Everyone strolled back in the direction of the house, where tea was awaiting them. Everyone except Miss Goddard and Lord Windrow, that was, who were walking slowly together in the direction of the lake, and Tresham and Edward, who were talking with each other beside the wickets.

And then, just before Angeline reached the house with everyone else, Tresham caught up with her, took her by the elbow, and steered her off in the direction of the formal gardens.

"You had better be warned, Angeline," he said when they were well clear of anyone else. "Heyward cannot take no for an answer, it would seem. He intends to ask you again. That must be why he went galloping after you yesterday and came back today actually inside Windrow's carriage with you — poor Windrow. He must have been trying to ingratiate himself with you. Be prepared."

"Oh," she said, "I will. Thank you for the warning. But are you sure? I thought he came after us because of Miss Goddard.

They are fond of each other, you know. They have been friends forever."

"He would do the world a great favor if he married her, then," he said, "which perhaps he will do after you have rejected him for a second time. Windrow has been acting strangely around her, but he must have turned queer in the head if he imagines that she will be susceptible to his sort of dalliance."

Angeline was not so sure. Well, she *was*. Miss Goddard would surely not dally in any way that would compromise her virtue. But was *dalliance* what Lord Windrow had in mind? Poor Tresh. He might start to feel vulnerable himself if one of his friends suddenly fell prey to love. Though it was doubtful. She could not quite imagine Tresham ever being either vulnerable or in love. When he married, as he must eventually, it would be a purely dynastic thing. He would choose just the right lady, and he would breed just the right number of children on her, and he would carry on with his life as if his marriage were no more than a pimple on the surface of it.

Sometimes she wished she did not love her brothers so much. They did not *deserve* her love. Except that no one would ever be loved if he had to deserve it. Including herself.

"I shall listen to his offer," she said with a sigh.

They had made love again last night — or, rather, early this morning, when dawn was already a suggestion beyond the windows of their room and one lone bird was doing its best to fill the sky with song. Edward had done it slowly and tentatively, prepared at any moment to stop if there had been too much pain. But really there had not, and the pleasure had far outweighed the little soreness there was. And once it had been perfectly clear to him that she did not want or need him to stop, then passion had swept them both away until they had emerged, much later, panting and sweating and all tangled up together and in the twisted bedcovers.

She could not say it had been better or more glorious than the first time. If she did, then she had the feeling she would be saying it every time they made love for the rest of their lives, and that would be ridiculous. It had been *as* good and *as* glorious.

And if Tresham knew . . .

"Good girl," he said. "This has been a surprisingly pleasant interlude, has it not? But it will be good to be back in London.

You will be swamped with admirers again once we are. And suitors. You must put me out of my misery and accept one of them one of these days, Angeline. It would be mortally depressing to have to face this all over again next year. *Not* that I would have you accept just anyone."

"Perhaps I will put you out of your misery today and accept Lord Heyward," she said with a laugh.

"Devil take it, Angeline," he said, "have *some* mercy on me. Imagine having Heyward as a brother-in-law for the rest of a lifetime."

"Imagine having him for a *husband* for the rest of a lifetime," she said.

And she felt a purely unexpected but quite identifiable aching sensation stab downward through her womb and out along her inner thighs.

Imagine Edward as her husband!

As they made their way back along one of the graveled paths toward the house and their tea, Tresham actually chuckled. And *of course* this had been a surprisingly pleasant interlude for him. Each day so far he had disappeared for an hour or two at a stretch — at exactly the same time Cousin Belinda disappeared. If there was not dalliance going on *there,* Angeline would be quite prepared to eat one of her hats, trimmings and all.

Edward found Lorraine and Fenner together in the conservatory half an hour before dinner. As good fortune would have it, his mother and his grandmother were with them, as were Alma and Augustine and Juliana.

"Edward," his mother said, "how did you find Lady Windrow? I used to consider her charming though I never knew her well, but she became reclusive after Windrow died. I believe they were exceedingly fond of each other."

"She was well, Mama," he said, hating the lie. Before he was forced into more of them, he turned to Lorraine and Fenner.

"I have spoken with Lady Palmer," he said, "but I must speak with the two of you too. This whole house party was arranged to celebrate your betrothal, after all, and it is only right that the main focus of attention be upon you. I may wish to take some of that attention away from you if Lady Angeline Dudley says yes to a question I hope to ask this evening and if she would not prefer that we delay an announcement. But it will be delayed if you would prefer it."

"Edward." Lorraine smiled warmly at

494

him. "You are going to propose marriage to her again. For the right reason this time — I can see it in your eyes. And she will, of course, say yes. How could any lady in her right mind *not?*"

Now there was a touching example of filial loyalty — in a mere sister-in-law.

"Edward!" The other ladies all spoke together. His mother pressed her clasped hands to her bosom.

Fenner got to his feet and extended a hand.

"Good luck, Heyward," he said. "And I am quite sure I speak for Lorraine when I say we will be delighted to have this gathering at my sister's made even more memorable than it already is."

"Thank you," Edward said and bent to hug his grandmother, who had extended both arms to him. "But she has not said yes yet."

And it would be *just* like Angeline to find some excuse to say no just so she could witness the extent of his wrath. It would be an extremely wrathful wrath. Good Lord, she might even now be with child — a mildly panic-inducing thought.

After dinner, by mutual consent, there was dancing in the drawing room again. The same three musicians had arrived after a hasty summons. And the Persian carpet had been rolled back from the floor again. The French windows were open wide again.

And once more, after a few lively country dances, which left everyone laughing and breathless, it was the waltz that everyone wanted. And once again Edward took Angeline as a partner and waltzed with her out on the terrace, twirling in and out of the candlelight with her.

Somehow his legs felt less wooden outdoors and his mind less intent upon counting out the rhythm and being careful to set his feet somewhere — anywhere — except on top of his partner's. The waltz really was rather a splendid dance. He smiled down at her.

"Another secret," she said. "You are the most divine waltzing partner in the world. No one else will ever know, and I shall not tell."

She smiled back into his eyes. He twirled her again, and it seemed to him that he could not miss a step or tread on her toes if he tried. He led a charmed existence.

She threw her head back and laughed.

And it sounded as if he had hurled a silent challenge at fate, which in his experience did not like to be tempted. He stopped dancing just out of the beam of a branch of candles on the mantel inside the drawing room.

"Come," he said. "It is almost as bright as day out here. Look at the moonlight on the lake. Let us go closer and feast on the sight."

She slipped her arm through his and they proceeded across the wide, sloping lawn, which was actually darker than he had anticipated. But the moonlit water was like a beacon ahead of them and there did not appear to be any clouds overhead that might obliterate it at any moment and plunge them into total darkness.

The air was still almost warm.

He slid his arm free of hers and took her hand in his own, lacing their fingers together. And he drew her closer to his side so her shoulder leaned against his upper arm.

Last night seemed a bit like a dream. It had been real, though. A dream could not possibly be so vivid. He still could not believe he had done something so . . . bold. Or that he *still* did not regret it or feel any guilt whatsoever.

The water was as smooth as glass. There was not a breath of wind. Beyond the lake were the trees and the hill and the tower folly at the top of it. Its silhouette was visible even now in the darkness. Moonlight

497

shimmered in a broad band across the water. It was not a silent scene, though. All around them insects were going about the business of their lives and making noise about it, darkness and night notwithstanding, and somewhere among the trees an owl hooted occasionally just to let the rest of the world know that it was there.

The sounds merely accentuated the calm serenity of the scene.

"Angeline," he said, his hand tightening slightly around hers, his eyes on the water, "will you marry me?"

"Yes, Edward," she said.

Just like that. And just like that they were betrothed and bound together for life.

It was surely the most moving marriage proposal and acceptance ever made. He smiled at the water.

He turned his head and she turned hers and their mouths met. Just like that. Their bodies did not turn. They did not wrap their arms about each other. There was no burning passion.

Only . . .

Well, only that thing beyond words.

Peace.

Rightness.

Love.

It was no use. There really were no words.

And it absolutely did not matter. There did not need to be words.

He spoke some anyway.

"I love you," he said.

She smiled softly in the light of the moon.

"I know," she said.

Which was by far the most eloquent speech he had ever heard from her lips.

CHAPTER 23

Angeline had chosen pale yellow muslin for her wedding dress. Her initial choice had been a bright sunshine yellow, like her favorite old day dress, but she had ended up taking the advice of Cousin Rosalie and Miss Goddard, who had both accompanied her to the modiste's and were in agreement with each other.

"The dress is to be worn on your *wedding* day," Miss Goddard had explained. "And on your wedding day all the focus of attention must be upon *you,* not upon your clothes. And really, you know, Lady Angeline, you are worth focusing upon."

"And you will be especially radiant on your wedding day," Cousin Rosalie agreed. "A bright dress will be quite unnecessary."

Miss Goddard had been at the modiste's on her own account as well as to advise her friend, and she had chosen pale blue and a simple design. She was to marry Lord

Windrow in Cambridge two weeks after Angeline's own wedding. Cousin Leonard and the Countess of Heyward, now Lady Fenner, had married at his country estate two weeks ago. There was a flurry of weddings now at the end of the Season, as there always was, and there were more to come. Martha's betrothal to Mr. Griddles had just been announced, and Maria was in imminent expectation of a declaration from Mr. Stebbins.

Angeline had resisted the urge to complete her wedding outfit with a flamboyant bonnet, though it had been a *very* strong urge. A wedding was a festive occasion, after all, and a festive bonnet ought to be . . . well, *festive.* However, all on her own, without even consulting the opinions of her cousin and her friend, she had decided upon a small-brimmed straw bonnet with a high crown, and had had it trimmed with white lace and white and yellow daisies and white ribbons. She had bought white gloves and white slippers.

And looking at herself now in the pier glass in her dressing room, she had to admit that she looked almost pretty. Except that the paleness of the garments accentuated the darkness of her hair and eyes and her dark-hued complexion. And there was nothing delicate about her features. But there was nothing she could do about any of that.

She wondered fleetingly what her mother would have thought about her today. Would she have thought the clothes tasteful? Would she have thought her daughter pretty? Would she have been *happy?*

"Mama."

Angeline formed the name with her lips but did not speak aloud. She supposed there would always be a sort of wistful sadness in her whenever she remembered her mother and the fact that she had never measured up to her mother's expectations. But she would use the memories in a positive way. When *she* had daughters, she would adore them from the moment of their birth, and she would shower them with love and approval no matter what they were like. They might be timid or bold, pretty or plain, it would not matter. They would be *her daughters.* And her sons would be *her sons.* Oh, she hoped there would be a dozen of each and that they would start coming soon. Well, perhaps not a *dozen* of each or even a dozen all told, but many of them anyway. She wanted to be surrounded by children. She wanted Edward and her to be surrounded by children.

"Oh, my lady." Betty was sniveling. "You

do look lovely."

Angeline spun around and hugged her impulsively, turning Betty's snivels to shrieks lest she crease Lady Angeline's dress or *drip* on it. But before any such disaster could occur, the maid had to turn to open the door of the dressing room, upon which someone had knocked.

"Well, Angeline," Tresham said, standing in the doorway and looking her over unhurriedly from top to toe, "you look unexpectedly . . . glorious."

"Unexpectedly?" She raised her eyebrows. And *glorious? Tresham* had said she looked *glorious?*

"I half thought of donning an eyeshade before knocking on your door," he said. "I expected . . . something different."

"Tell me again," she said.

He raised his own eyebrows.

"How I look," she explained.

"Glorious?" he said.

She blinked several times in quick succession. She would feel remarkably silly if she wept merely because her brother had paid her a compliment.

He stepped into the room and with one glance dismissed Betty.

"Angeline," he said, "you know that I believe you could do considerably better for yourself. Leaving a man standing at the altar, especially of St. George's with half the *ton* in attendance, would cause a scandal of astronomical proportions. But we are Dudleys. We could live it down. If you feel now that you made too hasty a choice, then tell me and I will extricate you before it is too late."

She gazed at him, at the brother she so adored. He just did not understand at all, did he? Of course, she had never told him, and she would not tell him even now. Some things — even *I love him* — were just too private. And how could she say *I love him because he is so different from you?* That was only a very small part of the truth, anyway. It might have been the starting point of her feelings for Edward, but it was not anything close to the ending point.

But Tresham was prepared to let her embroil him in scandal. And it would be a dreadful thing indeed even for the Duke of Tresham to live down.

Tears welled in her eyes after all and threatened to spill over onto her cheeks.

Tresham *loved* her.

"Devil take it," he said curtly. "I'll send directly to the church. I'll go there myself, in fact. Have Betty pack your things. I'll take you back to Acton this afternoon."

He had misunderstood her tears.

"Tresh," she said, "I am marrying Heyward because I *want* to, because I expect to be happy with him."

And it struck her suddenly that she had never called her elder brother by his given name — *Jocelyn.* He had been Everleigh — the Earl of Everleigh — until their father died when he was seventeen, and since then he had been Tresham. She wondered if he minded, if perhaps he too had felt some lack in his family life. But it was too late to call him Jocelyn now. To her he would always be *Tresham.*

He was looking at her very steadily with his almost black eyes.

"And I suppose," he said softly, "that is all that really matters when all is said and done."

He offered his arm and she took it.

She would not return to this room or to the bedchamber beyond it. Tonight she would sleep, appropriately enough, at the Rose and Crown Inn this side of Reading. Within the next few days she would be at Wimsbury Abbey in Shropshire. She would be the Countess of Heyward, a married lady, Edward's wife.

Her heart and stomach performed a vigorous pas de deux inside her. She did not look back.

Their night together at the Peacock Inn had not had consequences. Angeline had been able to assure Edward of that a month ago, and he was enormously relieved, for a hasty marriage by special license instead of by banns, and an eight-month child following after it, would tell their own story, and he would rather not have that story told even though he had never regretted that night. It had been something free and passion-filled and wonderful — and very private. Very *secret*.

He smiled at the memory of her eager, happy face poised above his as she had described herself as his *secret mistress* and sworn that she would use his name only in private. He had been *Heyward* to her ever since, for their betrothal had been conducted with strict propriety and they had hardly been alone in the six weeks since he had proposed to her and been accepted.

Tonight they would be alone together.

It seemed fitting that it would be at the Rose and Crown Inn. He had suggested it to her, and she had laughed and said that yes, it would be perfect. She had added that she would not even for a moment step alone into the taproom. He had replied, in all seriousness, that she had better not. And then they had looked into each other's eyes and laughed.

Edward was aware of the church filling up behind him. No one was so ill-bred as to talk aloud, but there were murmurings and rustlings and whisperings. Beside him, George Headley, his best man, cleared his throat and attempted to loosen his cravat. Headley was more nervous than *he* was. He had been dreaming for a week, apparently, that he would drop the ring when the time came to produce it and would be forced to make an idiot of himself chasing it as it rolled endlessly from pew to pew.

Edward was not nervous. He was *excited.* He was doing his duty, he was pleasing his family, and he was pleasing himself all at once. He was a happy man.

Provided, that was, Angeline did not have a change of heart at the last possible moment. He would not put it past Tresham to try to talk her out of this marriage, of which he obviously disapproved. He did not like Edward, which was perhaps fair enough, as Edward was not particularly fond of him either, or of Lord Ferdinand Dudley, who had seemed to enjoy the Season in a particularly carefree and often reckless manner. But they would all be civil to one another,

Edward thought — *if* Angeline did indeed marry him, that was.

He did not have a pocket watch and would not have drawn it out, he supposed, even if he had. But it seemed to him that she was late.

And he felt nervous after all. What if she did not come? How long would the congregation sit here before becoming restless and beginning to slip away? How long would *he* sit here before *slinking* away?

And then there was a heightened rustling at the back of the church and the clergyman appeared in front of him and the murmurings among the congregation swelled slightly and the pipe organ drowned them all out with an anthem.

She had come.

His bride had arrived, and he was about to be married.

Edward stood and half turned to watch her approach along the nave on Tresham's arm.

She looked like a ray of spring sunshine dropping its delicate touch onto the end of summer. The veil of her bonnet was in a cloud about her face, he could see as she came closer. But beneath it she was all vivid, radiant beauty and warm smiles directed at him. He clasped his hands behind him and gazed back.

Angeline.

The most beautiful woman he had ever set eyes upon. Not that he was biased.

And then she was at his side and the clergyman was speaking and Tresham was giving her hand into Edward's.

"Dearly beloved," the clergyman said in that voice only clergymen possessed to fill a large, echoing building without shouting.

The large building was unimportant. So was the congregation, even though it included all the people in the world most dear to him and to her. *Angeline* was here, her hand in his, and they were speaking to each other the words that would bind them in law for the rest of their lives, the words that would bind their hearts for a lifetime and an eternity.

It felt strange and strangely freeing to have discovered that after all he was a romantic. Half the people here would be deeply shocked if they knew that he actually *loved* the woman who was becoming his wife, and that she loved him. Such an extravagance of sensibility would seem almost vulgar to many people. And it amused him that Angeline had suggested they guard the secret of their deep love for each other while presenting the front of a conventional marriage to the world.

And then she *was* his wife. The clergyman had just said so.

She turned her head to smile at him, her lips parted in wonder, her eyes bright with unshed tears. He gazed back.

His secret mistress.

He almost laughed aloud with sheer joy at the remembered words. But that could wait for tonight when the door of their room at the Rose and Crown was firmly closed behind them.

There was the rest of a church service to be lived through first, and a grand wedding breakfast at Dudley House.

This was their wedding day.

She was his wife.

Epilogue

Seven Years Later

The snowdrops had been blooming for a couple of weeks or longer. The crocuses were starting to bloom. Even the daffodils were pushing through the soil ready to bud before February turned to March.

It was not a springlike day today, however. In fact, Edward thought as he stood at the French windows in the drawing room at Wimsbury Abbey, it was downright wintry. The sky was slate gray, wind was whipping through the bare branches of the trees, bearing a few sad remnants of last year's leaves before it, and a light sleet was trying to fall. It was a cold, cheerless day.

He hoped it was not an omen.

A blaze crackled in the fireplace behind him. His mother sat close to it, alternately holding her hands out to the heat and drawing her shawl more warmly about her shoulders. Edward was not feeling the cold

— or the heat for that matter.

He was restless and worried and, yes, frightened. He even caught himself at one irrational moment believing that he must surely be suffering more than Angeline was. She at least was *doing* something. She was laboring hard. He had nothing to do. Absolutely nothing but fret. And feel helpless. And guilty at having been the cause of her pain. And aggrieved that Alma was allowed in their bedchamber, and the physician and the nurse they had hired and even Betty — his mother too, when she chose to go up there, as she did every hour or so. Half the world was allowed into his bedchamber, but not he. Not the mere husband and lord of the manor. He was not allowed in there. He was not even allowed to pace outside the door. Angeline could *feel* him there when he did, if you please, and *his* distress distressed *her.*

A man could surely be forgiven if he became peevish at such moments in his life. Except that they were considerably longer than just *moments.* Angeline had woken him at one o'clock this morning with the news that she was experiencing pains that were so peculiar and so regular that she really believed they must be *labor* pains. He had shot straight up in the air in his panic and come down on his feet beside the bed — or so it had seemed — and he had not been allowed near that bed since.

It was now half past four in the afternoon.

"I have poured you a cup of tea, Edward," his mother said. "Do come and drink it while it is hot. And Cook has made some of her buttered scones. I have put two on a plate for you. Do eat them. You had very little breakfast and no luncheon."

How could one *eat* when one's wife was laboring abovestairs and had been for hours and hours? And when had the tea tray arrived? He had not heard it.

"Is this *normal,* Mama?" He turned to face the room though he did not move closer to his tea. "This length of time?"

So many women died in childbed.

"There is no *normal* when it comes to a confinement, Edward," she said with a sigh. "When Lorraine had Simon two months ago, she delivered after no longer than four hours. Yet Susan took three times as long to arrive, I remember, and Martin even longer than that. I was not with her when Henrietta was born three years ago."

They all continued to treat Lorraine, Lady Fenner, as though she were a member of their family. She had no family of her own apart from a reclusive father. Of course,

Susan, now age ten, really was one of their own.

But three times as long. Twelve hours. Angeline had been in labor for sixteen — and that was only since she had told him about it.

"Perhaps I should go up there," he said.

He had gone up a couple of times despite the prohibition, though not inside the bedchamber, of course. The last time was an hour and a half ago. He had listened through two bouts of heavy moaning and had then fled.

"What useless creatures we husbands are," he complained.

His mother smiled and got to her feet to come to him. She set her arms about him and hugged him close.

"You have waited *so* long for a child, you and Angeline," she said. "Wait an hour or two longer. She is strong, and she has been so very excited about this confinement, Edward. She has been happy enough since your marriage, of course. She has always been cheerful and always smiling and always full of energy. But there has been a core of sadness that I have sensed more and more over the years. She has longed for a child."

"I know." He hugged her back. "She has always said — we *both* have — that having

514

each other is enough. And for me it has been. I do not care the snap of two fingers about the succession — pardon me, Mama. But I *do* care about Angeline. I do not know how I would live without her."

Yet he had shared that core of sadness — if *sadness* was the right word. He had never wanted them to be a childless couple.

"It is to be hoped," his mother said, "that you will not have to live without her, or at least not for a long, long time. Come and drink your tea and then I will pour you another while you eat your scones."

But before they could move toward the fire and the tea tray, the door opened and Alma hurried inside, looking flushed and slightly untidy and very happy.

"Edward," she said, "you have a *daughter.* A plump and tiny little thing considering how large Angeline was, but with an excellent set of lungs. She is protesting her entry into this world with what appears to be typical Dudley bad temper — and those were Angeline's words, I hasten to add. Many congratulations, Brother. You may come up in ten minutes' time. By then we will have her cleaned and wrapped and ready to set in your arms."

And she was gone, closing the door behind her.

Angeline's words. She was still alive then. She had made a safe delivery and survived it.

And he had a daughter.

He set the fingers of one hand to his lips. But it was no good. The tears were coming from his eyes, not his mouth.

He had a daughter and Angeline was alive.

"Mama." He hugged her again. "I am a *father.*"

As though he were the only man in the world ever to have achieved such an astonishing feat.

"And she has the Dudley temper," he said. "Lord help me, she is going to lead me a merry dance."

He found the idea so alarming that he threw back his head and laughed.

"And now," his mother said, "you may relax at last. All is well, Edward. Drink your tea and eat one scone at least before you go up."

He did so just to please her, though the very last thing he needed right then was to eat and drink. He was taking the stairs two at a time long before the ten minutes were at an end.

Alma brought the baby out to him. He could not come in yet, she told him, as the afterbirth was a bit slow and Angeline needed to be made comfortable before he was admitted.

And she placed a bundle in his arms that was so light it surely weighed nothing at all. But it was warm, and it was the most precious commodity he had ever held. For a moment he held his breath lest he drop it.

His daughter was tightly swaddled in a white blanket. All that was visible of her was her head, downy with damp dark hair, and her face, red, scrunched up, beautiful beyond belief. She was crying with cross little mews.

He held her in the crook of his arm for a few moments until Alma had disappeared back into the bedchamber. Then he moved the bundle so that his right hand was spread behind her head and his other hand beneath her body. He tipped her slightly, bringing her face close to his own.

His daughter!

"Well, little one," he said, "this is the way it is, you see. You may have temper tantrums to your heart's content and they will have no effect whatsoever upon your papa. You are loved, my sweetheart, and that is quite unnegotiable from this moment until I breathe my last. You will find that your father has an implacable will when it comes to those he loves. You might as well settle down now to being a part of this family."

She had stopped crying. Her eyelids parted to narrow slits and she gazed at him with unfocused light blue eyes. Her mouth puckered into an O.

"Precisely," he said and smiled at her.

They were in silent accord — and a baby cried, at first with an indignant squawk and then with healthier protest.

Edward gazed in astonishment at his daughter, who gazed silently back.

And then the door of the bedchamber opened abruptly again and Alma looked out.

"Oh, Edward," she said, "you have a son. It was not the afterbirth but another child. Now we know why Angeline was so huge. Give us five minutes and then you can come in."

And the door shut again as abruptly as it had opened.

Edward stared, stunned, at his daughter, who looked curiously unsurprised.

"Well, little one," he said after several moments, his voice noticeably shaky, "it seems you have a brother and I have a *son*."

And an heir.

Angeline had been at the very point of exhaustion for hours, it seemed. She was moving past that point, would have already done so, in fact, if the pain had not been more powerful than the weariness, and the interminable urge to push had not been stronger than both.

It seemed so unfair. Her child had been born . . . how long ago? Forever ago. And that had been the end of that, she had thought. No one had told her about the afterbirth or that it would go on forever and be just as painful as the actual birth.

"One more push, my lady," the physician said for surely the five thousandth time.

They were unnecessary words. She had no choice, even though every time she was convinced it would be the last, that she could not possibly do it even once more. She wanted to sleep. She had never craved anything more. During her lowest moments she had even wanted to die, but that was no longer the case. *Her baby had been born.* They had a daughter, she and Edward, and dying was out of the question, pain and exhaustion notwithstanding.

Indeed, she would *not* die. Or be defeated by pain. Or give in to exhaustion. She gathered all her remaining strength, which she would have thought nonexistent even just moments ago, and pushed with all her might. And she was rewarded with a great gushing of freedom a moment after her ears half registered the astonished words of the physician.

"Oh, my," he said, "there is another one."

And then a baby was crying lustily and Angeline opened her eyes to see what had happened to her daughter — she had *thought* Alma had taken her out to Edward. But there was *another* baby, dangling upside down in the physician's hands, its little arms flailing helplessly, its body slimy from birth.

"You have a son, my lady," the physician said. "I have never delivered twins before. I did not understand what I was facing."

Which evidence of his inexperience might have made her nervous had she known it in advance.

Angeline reached up both arms, and he set the child down on her stomach in all his slime, and Angeline set her hands on him, one behind his head, the other behind his bottom, and felt his warmth and his human-ness before the nurse took him away to wash him and swaddle him.

The indignity of his birth over with, this baby fell silent. His hair was going to be fair.

"He is an Ailsbury," she said.

And her heart swelled with love almost to the point of bursting. And with yearning to hold her daughter again. And to see Edward.

She was a mother — twice over. And he was a father. After all this time. Seven long years.

She let her hands fall reluctantly to her sides when the nurse took the baby, and she fell half asleep while the physician finished with her and Betty cleaned her and the bed and Alma got her into a clean nightgown and brushed her hair.

Then she woke sleepily as the quiet little bundle that was her son was laid in the crook of her arm and Alma opened the door and Edward came in, an identical bundle in the crook of *his* arm.

He approached the bed and sat down carefully on the side of it, never taking his eyes off her.

"Angeline," he said, "how *are* you?"

"I was never better in my life." She smiled at him and then looked down into their daughter's face as he looked down into their son's.

He set his bundle down in the crook of her free arm and took the other into his own arms. He rearranged it so that the baby's face was close to his own and he gazed for several silent moments.

"Welcome, my son," he said softly at last, and he smiled with such tenderness that Angeline's heart turned over.

He looked back at Angeline.

"If someone had told me an hour ago," he said, "that it was possible to love two children equally and to overflowing, I would have said it was impossible. But it is not, is it?"

"No." She shook her head. "Love is infinite. You have your heir, Edward."

"Yes." He looked from one to the other of the babies again. "More important, we have our *son*. And our *daughter*. Not necessarily in that order. I have a strong suspicion that little Madeline is not ever going to let Matthew forget that she is the elder."

"We are able to use *both* names," she said.

Lady Madeline Mary Elizabeth and Matthew James Alexander, Viscount Leeson. Large names for two little bundles of new humanity.

"Angeline," he said, leaning slightly toward her, "thank you."

She smiled though even the effort to do that was exhausting.

"I love you so very much," she said.

He cupped the side of her face with his free hand and leaned over her to kiss her softly on the lips. He did not need to say anything. That was what seven years of marriage did for one.

There were those who said that the luster

went from a marriage before one year was over and that all but the legal and ecclesiastical bonds was dead within seven years.

She did not suppose it was possible that she was *more* in love with Edward now than she had been seven years ago, or he with her. That would be to insult what they had felt for each other when they married. But it was certainly true that she was *as much* in love. It was also true that the quality of her love had deepened. She knew him now in almost every way one human being could know another. *Almost* every way. No one could ever know absolutely everything there was to know about another, of course, and if it were possible it would not be desirable, because there should always be more to discover, always something new to surprise and delight.

Even she could not have guessed that Edward would have *tears* in his eyes as he looked from their son to their daughter and back again — and back yet again.

And of course *no one* else knew him as she knew him. To the world he was a dutiful, quiet, rather dull man. To his family he was a warm and loving and dutiful man. Only she knew the depths of passion that he poured out in his private and sexual relationship with his wife.

With his *secret mistress.*

She had never stopped being that. A wife could be a dull creature, as could a husband.

A lover and his mistress were endlessly exciting.

Except that excitement was just too wearying to be contemplated now. Perhaps later . . .

The little bundle that was Madeline was being lifted from her arm. Edward was holding her, she saw when she opened her eyes. The nurse beside him was holding Matthew.

"Sleep," Edward said. "And that *is* an order."

She exerted herself sufficiently to smile once more.

"Yes, my lord," she said and was asleep almost before the words were out.

ABOUT THE AUTHOR

Mary Balogh is the *New York Times* best-selling author of the acclaimed Slightly series and Simply quartet of novels set at Miss Martin's School for Girls, as well as many other beloved novels. She is also the author of *First Comes Marriage, Then Comes Seduction, At Last Comes Love, Seducing an Angel,* and *A Secret Affair,* all featuring the Huxtable family. A former teacher, she grew up in Wales and now lives in Canada. To learn more, visit the author's website at www.MaryBalogh.com.

We hope you have enjoyed this Large Print book. Other Thorndike, Wheeler, Kennebec, and Chivers Press Large Print books are available at your library or directly from the publishers.

For information about current and upcoming titles, please call or write, without obligation, to:

Publisher
Thorndike Press
10 Water St., Suite 310
Waterville, ME 04901
Tel. (800) 223-1244

or visit our Web site at:

http://gale.cengage.com/thorndike

OR

Chivers Large Print
published by AudioGO Ltd
St James House, The Square
Lower Bristol Road
Bath BA2 3SB
England
Tel. +44(0) 800 136919
email: info@audiogo.co.uk
www.audiogo.co.uk

All our Large Print titles are designed for easy reading, and all our books are made to last.